THE
UNDERTAKERS
RISE OF THE CORPSES

W9-BRY-001

TY DRAGO

sourcebooks
jabberwocky

Published by Sourcebooks Jabberwocky, an imprint of Sourcebooks, Inc.
P.O. Box 4410, Naperville, Illinois 60567-4410
(630) 961-3900
Fax: (630) 961-2168
www.jabberwockykids.com

Library of Congress Cataloging-in-Publication data is on file with the publisher.

Source of Production: Versa Press, East Peoria, Illinois, USA
Date of Production: March 2011
Run Number: 14630

Printed and bound in the United States of America.

VP 10 9 8 7 6 5 4 3 2 1

When writing about an adolescent boy, it's best to seek the advice of an expert. This book is dedicated to my son, Andy Drago, who read it and offered helpful (and often profound) insight into the realities of his age, his culture, and his mysterious language.

Son, I couldn't have done it without you.

"Children make the best heroes."

—Anonymous

CONTENTS

CHAPTER 1

DEAD MEN WALKING

On a sunny Wednesday morning in October—a day that would mark the end of one life and the beginning of another—I found out that my next-door neighbor was one of the walking dead.

The day had started typically enough, with Mom nagging me to get dressed. Emily, my five-year-old sister, was wailing because the cable was out and she couldn't watch *Dora the Explorer*. And me? I was in the bathroom, trying to get that "sticky-up" part of my hair to lay flat.

My name's William Karl Ritter—Will to the world at large. I'm twelve years old and just about as "middle of the road" as you can get. I'm not skinny or fat, not really tall or short, not butt-ugly or particularly good-looking. What I am is a redhead. See, I've got my mom's pale face and green eyes and my dad's freckles and mop of orange hair, which he had always called the "family heritage" dating back to the old country. If so, then it was one weird heritage. After all, who ever heard of a redheaded German?

I hated being a redhead—and still do. Sort of.

Back then, I guess I hated a lot of things. For example, I hated middle school. The classes were boring. I hated being called *Red* all the time. And I especially hated when the school bullies pinned me down and played "connect the dots" with my freckles and a ballpoint pen.

But most of all, I hated that my dad wasn't there to make it all right.

"Bus in ten minutes, Will!" Mom called from downstairs. "I've got a Pop-Tart for you!"

"Okay, Mom!" With a groan, I gave up on my hair, fled the bathroom, and bounded down the steps three at a time.

Mom was in the kitchen, calming Emily down with a glass of apple juice. "There's nothing I can do about the cable, honey. It'll come back on when it comes back on. Will, grab something to eat. You've got...eight and a half minutes!"

"I'll make it!" I said, shoving half a Pop-Tart into my mouth.

"Isn't today the deadline for the soccer sign-ups?" Mom asked, glancing sideways at me.

The Pop-Tart suddenly caught a little in my throat.

"I guess so."

She gave me her "mother" look. "I want you doing more with your free time than playing Xbox. A little exercise, maybe? Why don't you sign up?"

I made a sour face. "Soccer sucks."

"You loved it up until two years ago. Tell me again how many goals you scored that last season you played. Was it eight?"

"Yeah," I admitted. "But it's, like, different now."

"Will, your dad would want you to continue doing the things that interest you."

"I know," I sighed.

"Sign up today," Mom said firmly. "Emmie and I expect to see you in some games this fall. Got it, mister?"

"Okay, I'll do it," I relented, only half-meaning it.

Smiling, she forced a hug out of me, after which Emily dumped a sloppy kiss on my cheek. Then I snatched up my backpack from its place by the door and headed out.

"Have a good day!" Mom called.

I did *not* have a good day.

I leapt down the stoop, letting the door slam behind me. I was determined to get all the way up the hill to the bus stop in less than thirty seconds. But before I could get as far as the sidewalk, I heard Old Man Pratt call to me. He sounded pissed. He usually did.

Inwardly I groaned. What had I done *now?*

I turned around—and instantly all thoughts of school, soccer, and bus stops went right out of my head.

Pratt said, "You got your trash cans mixed up with mine again, boy!"

He'd moved in next door to us about two years ago. His house looked almost exactly like ours, which looked almost exactly like every other house on Grape Street, which looked almost exactly like every other street in the Manayunk section of Philadelphia: a two-floor, vinyl-sided row home with square windows and a flat, tarred roof. *The Manayunk Standard*, Mom always called it.

Pratt was the neighborhood grouch. Somewhere in his seventies, he lived alone, kept to himself, and got pissed off more often and with less reason than anyone I'd ever met.

"I'm talking to you, Ritter!"

I tried to speak—I really did—but no sound came out. When you turn around expecting to see something familiar—not particularly pleasant but familiar—and instead see something else altogether, it takes a little while for your brain to catch up with your eyes. Some people might call it shock. I call it the *holy crap factor*.

Ernie Pratt was dead—very dead—which didn't make much sense because as far as I knew, dead men didn't get pissed.

He was wearing what he usually wore in the mornings: a white terry-cloth robe and slippers, except the skin inside the slippers had gone as dry as old paper. His face was gray and pulled tight around his skull. One of his eyes was hanging out of its socket, dangling by a short length of thick, corded tissue. The other one, looking milky and sightless, nevertheless stared at me. His lips were gone, receded, revealing a black-gummed mouth with only half the teeth it should have had, and even those were as yellow as old eggs.

Which is also how he *smelled*. The stench hit me like a hammer. I actually staggered back a step. The reek of rotted flesh turned my stomach, threatening the Pop-Tart in my belly with a hasty and violent eviction. I kept it down, mainly because I could tell that Old Man Pratt was watching me, ogling me with that one "good" eye. Looking for what? Fear? Disgust? Right then, I felt plenty of both! My knees had gone weak, and the world—my safe familiar world—seemed to be slipping like sand through my fingers.

"What're you staring at, Ritter?" the talking corpse demanded. "What's the matter? Cat got your tongue?" Then he smiled, splitting what was left of his mouth open in a grimace that sent a chill down my spine and out through all ten of my toes.

Pratt wasn't just dead. He'd clearly been dead a while—weeks maybe!

But he hadn't been a walking cadaver yesterday. I was sure of that! So just what on Earth had happened to him?

"I'm...okay," I stammered, somewhat surprised that words could come out of my mouth at all.

The dead man regarded me, tilting his head at an odd, thoughtful angle. As he did, a series of black beetles bubbled up through a hole in his neck and ran down his collarbone, disappearing inside the white robe.

That was all I could take. Wide-eyed, I started stumbling away from him. It felt like my stomach was about to explode out of my mouth. I glanced toward the front door of my house, hoping my mother might be standing there to see me off. She did that sometimes. This, however, was apparently not one of those times. No doubt Emily was still griping. I was going to die because the cable TV was out.

"Okay, huh?" Dead Man Pratt replied. "You don't look it."

Then to my utter horror, he reached over and caught my upper arm.

I didn't scream. If I had, Mom might have heard it and come to the door. Then things would have turned out differently—maybe worse.

Instead I flailed and scrambled backward.

Pratt was strong. I could feel his strength in the clutch of his gray, dry fingers. He grinned another of those hideous grins, looking like a rotting corpse that had just won the lottery. His one milky eye gleamed like a beacon as he started to pull me toward him.

Then he spoke again. Except he didn't. His black, lipless mouth never moved. I seemed to hear the words coming from inside my head—disjointed, as if he were uttering them one at a time and making an individual sentence out of each.

"*What. Do. You. See. Boy?*"

Acting on pure animal instinct, I swung my arm in a wide arc and brought it down on his wrist. I didn't plan it. I didn't aim. I just did it.

I don't know what I expected to happen. But one thing I didn't expect was for Dead Man Pratt's hand to snap right off the end of his arm!

Suddenly freed, I stumbled backward, almost fell, regained my balance—and took off up the street in the direction of my bus stop. Halfway there, I noticed that the blackened dead hand was still clutching my shirt sleeve. Worse—it was twitching a little.

At that, I finally *did* scream.

Doing a panicked bee-in-your-shirt dance, I threw the gross thing off of me. It bounced into the bushes. Then I kept right on running, risking a quick glance over my shoulder.

Pratt was standing where he had been, looking after me. His smile was gone, replaced by a scowl as he examined what was left of his arm. If lopping off his hand had hurt him, he gave no sign of it.

I think I made it to the bus stop in less than thirty seconds. First time ever. There's nothing like raw terror to get your butt moving.

A handful of kids were already waiting there. One of them was Mike Reardon, a friend. As I reached him, panting and sweating, he asked, "You gonna die or what?"

"Look down the hill!" I exclaimed, trying to catch my breath. My heart felt like it was about to burst.

He looked. He frowned. Then he laughed.

"What'd you do to Old Man Pratt?" he asked. "He's standing there in his robe looking seriously pissed!"

I swallowed, steeled myself, and then faced down the hill.

The robe was there, but the thing inside them wasn't a man—or at least, it hadn't been for a really long time. As I watched, the cadaver waved with his one good hand.

This time the chill ran *up* my spine and squirted out my ears.

"Bus is coming!" someone announced.

My cell phone was in my backpack. Should I call the cops? Call my mom? And tell her what exactly? That Old Man Pratt died maybe a month ago and didn't know it? But then why hadn't Mike seen what I'd seen?

Shuddering a little, I dragged my eyes away from the thing down the block, watching instead the yellow school bus rumbling to a stop at the curb. As the accordion doors creaked open, kids lined up to climb aboard. I stood in the back, my mind reeling.

Am I going crazy?

CHAPTER 2

DEAD MEN TEACHING

The bus ride up to Ridge Avenue took just ten minutes. It turned out to be a long ten minutes.

By stepping onboard, I'd committed myself. Our driver, Mrs. Gardner, wouldn't let us off once we were on—not until we'd reached John Towers Middle School. So changing my mind and running home to Mom was off the table. All I could do was sit stiffly on the seat beside Mike, trembling and not saying anything as the bus trundled up the hill, picking up kids every few blocks or so.

And the more I sat there, the less sure I was of what I'd seen.

After all, dead guys didn't walk around, did they? They didn't grab you, only to have their hands snap off on your shirt.

Right?

I didn't know what had happened outside my house, but I was slowly managing to convince myself that it had been some kind of weird hallucination. A bad Pop-Tart maybe?

When we reached the school, I staggered from the bus in a daze of confusion and uncertainty. I bumped into Mike on the way down the narrow steps, making him snap, "Jeez! What's the matter with you?"

"I dunno," I replied, still feeling the dry clutch of Pratt's dead hand on my arm.

"You sick or something?"

"Maybe."

"Well…see you." And with that, Mike veered away, looking uncomfortable.

He thinks I'm nuts.

The student entrance was always manned by a couple of teachers whose job it was to make sure that everybody got inside before the bell rang. Today it was Mr. Lafferty's turn. Lafferty was a gym coach, a big impatient guy who kept ordering everyone to keep moving through the doors. Across from him, eyeing the lazy march of kids passing under his nose, stood Assistant Principal Titlebaum.

I wouldn't have recognized him if not for the stupid flower he always wore in the lapel of his fancy suit.

Because the guy inside that suit was dead.

He wasn't as dead as Old Man Pratt had been. Well—of course he was *as* dead—just not for as long. Where Mr. Pratt had been a dried-up husk, cracking open here and there when he turned his head, Mr. Titlebaum was still—juicy. His flesh appeared tight and transparent, the muscles beneath visible, the skin moist and faintly purple.

His head was moving slowly back and forth, his dead eyes scanning the crowd, looking for—what?

They settled on me.

Gasping, I stumbled sideways, trying to get as close to Mr. Lafferty's side of the student entrance as I could.

"Yo! Watch it, Red!" someone yelled as I bumped into him.

"Sorry..." I muttered.

Feeling dizzy with fear, I somehow managed to make it through the school doors.

"Hey, Will!"

There was Brian Kowalsky, one of my best friends. I tried to smile but couldn't manage it. Brian didn't notice. "You study for the math test?" he asked.

"Uh-huh," I replied. And the thing is, I had. But that had been last night, when my life had been a whole lot simpler.

"Not me. Fell asleep watching *CSI*. My mom freaked! Now she says I'm gonna flunk, and it serves me right."

It sounded like a mom thing to say.

"I'm ready anyway!" Brian unconvincingly declared. "But can I copy off you...in case I'm not?"

"Whatever," I told him.

A typical day at school.

Homeroom came and went. My homeroom teacher,

plump Ms. Carvelli, was clearly and blessedly unzombie-like. She led us through the Pledge of Allegiance and the morning announcements and then wished us all a good day when the bell rang. I considered talking to her and telling her what was happening to me.

I didn't.

Instead Brian and I marched off to first period math, with Brian still fretting over the test and me just praying that our teacher, Ms. Yu, would be alive and well.

She wasn't.

"Aw, crap," I breathed, staring at the corpse by the blackboard.

"Relax," Brian whispered. "I mean, you studied, right? I don't want to be copying off you if you didn't study."

Saying nothing, I averted my eyes and took my assigned seat in the third row. Brian sat catty-corner and two rows back. I heard him shift his chair a little closer.

"Get settled!" the Ms. Yu-thing said in her heavily accented English. "We have a test today!"

"Hey, Red," said a voice from beside me, and despite everything, my spirits lifted a little. Helene—spelled with three *e*'s but pronounced with three *a*'s—Boettcher dropped into the desk beside mine, just as she did every math class. At the sight of her, my mouth went a little dry, and all thoughts of walking dead people briefly receded.

She absently brushed a lock of wavy light brown hair away from her big hazel eyes. "Ready for the test?"

I struggled for words. It was a problem that happened only in front of her.

Well, and zombies, of course.

"I...think so."

"The Math Queen's tests are always so hard," Helene complained. "It's like she's not...human or something."

Another, rather different kind of cold shock ran down my spine. I gaped at Helene speechlessly as, from the blackboard, dead Ms. Yu declared, "Attention, class! Everyone look at me!"

It was the last thing I wanted to do. I did it anyway. What I was looking at was a dried-up carcass loosely wrapped in a floral print dress and clutching a pile of stapled papers in one gray bony fist. Bits of flaky skin fluttered off of her, covering the floor like weird confetti. There were beetles following her with every step she took. They seemed to be feeding on the confetti.

I glanced around at the other kids. None of them looked nervous, except for Brian, of course, who hadn't studied.

They didn't see that she was a corpse. They didn't even seem to see the bugs!

"There will be no talking," she said. "Your eyes will be on your papers. Forget the clock. Focus only on the test."

"You okay?" Helene whispered.

I nodded miserably, wishing I could confide in her but realizing that her remark about Ms. Yu had been just a joke—one of those things that, yesterday, we'd have laughed about and then forgotten.

Helene wouldn't believe me. No one would.

The telephone on the wall beside the door suddenly rang.

I actually let out a little startled yelp. A few of the kids around me chuckled.

"You don't *look* okay," Helene remarked dryly.

Her speech interrupted, Dead Woman Yu moved to the phone using an ungainly shuffle that sloughed more little gray skin flakes off of her decaying body. They left a gruesome trail across the tile floor that the beetles seemed to love.

Lifting the receiver in one bony hand, she uttered the phrase that, as always, earned her a laugh from the class: "I am Yu!"

I didn't join in the merriment. Neither did Helene.

The corpse flashed the class an annoyed look. Then she listened to the voice on the other end of the line. As I watched, her withered and blackened body grew stiff—no pun intended. She turned her head and looked right at me.

It's Mr. Pratt! He's called the school to tell Mr. Titlebaum and Ms. Yu that I can see them—that I can see them all!

Without really knowing why, I glanced at Helene, who met my eyes.

Amazingly, she whispered, "Don't panic."

Our deceased math teacher replaced the receiver. "William Ritter," she said, "you are to report to Mr. Titlebaum's office immediately."

I didn't move—couldn't move.

The corpse's rotted eye sockets narrowed. Something that looked horribly like a smile flashed across her skeletal face. "Did you hear me, Mr. Ritter?"

"Y-yes, ma'am."

Moving in slow motion, as though trapped in a nightmare, I collected my books and stood, ignoring the dismayed look on Brian's face. The classroom was as quiet as a graveyard. The other kids somehow sensed that something very bad was going down.

My dead math teacher watched me march slowly toward the door.

As soon as I'm in the hallway, I'll run for the nearest exit. I'll get home somehow—walk, or hitch, if I have to. I'll tell Mom what's happening. I'll make her believe me.

But as the classroom door closed behind me, I knew that wouldn't be possible.

Dead Man Titlebaum stood twenty feet away at the end of the corridor to my right. To my left, two more zombies were waiting. I didn't know who they were, although both wore janitors' overalls. They were the juicy kind, like the assistant principal. Together their three sets of lifeless yet malevolent eyes burned hungrily into me, their dripping, decaying bodies blocking any hope of escape.

"This way, William," Mr. Titlebaum commanded. He waggled one swollen purple finger at me.

I clutched my books to my chest, paralyzed.

"P-please..." I felt a tear trace down my cheek. "I... want my mom."

"*No. Mom. Boy*," the assistant principal said, this time speaking in that same strange way that Old Man Pratt had—without moving his lipless mouth. "*Go. On. And. Cry.*"

Suddenly I found myself praying that I *was* crazy. Crazy had to be better than what these things had in mind.

The zombies advanced.

I knew I ought to run, but my legs wouldn't budge.

Ms. Yu's classroom door burst open behind me. "Move!" a voice exclaimed. I was shoved roughly aside. My books crashed to the floor as a figure darted past me.

As I watched, thunderstruck, Helene Boettcher crossed the corridor at a run and yanked down on the fire alarm.

An electronic horn blared out of the school's PA system. The three zombies stopped. Seconds later, doors started opening up and down the hallway. Kids filed out, all wearing that interested, somewhat amused expression that comes whenever something unexpected breaks up the day's routine.

If they only knew.

I felt the first faint whisper of hope.

Then a dry bony hand dropped onto my shoulder. Ms. Yu's voice whispered in my ear, "What do you see, Mr. Ritter?"

A dozen feet away on either side of me, the zombies had recovered themselves and were focusing their attention on

Helene now. Dead Man Titlebaum charged at her, moving with surprising speed, his strong hands extended.

Seemingly unafraid, Helene reached behind her back and produced a gun!

Except it wasn't a real gun. It was molded plastic and dyed a pale blue color.

A water pistol?

Standing there with Ms. Yu's dead fingers digging painfully into my shoulder, the notion struck me—crazy though it was—that Helene would be expelled for bringing that thing to school!

As the assistant principal neared her, Helene fired a stream of water right into his face. To my astonishment, the dead man staggered back, clutching at his eyes as though blinded. Then, spinning on her heel, she fired twice more at the deceased janitors. This time she aimed low, catching them in the pants legs.

One of them changed direction and marched right into the wall, knocking off a mounted fire extinguisher. There he stood, twitching helplessly. The other one's legs stopped altogether. The corpse overbalanced and—his arms pinwheeling—crashed to the floor. When he tried to get up, I saw with horror that some of his face stuck to the floor and peeled away, revealing the underlying muscles.

Helene ignored them, crossed the hall, and fired another stream over my shoulder. It nailed Dead Woman Yu full in the face, driving her back through the open classroom door. I stood stunned, barely able to register what was happening.

A small, warm hand closed around mine.

"If you don't want to die," Helene said, "follow me."

CHAPTER 3

DEAD MEN HUNTING

Wait…a…minute!" I cried.

Helene ignored the protest, dragging me roughly back into the classroom, her water pistol trained on Ms. Yu, who had pressed her back to the blackboard and was now spasming as if in some kind of fit.

Around us, most of the kids were standing beside their desks—probably in response to the fire alarm. They were watching their math teacher jumping and thrashing like a hooked fish, their expressions ranging from astonishment to fear.

Only Brian seemed to have a voice. "Will? What's… going on?"

I had no idea what to tell him.

Abruptly Helene dropped my hand and snatched up a nearby desk chair. "Stand back!" she ordered. Then as we all watched in shocked silence, the girl I'd liked since September swung the chair in a wide arc and smashed out the nearest classroom window. What's more, she did it easily, smoothly, as if she shattered school windows all the time.

"Climb through!" she ordered me. "Watch out for broken glass."

"She broke the window!" Brian cried.

"No!" Our math teacher shrieked. She stumbled forward, reaching for us with her mummified hands, her skull's face twisted with rage.

I thought, *What on Earth are these other kids seeing right now?*

Helene didn't even look at the approaching corpse. She simply raised one arm and fired her pistol into the dead woman's right knee, just below the hem of the flowered dress. Ms. Yu suddenly veered to her right and began turning in a sloppy, frustrated circle around a leg that now seemed to have been rendered useless.

Still trailing behind her, a bunch of beetles got stomped.

"Get going!" Helene told me.

Feeling numb, I obeyed, gingerly avoiding the shards of glass that lined the window frame like shark's teeth.

The outside air was crisp with autumn's chill. The trees along Ridge Avenue were turning orange and yellow. Fifty yards to the left, the busy Shurs Lane intersection buzzed with late morning traffic. To the right—

To the right, three more zombies rushed toward me from the direction of the school's main entrance. They were all dressed like teachers and looked to be in varying stages of decomposition. One was so far gone that some of his body parts seemed about to fall off of him. Still he kept coming. They all did, closing in on me with terrifying speed.

"*There. Catch. Boy. Kill. Girl. Catch. Boy.*"

I heard Helene exclaim, "Run for Shurs! I'm right behind you!"

"Wh-what *are* those things?"

"Just run!"

So I ran, looking over my shoulder long enough to see Helene spring through the broken window after me. Behind her, the remaining windows of our mathematics classroom were filled with the pale faces of frightened kids. Brian's was among them.

No test today, dude.

We reached the intersection. The light was red, the traffic heavy. I stopped, panting and clutching a lamppost for support. Helene hardly seemed winded at all.

"Now will you tell—?" I began.

"Keep going!" She grabbed my hand again and pulled me down Shurs Lane in the general direction of home. "They'll be spreading the word about us! We've got to get off the main roads!"

A couple of blocks later, we turned left onto Mitchell Street, darting across the busy road and earning ourselves some angry horn blasts. Mitchell was a more typical Manayunk street, narrow and lined with houses. Through open windows I could hear TV's and radios playing—the sounds of normalcy.

After another block, Helene turned again and then again after that, leading us gradually downhill toward Main Street and the river. We ran until our hasty footfalls were all I could hear—well, those and my labored breathing.

"Where...are...we...going?" I croaked. She didn't reply. Somewhere off in the distance, police sirens blared. I swallowed and asked a different question. "They're hunting for us, aren't they?"

Helene treated me to a look that seemed to say *Duh!*

"My house is close by," I offered. "My mom—"

"No," she said flatly. "You can't."

"Why *not?*"

"There's no time to explain. Just—please, we have to keep going!"

She led me down a series of alleys and side streets, all of which finally dumped us near St. John's Church and the empty playground at Manayunk Park across from it.

"There!" Helene exclaimed. "Quick!"

She crossed the street and vaulted the playground fence like a hurdle jumper. Feeling outclassed, *I* had to climb it. Once inside she yanked me wordlessly to the ground—and just in time too. Lying there in the bushes, we both watched as a police car buzzed slowly down Churchview

Street, coming from the direction of the school. Its lights were flashing, but its siren was off. I could see two uniformed policemen sharing the front seat.

The one on the passenger's side was clearly dead.

I almost cried out, but Helene clamped a small hand over my mouth.

The police car slowed briefly in front of the playground. I could almost feel the corpse's milky eyes scanning the empty swings and monkey bars. It made my skin crawl. Surely the thing had spotted us!

The cruiser disappeared around the next corner.

Pressed so close beside me that I could almost feel her heartbeat, Helene sighed with relief. "They're gone. Let's go."

"Okay," I squeaked.

We finally reached the bottom of the hill. Here, Main Street ran the length of Manayunk, following the path of the Schuylkill River. Lined with hip shops, antique stores, and fancy restaurants, this part of town was almost always busy. Huddled together along a narrow side road, we peered out at the pedestrians and passing traffic.

"Two cop cars," Helene reported. "One three blocks south and heading away from us; the other coming this way and stopped up at the Cotton Street light."

"Are they all…zombies?" I asked.

"Don't call them *zombies*."

"Why not?"

She just shook her head.

"Okay—are they all dead?"

"No."

"Then can't we find one who isn't and, like, ask for help?"

She scowled at me. "And who do you think that cop's gonna believe? A couple of kids who just attacked some teachers and took off from school...or another cop?"

She was right, of course. It made me feel sick.

"So...what do we do?" I asked.

"We wait til it looks clear. Then we cross Main and head down to the tow path."

"The tow path?"

She nodded.

"But where are we going?"

"For now, just to a place where we can be safe for a little while."

I nodded. My side hurt from running. Hesitantly I asked, "Helene?"

"What?"

"Why are you helping me?"

She gave me a long look. "I'm an undertaker," she replied.

"What?"

But instead of explaining, she peeked around the corner again and declared, "The second cop car just turned down Cotton Street. Let's go!"

We went.

The tow path was a boardwalk that ran behind and

below Main Street, right along the hundred-year-old Manayunk Canal. Popular with joggers and cyclists, it ran the length of the neighborhood and was spanned by a handful of bridges that connected Manayunk with some old factories that were perched between the canal and the Schuylkill River.

We hurried along the boardwalk, seeing no one, and crossed one of the bridges. On the far side, Helene led me to a weedy vacant lot that sat in the shadow of a huge concrete railroad trestle. To our right was the canal and, beyond it, Manayunk. To our left, the Schuylkill River gurgled through the trestle supports and under the Belmont Avenue Bridge. Traffic noise rumbled close by.

I followed Helene down a makeshift stairway of broken concrete that reached almost to the edge of the river. Down there a large cement pipe lay half-buried in the bank, probably left over from some construction project.

Inside the six-foot-high pipe, a big hunk of plywood had been laid flat, creating a floor of sorts. On it were a sleeping bag, a big backpack, and a camper's kerosene lantern.

Helene produced a lighter and lit the lamp. Its yellow glow filled the space.

"Where are we?" I asked.

"It's where I sleep."

"You sleep *here?*"

She nodded absently and went to work shoving the meager assortment of personal effects into the backpack, leaving me to look around, feeling bewildered. What had she planned to do when winter came?

"Helene—" I began.

"I like that," she interrupted.

"What?"

"My name. You pronounce it right...with three *a*'s and no *e*'s. Most people don't. I like that."

"So is that why you helped me—because I say your name right?"

She laughed but without humor. "No."

"Then why—?"

"There'll be time for that later. They're gonna keep looking for us, and sooner or later, they'll come down here."

"Helene, I wanna go home."

She paused in her hasty packing, giving me a look of such regret that I went cold inside. "I know you do," she said. "But you can't—at least not right now."

I didn't want to hear that, and it suddenly occurred to me that I didn't have to listen. I could just take off and run home. It was still early in the day. Mom might still be there. I could almost *feel* her hug me. Heck, right now even one of Emily's sticky kisses would have seemed like paradise.

"You'd put them in danger," Helene said as if reading my mind. "Right now the best thing you can do is come with me."

"Where are we going?"

"Center City."

Center City Philadelphia, with its skyscrapers, museums, and monuments, lay a few miles to the southeast, along the river.

"What's in Center City?" I asked.

"You'll find out when we get there," she replied. "Look, Will, I know you're scared. If it makes you feel any better, *I'm* scared. But you've got to trust me. I know what I'm doing."

That seemed quite a promise coming from someone who lived in a pipe. Was Helene homeless? She didn't look homeless—she was always dressed neatly, her hair clean and brushed. And homeless children didn't go to school—at least not in Manayunk.

Besides, weren't homeless people sometimes crazy? Helene wasn't crazy.

Then, as I watched, she started talking into her wrist.

"This is Manayunk One," she said. "I'm coming in."

I blinked.

There was a crackle of static, followed by a male voice. "This is Haven, Manayunk One. What's your situation?"

"I've got a Seer with me. We've been blown, and the Corpses are looking for us."

"Okay, Manayunk One." There was a pause. "The Chief's here. He wants to know if it's Ritter you've got."

Helene smiled slightly. "Tell him yes."

Another pause. "The Chief wants you to bring him here."

Helene frowned. "To Haven?"

"Affirmative."

"Not First Stop?"

"Not First Stop, Manayunk One."

"Okay..." she replied, clearly taken aback. "But we still need a way outta here."

"Looks like the nearest train station is at Shurs Lane and Manayunk Avenue."

"They'll be watching that."

"Okay. How about Bala Station at Bala and City Line?"

"Isn't that just the other end of the R6 line?"

"It's a different route with the same number. That should throw the Corpses off."

"Cool. That works."

"Come up at Tenth Street and expect a Number Twenty-Four."

At that, Helene actually laughed a little. "Okay. Thanks, Haven. I'll signal when we're at Market East."

"Understood. Good luck. Haven out."

Helene rubbed her face with her hands.

"Who was that?" I asked.

"I'll explain later. We've got to go." She scooped up her loaded backpack and headed for the mouth of the pipe.

"Wait!"

She sighed impatiently. "What?"

"Those things back there—those dead people..."

"What about them?"

I swallowed. "You...can see them too?"

She studied me. Then she smiled. "Yeah, Will. You're not insane. I can see them too. Now, let's go. I promise to answer all your questions but not yet. Wait until we're someplace safe."

"Is there such a place?" I asked a little desperately.

Her smile widened. "You bet there is!"

CHAPTER 4

INTO THE CITY

We didn't reach the Bala Train Station until mid-afternoon, after a long hike that took us across the river, along narrow tree-lined roads, and through fancy neighborhoods. At last, tired and hungry, we staggered out onto City Line Avenue, so named because it marked Philadelphia's northeastern border. It was a wide street—far wider than anything in Manayunk. Its six lanes were choked with cars and buses.

"Which way?" I asked wearily.

Helene pointed north.

City Line was a big business spot, so there were plenty of people around. Thankfully nobody paid any attention to us as we trudged along the sidewalk.

"I don't see any of them here," I said.

"Me neither."

"They're not all in Manayunk, are they?"

"You wish."

"Then why are there zombies—?"

"Don't call them zombies," she said again.

"Why not?"

"Because zombies are slow and stupid, and the Corpses *aren't*. You want to remember that."

"Okay," I relented. "So why don't I see any…Corpses… around here?"

As if on cue, a limousine rolled to a stop half a block up. One of its shiny black doors opened, and a man in a three-piece suit emerged. Laughing, he turned to his companion, who was following him out of the car.

The second guy was dead.

As dead people went, he was freshest I'd seen. His body was straight and tall as he and his friend stood face to face on the sidewalk outside a big glass building that bore the sign *NBC-10,* complete with the familiar peacock logo.

"Spoke too soon," Helene remarked.

"He looks like someone important."

She looked pointedly at me. "That's Kenny Booth."

I was stunned. "The TV news guy? Mr. 'Get to the truth with Kenny Booth'?"

She nodded.

"He's…dead?"

"He's a Corpse."

"Isn't that the same thing?" I asked.

"Not exactly."

"Does he look like *that*...on TV?"

She shrugged. "Sure, if you're a Seer."

"Like us?"

"Like us," Helene said.

"But how can you tell?" I asked. "I mean, he looks—dead, just like all the rest of them. How can you tell he's Kenny Booth in particular?" Sure, he had a nice suit, but weren't there a lot of nice suits on City Line Avenue?

"I can see his Mask," she replied.

I blinked at her and then glanced over at the living man and dead man still standing on the sidewalk, chatting away like old pals.

"Try this," Helene told me. "Ever do one of those Magic Eye posters? You know, the ones where there's a picture *within* a picture, and you can only see the second picture if you hold your eyes a certain way?"

I nodded. My dad had brought one home a few years back, and Mom and I had spent half the night trying to spot the 3-D basketball player that he promised us was hidden inside the 2-D picture of a globe. Mom couldn't get it—but I could. It took some practice, and it gave me a headache after a while, but I finally saw the guy dribbling the basketball. An *autostereogram*, my father had called it.

It was pretty cool.

"Do that," Helene said. "Look at Booth again, but this

time try to look just in front of him. Let your eyes lose focus and wander a little bit. See what happens."

So I did. Standing there on that sunny sidewalk, with heavy traffic to our left and people moving past us on the right, I locked my gaze on the fancy-dressed cadaver. Then I kind of crossed my eyes the way I had with Dad's poster.

And it was just that easy.

Floating on top of the purple, bloated face appeared the familiar image of Kenny Booth, Philly's favorite TV news guy. His hair was perfectly styled, his teeth pearly white.

Seeing him like this—for the first time, I really understood just how well these Corpses had disguised themselves.

And it terrified me.

Then I blinked, and Booth's Mask disappeared, leaving behind an animated lump of dead flesh that was just now laughing at some comment his friend had made.

"Come on," Helene said. "We shouldn't stay out in the open too long."

Agreeing wholeheartedly, I followed her across the street, giving Booth and his buddy a wide berth.

Several blocks later, we reached the train station.

In half an hour, we'd be in Center City. By now, of course, my mother was already there. She worked as a nurse at Children's Hospital and would be doing the noon to eight shift today. Emily would be at Grandmom's as usual. My life. So normal. So boring. What I wouldn't give to just step right back into it!

As we stood on the platform waiting for the next train, I glanced nervously at Helene. Who was this girl? She'd simply shown up for school in September, a little over a month ago. *New to town*, the teachers had said. Pretty and friendly, she'd quickly become popular. But she'd never been one of those girls to join cliques with her friends and treat everybody else like dirt. And she'd always been especially nice to me—although before today, I'd lacked the courage to say more than a dozen words to her.

Now she had saved my life, and she ran around as if fighting zombies—Corpses—and evading the police were everyday activities for her. On top of that, she lived in an abandoned pipe on a riverbank!

Where were her parents?

And what on Earth had she meant when she'd called herself an *undertaker*? Wasn't that a funeral director or something?

The train arrived, and we boarded it. Within minutes we were headed into Center City, leaving my entire life behind us.

I turned to Helene, determined to finally get some answers, but she beat me to the punch. "Your dad was a cop, right?"

I blinked. "What? Oh. Yeah."

"He died?"

"Two years ago."

"Killed on the job?"

I nodded. This wasn't my favorite subject. My dad's death had hit me hard.

She studied me thoughtfully. "Sorry."

"Not as sorry as I am," I replied flatly.

"Guess not. You ever think about becoming a cop?"

"Sometimes."

"You'd be a good one," she said, surprising me. "You're brave."

"I don't feel brave."

"Brave people never do. But you kept your cool back there in the classroom. A lot of kids would've run away screaming."

"I wanted to," I said.

"Sure, but you didn't. That's brave."

"Not as brave as you."

She actually blushed a little. "Well—it's easier when you know what's going on."

"So how about helping me out? What *is* going on?"

"You'll find out later."

I frowned. "Why can't you tell me now?"

"Rules," she said. "Sorry. We have to wait til we get there."

"To Haven?" I asked, remembering the weird wrist radio conversation.

"Yeah."

"Is that who you were talking to...back in the pipe? Haven?"

She nodded.

"Uh-huh. But you can't tell me what Haven is?"

"Nope. Not until we get there."

"Fine," I said, frowning. "Can you at least tell me about the Corpses?"

She nodded.

"Good," I said, feeling annoyed. "Let's start with why they're dead."

"The Corpses aren't dead people. They're reanimated bodies that have been possessed."

"Possessed...by whom?"

"We don't know," she said with a shrug.

"Okay, then...how?"

Another shrug. "We don't really know that either—not for sure."

"Fine..." I said again, feeling frustrated. "Then let's try this: how can you and I see them when nobody else can?"

"The only people who can See them are kids," Helene replied. "But only a few, rare kids—and no adults at all."

"No adults?"

She shook her head. Then, turning away from me, she added quietly, "At least not anymore."

"Why not?"

"We don't know."

"You don't know much, do you?" I remarked bitterly.

"Sorry."

"How many Corpses are there?" I asked.

"Thousands. Maybe tens of thousands. They started showing up about three years ago—just a few at first but more all the time. Now they're all over the city."

"Is it some kind of invasion?"

"That's what it looks like."

"And what would happen if I went home?"

"They'd kill you," she replied simply. "And probably your family too—just in case. They go after anybody who can See them."

"My neighbor's one of them," I said.

She smiled thinly. "I know."

"I thought I was going nuts!"

"I'll bet you did," Helene said gently. "I could tell that in class this morning. From the way you were staring at Ms. Yu, I figured that you'd finally started Seeing."

"*Seeing?*"

"That's what we call it when you start recognizing the Corpses for what they are."

"So you could See Ms. Yu too," I said.

She nodded.

"And it didn't bother you?"

"I'm used to it."

"Has she always been—you know, dead?"

Helene nodded.

"From the beginning of the school year?"

Another nod.

"Why would a Corpse be teaching math at our middle school?"

"It's a cover," she said. "They all have to pretend to lead ordinary lives—to be like the humans around them."

"But they're everywhere!" I exclaimed.

"There are a lot of them in Manayunk," she said. "More than in most other parts of the city."

"Why? What's so special about a little neighborhood like Manayunk?"

She shook her head. "I'd better let Tom answer that one."

"Tom?"

She didn't reply.

"Tom who?"

She only shook her head again.

"He's at Haven?"

"Yeah. Hang in there, Red. We'll be there soon."

I sat back and closed my eyes, listening to my heartbeat. It sounded really loud. "Do me a favor," I said.

"Sure."

"Don't call me Red."

A pause. "Okay."

We spent the rest of the ride in silence.

CHAPTER 5

NUMBER 24

When I was ten, my dad took us all sightseeing in Center City Philadelphia. We visited Independence Hall, Betsy Ross's House, and the Liberty Bell in its glass pavilion. But my favorite part was the trip to the top of City Hall Tower, where a huge statue of William Penn, the city's founder, stood overlooking everything.

The view amazed me, although it scared Emily, who'd been only three at the time. So Mom took her back to the elevator, leaving me and Dad alone on the small observation platform that encircled the base of the statue, high above the city.

Dad pointed out all the surrounding skyscrapers and told me that when he'd been a kid, City Hall had been the tallest building in town. Apparently there used to be this law saying that nothing could be taller than the top of Billy Penn's head. I remember the two of us looking up at the statue: a man with a long coat, funny shoes, and curly locks of hair half-hidden by a wide-brimmed hat. He seemed big, old Billy Penn.

But not as big as my dad.

I'd grown up thinking my father was invincible and eternal, just like Penn's statue. But he'd also been a great guy, quick to laugh or tease or tickle—always good for a game of chess or a story of his policeman's adventures on the Philly streets.

Standing there that day, side by side, neither of us knew that Detective Karl Ritter had just six months to live.

I'd been fatherless now for two years. Sometimes it felt like forever. Other times it seemed like he'd died only yesterday. It was something that Mom always told me I'd get used to. She was wrong.

"Will?" Helene asked, interrupting my memories. "You okay?"

I nodded.

We'd left the subway and had come up onto the streets of Philly. The two of us now stood on the corner of 10th and Market streets, waiting for the light to change. I'd forgotten how much bigger everything was here in Center City: the buildings, the traffic—even the air felt heavier. It was a little dizzying.

Helene whispered, "Don't look around so much."

"Why not?"

"Because there are Corpses closing in on us."

So of course I had to look around.

A dead woman was strolling along the street toward us, clutching a Macy's shopping bag in one dripping, decaying hand. She was trying to look casual, but her lifeless eyes kept flitting in our direction. A second cadaver—this one dressed like a construction worker, including hard hat, stood across the wide street. He was waiting—as we were—for the traffic light to change.

Swallowing, I spotted a third Corpse. This one was another cop, and he sat inside an idling police car maybe thirty feet away.

Watching us.

"Helene!" I muttered.

"I See them," she replied calmly. "Just stay close."

The light changed.

Helene raised her wrist to her lips and whispered something into her radio that I didn't catch.

The crowd of pedestrians stepped off the curb, pushing us along with them, moving hurriedly across Market Street.

Dead Man Cop stepped out of his car.

The shopper fell into step just a few clueless people behind us. Ahead, the construction guy advanced, his purplish skin stretched tight, his lipless mouth open in a sneer that no one but us could See.

Helene said, "When someone tells you to move—move."

I nodded, struggling to remain calm. Corpses closed in

on three sides of us. The cop placed one slimy, skinless hand on his nightstick.

They've trapped us! They expected us to take the train into town, and they were waiting!

We were halfway across the intersection now, each cadaver only steps away. My heart was hammering.

Would they simply snatch us and whisk us away to the waiting police car? Why not? We could scream ourselves hoarse—who would believe us? Who would defy a uniformed cop on the say-so of a couple of truant middle-schoolers?

The net was almost closed now. The cop had started to snap his rotting teeth open and closed, as if he planned to *eat* us. As he did, one of his eyes popped out, landing on the ground beneath his booted feet.

When, a moment later, he stepped on it and squashed it, I thought I might vomit.

"Coming through!" a voice suddenly called.

Around us, people cried out in alarm as a dozen kids on bicycles burst out from behind an idling bus. Ranging in age from fourteen to maybe seventeen, the cyclists weaved expertly through the stopped cars at the Market Street red light before pedaling right into the tangled mass of pedestrians.

Everybody scattered.

Dead Cop uttered an unearthly cry of rage. The other two Corpses suddenly leapt forward, reaching for Helene and me and moving incredibly fast. But the cyclists were faster. The nearest of the kids, a tall, dark-skinned girl with long dreadlocks pulled something off her back.

It was a Japanese sword.

As I watched, dumbstruck, she swung it savagely at Dead Construction Guy, lopping off both his outstretched arms at the elbows. The severed limbs dropped to the asphalt. The Corpse stared at the stumps, looking more annoyed than anything else. An instant later, twin streams of pistol water, fired by two of the other riders, caught him and the woman shopper full in the face.

The pedestrians all ran, some cursing, some screaming—but all seemingly oblivious to the amputation that had just taken place in their midst.

The next thing I knew, I was surrounded by bicycles. They stopped around us, forming a tight circle, every one of their riders brandishing a water pistol. They were each, I saw, riding a Schwinn Stingray—the coolest thing going these days, a muscle bike with V-back drag bars and a banana-shaped, low-ride saddle. The nearest rider, an older kid wearing a leather jacket and dark sunglasses, grabbed me and pulled me up onto the back of the bike's long seat.

"Hang on!" he commanded.

I gratefully wrapped my arms around his waist.

Dead Cop made one final grab for me. The cyclists all fired at once, soaking him. He tumbled to the street, twitching spastically.

Then we pedaled away with surprising power, making a sharp left turn onto 10th Street and heading north, leaving the chaos and carnage behind us.

"Nothing to it!" Helene called, grinning at me from the back of another bicycle, her brown hair flying behind her.

Despite everything, I grinned back.

Because there *had* been nothing to it. Whoever these people were, they were good!

We navigated the Philly streets at a breakneck pace, making sudden, sharp turns that took us down narrow roads and through back alleys. Within minutes, we'd left behind the skyscrapers of Center City, entering instead an urban neighborhood that seemed to include little more than warehouses, factories, and vacant lots.

I'd never been in this part of the city before. There was less traffic, and the shadowed streets grew darker. And there were homeless people everywhere—some huddled in doorways; others meandering along the sidewalks.

With a final turn, we spilled onto Green Street. Several yards up ahead, a plywood ramp led from the street down into the entrance of a dilapidated underground parking garage. The six-story building above was splattered with red warning signs, its windows boarded up.

This building condemned by the City of Philadelphia. Trespassers will be prosecuted!

The bikes buzzed down into the parking garage like bees returning to their hive.

CHAPTER 6

HAVEN

Beyond the ramp, the light diminished, and the cyclists began wheeling their way down a long, spiraling concrete tunnel. I glanced behind us just in time to see the ramped entrance closing somehow.

"Will?" Helene called. "You okay?"

"Yeah!"

Then my driver added, "Chill out, Helene. I've got your boyfriend!"

Some of the other riders laughed. I felt my cheeks redden.

The girl with dreadlocks spoke. Her Japanese sword had been returned to a black sheath that she wore on her back. "Shut it back there, and get ready for the jump!"

"Jump?" I asked.

"Jump," my driver replied.

A moment later the tunnel abruptly straightened, running for a final fifty feet before hitting a solid brick wall. In front of the wall, someone had erected a wooden bike ramp.

"Uh—" I began.

The dreadlocked leader hit the ramp first. With a cry of sheer abandon, she and her bike took flight, colliding with the wall at terrifying speed—

—and vanishing.

The wall seemed to *ripple* a little bit but then settled right back.

I stared in disbelief. Off to my left, I heard Helene laughing. "Faster, Burton!" she exclaimed, smacking the boy's helmet. "Watch this, Will!"

She and Burton made their jump, and exactly the same thing happened—the brick wall just kind of swallowed them up.

"How…? What…?" I stammered.

"It's magic, kid!" my driver replied. Then with a final, powerful kick, we followed the rest of the cyclists up the ramp and into empty air.

I squeezed my eyes shut, but there was no crash. Instead something like stiff plastic brushed my face and then we were on solid ground again. Warily I opened one eye.

We were in a brightly lit room as big as a soccer field. The ceiling looked fifty feet high, lined with pipes and hanging fluorescent lamps. Along the walls, plywood partitions had been erected, closing off small sections from the rest of the open space. The floor was gray-painted concrete.

Feeling dizzy, I looked back the way we'd come. There was no brick wall. But there *was* a doorway—one big enough for a truck to pass through—with a strange curtain draped across it. It seemed to be made of dozens of strips of heavy plastic, all painted to look like bricks.

From this side, the illusion was pretty obvious. But in the dimly lit tunnel, those strips of flexible plastic looked exactly like an impenetrable brick wall.

The cyclists all parked their rides in a designated area. Around us, people rushed forward to accept the riders' gear and help them dismount. I gaped at all the activity. Everyone was in motion. Everyone was busy.

And every one of them was a kid—many not much older than me.

The dreadlocked leader pulled off her helmet and tossed it to a younger girl, thirteen maybe, who was collecting them. Then she dismounted and hurried over to a tall, dark-skinned boy her own age, who interrupted his conversation with two other kids in order to greet her.

"Any problems, Sharyn?" I heard him ask. His voice was deep and authoritative.

"Nothing to it, bro." Sharyn grinned. "Credit's all Helene's though. She tipped us off, and we made the grab and split before the Deaders even knew what happened!" Then she laughed—the sound strangely musical.

I climbed unsteadily off the rear of the bike. My driver slapped my back. "Good ride, kid. I'm Chuck Binelli."

"Will…Ritter."

He grinned. "I know. Welcome aboard, Will."

I wanted to ask "Aboard *what?*" but suddenly Helene was there, grabbing my arm and pulling me across the floor.

"What *is* this place?" I asked her.

"This is Haven!" she replied. "Yeah, I know it's kind of a stupid name, but it goes back to the beginning, so we're kind of stuck with it. This big room here is where most of the work gets done. We pretty much just call it the Big Room. Imaginative, huh? Anyway, come on—there are some people who've been waiting a long time to meet you."

A long time?

"Tom…Sharyn, this is—" Helene began, dragging me over to the tall boy and the dreadlocked girl. I suddenly noticed how alike they were, even down to their identical brown eyes.

"—Will Ritter," the boy finished. He smiled and stuck out his hand. "Tom Jefferson. This here's my sister, Sharyn."

He shook hands with me—something I wasn't very used to doing.

"Um…hi" was all I could think of to say.

"He wants to be a cop!" Helene declared. I looked at her, a bit surprised that she would just blurt that out.

"That right?" Sharyn remarked. She elbowed me playfully. "Straight or bent?"

"Sharyn!" Tom said sharply.

"Just kidding!" The girl winked at me. "A straight cop, huh, Will?"

"Just like his old man," Tom added.

"How do you know about my dad?" I asked.

Tom glanced at Helene. "You didn't tell him?"

"Didn't feel right," she replied. "I didn't know the guy. You two did."

"Thanks, Helene," said Sharyn, looking as if she meant it.

Her brother nodded gravely. "Will, there's a whole mess of stuff that you need to know. But we ain't got time for all that. Right now I'm guessing that you're freaked out. I don't blame you. So let's keep things going on low gear for a while. When did you start Seeing Corpses?"

I said, "This morning."

Tom nodded again. With his thick neck and broad shoulders, he looked like a varsity football player. Beneath the closely cropped mat of kinky black hair atop his head, his dark eyes were filled with warmth, sympathy, and a fierce perception.

Quietly, he said, "Sucks...don't it?"

The question carried such sincerity, such understanding, that I had to swallow back a sob. "Yeah."

Helene patted my back.

"You must've figured you were crazy," Tom remarked.

"Who was it? Some teacher at school?"

"And my next-door neighbor," I muttered. "And some cops."

"And Kenny Booth," Helene chimed in.

Sharyn laughed. "Yo, Red! You *have* had a busy day!"

Beside her, Tom said soberly, "By now, Will, you must've figured out that you ain't alone in this. See all these kids around you? We're *all* Seers. And one way or another, every one of us has had a day like yours—the day when we found out about the Corpses."

I nodded, too overcome to speak.

"I wish I could answer all your questions right away," Tom continued. "But Helene did her job at your school and blew her cover doing it. I got to debrief her. That cool with you, Helene?"

"It's cool," Helene replied.

Tom nodded. "For now, Will—just chill. Sharyn, how's about hooking up our man here with some food and a bed?"

"I'm there," his sister said.

Sharyn spun me around and pointed me toward the rear wall of the Big Room. I glanced back at Helene, who smiled at me. "Let's go, Red," chirped Sharyn. "Some eats and you'll feel a whole lot better. Trust me!"

But I resisted, calling to Tom, who had already started off in a different direction with Helene in tow. "Wait! You said something about my dad?"

He looked back at me. "It'll keep," he said. "But I'll tell you two things right now. First: none of this"—he gestured around at the Big Room—"would be here without your dad. Yeah, Sharyn and me knew him well. And second: your rolling in here today was expected, Will. Fact is, we've been expecting you for a long time."

I absorbed this as best I could.

Too much too quickly.

Half out of fear and half out of frustration, I blurted, "Who the hell are you people?"

Tom smiled.

"You've met the Corpses," he said. "Well—we're the Undertakers."

CHAPTER 7

SHARYN

So...how's it hanging, Red?" Sharyn asked as she led me across the Big Room. All around us, Haven was alive with activity.

"Don't call me Red," I said wearily.

Sharyn's dark eyebrows rose. "Not hanging so good, huh?"

I didn't answer. She shrugged. "Not much for talking either, I guess."

"Yo, Sharyn!" someone called.

A short, rather chubby girl with curly brown hair ran up to us, rubbing greasy hands on the stained mechanic's apron she wore. "What did you think of those new shocks Alex and me slapped on the Stingrays?"

"They were fierce, Tara!" Sharyn replied enthusiastically. "Like riding on air! You should've seen those Deaders bail when we pedaled through!" She touched the hilt of her sword, which she still wore on her back. "I even got a piece of one with Vader here. And—oh!" She threw a surprisingly strong arm around my shoulders. I didn't like it. "This here's Will Ritter—Karl's kid. Got the Sight today, and him and Helene had to split his school shooting! Will, this is Tara Monroe. She's our Monkey Boss."

"Monkey Boss?" I asked.

"He *is* new!" the smaller girl said. "No First Stop?"

"Will's special," she replied. "Tom just had to meet him first."

"I'll bet he did!" Tara said, laughing. She turned to me. "*Monkey*'s our word for mechanic or handyman. And *Boss* just means that I tell whom when to fix what—like the bikes and other things."

"Oh," I said. "Hi."

"Not much for talking," Sharyn remarked.

"Give him a break," replied Tara. "He just started Seeing today!" Then to Will, "Your head must be, like, spinning, huh?"

I nodded.

"I got the Sight about eighteen months ago. It's, like, a miracle that I found my way to Haven before the Corpses got me. And even then it still took, like, a week before the shock wore off!"

"Yeah," I muttered.

"You get used to it," Sharyn remarked cheerfully.

Tara waved over a tall, blond-haired boy. "Hey, Alex! Check this out! Karl Ritter's kid just joined up today."

I managed a smile.

Alex didn't.

"Today?" the boy asked sharply. "Why's he here?"

Sharyn's expression darkened. "What do you mean, *Why's he here?* He's here because Helene brought him here."

Alex faced her. "Yeah? And why'd she do that? Funny, when I first got the Sight, I got dumped for two weeks in a boarded-up dry cleaners—getting *trained*."

Tara frowned. "Will's a special case—kind of like a celebrity!"

"Or a mole," Alex said.

Something told me I'd just been insulted by this jerk, although given the circumstances, I couldn't seem to muster up the energy to be angry.

"Will ain't no mole!" Sharyn declared. "And of course he'll do First Stop. Helene brought him here because Tom told her to. This ain't no stranger! Ain't we been watching him for years, waiting for today?"

Alex snorted, clearly unimpressed. He gave me a quick visual inspection. "All I see's a skinny, redheaded kid who won't be much good til he puts on some weight."

"And all *I* see is an obnoxious crud!" Tara snapped. "Go finish greasing those bikes!"

Alex smiled a smile that really had nothing to do with

smiling. To me he sneered, "See you around—celebrity." Then he stalked off.

"Um...sorry about Alex," Tara said awkwardly. "He's a great monkey. He's just—"

"What Tara here's saying," Sharyn cut in, "is that Alex Bobson's a jackass."

I couldn't have cared less about Alex Bobson. "What's First Stop?" I asked.

"Plenty of time for that!" Sharyn insisted. "Let's go, Red! See you, Tara!" Then she headed off without looking to see if I was following.

As I turned, a greasy hand touched my arm. "Listen—about Alex," Tara said. "He's had it worse than most. The Corpses killed both his parents trying to get him. He just barely got out alive and wandered the streets for, like, three months before we found him. That was more'n a year ago. The whole thing's kind of messed him up."

"It's okay," I told her.

She nodded. "Look, Will. I know you're shook. In my old life, my dad was a retired army sergeant. And his motto, as far back as I can remember, was *Be brave*. No matter what happens, a little bravery'll get you through it. So I guess, like, there's my advice, for whatever it's worth. Be brave."

Shrugging weakly, I replied, "I'm trying."

"Quit hanging back, Red!" Sharyn bellowed from some distance away.

"I wish she wouldn't call me Red," I muttered.

Tara rolled her eyes. "You're getting a pretty heavy dose of Sharyn today, huh?"

I shrugged, which she took as agreement.

"Yeah. She can take some getting used to. But once you get to know her, Sharyn's, like, awesome! The thing is, Tom and Sharyn both got orphaned real young and were out on the streets alone long before they got the Sight. Because of that, Sharyn sometimes doesn't quite get what the rest of us left behind. Tom's better at reading people than she is. Sharyn's cool, don't get me wrong. But she's, like, Sharyn."

I nodded.

"Well, I got work to do. It's gonna be okay, Will. Really."

"Sure," I replied, not believing a word of it.

"Yo, Will!" Sharyn called again. "You coming or what?"

Tara smiled and walked off, leaving me to catch up with my dreadlocked escort at a run.

"There you are!" she said, grinning. "You play sports?"

"What?"

"I watched you run just now. Nice form. You play sports?"

I remembered the three Most Valuable Player trophies on my bedroom shelf, all for soccer.

"Not really," I said.

"Your dad played football, didn't he?"

"Yeah. In college." I'd grown up hearing the stories.

"Ain't never seen him play, 'course," the girl said. "But I did get the chance to see him run more'n once. Sweet form. Same as you."

"Um…thanks."

She grinned again.

"Sharyn?"

"Yeah?"

"When's Tom gonna tell me about my dad?"

"Soon as he can. Tom's the man 'round here. He runs this place, top to bottom, and he ain't exactly big on free time."

"So…he's, like, the Head Undertaker?"

"Chief," she corrected.

"Chief Jefferson?"

"Chief Tom. But just call him Tom."

"I want to know what my dad's got to do with this place, Sharyn."

She looked hard at me. Then, as if reaching some internal decision, she replied, "Yeah, I guess that's cool. We owe you that much at least."

CHAPTER 8

TOM AND SHARYN

Karl Ritter was this cop who was tight with runaway kids—like me and Tom." She sighed. "Your old man was cool, Will…I mean, for a cop. And of course he's the first and only adult we know of to ever get the Sight."

"What?" I cried so loudly that Sharyn actually jumped.

"What'd I say?" she asked.

"My dad could See the Corpses?"

She nodded.

I experienced an almost dizzying sense of unreality. For the last two years, I'd been a boy without a father—and my memories of my dad had gotten me through a lot of sleepless nights. But now I'd just learned that there'd been a part of my father's life that I'd never heard about. Did my mom know?

"Freaked you out, huh?" Sharyn said. "Sorry. Figured Helene would've told ya that."

"She didn't. It's okay. Keep going."

With a shrug, she continued. "Well…me and Tom are twins. Got orphaned at two. Never knew our folks. Just went through this long string of foster homes—so many that we lost count. Anyway, by the time we were your age, we'd had enough. So we bailed out of the last gig and hit the streets. Been on our own ever since."

She shook her head at the memory. "The streets are hard, Will. Growing up in the 'burbs the way you did, you got no clue. Every scumball we met wanted something from us, and most of it wasn't what you'd call nice. Tom and me figured out quick that surviving meant looking out for ourselves. No cops. No social workers. Just us doing what we had to do. Get it? And that meant… well…crime.

"Just small stuff at first. Shoplifting. Purse snatching. Then later we started boosting houses over in Society Hill and Rittenhouse, where the money is. First, smash-and-grabs—nickel-and-dime stuff. But the more we did, the more we learned to do. Before long we were about the choicest pair of juvie thieves this city ever saw! I'm talking some serious game here—Tom especially. Got an eye for detail, my bro. Planned out every job carefully ahead of time. Cops never touched us. Til one night, that is."

Sharyn smiled wistfully. "We were down near Penn's Landin', breaking into this sweet redbrick townhouse. BMW in the drive. River view. We could almost smell the scratch! We hit it one night while the owners were off on some island someplace. Picked the lock. Aced the security system. No sweat. Except that when we split out the back door with the spoils, your dad was waiting for us."

"My dad? What did he do?"

She chuckled. "Guess you could say he made us an offer we couldn't refuse. But I should let Tom tell you the rest. He's better at telling stories than me anyway. 'Sides, here's where we eat."

Disappointed, I almost complained. But then I smelled food, and my stomach grumbled. I'd skipped lunch completely, and that Pop-Tart felt like a lifetime ago.

We'd reached a roped-off section of the Big Room that had been turned into a makeshift cafeteria. There were a few old refrigerators, some microwaves, a hot plate, and even a soda fountain. Long metal tables had been lined up. A few kids sat at one, sharing a freshly nuked bag of popcorn.

"You like Hot Pockets?" Sharyn asked me.

"Huh? I guess."

Nodding, she pulled a couple of the frozen wraps from the nearest freezer and popped them into a microwave. As they cooked, she introduced me to the kids at the table, whose names I immediately forgot.

"How many Undertakers are there?" I asked her.

"We're at about 120 or so, what with new recruits like you and all."

"I'm not a recruit," I said.

"Whatever."

"And all these kids can See the Corpses?"

"That's why they're here."

"But...how did they all get here? What do you do, put an ad in the papers? *Seeing dead people? Come join the Undertakers!*"

Sharyn laughed. "No—but I like it. Most come in the same as you. They start Seeing one day. It freaks them out—and that, in turn, flags the Deaders. So one of us slides in and does the rescue thing."

"But how do you know to be there to rescue them in the first place?"

"We keep an eye on the middle schools in town."

"All of them?"

She nodded. "Each one's got at least one schooler on site, looking out for Seers."

"Schooler?"

"Undercover Undertaker. They're trained to impersonate real students."

"Like Helene?"

Sharyn nodded.

"So—none of these kids can go home either?" I said.

"Nope."

I swallowed back a desperate moan. I didn't want to stay here! However grateful I felt to these people, there was no way that I was giving up my life to join this—well, *gang* was the only word I could think of.

"After this I'll introduce you to Steve-o," Sharyn said.

"Steve-o?"

"Steven Moscova. Our tech whiz. He dreams up all our gadgets. You know—like Q in the James Bond movies. He's a total nerd, but we love him anyhow."

The microwave beeped.

We sat and ate our food, although it didn't seem to have much taste. Funny—a couple of minutes ago, I'd been starving.

"I don't like the name," Sharyn said offhandedly.

"What name?"

"*The Undertakers*. Tom came up with it after your dad died. I get the idea—burying the dead and all. But I still think it lacks style."

I shrugged.

"How about something cooler," she suggested, "like *the Kid Kadets*...with a *K*?"

"Isn't *cadets* spelled with a *C*?"

"Well, yeah...but it's cooler to cap two words with the same letter. Like *Undercover Undertakers*. Alliteration. Didn't they teach you nothing in English class?"

"Guess not."

"Anyways, it'd be awesome," Sharyn said. "Don't you think?"

"Sure. Awesome."

She grinned. "Done eating?"

I nodded.

"Grab some candy then."

A number of colored candies filled a bowl in the center of the table. I picked one up. "What is it?"

"Candy-coated chocolate," Sharyn replied. "Homemade! Try one. Way better'n M&M's."

I tasted the candy. It *was* good. "You make these here?"

"One of the moms does."

My head shot up. "Moms?"

"They ain't real moms," she told me. "That's just what we call them. Actually it's this kid named Nick who makes them. He wants to be a baker someday, so he's figured out this way to candy-coat lumps of chocolate, sometimes with nuts. Good, ain't they?"

"Yeah. Can I have another?"

"Take as many as you want, Red. No parents here. 'Course, no dentists neither—which turns out to be a problem sometimes." Another grin. "But nothing's perfect."

I popped a fistful of candies into my mouth.

Sharyn laughed. "I'd say fill up your pockets, but I've done it, and they just melt. Ready to go?"

I nodded, my mouth thick with chocolate.

"Cool! Let's do it!"

CHAPTER 9

SALTWATER

In the southwest corner of the Big Room, a series of long tables had been set up around an area of open space so that they formed a big square. Atop these tables stood an assortment of computers, Bunsen burners, test tubes, and other gadgets. A half-dozen kids of varying ages busied themselves at assorted workstations, tapping keys, turning dials, tipping test tubes, or taking notes.

In the middle of all this scientific chaos, a skinny kid with straight dark hair and thick glasses moved among the workstations. In each case, he either offered approval or corrections.

"Yo, Steve-o!" Sharyn announced. "This here's Will Ritter, Karl's boy. He just joined up."

I almost reminded Sharyn that I hadn't *joined up* for anything.

The kids at the tables all stared curiously at me.

Then Steve asked distractedly, "Karl who?"

Subdued laughter rippled among his coworkers. Sharyn's face darkened. "What do you mean, *Karl who?* Karl Ritter!"

"Oh. Right. Hi."

"Hi," I said.

Sharyn groaned. "Sorry, Will. This here's Steve Moscova, and we call this little nest of his the Brain Factory. Steve's little bro, Burton, rode with my crew today."

I remembered the boy who'd shared his bike with Helene.

Sharyn continued, "They're the Moscova Brothers! Except that Steve ain't quite so…I don't know…"

"Jock-ish?" Steve suggested. "Or maybe Jock *Itch* would be more accurate."

Sharyn snorted out a laugh. "Steve dreams up all our anti-Deader stuff. Whenever we need something, he's our Mr. Wizard."

"I've got work to do," Steve said flatly. "Nice to meet you, Bill."

"Will," I corrected.

"Right. Sorry."

Irritated, I looked away. Then something caught my eye: a set of plastic rifles mounted on the wall—more than a dozen of them.

"Hey!" I exclaimed. "Are those Super Soakers?"

Steve nodded absently.

"What are they for?"

He made a face. "Shooting Corpses. What else would they be for?"

Recalling Helene's water pistol, I asked, "What's in them?"

"Nothing," Steve said. "They aren't loaded."

I gave him a look. "Okay...then what *would* be in them if they *were* loaded?"

"H-2-O," Sharyn replied, smiling slyly. "Tap water."

"Water hurts Corpses?" I asked.

"Sure!"

Steve sighed. "Sharyn's messing with your head. She likes to tell new recruits that the Corpses are like those stupid aliens in that movie *Signs.* The truth, however, is that regular water is harmless to them. What we use is a solution of water and sea salt."

I blinked. "Saltwater?"

"You know it, Red!" Sharyn replied, slapping me on the back. "Steve discovered it! You shoot a Deader in the arm or leg and it goes numb. Shoot them in the face and they go blind and start bouncing off the walls!"

I remembered Ms. Yu and Assistant Principal Titlebaum. "Would enough of it kill them?" I asked.

The Brain Factory went quiet. Finally Sharyn said somberly, "We ain't got a way to kill a Corpse, Will...at least not yet. Saltwater slows them down, but it don't do nothing permanent."

"They usually recover within a few minutes," added Steve.

I looked from one to the other. "But—back on Market Street, Sharyn, you chopped the arms off of one of them with that sword on your back."

"Vader," she said, reaching up and patting the hilt.

"Whatever—that's *got* to do some damage! Don't tell me the arms just grow back!"

"They don't," said Steve. "But that Corpse will just Transfer."

"Transfer?"

"You haven't been to First Stop," he said.

Sharyn and I said "No" together, although I still didn't get what this First Stop thing was.

Steve nodded. "Then I'll give you the short version. Corpses aren't dead human beings. They're invaders who take possession of cadavers, the fresher the better, and animate them somehow. The bodies are like vehicles to them—ways to get around in our world. They keep each one for a while, until it starts really falling apart. Then they just Transfer to another one. The body you described—armless—will be pretty useless to that particular Corpse. So he'll Transfer."

"Probably already has," said Sharyn.

"Oh," I said. "But what about the body he's in? I mean, why don't people see the arms that Sharyn chopped off?"

Steve explained, "The Corpses have a way of blocking

what people see. But you'll learn more about that at First Stop."

"You mean it's part of their Masks," I said. "Helene told me about Masks. She even showed me how to spot a Corpse's Mask by holding my eyes just right."

Steve nodded. "Same technique for seeing an autostereogram. It's part of the First Stop training."

"Yeah," Sharyn added. "But it's good to know you got the knack for it down already. That'll speed things up for you."

Great, I thought bitterly.

Steve said, "You know, I remember giving your father a Magic Eye poster that I'd designed and printed out. This was a while back, when we were just beginning to understand the Corpses. He was the only adult that we know of to ever have the Sight—but he had some trouble spotting a Mask. I thought practice with it might help. Then of course he..." His words trailed off. When his eyes regained focus, he found Sharyn and me staring at him.

"Sorry," he muttered.

"Forget it," said Sharyn. "Red, don't you sweat none of that for now. Come on, I'll show you the dorms."

I frowned at them both, my mind spinning with questions. Where had these *invaders* come from? How had my dad found out about them? Why had he been the only adult who could See them?

And why hadn't I known about any of this?

That was the question that hurt.

Suddenly I didn't feel like asking it. I didn't feel like asking anything.

I turned to follow Sharyn.

"Wait a second," Steve said. "Before you go, help me test something."

Sharyn groaned again. "The last time you conned me into playing lab rat, my skin turned green for a week!"

"This isn't like that. I've been working on a new salt-water delivery system. Tom's worried that pistols draw too much attention for Schoolers. He asked me to come up with something less—conspicuous. Besides, I don't want you anyway. My prototype is for somebody a little—well, smaller. Bill here will do."

"Will," I corrected impatiently.

"Right. Sorry. Come around here."

I glanced at Sharyn, who shrugged. Then, feeling vaguely uneasy, I stepped around one of the lab tables and officially entered the Brain Factory. Steve looked me over. "We're about the same size. How old are you?"

"Twelve," I replied. "How old are you?"

"My age isn't relevant."

"He's fifteen," Sharyn offered.

"Take your shirt off," Steve said.

"What?"

"Take your shirt off."

"Why?"

"Look, do you want to help or not?"

The fact was that I didn't particularly want to help. I didn't particularly care about water pistols at the moment. I just wanted to go home.

Nevertheless I said, "I'll help."

"Then take your shirt off."

"Can I, you know—keep my pants?"

"Of course you can keep your pants!" he exclaimed.

I pulled my shirt over my head and tossed it to Sharyn, who sniffed it. "Phew! We've got to hook you up with some fresh clothes!" I almost said that I had a whole closet full of clothes back home, but I didn't.

Steve reached into a nearby box and pulled out a flat, rectangular plastic container with two long clear plastic tubes sticking out of either end. This he fitted around my stomach with a strap so the plastic container pressed against the small of my back. It was filled with water and felt cold against my skin. Then he fastened the tubes to my upper and lower arms with Velcro so each tube ran from my hand to the container against my spine. Each tube ended with a little plastic squeezable bulb that fit neatly in my palm.

"Now," Steve said, "put your shirt back on."

I did. The shirt hid the whole setup except for the plastic bulbs.

"What's it do?" I asked.

"The reservoir at your back holds saltwater. The pumps in your palms draw the water through the tubes and fire it out the ejectors behind them at high pressure. Try it out on the practice target." Steve pointed to a mannequin that stood in front of a nearby concrete wall.

"How much'll it hold?" Sharyn asked.

"About a pint. But the reservoirs can be daisy-chained together so a person could wear up to four at once. That would give you about half a gallon."

Sharyn frowned. "Pretty heavy."

Steve nodded. "Well, weight's always been a problem, hasn't it? No way to make water lighter, after all. Go ahead, Bill—give it a try."

I sighed and raised my right arm, pointing my wrist at the target. Bending my middle and third fingers, I pressed down on the bulb.

A spray of water shot from the curly antenna, hitting the mannequin square in the face.

"Sweet!" exclaimed Sharyn. "Try the other wrist!"

Impressed, I switched arms and did it again. Another hit. Despite myself, I laughed. "I feel like Spider-Man."

Sharyn chuckled. "Do both hands together."

Steve protested, "No! Wait!"

Too late. I raised both arms and fired—and the plastic reservoir on my back exploded, soaking my shirt and the seat of my pants. I cursed as cold water seeped into my boxers.

Sharyn burst out laughing.

"You can't fire both off at once!" Steve moaned. "To

force water out one side, the other side has to be free to take in air! Otherwise you put too much pressure on the reservoir, and it pops its seams. Ugh! Look at this! Hold still, Bill—let me get it off of you."

I spun around, wet and irritated and suddenly very angry. "My name is Will!" I screamed into the older kid's startled face. "Not Bill! Will!"

Steve's face paled, and he retreated. Behind him in the Brain Factory, the other kids stopped what they were doing.

"Sure," he muttered. "Sorry."

Suddenly Sharyn was between us. "Chill out, dudes! Yo, Will, let Steve get that crap off of you and then we'll head off someplace to get you dried and dressed. And Steve-o, get the dude's name right, okay?"

This from the girl who insists on calling me Red.

"Sure," the boy in glasses said again. "Will it is. Got it."

"Good," I muttered, feeling tired, embarrassed, and surprised at myself. I didn't usually go off on people like that.

Evidently things were changing—and so was I.

And just like that, I knew that I couldn't stay here anymore.

CHAPTER 10

ESCAPE

An hour later, I sat on a canvas folding bunk, dressed in borrowed clothes and staring down at my shoes.

Haven had two dormitories—one for boys and one for girls. Both were just pieces of the big room that had been sectioned off with unpainted plywood. Every kid in this place had an assigned bunk, although mine would be temporary. Apparently I would be spending the night here and would then go to First Stop—whatever that was—in the morning.

Spending the night here—with the Undertakers.

By now my mom must know some of what had happened at school. She had to be worried sick. She was probably home right now, calling in favors from all of Dad's old friends on the police force to help find her missing son. Except that I was here, in this unfindable place deep below a condemned building with a gang of runaways who seemed determined to make me one of them.

Besides, how many of those old friends might be *Corpses?*

I have to go home!

Coming here—allowing myself to be brought here—had been a terrible mistake.

That had suddenly become very clear to me. Forget what Helene had said about putting my mom and Emmie in danger. She was my mom! She'd know what to do! Mom always knew what to do.

I looked up. There were two other boys in the room, playing cards and laughing like friends.

I didn't want to make any friends in this place! I didn't want to See Corpses. And I sure as hell didn't want to be an Undertaker.

I stood up, my heart pounding. The card-playing boys ignored me. Slowly, afraid of being suddenly challenged—*grabbed*—I walked out of the room.

The Big Room was as busy as ever. Over to the left, I noticed an indoor skateboarding track, complete with slopes and quarter pipes. This place almost seemed like a kid's paradise. Free candy. Cool bikes. Junk food. Skateboarding. No parents. Heck, there was probably a rocking video arcade around here somewhere!

I felt nauseated.

There were Undertakers everywhere.

I walked through them, around them, amid them, and

no one called my name or asked me what I thought I was doing. No one really noticed me—not even when I circled around the corral area where they kept the Stingrays and stepped through the disguised plastic curtain that hid the entrance.

So simple.

I'd find a pay phone and call my house. Mom would come and get me. Mom would believe me about the Corpses. Mom would make it all right.

Once I was through the curtain and in the spiraling tunnel, I had to climb over the lip of the ramp that Sharyn and the rest of the cyclists had jumped off when we'd arrived here. After that I just started running. It was a long run, and all uphill, but I didn't care. I ran until my breathing came in painful gasps and my vision blurred, and still I didn't slow down. Finally I staggered into the late afternoon sunshine on Green Avenue, blinking and sweating, and headed immediately for the nearest corner.

There were people around, but thankfully no Corpses. No one noticed me. It was almost as if I were invisible or something. I liked it. I felt as if it protected me.

It took a while to find a pay phone. The neighborhood wasn't a good one.

I finally wandered, half-exhausted, into a Laundromat and spotted a phone on the wall. Silently grateful, I ran to it and snatched up the receiver. It dawned on me at that moment that I could count on one hand the number of times I'd used one of these things! These days everybody carried a cell phone. If my own hadn't still been in my backpack in Dead Ms. Yu's classroom, I wouldn't have come in here at all!

It made me wonder if pay phones like this even worked anymore.

It did. I could hear a dial tone.

After fumbling in my pockets for loose coins, I finally wised up and read the instructions. Then I dialed *0* and waited until a woman's voice asked me if I wanted to make a collect call. I did, and I gave the voice my name and home phone number.

"Please hold," she said. There came a pause, followed by some clicks.

There was no ringing—just a short silent wait that almost drove me insane.

Then: "Will?"

"M-Mom?" I choked, squeezing my eyes shut.

"Will? Honey? Is that you?" Her relief and terror nearly broke my heart. "Where are you? What's happened? Are you—?"

I opened my eyes, wiping at the tears that filled them—and froze.

A Corpse was looking down at me.

Remember the *holy crap factor?* Well, at that moment, I came pretty close to factoring into my pants.

She was a *ripe* one, tall and thin, her gray skin oily and

hanging loose off her bones. Her hair fell from her scalp in thin, dark wisps—and her milky eyes locked right on me.

I dropped the receiver. I could hear my mom calling my name.

The Corpse grinned. Then she spoke. "William Ritter, I presume?"

We were alone in the Laundromat. I'd been in such a hurry to get to the phone that I hadn't even bothered to scope the place out. Around us some of the big dryers were rumbling loudly, drowning out whatever noise I might make.

I tried to run, but the dead woman was too fast—way too fast. She shoved me hard in the chest, sending me staggering back against the wall, knocking over a trash can.

Then before I could steady myself, she closed on me again. One of her hands, smelling of rotten eggs, seized my throat.

I gagged as the fingers tightened.

Within moments I felt my sneakers leave the floor. I hung in her grasp, my eyes bulging, thrashing as helplessly as a fish on a hook.

The Corpse grinned wider.

"Don't worry, little one," she hissed. "I won't kill you."

Then, as my vision blurred, my eyes involuntary crossed, letting me glimpse the Mask hovering atop the rotting lump of meat that had me by the throat.

The gray curly hair. The wrinkled, spotted face. The kindly expression.

I was being choked out by a monster pretending to be a little old lady.

Darkness closed in around me.

"We have plans for you, William Ritter," Dead Old Lady whispered.

Then her head came off.

One minute, she was grinning at me with her black lips and yellowed, decaying teeth. The next, this look of surprise flashed across her face as her head went spinning through the air in a flash of silver. There wasn't much blood. After all, her heart hadn't been beating. Her arteries had probably dried up days ago.

For one horrible moment, the hand around my throat continued to choke me. Then its grip loosened, and it fell with the rest of her to the tile floor. I dropped back down onto my sneakers, the world seeming to tilt around me. I had to clutch at the wall to steady myself. Gradually my vision cleared.

Sharyn spun her sword smoothly and sheathed it on her back.

"Out for a walk, Red?" she asked with a smile.

I didn't know what to say.

She shrugged. "Still not much of a talker, huh? No sweat. Saw you split Haven and figured I'd better follow along. This can be a rough part of town."

I looked at the phone and then down at its dangling receiver. Before I could reach for it, Sharyn hung it up without a word. Through it all, I could hear my mother calling—screaming—my name.

My throat, already sore from the Corpse's attack, now closed up for another reason.

"I want to go home," I whispered.

Sharyn nodded, still smiling. "Why don't you talk that one over with Tom, huh?" She looked around the Laundromat. "Let's go. Even Deaders got to do the wash thing, I s'pose—but I don't figure this one was using all these machines. Somebody'll come by."

"They'll find the body?" I asked hopefully.

"Not unless she wants them to—and she doesn't."

I blinked."I…don't understand. You said you couldn't kill a Corpse."

"You can't, and I didn't. She's still in there. But we don't got time to get into all that. Come on." She took my arm and led me, gently but firmly, back out onto the street.

We returned to Haven walking side by side, Sharyn humming some tune I didn't know and me once again staring down at my shoes.

"Am I in trouble?" I asked finally.

"For what?"

"For trying to go home."

She chuckled. "Will, if every new recruit who bailed got into trouble, Tom and me would probably be alone in there. Don't worry over it." Then, looking sideways at me, she said, "Hey, you never asked me about Vader."

"What?"

"My sword. Ain't you curious about it?"

Right then, I both was and wasn't. But I supposed talking about that was better that thinking about what my mom was going through at the moment. "It's a *katana*, isn't it?" I asked.

"Nope. It's a *wakizashi*. That's a Japanese word that means 'sidearm.' It's smaller than a katana—easier to hide under a jacket or something."

"Why do you use it?"

"Because I don't like squirt guns," she said. "Besides, when Corpses get doused, they can pretty much shake it off. But lop something off their sorry butts, and there ain't nothing for them to do but Transfer. Keeps 'em down longer."

"Then why doesn't everyone in the group carry one?" I asked.

Her grin widened. "Can you figure a hundred kids all running around with swords?"

I had to admit I couldn't.

"I'm a special case," she added.

No argument there.

"Where did you get it?" I asked.

I expected her to tell me she'd stolen it, maybe back in the days when she and her brother had been boosting houses to get by. But instead, she said, "Your old man gave it to me."

My father gave her a sword?

One more painful mystery. One more thing I didn't feel like exploring.

I fell silent. She let me be. And we finished our walk that way.

When we got back to Haven—once again traveling down that long, spiraling tunnel and through the curtain of "bricks"—everything was pretty much as it had been. If my escape had made any kind of splash, it didn't show—at least not until Sharyn escorted me back into the boys' dorm.

Helene was waiting for me.

One girl saw the other, and something passed between them. Sharyn patted my shoulder. "Good luck," she said to me. Then she turned and left.

The card players were still there, ignoring us completely. Otherwise the room was empty. Helene stood beside the bunk that had been assigned to me. Her hands were on her hips. Her eyes locked on mine almost as fiercely as the Corpse's had back in the Laundromat.

Then she marched right up and punched me in the stomach.

CHAPTER 11

FACING FACTS

Gasping, I doubled over, feeling all the blood drain from my face.

Helene exclaimed, "Do you know what you almost did?"

I gulped for air. Helene had hit me pretty hard, but something told me it wasn't as hard as she *could* have hit me, so I figured maybe keeping quiet was better than trying to defend myself just now. She didn't seem to need my half of the conversation anyway.

"They're looking for you, you idiot!" she cried, waving her hands in the air. "They're out there right now. Hundreds of them! Maybe thousands! And by this time, every one of them knows what you look like! How many did you run into? Well? How many?"

With an effort, I found my voice. "Just one."

"Where?"

"Laun...Laundromat."

Helene blew out a sigh. "You got that far? Good. At least they didn't close in on you too close to *here*." She stomped away, back toward my cot. With a groan of effort, I straightened.

She said sharply but with less anger, "Will, if they'd caught you, they'd have made you lead them right back here. Don't you realize that? If the Corpses ever find out where we are..." Her words trailed off. "I'm sorry I hit you," she said after a long moment.

"Me too," I replied.

At that she almost smiled. She had a nice smile, but right then, I wasn't interested in it or her.

Helene sighed again. "I guess I...kind of forgot what it's like on your first day. You okay?"

"Yeah."

She conjured up an awkward laugh. "Hey—I hear you had some fun with Steve earlier. Here's a tip: don't test anything he gives you unless you've seen at least three other people test it first."

Then when I didn't reply, she made an exasperated face. "I said I was sorry."

"I know."

"Will you please talk to me?"

"I wanna go home, Helene."

"I know how you feel."

"No, you don't," I said.

"Yeah, Will, I do. What do you think—that I was born here?" Helene stepped up to me and took my arm, looking dismayed when I flinched. She led me to my cot, sat me down, and then settled herself beside me. Quietly she explained, "I grew up in Allentown. That's about an hour northwest of here. Ever hear of it?"

I took a deep breath, still hugging my stomach. "It's where Dorney Park is," I remarked. That was a local amusement park.

She nodded. "We used to go there a lot when I was a little kid."

"How'd you end up here?" I asked.

"One morning I started Seeing dead people. Not a lot of them—just a few here and there. Scared the crap outta me! I told my mom and dad. They thought I was nuts. Gave me all these tests—all these pills. That's happened to a lot of kids around here. Of course, none of it did any good. The Corpses were still there.

"So they stuck me in a nuthouse—only they called it a hospital. Doctors would jab me with needles and ask me about my dreams. I was there about a month when a new nurse showed up: Mrs. Greer. But Mrs. Greer wasn't alive." She looked pointedly at me. "Can you guess where I'm going with this?"

I nodded.

Helene continued, "I found out later that the Corpses infiltrate nuthouses that handle kids. They're looking for

Seers like us—the ones who get locked away for saying that they can See the Corpses for what they really are."

"What do the Corpses do when they find one?"

She grimaced and then ran a finger under her throat from ear to ear.

I swallowed dryly. I didn't want to believe this.

Helene went on. "One night after lights out, Mrs. Greer came after me—ready to put a pillow over my face and then fake some kind of accident or something. All of a sudden, this boy and girl, both dressed like orderlies, burst through the door. The boy shot a water gun into Mrs. Greer's face and then the girl chopped her head off with a sword! I never saw anybody move so fast!

"Then the boy said to me, 'Helene, you're not crazy. And if you don't want to die, come with us now.'"

"Tom and Sharyn?" I asked.

"Yeah. Back then they still did a lot of the Seer runs themselves. See, the Undertakers watch the nuthouses for the same reasons the Corpses do. I mean, we can't put people on the staff, but we *can* hack into the patient files.

"Anyway they brought me here. That was nearly two years ago, not long after your dad..." Her words trailed off.

Swallowing, I did some math just to distract myself. "So...how old were you when you started Seeing Corpses? Ten?"

"Eleven. I'm thirteen, Will."

"Oh," I said, surprised. I'd assumed that she was twelve, like me. "Don't you miss your parents?"

"Sure. Every day."

"Then why don't you just go home?"

"Because I love them, and I don't want anything to happen to them. The Corpses have been known to kill whole families if they think their secret might be in danger. Besides, as much as I know they love me, there's nothing—absolutely nothing—I could say that would make them believe me. Adults don't believe kids about stuff like this. They never have, and they never will. The Corpses know that. They count on it."

"I'll bet my mom would believe me," I insisted.

"I'll bet she wouldn't."

This time it was my turn to get angry. I jumped to my feet.

"Look!" I snapped, glaring down at this girl who'd saved my life today. "Just because *your* mom didn't believe *you* doesn't mean that mine wouldn't believe *me!* She's better than that! I'm telling you she'd believe me!"

Helene's expression hardened again. She stood and faced me, her fists back on her hips. "I wish we could let you leave! I'd like to watch you run home to your mommy and ask for help! Just see what happens next! See if you don't end up in a nuthouse, with a stick in your mouth and wires glued to your body and some guy in a white coat telling everyone to stand clear—right before he hits the switch!"

"She wouldn't do that to me!" I screamed, tears stinging my eyes.

"Yeah, she would! She's a grown-up, just like all the rest! She'd tell you she loves you and that it's *for the best*. You could yell and kick all you wanted, but still they'd strap you down and tell you to relax—and then, *zap!*" Helene snapped her fingers in my face before stepping right up to me, bringing her nose within inches of mine.

"Don't you think all the kids here wish they could go home? Don't you think the dozens of Undertakers who are watching the schools and sleeping in sewers wish it too? Don't you think the kids who See Corpses and end up dead wish it most of all?

"You want to feel sorry for yourself, then fine! But don't you dare—don't you *dare!*—tell me that your mom would believe when mine didn't!"

For a few long seconds, we just stood there glaring at each other. I half-expected her to hit me again and wondered what I'd do if she did. My father had warned me more than once about hitting girls—about hitting anybody.

But then, my dad had said a lot of things. And one look around this place suggested that my dad hadn't been who I thought he was.

Helene said, "You shouldn't be here."

"I know."

"You should've gone right to First Stop. I don't know why Tom wanted me to bring you straight to Haven."

Then after a moment's thought, she said, "Yeah, I do. He figured you were different. You're Karl Ritter's kid, so he figured you'd be better than just any old middle-schooler."

"I'm not," I said.

"No, you're not." She then gave me a pitying look that somehow seemed much worse than her anger or even her punch. "One more thing," she told me. "If you ever again put the rest of us in danger like you just did, I'll kill you myself!"

Before I could reply, she ran from the room. To my surprise, I could hear her crying.

"Nice job, Red," one of the card players taunted.

"Yeah—swift move!" added the other.

"That's enough," said a third voice, and the two of them instantly went quiet.

I looked back at the doorway.

Helene was gone. Tom had taken her place.

He pointed a finger. "Come with me."

CHAPTER 12

THE SHRINE

So—word is you tried to bail on us," Tom said as we walked side by side through the Big Room.

I grimaced but didn't see any point in denying it. "I guess so."

"Well, I don't blame you."

"You don't?"

"Hey, after the day you've had?" he said.

"I wanna go home, Tom."

"Well, we'll talk about that. But first, why don't you let me show you 'round a bit more. We're a pretty amazing operation."

I shrugged unhappily. "Okay."

Tom grinned as if my answer had sounded a lot more enthusiastic than it was. Then he made a sweeping gesture with his arm, motioning toward all the activity around us. "Know what these kids are doing?"

I shook my head

Tom pointed. "Those dudes over there are cutting wood for building materials. We're trying to break this place down into smaller sections a little bit at a time. It's a privacy thing. Now, over there—those dudes are upgrading our wiring. We got piles of electronics already, with more getting hooked up all the time. But we keep popping fuses. And those dudes—we call them the Hackers and the Chatters. The Hackers run all our computer jobs, anything from legit stuff to breaking into secure systems. The Chatters—now, they're the communication pros. They keep us linked with the Undertakers out in the field."

"And all the Undertakers are kids?" I asked.

Tom nodded.

"Because they're the only ones who can See the Corpses?"

"That sorta *is* the main qualification for membership."

"But my dad could See them."

Another nod. "Yeah, but he's the only adult who ever could. We don't know why. The rules about Seeing are pretty mysterious, although it looks like it runs in families. If one kid in a family gets the Sight, odds are good that the others'll get it too, sooner or later. Steve thinks it's a gene."

I knew a little something about heredity from science class. "So you think I inherited the Sight from my dad?"

"It's one theory."

"Then why'd I only start Seeing them today?"

"Girls start Seeing around eleven," Tom explained. "Boys around twelve. Might have something to do with the start of puberty. Nobody knows for sure—yet. But we're working on it. The real worry is that the Corpses are working on it too."

"What's that mean?" I asked.

Tom smiled thinly. "You think it's a coincidence that you ran into so many of them this morning? That you bumped into the woman in the Laundromat that Sharyn decapitated? Doesn't it kind of seem like they're everywhere around you?"

I blinked. "I guess so..."

"The Corpses have been watching you."

A chill raced down my spine. "What for?"

"Because they knew your dad could See them—was, in fact, the only known adult who ever could—and they wanted to know if you'd start Seeing them too. So they set things up to stay close to you, just waiting for today to come along."

"Oh," I replied. "Then I guess I'm lucky that Helene was there."

Tom's smile widened. "That wasn't luck either. I *sent* her there, Will. We knew you'd turned twelve, and we figured that you'd probably get the Sight sometime in the new school year. So Helene went into your school undercover, with orders to keep an eye on you. If you rolled in one day with the Sight, she was supposed to bust you both out of there fast and bring you to us. And she did one serious job of it too!"

"Yeah, she did," I admitted. "So she was like my—bodyguard?"

"Something like that. We've got Undertakers in every middle school in town, all looking for kids like you."

"Schoolers," I said.

He nodded.

"And how long have you all been doing this?" I asked.

"About three years."

"Have you always been in charge?"

"Nope. Up front, your dad was the man. I kind of took over after he got—after he died."

"My dad died more than two years ago."

"I know," he replied.

"So for a year before that, he was, like, a general, fighting against the Corpses?"

"Well, yeah," Tom said. "But that ain't the way it started."

"Huh?"

"Hang on. I was holding off on showing you this, but all of a sudden, now feels like the right time." Putting an arm around my shoulders, he led me toward one of the small plywood "rooms" that lined the walls of Haven. As we neared it, the Chief stepped aside and motioned for me to go in first.

Feeling bewildered, I did—and gasped.

The room, like the dorms, had no ceiling, just eight-foot walls enclosing a single army cot, a small footlocker, a desk, and a wall of pictures—

—all of *my* father.

I suddenly felt light-headed. Slowly, as if in a dream, I examined each of the photos, trying to wrap my mind around what I was seeing.

In one, Karl Ritter was standing in the Big Room, which looked much emptier than it did now. He had his arms around a somewhat younger-looking Tom and Sharyn. All three were smiling.

"We took that the day he got us this place," Tom said wistfully, coming to stand at my shoulder. He towered over me. "Back then it was just us three. The camera was on a timer, stuck up on top of a stack of boxes."

How happy my dad looked! I felt a sudden, sharp stab of jealousy. This had been *my* father, not theirs, and yet these strangers had claimed a portion of Karl Ritter's time that he might otherwise have spent with his family.

With me.

"Sharyn told me that you first met him after the two of you robbed some house," I said.

Tom laughed. "Yeah. We'd boosted the place clean, and we were slipping out the back when he just kind of whistled. It's probably the only time in my life I ever heard Sharyn scream. We turned around, and there he was—this redheaded plainclothes cop, leaning on a lamppost and wearing this funny smirk. He didn't pull his gun or nothing."

"Did he arrest you?"

"He played it that way up front. Cuffed us. Stuck us in the back of his car. I was already thinking what kind of lawyer we could get. By then we'd been ripping off rich houses for a couple of years, and we'd saved up some dough. So I figured we could afford somebody good. Thing is, all we really had was maybe two grand, and *that* was buried in a mayonnaise jar under an overpass near Callowhill Street. When you're looking to hire top legal muscle, two grand don't even buy them lunch!"

He shook his head, lost in the memory.

"If your old man had played it straight, Sharyn and me'd still be in a juvie lockup someplace, waiting to turn eighteen. 'Stead he *talked* to us—the first time anybody'd done that in longer than we could remember. And not social worker crap about 'the challenges of orphanhood' neither. We'd had that stuff shoved down our throats back in the fosters. Nope, Karl talked about brains and talent and the guts it took to do what we did and pull it off for so long." Another laugh. "At first Sharyn and me figured that he might be after a cut of the action!"

"What *did* he want?" I asked.

"For us to use our talents in a better way. He said he had connections with the city government—that he could hook us up with a gig that'd challenge our skills, keep us in green, *and* be legit."

"And you said yes?"

"Not right off. We'd been on the streets for years by then. We had what you'd call trust issues. But when he didn't dime us out and instead just kept tabs on us and talked with us every chance he got—" Tom shrugged. "After a while we started seeing that he was on the level. And once we saw *that*, we finally understood just how sweet a thing he was offering us."

Another of the photos showed my dad wearing his police uniform—something he rarely did once he'd made detective. In this shot he was surrounded by a half-dozen kids, all standing at attention and saluting the camera. Tom said, "That one got took about a week before he died. By then we'd been fighting the Corpses for a while, and this was a rare chance to chill. Burt Moscova—that's him there in the back—wanted to see Karl in his old cop outfit. And your old man did it, just that once, just for us."

I frowned at the photo, hurt, but not quite sure why. I could remember a time when I hadn't wanted to share Dad with my new baby sister! The idea of him spending so much time in the company of these thieves when his son—*his own son!*—had been waiting at home…

"You okay?" Tom asked.

"What *is* this place?" I asked, trying to hide my feelings. *He was* my *dad!*

"Ain't you guessed?"

I shook my head, although in truth I had.

Tom said, "This was Karl's office after we opened this place."

His office. His secret office in his secret clubhouse where he did his secret work.

"Uh-huh," I said sourly. "Okay, so then what *was* his work? What was Haven? Before the Corpses showed up, I mean."

"A shelter for runaways. We'd get them here, feed them, give them a safe place to sleep, try to hook them up with some counseling. Back then we called it Haven House. Sharyn and me kept the place clean, running, and organized. Officially, we were 'helping Karl out.' But the truth is that he had you and your mom and your sister, so most of the time, it was just the two of us here alone."

Hearing that made me feel a little better. Maybe our family had been a priority in my father's life after all.

A thought struck me. "Tom, did my dad own this whole building?"

The Chief shook his head. "Nope. City owned it. Still does. Your dad set things up for us to lease it—for charity purposes. It's a little complicated. Let's just say your old man knew how to work the system."

"But how do you pay for everything? I mean...you've got to have money, right? Who buys the food and the blankets and the computers—"

"—and the telephone system, the utilities, the annual lease payments on the building," Tom finished for me. "All that?"

"Yeah."

He gazed at the pictures of Karl Ritter. "About six months before he died but long after we'd dropped the charity stuff and started fighting Corpses full time, your dad took out this life insurance policy on himself—a big one. They ain't easy to get when you're a cop, leastwise outside the department. And he couldn't do it the usual way because he couldn't risk anybody finding out about us. So he kept it on the sly, and it cost a load of cash, but he did it. Then later, after he got...well...just when we figured we'd have to give up the war, this check rolls in." He looked me in the eye. "A quarter-million dollars."

I stared stupidly at him—the *holy crap factor* at work again.

Tom continued, "Yeah, we couldn't believe it either. It was all rigged to go into this fancy trust that only Sharyn or me could hit for money. And owing to some serious financial management, the Undertakers have been getting by just fine on that dough ever since."

I understood maybe half of this—but it seemed clear enough that my father had believed in this cause, believed with all his heart. And that he'd kept it a secret—at least from me.

"Does my mom know about this place?"

"She used to, back when it was just a shelter," Tom replied. "Then later, after the Corpses showed up, Karl figured that he had best protect her. So he told her the shelter'd been closed down. After that all our business was done on the sly."

"Even from her?"

"Especially from her," said Tom. "Since he's been gone, we've kept doing what he taught us. Karl rigged it with City Hall so we could renew our lease every year without no trouble and with no questions asked. We just fill out the right forms and pay the right fees."

"But the signs outside!" Will protested. "This building is condemned."

The older boy shook his head. "*We* made those signs, man. Helps keep folks from sniffing around. Even the street people pretty much stay clear of us these days. Besides, we got ways of handling trespassers.

"Will, the thing you need to get is that everything the Undertakers are…is because of your father. He's our founder and our inspiration. He may only have fought in this war for a year, but in that year he taught us what we needed to know to keep on fighting it without him."

I looked from the photos to Tom and back again.

My dad had this whole part of his life that I never knew about.

Then another thought struck me.

But he must have known that—someday—I'd find out.

Maybe he even counted on it.

Without even knowing I was going to, I asked, "How'd he die?"

Tom was silent for maybe half a minute. "What'd they tell you?"

I would never forget the day: the policemen who came to our house; their somber faces; the way Mom had cried. "They said he'd been sent to investigate a break-in in North Philly, that something had gone wrong, that he'd been stabbed and found dead at the scene." All that had been two years ago, and the pain still felt sharp and fresh, as if it had happened just yesterday. Suddenly and against all my best efforts, familiar tears stung my eyes.

Tom nodded grimly. "Like I said, your dad fought with us for a year after the Corpses showed up. He wrote most of the rules and regs that we still follow. He showed us what to do and how to *think* so we could survive. But more'n that, he got involved. When we found a Seer in a jam, he led us on the rescue, sometimes going head to head against the Corpses himself.

"As near as we figure, one of them must have ID'ed him. He was set up that night, Will. There wasn't no burglar in that North Philly shop. It was a Corpse—maybe more'n one. They iced your old man and rigged it to look like some random street killing."

I stared at him. "How do you know that?"

Tom replied, "Because he called us before he died."

"Called you?"

"We got special wrist radios that we use. Maybe you've seen them. Well, after that Corpse shivved him and left him for dead, he somehow found the strength to call us and spill what went down and where he was. Sharyn and I got there as fast as we could, but by then the cops had already surrounded the dump. We couldn't do nothing but watch from an alley as they carried him out on that stretcher with a sheet over his face." He looked down at me. "I'm really sorry, bro."

"It's okay," I said, although it wasn't.

"No, it ain't. Now all we can do is honor what he was. Your dad changed everything for my sister and me. He took a couple of juvie felons and turned us first into reformers and then into soldiers. That's why we set up this room for him. It's a shrine—a memorial. We loved him, Will. I guess I just wanted you to know that. That's why I brought you in here."

I looked at the pictures and thought about what Tom had said. A lot of this still felt like a betrayal, although I was starting to get why my father had kept it secret. Since coming here, everyone had been badgering me about how important it was that I not go home, that doing so would put Mom and Emily in danger. For the first time, I understood that those were actually my dad's words being passed down to me through the mouths of strangers. I began to see the truth in them.

It broke my heart.

"I don't want to stay here, Tom," I whispered.

"I know it."

"But I have to…don't I?"

"No, bro. You don't. You can bail anytime you want. Nobody'll come after you a second time, I promise."

"But doing that'll probably put Haven in danger, right?"

"Right."

"And my mother and sister too?"

"Yeah." Again that strong arm settled around my shoulders. My dad used to hold me that way. Since his death, I couldn't remember anyone else doing it.

"Thing is," Tom said, "we don't think the Corpses know why some kids can See them when everyone else can't—but we know it's got them freaked. You, me, Sharyn, Helene—all the Undertakers—we're the flies in the ointment, the bugs in the system, the ghosts in the machine. Get it? They can't afford to let us keep breathing. So when they find kids with the Sight, they kill them."

"How many have died?" I asked.

He shrugged. "Ain't no way of knowing that. Not every boy or girl who suddenly starts Seeing Corpses ends up an Undertaker. Most of them end up dead.

"But ruthless as they are, the Corpses ain't stupid. They don't kill for killing's sake or folks would start asking questions. That's why they didn't grab you or ice you right off. They waited to see if you'd get the Sight—waited til you became a danger to them. Once that happened, they tried to snatch you, probably to arrange one of their little 'accidents.' It's the same with your family. So long as the Corpses got no reason to think they know something they shouldn't, your mom and little sis are safe."

I put my face in my hands. "I can't go home."

"Nope."

I looked up at him. "Can I stay here?"

Tom actually laughed a little. "Will, that ain't never even been a question."

"But what can I *do* here? I don't know anything about wars! I can't fight, and I sure can't build walls or rewire things. What good would I be?"

"We'll teach you the skills you need," Tom assured me. "And for whatever its worth, I believe in you. You're Karl Ritter's only son, and that's saying something in my book. Be an Undertaker, bro. Help us fight the Corpses. In return we'll help you get home someday."

With that he stepped back and held out his hand.

I looked at it, somehow understanding that this wasn't just a *Hi, how are you?* handshake. This one meant something. This one was *binding*.

After a moment's thought, I shook it.

CHAPTER 13

FIRST STOP

When I awoke after my first fitful night as an Undertaker, my pillow was damp with tears. Most of the other kids were already awake and gone from the dorm. Stiffly I followed them.

Breakfast consisted of cold cereal, milk, and juice. It made me long for Mom's cooking. Today was Thursday. My mother had the afternoon shift, which meant she'd be home making pancakes, this time just for Emily.

Except, of course, she wouldn't. She'd be out looking for me.

I wondered if she'd slept as badly as I had.

The idea made me sick to my stomach.

Overall the Haven dining experience was a lot like lunchtime at school. Everyone sat with their friends, leaving me to pick a lonely spot near the end of one of the long tables. There I sat, trying to dredge up some interest in corn flakes and a bruised apple, when Sharyn plopped down across from me.

"Mornin', Red! You ready to start your training today?"

Training? Tom had mentioned that yesterday when I'd promised to become an Undertaker. At the time it had seemed like a vague thing, not quite real. Apparently it was.

"I guess."

"Cool! Hey, I dug up some fresh clothes for you. Should fit you better'n what you've got on now. It's all here." Grinning, she showed me a lumpy plastic trash bag.

"Oh," I said. "Thanks."

"No sweat. So eat up, and let's roll!"

Curiosity briefly overshadowed my despair. "To First Stop?"

"You know it!"

"What exactly is First Stop?"

She grinned. "It's this cozy little spot we keep for training new recruits. We run classes about twice a month. A new one just kicked off, but I figure we can slip you in with no hassle."

"But—why not just train people here? There's plenty of room."

"It ain't about room," Sharyn said. "It's about security. Sometimes the Corpses snatch some poor Seers before we can get to them. Then the Corpses somehow brainwash them and send them to find us as spies. We call them *moles*. Their mission is to scope out Haven's locale and then drop the dime on us. And if the Corpses ever get a hold of *that* bit of info, they'll roll in and ice the whole place!"

Helene had said as much to me yesterday during our fight. I tried to imagine the Big Room overrun by the walking dead—and shuddered.

Sharyn continued, "So early on, your dad and Tom rigged up this place for training recruits off-site. That way if a mole does slip in, we just close down that First Stop and find another."

"And what happens at this...training camp?" I asked.

"Loads! You learn how we fight, our gadgets, our rules and regs—all things Undertaker. On the flip side, we scope you out and make sure you're on the level and not just a Deader stooge."

"But I'm not a mole!" I insisted.

Sharyn reached across the table and tousled my hair. I didn't like it. "Of course you ain't, Red! When I said *you*, I meant like the general *y*ou. No way we'd have let Helene bring you straight here instead've to First Stop, like usual, if we'd figured you might be bent!"

Special treatment. No wonder that Alex Bobson kid had given me such a hard time yesterday.

"How long do I have to be there?"

"You'll roll on back to Haven a week from Tuesday, along with the rest of your class."

"Oh," I said glumly.

"Hey—it's cool! First Stop don't suck much. We keep you hopping, and the time flies. 'Sides, you get to learn all our tricks! Don't get better'n that!"

I studied her, trying to figure out if she was being ironic. With Sharyn there was no telling.

"Can I see Helene before we go?" I asked. I wanted to apologize for yesterday's fight.

Sharyn's smile faltered. "No go. Sorry. Tom sent her back up to Manayunk to scope out things since you two split yesterday. She ain't gonna be back til past midnight."

"Isn't that dangerous?"

Sharyn leaned over the table and said quietly but firmly, "Will, everything we do is dangerous. Now eat, and let's bail. You got a big day ahead of you."

Twenty minutes later, the two of us were making our way up the spiral ramp and back onto Green Street, this time riding two Stingrays—an opportunity that would have thrilled me before yesterday.

From there Sharyn led me along a complicated route that finally ended at a boarded-up storefront in a run-down neighborhood somewhere north of Center City. The sign over the door read *Professional Dry Cleaning*, although the place looked like it had been out of business for years. After a careful look around, she and I walked our bikes down a side alley and stopped outside a grimy old service door.

"Listen up," she said. "Before we go in, there's a couple things I got to tell you. First, this is Day Three for most of the recruits. Day One, we get them settled. Day Two, we get them talkin', telling us how they ended up wanting—or needing—to join the Undertakers. Get it?"

"Yeah," I replied.

"Except that ain't all we're doing. We're also scoping them out and checking if any of them got the makings of moles. Today, Day Three, the real stuff starts, and first off is what Tom calls his *orientation speech*.

"Now, til this mornin', none of these dudes have met the Chief. So when you get in there, remember: you ain't met Tom before neither. The story is that you just got boosted, and we're bringing you right in. You cool with that?"

I shrugged. "Sure."

She nodded. "Now, the second thing—you're gonna be living with these kids for a while, and you're probably gonna get friendly with them. That's cool. Only when you do, don't spill no info on Haven. That's important, Red."

"Security?" I asked.

"We've got to watch our backs."

"What if one of the recruits *does* turn out to be a mole?"

She grinned. "Then we tag them, bag them, and drop them at a hospital ER. After that we ditch the First Stop and find a new one."

I looked at her, astonished. "And that's happened?"

"Twice."

Sharyn opened the service door with a key and ushered me into a poorly lit room about the size of the boys' dorm at Haven. Half the floor space was roped off and layered in mats. A dozen rusty old folding chairs had been lined up on the other half. A single hanging bulb over the matted area provided the only light.

Five kids sat in the folding chairs watching Tom, who stood atop the mats looking tall, powerful, and thoroughly in charge. The Chief was speaking, although he paused for just a moment as we entered. As his eyes found mine, Tom offered me only the barest hint of a smile.

"—ain't alone in this," he was saying. "You're just five outta hundreds of teens and preteens who picked up what we call the Sight—the ability to cut through whatever scam the Corpses pull that keeps everyone else from recognizing them for the rotting carcasses that they are.

"I wish I could say we got it all figured out. We don't. I wish I could say this war'll be over soon. I can't. But I *can* promise you two things straight up. The first is that you're safe here. We'll teach you everything you need to help us fight the Corpses. The second is that if you do decide instead to bail, you'll be facing major risk. Corpses hunt Seers, and when they find them, they kill them.

"I know this ain't fair. I know most of you got homes that you miss. I know you're scared. But this is war, and in war, sometimes children got to grow up fast—in this war, especially, because the only ones fighting it is *us*.

"But understand this: it's a war we can win. This place you see here may not look like much. But trust me, it ain't all there is. This dingy old place is kind of like a small gear in a much bigger machine—a machine that was assembled by a great man as a way to fight back against this invasion. We are that machine. We are the Undertakers.

"Work hard, learn your lessons, and sooner than you think, I'll show you what I mean."

The Chief of the Undertakers stood tall atop the mat, his strong face illuminated by the light of that single hanging bulb. He gazed down on the recruits, somehow appearing larger than life—filling the mat, filling the whole of the available space in First Stop. When he spoke, the kids listened in rapt attention. They believed him. They believed *in* him.

This is what a leader looks like.

Tom said, "Remember, you ain't alone. You got us, and we all got a job to do. Because in this war, we ain't the first or last line of defense. We're the *only* line of defense."

CHAPTER 14

STREET KARATE

In the silence that followed, I looked over the recruits. There were two boys and three girls. The smallest girl was a tiny blond who barely seemed old enough to be Seeing Corpses. She looked like she might be crying.

Tom nodded to Sharyn and me. "A new recruit joined up today," he said. "His name's Will Ritter. Now, I know y'all got a couple of days' head start on him here, so I hope you'll help him along. Will, why don't you grab a chair?"

I obediently took a seat beside the little blond girl, who gave me a shy smile. I did my best to smile back.

There were definitely tears on her cheeks.

I knew just how she felt.

Tom said, "Today we get down to the real deal. I'm gonna turn y'all over to my sister Sharyn now—she's gonna demo some of the Undertakers' customized combat techniques. But before I go, I'll take some questions. Anybody?"

A thin boy wearing wire-rimmed glasses raised his hand. "Has my mom's hairdresser always been, well...dead?"

"Solid question, Ethan," Tom replied. "How long's your mom been seeing this dude?"

Ethan shrugged. "A little over a year, I guess."

Tom nodded. "That jives. See, Corpses ain't really dead people. They're invaders from somewhere else who inhabit dead bodies. We think it's how they survive and get around in our world. They slide into a dead person, take the body over, and wear it like a suit until it rots around them. Then they Transfer to another. But whatever body they're wearing, they always somehow project an image of the same false identity. That's why it's handy to be able to recognize individual Corpses by the Masks they wear rather than the bodies they're in. There's a trick to doin' that. We'll be showing it to y'all.

"So, yeah, man, your mom's hair dude's always been a dead body—but probably not always the same dead body."

Ethan didn't look happy about the answer.

A tall girl with short dark hair and an olive complexion raised her hand. "Some Corpses are women, right? I mean, they look like women—dead women. But underneath are they, you know—female?"

"We're not one hundred percent sure about that one, Maria," Tom replied. "But we think the Corpses got gender just like humans do. Male Corpses possess male dead bodies and pose as dudes; female Corpses pose as women."

The last boy in the group looked bigger and older than the rest. His round face, half-hidden beneath a long mop of yellow hair, seemed to wear a perpetual scowl, as if he were mad at the world.

The kid had *bully* written all over him.

"Well, duh!" the big boy chimed in. "What else would they do?" Then he looked around as if expecting everyone to laugh at what he figured was a funny joke. When nobody did, he sulked.

Ethan raised his hand again. "Um…are the Corpses just here—I mean, in Philly? Or are they everywhere?"

Tom replied. "Near as we know, the invasion has started here in Philly, and most of them are still in this area—although, in the last year, more of them have spread out to New York, Baltimore, Washington…"

Ethan gulped, but he didn't lower his hand. "Then there must be other groups like this one in those other cities, right?" he asked, sounding almost desperate.

He wants the Undertakers to be big, I thought. *He wants to believe he's safe inside a really huge organization.*

But Ethan came away disappointed. "Maybe there *are* other groups like ours out there," Tom replied. "But so far, we ain't found any. And believe me, we been looking. Sorry, Ethan."

The boy paled and lowered his hand.

"Any more questions?" Tom asked.

"I've got one," I said almost without thinking. "How

can we win this war when we don't even know how to kill a Corpse?"

A nervous murmur rolled through the rest of the recruits, and I realized I'd just fouled up. I was supposed to be new here, right? So then how did I know that the Undertakers had no way to kill Corpses? Inwardly I cringed.

Somewhere in the shadows, I heard Sharyn groan softly.

"We got ways to hurt them," the Chief replied carefully. "We can even force them to Transfer to other dead bodies sometimes. But it's true that nothing we got yet has done any Corpse permanent damage. Not that we ain't working on it." Then, treating me to a hard look, he said flatly, "What I don't get is just how *you* knew about it, Will."

I swallowed.

Tom understood full well how I knew what I knew. I could only figure that putting me on the spot like this was a kind of test. It had been my mistake, so I had to fix it.

I thought furiously. Around me the other recruits were silent, expectant.

Finally, faking a shrug, I replied, "When they came for me, I had my dad's service revolver. I emptied it into one of them, and he just kept coming. How are you supposed to kill *that?*"

Tom held my gaze, his expression grave. Then he smiled. "Sounds like you had yourself a time, Will. Now, if there's no more questions, I'll pass you over to Sharyn. Listen up, learn what you got to learn, and I'll see y'all again soon."

He left the mat, stepping over the rope boundary. There was no applause.

His sister emerged from the shadows and offered her brother a high five. He accepted it, although I got the impression that he wished she wouldn't do that.

Then Sharyn fairly bounded onto the mat, her dreadlocks dancing around her head like tight black springs. Since our arrival, she'd pulled off her sweatshirt. She now wore jeans and a black tank top with the words *Mopey Teenage Bears*—whatever *that* meant—splashed across it in big pink letters. Her arms were long, lean, dark-skinned, and muscular: an athlete's arms.

Sharyn positioned herself near the center of the mat and rubbed her hands together. "I'm Sharyn Jefferson, and I'm gonna be showin' y'all what we *can* do to Corpses!"

Instantly the big kid's hand went up. "Um...but you're a girl."

Sharyn nodded. "So I am! Thanks for noticing!"

"And *you're* gonna teach *me* how to fight?"

She cocked her head curiously. "You're the dude who came in yesterday, ain't ya? What's the name? Dave Hot Dog?"

The boy frowned. "Burger."

"Oh. My bad. Burger Hot Dog."

The boy leapt to his feet. "My name's Dave Burger! And I don't got to take—"

Sharyn's smile vanished. "Chill out, Hot Dog."

"I didn't come here to take no crap!" Dave exclaimed, red-faced. "And I didn't come here to learn fighting from no girl!"

"So you got nothing to learn from me?" Sharyn remarked. "Figure you can drop me easy?"

"This is stupid!" the boy declared.

"That right? Well, how's about you prove it. Like you said: I'm just a girl. So bring it! Lay me on my butt, big man. Bust a move like that, and *you* get to play teacher!"

The other recruits nervously watched this exchange. Although clearly taken aback by the challenge, Dave was either too proud or too stubborn to back down.

Finally, smirking, he stepped up onto the mat, looking the very picture of confidence. "Don't think I'm gonna go easy on you just because you're a girl."

Sharyn's grin returned. "Never even occurred to me."

"Just remember, this was your idea."

"I'm shaking with fear."

Dave blinked, unsure if she was making fun of him or not. Then he suddenly advanced, his fist hurtling toward the girl's face. He wasn't nearly fast enough. In a blur of motion, Sharyn pivoted, easily sidestepping the rushing boy, and delivered a sharp kick behind his knee.

Dave yelped in pain, dropping to a crouch. Sharyn then

yanked his collar hard, twisting him around and down onto his back. He landed awkwardly, pinning one of his bent legs painfully beneath him.

The yelp became a cry.

The girl pressed one bare foot on the boy's broad chest, leaning down.

"Get this, Hot Dog—that was easy," she said. Just before the boy starting screaming in agony, she removed her foot, straightened up, and faced the rest of the recruits. "Corpses are stronger than us. They're also faster and a whole lot meaner."

The recruits exchanged nervous looks.

Sharyn continued, "Think that makes them too tough? Well, I've gone up against more Deaders than I can count. You don't beat them with strength. You beat them with speed, brains, and precision."

Behind her, Dave had struggled back to his feet. His cheeks were burning, and his blond hair looked layered in sweat. Seeing the girl's unguarded back, he grinned and charged, all fists and fury.

I started to shout out a warning—but I never got the chance.

Sharyn ducked, spun, and hit the advancing boy once in the stomach with the blade of her hand. The blow was hard and lightning quick. Dave's lungs emptied in a *whoosh* of air. His eyes went wide. Then Sharyn dropped to a crouch and swept her leg smoothly across the mat, catching him at the shins.

He went down again—hard. This time he stayed down.

The girl stood up and casually explained, "Corpses don't feel pain. You can shoot them, knife them, break their bones, and they'll just keep coming. That's the plus of being dead—maybe the only plus.

"But that don't mean they don't got weak spots, dig? They're walking around in stolen bodies—stolen *human* bodies—which means they've been stuck with the human nervous system. There's parts of the body that control movement of an arm or a leg or even the whole body. They're called *nerve centers*, and pain or no pain—dead as they are—the Corpses rely on them just as sure as we do.

"There's one here." She raised her arm. "Tag a Corpse with a good kick to the armpit, and the whole arm goes limp for a while." She lowered the arm and touched her nose. "A hard punch to the bridge of the nose temporarily blinds them. And best of all: plant your fist right here"—she tapped the back of her head—"at the base of the skull, and you'll paralyze them for a time. You'll all be learning these moves over the next week or so.

"Bottom line? Fighting a Deader is all about staying calm, picking your moment, and then applying the right force. Over the next couple o' days, we'll be working on stance and balance. Once you're down with that, we'll roll into moves and attack styles. Before we're through, y'all will have a solid understanding of how we dance this dance. Any questions?"

I raised my hand, amazed. "What kind of karate is this?"

Sharyn pondered the question. "Well, I guess you'd call this MMA," she finally replied. "That's *mixed martial arts*. It's part boxing, part tae kwon do, part kandoshin." Then she grinned. "But 'round here, we just call it *street karate*."

CHAPTER 15

APT PUPIL

Five days later, on Tuesday morning, I stood on the mat in First Stop staring down a pimple-faced thirteen-year-old named Ethan Maxwell who wanted to beat the crap out of me.

The other recruits were all watching from their chairs, having already faced their own sparring partners—except for Dave, that is, who was occupying a bench against the rear wall. He was sullenly hugging an ice pack—a souvenir from his latest bout with Sharyn. He always sparred with Sharyn because pitting the enormous boy against anyone else would have been, in Sharyn's words, "like siccing Shrek on one of the seven dwarves."

Usually the three girls—Harleen, Maria, and the little blond, Amy Filewicz—only sparred among themselves, leaving Ethan as my regular partner. So far I'd won every match—a fact that was apparently frustrating Ethan more and more.

And it was starting to show.

He danced around me, moving altogether too fast, his fists held up aggressively before him. Turning in a slow circle, I followed his movements, watching his eyes, looking for the "tell" that would announce a swing. I saw it and immediately raised my arm, blocking a right-handed punch. Instantly Ethan swung his left fist, his arc too wide. I blocked that too. Again he came at me with his right, this time going for my stomach. I jumped back and gave him a shove—just hard enough to push him off balance and send him staggering across the mat.

Ethan uttered a little curse.

From the sidelines Sharyn scolded him. "Don't be so fast to attack. Pick your moment—but don't miss it when it comes!"

Ethan glowered at me. "This time you're going down, Ritter," he said, just a little too loud.

He's scared, and he's trying to hide it behind fake courage.

I wasn't sure where this realization had come from. After all, I didn't have any more experience fighting than he did. Nevertheless the feeling was strong.

Ethan came at me again, this time with an all-out charge, his head down and his arms pinwheeling. I wasn't sure if he meant to club my skull or bowl me over, and I didn't care. I waited until just the right second. Then I ducked under the swinging arms and gave him one hard jab in the midsection.

Ethan's breath exploded out of him. The wire-framed glasses tumbled off his face as he fell to his knees, gasping.

"Oh, crap! Ethan, I'm sorry!" I exclaimed. I dropped into a crouch beside the fallen boy, who was gulping like a landed fish.

"It's cool," Sharyn said at once. She knelt and cupped Ethan's face with her strong hands. The boy's eyes were glassy, the skin beneath his pimples suddenly pale. "You just got the wind knocked outta you, that's all. I know it's scary, but it ain't nothing to worry about. Just chill out, and you'll catch your breath."

She kept talking in that reassuring tone until the boy's color returned and he started breathing normally again. Sharyn smiled, patted Ethan's shoulder, and then stood up to face me.

"I'm really sorry!" I told her. "I didn't mean to hit him that hard!"

"It ain't about how hard you tagged him. It's about where you tagged him. There's this sweet spot"—Sharyn tapped her midsection, just above her belly button; she was no longer speaking just to me, but to all the recruits—"called the *solar plexus*. Tag it right, and you can mess up the body's rhythm for a time, making it tough to catch any air. Problem is that Corpses don't breathe, so hitting them there don't mean much. Y'all want to remember that."

She looked back at me. I nodded.

Sharyn helped Ethan to his feet and returned his glasses. "Go plant yourself," she told him gently. Then to my horror, she gestured toward Dave. "Yo, Hot Dog! Feel up to a quick dance with Will here?"

"Sharyn?" I whispered.

She winked. "You're better than you think you are, Red. Fact is, you might just be a natural."

Dave rose from his bench on his tree-trunk-sized legs and made his way toward the training area. I gulped.

A natural?

I could count on one hand the number of fights I'd been in, and three of those fingers would have been sparring matches with poor Ethan! Outfighting that skinny, inexperienced kid was one thing. But this—walking bulldozer—was another!

As Dave stepped onto the mat, I suddenly thought, *Sharyn beat him*. So why can't I?

But that was just crazy. I was no Sharyn! Not even close.

Dave eyed me without expression. His wordless message was simple: *I'm still embarrassed over losing to that girl, so I'm planning to take it out on you. I'm going to squash you like a bug!*

I felt my stomach knot up.

Dave pulled a sparring helmet over his head and wrapped his fists with tape. We didn't use gloves.

Calmly Sharyn said to me, "'Member, it ain't about

size or strength. It's about speed, precision, and—mostly—belief."

"Belief in what?" I croaked.

She grinned. "Yourself, Red!"

Then she left the mat.

From ten feet away, Dave grinned at me.

I tried to smile back, tried to believe. It just wasn't happening.

"Do it," Sharyn called.

Dave advanced but slower than Ethan had—more confidently.

I watched him, unmoving. I felt like a deer in headlights.

"Get your guard up, Will!" Sharyn called.

Too late. Dave's huge fist lashed out, cuffing me on the side of my head. Something told me it wasn't half as hard as the kid was capable of hitting, but it was still enough to knock me to the mat.

Dave guffawed and stepped back.

For a long empty moment, I just lay there, my head ringing.

Some natural fighter!

Sharyn said, "Get up, Will."

I pulled myself to my feet and, reluctantly, faced Dave again. He was smirking and slamming his right fist into his left palm rhythmically. *Thump. Thump. Thump.*

I frowned.

He thinks I'm a pushover. A wimp. Is he wrong?

Yeah. I think maybe he is.

And just like that, the fear faded. It wasn't gone. I'd simply tucked it someplace inside my head where it wouldn't get in the way. Then I focused on Sharyn's teachings over the last few days: stance, balance, confidence, timing, speed, and precision.

Dave grinned at me again.

This time I grinned right back. Then I spread my legs, raised both my fists, and looked him squarely in the eyes.

Dave's face darkened. He came forward slowly, warily.

I expected the right roundhouse, just like last time, and he didn't disappoint me. This time, though, I ducked under it and jabbed him in the right armpit. Dave didn't seem to feel the blow, but I saw his arm go limp—just like Sharyn had told us it would.

But the kid was quick. He spun around and swung at my temple with his left fist. Fortunately I saw it coming with a split-second to spare and managed to pivot clear.

Dave spun around, angry now. His right arm hung uselessly at his side.

"Okay, shrimp!" he growled. Then he charged forward, all power and menace.

I gauged his footsteps across the mat, picking my moment. At the last second, as Dave unscrewed a powerhouse punch clearly intended to knock my teeth out of my ears, I sidestepped and swept out with one leg, catching him right below the knee of his advancing foot.

Dave went down face-first onto the mat.

I waited for him to push himself impatiently up onto his hands and knees—

—and then I kicked him in the ribs.

Dave's huge body flipped over onto its back, and this time he didn't get up. Instead he just lay there, groaning and hugging his midsection.

I dropped down beside him. "You okay? Can you breathe?"

"Yeah!" Dave grunted. "I'm good. No sweat!"

"That'll do," Sharyn said. "Hot Dog, you cool?"

The boy rolled over again and, treating me to a suspicious glare, climbed unsteadily to his feet. Once there, still hugging his stomach, he said, "Yeah, I'm great. I'm, um...just gonna go sit down in the back again."

Sharyn smiled. "No problem."

Dave gave me a funny look. Then he left the mat. I watched him go, not quite able to believe what had just happened.

I won.

I actually won!

CHAPTER 16

THE BURGERMEISTER

Lesson's over!" Sharyn announced. "Grub's in half an hour. Rest up. Y'all doing great. Best bunch I seen in months! So great, in fact, that me and Tom got a surprise for you this afternoon!" Then she headed over to the alley door, where Tom was already waiting in the shadows.

I wondered how long the Chief had been there.

The three girl recruits headed off toward their shared bedroom. Ethan left too, looking crestfallen. With a sigh I started after him.

Tom called, "Will—hold up."

I obeyed, watching curiously as the Jeffersons approached the mat. It was just the three of us now in the training room.

"You got a knack for fightin', bro," Tom said.

"I got lucky," I replied.

Sharyn shook her head. "Uh-uh. I've seen lucky. You got your dad's talent for hand-to-hand."

Had my father been good at this kind of fighting? I wasn't sure. The Karl Ritter I knew had always carried a gun and a policeman's nightstick.

He'd always seemed invincible.

"Mind you, Ethan ain't much of an opponent," Sharyn continued. "Nice kid, and I figure we got a place for him, but it ain't gonna be in combat. Harleen, now she's got more game. As for Amy and Maria—well, I can't tell yet. Still too early."

"What about Dave?" I asked. "I can't believe I beat him!"

The girl chuckled. "You sure did—once you figured out how not to be scared of him."

Tom frowned. "I got my worries about that kid. He's all attitude."

Shrugging, his sister replied, "It ain't his 'tude. That's more talk than anything else, and he sure ain't the sharpest knife in the drawer. What worries me is his age. He says he's fourteen, but that's pretty old to be just getting the Sight, even for a boy. Think maybe he's a mole?"

"Could be."

I was shocked. Dave could be a bit of a bully sometimes—but a spy for the Corpses? I couldn't believe that.

"So how do we find out for sure?" I asked them.

Tom and Sharyn shared a smile. "Hear that?" the sister said to the brother. "Now it's we."

I scowled but didn't reply.

"Don't sweat it," Tom told me. "We got rules and regs for this. Over the next week, we'll be giving y'all a few coping exercises, and we'll tell you that they're to help you get past your fear of the Corpses. But what they really do is make sure that each of you actually has a solid, healthy fear of them. Because if you don't, then you're most likely a mole."

"Or an idiot," his sister added, "which might be right where Hot Dog's at."

"Is there anything *I* can do?" I asked.

"Keep trainin', bro," Tom replied, "and keep your eyes open. If you see anybody sneaking around after hours, drop a dime on them. There's an Undertaker named Kyle Standish who lives here and looks after the place. We call him the First Stop Boss. If you haven't met him yet, you will. He's always here at night, and we usually have at least one other senior Undertaker here too—just in case of problems. Flag any of them, and they'll drop everything and help you."

"Okay."

"Go get cleaned up with the rest of 'em," Sharyn told me. "Y'all got a big afternoon coming up."

"Yeah?" I asked. "The big surprise you talked about?"

It was Tom who replied. "A field trip to Haven."

"We're going to Haven?"

They both nodded. "Just for the afternoon," said Sharyn.

Tom explained, "It's the first time we've ever tried it. Kind of an experiment. Show you around the Big Room and let y'all see the operation that's waiting for you. You'll learn a bit about each of the crews and find out everything we know about the Corpses. Then we get you back here before supper."

"But what about the security?" I asked. "The whole *mole* thing?"

"Don't sweat it," Sharyn said. "You'll be getting a ride from here to there and back again. First-class seating! Well—'cept for the bags over your heads."

I looked at her. "Bags?"

"We can show 'em *what* Haven is, Will," Tom explained, "but not *where* it is. So we take you there and back by a nice, crazy, complicated route. That way, if there's a mole, they won't have no way to figure where we took you."

"But why risk it at all?"

Tom shrugged. "Morale. You saw how down Ethan looked a few days back when he asked about other Undertaker groups? Well—all the recruits are feeling that same way to one degree or another."

Sharyn added, "This trip'll show 'em that there's more to being an Undertaker than this smelly old dry cleaners. Does a world of good. Trust me. I've seen it plenty."

"Sounds great to me," I said, meaning it.

After all, I might get to see Helene again, even briefly. I might get to apologize.

"One more thing, Red," said Sharyn. "Tonight after lights out, I want you here on the mat for a private session."

"What for?"

"You got yourself a knack for fighting. Let's see out how good you dance with a cooler partner."

I didn't like the sound of that and left the mat feeling a mixture of unease and guilty excitement.

A good fighter? Where had *that* come from?

I found myself almost looking forward to facing this *cooler partner*. And it was the first time in days that I had really looked forward to anything.

Mom would never approve, of course.

But then, my mother wasn't here.

That thought brought with it a fresh stab of desperate loneliness, washing away my budding optimism.

I opened the door that connected the training room with the dorms and kitchen area.

Dave filled the threshold.

Glowering, he took a step toward me. I didn't move. This guy was huge—as tall as Tom and much heavier. Not so long ago, I would have felt intimidated. Those days, I realized with some surprise, were over.

Anyway, a second look made it clear that this kid was in no condition to start another fight. He was clutching a fresh ice pack to his stomach.

I've seen the walking dead! I can't believe I once thought guys like this were scary!

Almost absently I scanned Dave's face, neck, and body, silently reviewing my combat training.

It would be so easy. One jab at the base of his skull would bring him down like an elephant.

Except that Dave's not the enemy, is he?

Besides, the Dave Burger looming over me no longer seemed like a bully. His manner was subdued, almost anxious. "Your name's Will, right?"

"Yeah." I replied, wondering how, after two days together in this place, anybody's name might still need confirming.

"I'm Dave Burger," he said. Then he scowled. "Not Hot Dog. Burger."

"I know."

"But everybody calls me the Burgermeister."

"Yeah? How come?"

He shrugged. "A teacher started calling me that back in first grade, and it kind of stuck. It means *mayor* or *boss* or something in German. All my friends use it."

"Okay—Burgermeister."

"You got a handle?"

I shook my head. "Just don't call me Red, and we're cool."

"Sharyn calls you Red."

"Yeah, well, I've kind of given up on her."

"Right. No Red." Dave shuffled his feet a little nervously. "Did...you guys talk about me?"

"Who?"

"You and Tom and Sharyn just now."

"No," I lied, figuring that it wouldn't do much good to tell this kid that Tom thought he might be a Corpse spy. "They, um—want to give me a little extra training."

"What for? You don't need it."

I stared incredulously at him. "What?"

"You kidding me? Once you got past the shakes, you were so cool up there that if somebody poured boiling water down your throat, you'd probably piss ice cubes."

I burst out laughing. So did he.

I said, "Would you believe that's, like, the first real fight I've ever had?"

"No way!" Dave exclaimed. "Jeez! You're a natural! And I've been in enough fights to know."

All of a sudden, I felt an unexpected rush of pride. "Thanks. That's kind of what Tom and Sharyn just said. They want to try me out against somebody—else." I almost said *somebody better* but caught myself.

"Yeah? When?"

"After lights out."

"Think they'd let me watch?"

"Sharyn called it a private session."

He frowned, looking disappointed. "Oh."

"I dunno. I could ask."

"Yeah? You'd do that?"

"Why not?" I shrugged. "Worst they can do is say no."

"Hope you're not gonna be going up against that Sharyn girl," Dave remarked warily. "She's like a wrecking ball." He shifted the ice pack, grimacing a little. "When you hit me, it hurt. But I'm still feeling those first bruises she gave me back on Thursday!"

I laughed again.

But Dave shook his head. "I'm serious. I've been in a ton of fights. I guess you'd say it was kind of my hobby. And I never lost one—not one—til I came here. Will, I'm telling you, I ain't never in my life seen nobody move as fast as Sharyn. Well, except for that Corpse the other day, 'course."

"Corpse?"

He nodded. "Yeah. I started Seeing them about six months ago. Not many. Just a few around Collegetown. That's where I'm from. At first I thought they were wearing Halloween costumes—like it was some kind of goofy joke. Then I realized that they weren't and that I was the only one who saw them. Jeez, what a mindblower!"

"And you kept going like that for six months?"

Dave shrugged. "What else could I do? I live—lived—with my grandma, and if I'd told her, she'd have just made me go to church or something. No way was I going to the cops—not after finding out that a couple of *them* were Corpses! And I couldn't tell my buds because, well, they'd figure I was nuts. Know what I mean?"

"Yeah, I do." And I did.

"So I just kind of tried to stay away from them. Whenever I had to talk to them, I'd keep it short and wouldn't look them in the eyes—those weird milky eyes of theirs that seem to see you and not see you at the same time. You know?"

"I know."

He continued, "Then five nights ago, I bumped into one of them on the street while I was coming back from the arcade. A real slimy one. You know what I mean by that? Slimy?"

I thought of spotting Kenny Booth on City Line Avenue. "Yeah," I said.

"I still don't know who he was or was pretending to be—just a guy in jeans and a flannel shirt. I guess I was feeling tough that night because I finally mouthed off and called him a zombie."

"You don't want to do that," I said.

"Do what?"

"Call them zombies."

Dave looked at me. "Why not? Ain't they zombies?"

I remembered what Helene had told me. "Zombies are stupid and slow in the movies. You don't want to make the mistake of thinking these things are."

He considered that. "Guess I can't argue with that—not after what he did."

"Tried to kill you?" I asked.

"Hell yeah!" Dave raised his shirt. I gasped. Bruises

covered most of his muscled chest and washboard belly. Some of them were new—probably Sharyn's work. But others had already turned yellow, which meant they were more than a few days old.

"That zombie—sorry, Corpse—hit me like a freight train. Sent me flying!"

"Well, no wonder it hurts so bad when Sharyn hits you!" I exclaimed.

"Yeah!" Dave's expression brightened. "Maybe *that's* what it is!"

"So what happened? With the Corpse, I mean."

"We fought. I hit him with everything I had—went at him until huge clumps of rotted flesh were coming off in my hands. But nothing I did seemed to faze him. Finally he picked me up—right off my feet, lifting me up over his head. And he did it quick! So quick that I could hardly see it!

"Don't remember too much after that. He threw me right off the road and down a gully that emptied into a creek. The Corpse must've figured I was dead because he didn't come down to finish the job."

"Wow..." I muttered.

"Yeah." The Burgermeister forced out a shaky laugh. "Woke up the next morning and headed home. Cops were already there on the porch, talking to my grandma. Watched them from the bushes. I couldn't hear what they were saying, but I knew right away that I had to get outta town."

"How come?"

Dave's face darkened. "Both of them were Corpses."

"Oh," I said.

"After they left, my grandma went over to our neighbor's, probably to tell her what happened. I sneaked inside the house just long enough to grab some dough and leave behind a note. You know, so she wouldn't worry. 'Course, she'll worry anyway."

"Yeah," I agreed, thinking of my mom. *She* hadn't even gotten a note.

"Then I caught a train into Center City. I figured I'd lie about my age and join the navy or something."

"Good idea."

"Except the jerks wanted a birth certificate! Can you believe that?"

I supposed that I *could* believe it. Adults always had ways of locking kids out of places they thought they shouldn't go.

"So I just kind of wandered around. That night I had to sleep in a Dumpster. I was in big trouble. My money wouldn't last long, and even worse, it turns out there are even more Corpses in Philly than in Collegetown!"

"You should see Manayunk," I told him.

"Yeah?"

"Yeah."

Dave actually shuddered.

"How'd you end up here?" I asked.

"Got lucky for a change. I was on Market Street on Wednesday when I spotted a bunch of these kids on majorly cool bikes hiding behind a bus. All of a sudden, they peeled away—right through a crowd of people crossing the street—snatched up a couple of other kids and then took off down Tenth. The thing is, there were three Corpses there, and these guys shot them in the face with squirt guns! One of them even had a sword. I think maybe it was Sharyn, although I didn't know it at the time."

I smiled but said nothing.

Dave continued, "So I figured anybody who could do that to those walking fly bags was who I wanted to hang with. So I started asking everybody who was there—all the 'bystanders'—and I finally ran into this kid named Jonathan who turned out to be with the guys on the bikes. Some kind of spotter. Once I told him I could See the Corpses, he offered to bring me here. Got to admit though," he concluded, looking around, "I expected better."

For a moment I considered telling him about the field trip this afternoon. Then I changed my mind. Tom and Sharyn thought this dude might be a mole, and if he was, it probably wouldn't be smart to make him think I knew more about the Undertakers than I'd let on.

Except... he doesn't seem *like a mole.*

I said, "You wanna grab some lunch, Burgermeister?"

"Sure."

I looked at him. He looked back at me.

"Um...you kind of have to move," I added.

He blinked. "Oh! Sorry." Then he stepped aside, and to my surprise, he made a funny *after you* gesture with a swing of one of his huge arms.

I smiled.

And realized with some surprise that I kind of liked Dave "the Burgermeister" Burger.

CHAPTER 17

FIELD TRIP

That afternoon the six First Stop recruits were once again herded into the main room—fresh from a hearty lunch of nuked hot dogs, nuked macaroni and cheese, and apple juice. Instead of taking chairs, however, we were lined up near the dry cleaner's rear door and each handed a black sack.

"Today," Sharyn announced, "we're all gonna go out for a few hours. Now, y'all want to pull those bags over your heads. Then I'll lead you, one at a time, through the door and into the back of a van. The van's got bench seats on both sides with ropes for seat belts. Once you're in there and tied down, we'll split."

"Where are we going?" Amy asked.

"That's a surprise. But don't worry. Y'all will be back here by dinnertime. Cool?"

Harleen and Maria nodded. The Burgermeister frowned. Amy and Ethan looked nervous.

"Good," Sharyn said. "Not…you don't take off those bags until I tell you it's okay. Got it? I'll be sitting in the back with y'all, and if one of you tries breakin' that rule—well, let's just say you'll be getting a personal training session first thing we get back. Everybody down with that?"

Dave, who knew all about personal training sessions with Sharyn, was the first to don his black sack, pulling it over his big head so quickly that I had to suppress a smile. The rest followed suit. Finally, with a grin and nod from Sharyn, I did the same.

It was stuffy inside—and dark. I couldn't see a thing, which I supposed was the point.

Ten minutes later, we were all in the back of a creaky metal van, perched on hard benches. "Just sit tight," Sharyn told us as the doors shut loudly. "This'll take about half an hour."

And maybe it did, but it was a long half an hour.

First of all, I was uncomfortable, although it was easy enough to breathe in the sack. Second, whoever was driving this thing wasn't particularly good at it. Tires seemed to squeal with every turn, tossing us to and fro on the benches and knocking us into one another time and time again. And there were a lot of turns. Whatever complicated route Tom had worked out for taking us from First Stop to Haven, it involved a lot of twists and doubling back. I didn't think the best spy in the world could have tracked us.

By the time the van rolled to an abrupt halt, I'd lost all sense of direction. We could have been anywhere from the art museum to the Philly airport.

"Jeez," Ethan muttered from beside me. "I feel sick."

Frankly so did I—probably had something to do with riding around in a bouncy van with a bag over my head.

"Chill out, y'all," Sharyn said, sounding as cheerful as ever. "We're here!"

The doors opened, and out we came. Sharyn helped each of us out in turn, lining us up and then marching us—still bagged—down a short hall and into an open area that, by the echo, could only be Haven's cavernous Big Room.

No ramp. No brick wall. Apparently there was more than one way into the Undertakers' secret headquarters.

A door shut, and Sharyn pronounced, "Okay, dudes. Lose the bags!"

Gratefully we obeyed.

I did my best to mimic the amazement the other recruits clearly felt at witnessing the beehive of activity around us. It wasn't hard. Seeing it now without some of the shock and fear that I'd been drowning in the first time, the operation *was* impressive. The high ceiling; the corral of muscle bikes; the rows of sectioned-off rooms and offices that lined the walls—they made the whole Undertakers concept seem somehow more reliable.

More *real*.

And I started to see the point of this field trip.

"Welcome to Haven," Tom said, stepping through the same door that we'd all just used. "Hope y'all enjoyed the ride. You're the first recruits to ever get this chance before graduating First Stop, so make the most of it."

I looked at him, my stomach only now settling down, and thought, *Was he the driver?*

Did any of the Undertakers have a license? And where had the van even come from?

Questions for another day, I decided. For now I needed to play the newbie and go along with everybody else.

"Listen up," Sharyn said. "We're gonna spend some time taking y'all around this room to show you how the Undertakers are set up and how we roll. Maybe some of you'll get a feel for what you might want to do after First Stop. After that comes a little break, and then a bit about the Deaders that we like to call *Corpses 101*."

Grinning, she marched across the expansive floor, waggling a finger for us to follow.

The Undertakers, it turned out, were arranged into crews, with each crewer reporting to a boss who either answered to Tom or to Sharyn as Deputy Chief. Most crews maintained a station in the Big Room from where they did their job. And that afternoon the First Stop recruits spent anywhere from fifteen minutes to an hour at every single one of them.

First came the Chatters, who occupied a square of tables set up at what their boss—a short, dark-haired boy named Sammy Li—defined as "the exact geographic center of Haven." Apparently that made the building-wide Wi-Fi work better. The kids on this crew were the communicators. They remained in constant contact with the Schoolers—Sharyn's Undercover Undertakers. They also monitored Corpse activity in the newspapers and on local television.

During our visit, Sammy let a few of us take turns flipping through the *Philadelphia Inquirer*, looking for photos of cadavers mugging for some journalist's camera. Ethan actually found one and seemed really jazzed about it.

The Hackers manned three banks of computers set up against Haven's rear wall. They spent their days worming into all kinds of systems, securing false identities for Schoolers, researching known Corpses, and keeping track of the Undertakers' finances. Their boss was a sixteen-year-old girl named Elisha Beardsley. "Work for me," she announced with the enthusiasm of a candidate for class president, "and we'll show you how to break into every system on the East Coast! It doesn't get better than that."

I thought that maybe it did, but some of the others looked excited—especially Maria.

After that came the Monkeys, Haven's mechanics,

plumbers, carpenters, and electricians. They were bossed by Tara Monroe, the short, slightly heavy girl who'd been nice to me during my first confusing minutes in Haven. "My crew keeps the bikes running," she explained as we gathered together near the Stingray corral. "We also take care of the building itself, making regular improvements. So if you got a way with tools, we could definitely use you."

"Cool," I heard the Burgermeister mutter from beside me.

Toward the end of her talk, Tara's eyes briefly found mine. She offered me a small smile of recognition. I managed to smile back. It was nice to have a friend.

I wonder where Helene is.

"Schoolers and Angels are different kinds of crews," Tom told us a few minutes later. We'd left the corral and were now standing near the cafeteria. "For starters, Schoolers don't have a station in Haven because—well, most of the time, they're not here. They're out in the world, hiding in the local middle schools, playing normal. They have a tough job: to keep an eye out for Seers and, when they find one, get to them before the Corpses do. Schoolers are trained to fight, to fend for themselves, and to keep cool no matter how hairy things get. It's a high-power, high-risk gig—which is why they're the only crew I boss personally.

"Angels, on the other hand, are our search and rescue

team. Most of the time, they're the ones goin' toe to toe with the Corpses. When a Schooler needs backup, Angels ride in. When some Deader is up to something, it's the Angels who tail 'em and get the 411. Sharyn bosses that crew, and getting on it ain't easy. You get trained in combat, weapons, and how to handle yourself on a bike and a skateboard, and you keep funny hours. It ain't easy, and it ain't for the timid.

"So—if any y'all think you might be Schooler or Angel material, let Sharyn or Kyle know, and we'll see what's what."

There didn't seem to be any immediate takers, and Tom didn't seem to expect there would be. So he nodded to Sharyn, who stepped up, rubbed her hands together, and announced, "Okay, break time! There's candy and popcorn, and I think Nick's even whipped us up some pie. Go seat yourselves down in the caf, and I'll check the back."

This we did, with the Burgermeister dropping heavily into the chair beside me. He tried one of the homemade candies. "These ain't bad," he said after a half-dozen disappeared into his huge maw. "But I was hopin' for some real food."

"We had lunch before we left First Stop," I told him.

"Yeah, I know. But I'm hungry!" Another handful of colored candies met their maker.

Sharyn reappeared a moment later, tugging along a

tall, skinny blond kid of about sixteen. "Dudes, this here's Nick Rooney. He's our Mom Boss."

Harleen and Maria giggled as Dave whispered into my ear, "He don't like no Mom *I* ever saw." Then he noticed that the blond kid was carrying a steaming apple pie in his oven mitt–covered hands. "Hey, dude!" he suddenly exclaimed to Nick. "Get me some of that!"

The Moms, it turned out, kind of sat at the bottom of the Undertakers' unofficial crew totem pole, and it was with them that most new recruits started out. These kids did the thankless drudgery jobs: shopping, emptying trash, doing laundry, and generally picking up after everyone else. Nobody liked being a Mom, and most kids rotated off the crew as soon as newer recruits came in to take their places.

Nick Rooney seemed to be the only exception; he'd been a Mom since joining up almost two and a half years ago, and he apparently showed no interest in doing anything else. Nick was also the baker wannabe who personally made, in addition to pies, the candies that everyone around me—especially Dave—was currently inhaling.

But I didn't have too much of an appetite. Instead I found a quick moment during the break to lure Sharyn aside.

"Where's Helene?" I asked her.

"Helene?" the Deputy Chief replied. "The girls' dorm, I think. Said she was tired."

"Oh." I tried to hide my disappointment. "I was afraid she might be back out on a new Schooler assignment."

Sharyn shook her head. "Nope. Not yet anyhow."

"Okay. Well—tell her I said hi."

She treated me to a thin, knowing smile. "Tell her yourself, Red—the next time you see her." Then she turned and addressed the rest of the recruits. "One more stop, dudes! We're off to the Brain Factory, where y'all will be hearing from Steve Moscova, who runs that crew with an iron pocket protector! So line up! This one's going to be a blast!"

CHAPTER 18

CORPSES 101

Ahem," Steve said loudly. "My name's Steven Moscova, and I'm the Brain Boss for the Undertakers. I've dedicated myself to understanding these invaders because only through understanding them can we hope to defeat them."

We were gathered outside the Brain Factory, occupying chairs that had been set up just out of reach of the half-circle of long tables that marked the boundary of Steve's domain. His crew was nowhere to be seen, although a big cracked blackboard had been set up beside the nearest table. On this blackboard, Steve had taped up an assortment of photographs—each one showing a different Corpse in a different stage of rot.

I felt my stomach roll over. It was the bumpy van ride all over again.

Beside me, Dave groaned, "I shouldn't have eaten so much candy!"

Steve said, "It's okay to ask questions—just please raise your hand. Let's get started." He tapped the first picture on the blackboard. It looked like Old Man Pratt—at least, the way he'd been the morning I'd left home. Dried up. Almost a husk. Beetle food. "This is a long shot of a Corpse inhabiting a Type Five cadaver. Because of its advanced state of decomposition, it is nearing the end of its usefulness. This particular body has probably been dead for more than two months. All the fluids are gone, leaving behind brittle bones and skin like old parchment. These cadavers are pretty worthless in combat. They break too easily. Soon the Corpse inside this body will be looking for something fresher. We call this *Transferring*, and it brings me to the first point I need to make today.

"Corpses are *not* the souls of the bodies they inhabit. The bodies are simply, normally dead. The entities that we call *Corpses* come in afterward. We don't know where they're from, but the best guess is another plane of existence—what you might call another dimension."

I asked, "Why can't they come from—I dunno—outer space?"

Steve said, "That's a good question. But—Will, is it?"

I felt my face redden. Of course Steve should recognize me! But then I remembered the role I was supposed to be playing. "Yeah. Will."

"Next time raise your hand if you've got a question."

My face stayed red. "Sure."

Steve said, "Anyway, the answer is: maybe they *could,* but they *don't*. We're pretty sure that they enter our world as beings of pure energy. That's why they need to inhabit cadavers in the first place."

He rapped his knuckles on each of the remaining four photos, moving from left to right. "We categorize each level of continuing decomposition." He stopped at the last. The animated cadaver in this one looked fresher than the rest—slimier.

"When possible, the Corpses try to pick what we call Type One bodies," Steve said. "Type Ones are less than a week dead. Such bodies are stronger, more resistant to damage, and of course last longer. The Corpses take good care of these bodies, even going so far as embalming themselves if that hasn't already been done."

Amy raised her hand. "What's *embalming*?"

Steve said, "It's when the blood is drained and replaced with a formaldehyde mixture."

We were all overcome by a general sense of *ewww*.

"What for?" Amy asked.

It was Dave who answered her. "Keeps the body from rotting too fast."

Steve cleared his throat. "Simply put, yes. It fixes the cellular proteins, making it harder for bacteria to feed on them. Without that feeding process, decomposition is curtailed."

Amy looked blankly at him.

Dave muttered, "I liked my answer better."

Steve cleared his throat again.

I thought about the cadavers I'd Seen. Kenny Booth had clearly been a Type One. Mr. Titlebaum, the assistant principal—he'd been maybe a Two or Three. And Ms. Yu? A Four at best. She'd been awfully flaky. The woman in the Laundromat? A Type Two.

I shuddered at the memory of how strong she'd been.

"However," Steve continued, "while Corpses prefer Type Ones, in a pinch they'll take whatever's nearby. Most of their bodies are either stolen from freshly dug graves or from the city morgue, which they now control. We don't really understand the Transfer process, but there do seem to be some rules to it. For one thing, the range is limited—maybe even to line of sight. Corpses can't Transfer into living bodies, and if no new *dead* body's available, then the Corpse is trapped, regardless of the condition of its host cadaver. Something to remember."

"How does the illusion work?" I asked. Then when Steve looked pointedly at me, I raised my hand and asked again.

"Well, that's the big question, isn't it?" he asked. "If we knew that, we'd obviously be able to fight them better. Unfortunately the best I can give you are a few ideas.

"Each Corpse projects a false image. We call it a *Mask*. It might be technology or telepathy—we just don't know. But it's important to understand that the illusion has nothing to do with the bodies they inhabit. Corpses don't try to impersonate deceased people. Instead they use the bodies as shells to move around in—and then project the image they want the world to see on top of it. Let's do an experiment..."

He nodded to Sharyn, who rolled her eyes and began passing out manila folders. Inside mine I found two more Corpse photos. One showed a Type Five and the other a Type Two. Different dead bodies, but both male, and both wearing Philly police uniforms. From the moans and retching sounds around me, it seemed clear the others were looking at the same images.

Sharyn chuckled, but Steve seemed completely unmoved by our distress. "Now, I want everyone to look at these photos—really look."

Beside me, Ethan had turned totally green. On the other side, Dave glared at the faces as if they might attack him.

"Good," Steve said. "Now, relax—"

Somewhere behind me, Maria gagged a little.

"—and let your eyes lose focus."

Of course I knew what he was doing. But would it really work with a picture? So I stared at the Type Five for a moment and then crossed my eyes.

And there it was: the image of a man in his forties with thinning hair and a smooth face floating atop the Corpse's papery visage. Keeping my eyes like that, I turned my attention to the second photo. And there was the same face—the same Mask—superimposed over the image of a different, fresher dead body.

Two different bodies but one Corpse.

"I see it!" I heard Amy say.

"Good," Steve said again. "Anybody else? Raise your hand."

Everyone did—except the Burgermeister, who looked suddenly red-faced and frustrated. "What am I supposed to see?"

Steve continued, rolling right over him. "A Corpse's Mask is maintained, unchanging, regardless of the cadaver a particular Corpse is wearing. What's more, this disguise even carries over to any traces of themselves: shadows, fingerprints—and obviously photographs and videos. That's why no Corpse has ever been revealed on camera."

"Like Kenny Booth!" Ethan exclaimed. "He's been a Philly anchorman for almost three years!"

"Right," said Steve. "But Ethan, next time please raise your hand."

"But that wasn't a question," Ethan protested. "You said to raise our hands if we had a *question*."

Steve blinked. Sharyn laughed. After a moment the Brain Boss pronounced, "New rule. Nobody talks unless they raise their hand first."

We all nodded in agreement.

Steve went on. "But Masks have their limits—"

Ethan interrupted, fighting a smile, "You didn't raise your hand."

Steve blinked. "Except me. Nobody talks except me."

A few recruits chuckled.

"Anyway," Steve said with a sigh, "Corpses can't fake clothing. They have to buy it, just like everybody else. They also seem to be stuck with a gender—male or female."

Amy raised her hand. "So why doesn't this illusion work on us?"

"There are a number of theories," Steve replied. "Maybe we all have a gene that somehow blocks the transmission—a gene that gets activated at some point during puberty. That could be why none of us got the Sight until we were at least eleven or twelve."

Harleen Patel raised her hand. She was a skinny twelve-year-old with a round face, short dark hair, and braces. "What about the crazy way they talk—without moving their lips or anything?"

"We call that *Deadspeak*," Steve answered. "And it isn't speech as we understand it. For example, the sounds can't be recorded, which proves they aren't made of air vibrations, like real sound. They might be another form of telepathy—maybe even the way Corpses ordinarily communicate in their natural environment, wherever that is."

I raised my hand. "Why does it sound so, um...disjointed when they talk? Almost like they're saying one-word sentences."

Steve nodded. "Because it must be a *limited* form of telepathy. For example, it doesn't work over long distances. But it *does* use mental images—pictures, not words—to transmit ideas. Apparently we Seers somehow tap into these images, which our brains automatically translate into something understandable—English words."

I kept my hand up. "And what happens to a Corpse when something gets chopped off? How do they manage to keep up their Mask when, like, some body part is rolling around on the floor? I mean, they can't move around without their heads, can they?"

Steve pointed at me, as if he'd liked my question. "Corpses animate dead bodies, but they're still stuck with the limits of those bodies. You're right, Will. If a Corpse loses its head, it's immobilized. It can't go anywhere, and it can't Transfer—not without having another suitable cadaver nearby. To a lesser degree, the same is true if they lose an arm or a leg. They might still be able to move, but they generally don't—probably because they can't maintain their illusion if they wander too far from the severed limb.

"In such cases, Corpses support each other. If one of them is incapacitated, other Corpses instinctively know this. Maybe it's yet another form of telepathy. However they do it, the other Corpses find their fallen comrade, collect it and whatever pieces of it are lying around, and then take them someplace safe to Transfer. In the meantime, the downed Corpse keeps up its illusion, making any human witnesses think it's only fainted or something. We've observed this happening a few times.

"By making such observations, we're better able to understand the way these beings behave—their language, their culture, and their methods of attack."

"And what are their *methods of attack?*" Ethan asked.

"Ethan..."

Groaning, he raised his hand.

Steve said, "As most of you know, a lot of Corpses are policemen. But the fact is that they don't use guns. In fact, Corpses don't generally use any weapons at all. They prefer to strike their victims, choke them, or sometimes bite them..."

I felt a now-familiar chill race down my spine.

He continued, "Most of the kids whose bodies we've found died from blunt trauma."

"What's that?" Amy asked in a small voice.

Again it was Dave who answered. "They got beaten to death."

"Yes," said Steve, looking uncomfortable.

Maria began to cry.

"And that's not the worst of it," Steve said. "I'm sorry, but you need to know it all. The Corpses often take bites out of their victims. They..." His voice trailed off.

"What?" Amy asked.

"Eat them," Steve said.

We all went quiet.

Steve cleared his throat yet again. "Of course, nutritionally it's meaningless. Their stolen bodies can't digest anything. But we've nevertheless witnessed Corpses eating regular food in public—hot dogs, popcorn, et cetera—and apparently enjoying it. There may be some cultural significance. We don't even know for sure what they can taste."

"*Madre de Dios!*" Maria whimpered. She crossed herself.

I didn't blame her.

"How can they be so strong?" I asked, remembering to raise my hand. "If they're just normal people—normal dead people..." I let my words trail off.

Steve replied, "The human body is stronger than you think. Haven't you ever heard of a panicked mother lifting a car off a baby? That kind of emergency strength comes from a chemical in the body called adrenalin. Well, it seems that a Corpse can generate the same level of strength in its host body whenever it wants to. It's not adrenalin—the body's dead and so can't generate hormones of any kind—but it's something like it.

"However, the Corpses pay for all that speed and strength. The harder they work, the quicker their stolen bodies decay around them."

Ethan chimed in. "I know some of the Corpses are cops. What I don't get is how they become cops. I mean, don't they have to prove they're...people? With birth certificates or driver's licenses or something?"

Steve visibly relaxed. This was evidently safer ground than Amy's question. He didn't even seem to mind that his hand-raising rule had once again been forgotten.

"The Corpses are master forgers," he explained. "Each one has set up a perfect paper trail, including birth records, educational background, and tax history. We don't know how they do it, but every Corpse appears in our world with full credentials. Then it's simply a matter of stepping into this life. The thing to remember is that this false identity has nothing to do with the bodies a particular Corpse may inhabit over time. As I've said, Corpses aren't impersonating anyone who has ever really been alive. The cadavers are just temporary shells. Their ready-made lives, like their Masks, stay the same from host body to host body—and are jealously guarded. In our experience, a given Corpse is far more worried about public exposure of its fake human self than about injury to its current host."

"If they're so well set up," Dave demanded, "how do we beat them?"

"By *understanding* them," replied Steve. "And of course, by effectively arming ourselves."

The Burgermeister clapped his huge hands. "Now that's more like it! Arm ourselves with what?"

Steve held up a green water pistol. "Saltwater. For some reason even small amounts of salt interrupt the control that the Corpses have over their host bodies, temporarily incapacitating them. A shot in a limb makes the limb useless for a while. A shot in the face blinds the Corpse, disrupting motor skills. Enough saltwater, in fact, has been known to force a Corpse to Transfer."

"But it doesn't kill them," the Burgermeister pressed.

"No—I'm afraid it doesn't."

"So how do we beat these things," Dave demanded, "if we can't even kill one?"

Steve said patiently, "If you have a question, could you please raise your hand?"

The Burgermeister glowered. Then with an irritated grunt, he raised his hand.

"Yes?" said Steve.

"What?"

"You have your hand raised."

"That's what you told me to do!"

"So what's your question?"

Dave's face reddened. "I already told you my question!"

Steve blinked. "I think I forgot."

The Burgermeister looked ready to explode. "How can we beat the Corpses if we can't even kill one?"

"Oh, yes. Actually that's a pretty good question."

I leaned over and whispered to Dave, "Don't hit him."

"Solving that problem is our highest priority," Steve said. "And we're exploring a number of very promising theories. Maybe if any of you decide that field work isn't really your thing, you'll join the Brain Factory and work on it with me."

"Not me," Dave grumbled.

"Good call," I muttered.

"I mean, this guy looks like the king of Nerdsville!"

That last had been said too loudly. Steve heard it and blanched. At the same time, Sharyn burst out laughing. Within moments the First Stop recruits were laughing too, but poor Steve looked like he'd bitten into something sour—

All of a sudden, I realized something.

The Undertakers were kids.

Kids. Every last one of us. Well organized, sure. Maybe even halfway capable. But *kids*—who could still be distracted by a dumb joke made about one of our members.

And with this understanding came an awful sense of dread.

We don't stand a chance.

CHAPTER 19

AFTER HOURS

We returned to First Stop a short time later—once again bagged and bounced around in the van. After a dinner of nuked chicken pot pies, we all spent next the two hours in our dorms. Ethan couldn't stop yabbering about the Hackers and how cool that job would be, while Dave just stared unhappily at the little TV that came with our room, watching sitcom reruns.

"Doesn't even get cable," the Burgermeister grumbled.

I lay on my cot, thinking about the day and wondering what my mom had made Emily for dinner that night.

For the umpteenth time, I considered sneaking out and calling her again. There must be a pay phone out on the street somewhere. Another Laundromat maybe.

Um...hi, Mom. It's me. I'm okay. I'm staying with some kids in Philly. We're kind of like an army, except I don't think we stand a chance. What? Oh, didn't I mention that? See, there are these zombies. Except they're not zombies. They're kind of animated dead bodies that have been possessed by beings from another dimension. We call them Corpses, which I guess sounds a little—I dunno—simple, but what do you want? We're just kids, after all. Oh, and Mr. Pratt next door is one of them. So's my math teacher. And only kids can See them for what they really are. Well, actually, Dad could See them. Yeah, that surprised me too. But now that he's dead, it's only kids. And since you know as well as I do that nobody ever believes kids, we kind of have to fight them on our own. So that's what's happening. I'll be in touch. No, I don't know when. Give Emmie a kiss for me, okay?

And, Mom, I love you. In fact, I'm staying away because I love you.

I expected to feel familiar tears on my cheeks. For the first time, there weren't any.

Seven o'clock finally arrived.

The door opened, and Kyle Standish poked his head in. "Lights out, dudes."

As the First Stop Boss, Kyle's job was to run this ratty old place, make sure there was food for the recruits, and keep an eye on things after hours. He spent most of the day sleeping in his private bedroom at the end of the hall and usually only came out at night. A few of the kids half-jokingly called him the local vampire—but he didn't look like a vampire. Kyle was tall and pretty muscular, with hair not quite as red as mine. He smiled a lot—too much, in my opinion, given the lousy work he had to do.

"Why can't we still watch TV?" Ethan asked.

Kyle shook his head. "You know the rules. We've got to shut off all power at sunset."

"This sucks," Dave groaned.

"Yeah, it does," Kyle replied. "The thing is that after dark, any lights might get noticed from the street. This place is supposed to be closed, remember? We don't want any of Philly's Finest poking around, do we?"

"Guess not," Ethan admitted.

"This sucks," Dave said again—but then he stretched out on the bunk.

"You'll get over it," a new voice said.

Kyle wordlessly stepped aside as Tom entered the room. Tall as Kyle was, Tom dwarfed him. The Chief had his hands on his hips as he surveyed us like a drill sergeant. His dark eyes found mine. "You ready?"

I nodded glumly and stood up.

"I want to watch Will fight," the Burgermeister said.

"Me too," Ethan added.

"Maybe next time," Tom told them. "This one's private."

"So he gets to have fun while I lay here and stare at the ceiling?" Dave asked sourly.

Tom smiled. "He won't be having fun. Trust me." Then he led me out the door.

"It might've been smarter not to tell Dave about tonight's special session," Tom whispered once we were alone in the hallway. "He ended up spilling it to everybody else."

"I know," I replied. "Sorry."

He shrugged. "Nothing for it now."

The short corridor led past the kitchen and out into the shop's back room—the training room. Tom started off in that direction, but I caught his arm. "Can I talk to you for a second—before we go out there, I mean?"

Tom studied me curiously. "Sure thing. Let's hit the kitchen."

First Stop's kitchen was really nothing more than several old plastic chairs, a sink, a beat-up microwave, and a noisy old refrigerator. Not even a table. A pile of threadbare rags did triple duty as napkins, paper towels, and place mats. A single bulb hung from the ceiling.

"Sit," Tom said.

I sat.

"So what's up, bro?" the Chief asked, taking the chair beside mine.

As I struggled for the right words, there came a loud mechanical *click* from deeper in the building. The lights went out, leaving us in almost perfect darkness.

I jumped. "Jeez!"

"Just Kyle killing the power," Tom explained. "You know the deal. From now until morning, we're on battery lamps—and only when absolutely necessary. Don't sweat it. Give your eyes a few seconds, and they'll adjust."

The thing was, I kind of welcomed the sudden darkness. Somehow not having to look the Chief in the eyes made saying what I had to say easier. "Tom, I don't think we can beat the Corpses."

There was a long silence. I swallowed.

"How do you figure that?" His tone was patient. At least he didn't sound pissed.

"Well—we're just kids!"

I could barely make out Tom nodding. My eyes were adjusting to the dark, just as promised. "Are we?"

"Yeah!" I replied. "I mean—aren't we? This afternoon at Haven, Steve was giving us his Corpse talk when Dave and Sharyn started messing with him, cracking jokes, and—you know, it just suddenly hit me, Tom! I'm twelve years old! You're only seventeen! No offense."

"None taken."

"The Corpses are all over the place! Some of them are even cops! What chance have we got?"

Another pause, longer than the first.

"Will, I'm impressed."

"Huh?"

"It takes maturity to spot the immaturity in others."

I frowned. "I don't—"

He silenced me with a gesture that I could barely see. "There are children in the Undertakers, Will—but not a lot of childhood. We all have to grow up much faster than is really fair. What you saw today was a crew of recruits who ain't yet learned that lesson. They're confused, and they're scared. This afternoon, back in Haven, y'all found yourselves in a classroom situation—something you're familiar with—and so familiar behaviors kicked in. You messed around. You got to be kids again."

"But Sharyn—"

Tom chuckled. "Sharyn's *Sharyn*, Will. The rules go out the window where my sister's concerned. Ain't nobody on Earth I'd rather have with me in a fight, but she's always been a big kid."

"Oh," I said.

He could tell I was unconvinced.

"Look—just between us, I ain't saying we *can* beat the Corpses. After all, we're outnumbered and outgunned. But I do know that I'd put our crew up against any underground resistance that's ever existed. We got Schoolers in twenty middle schools across the city, all on the lookout for Seers. And do you know how we get 'em into those schools, bro?"

I nodded. "The Hackers—they rig them up with fake identities."

"Right. The Schoolers all report direct to me. I pick 'em, give 'em their assignments, and send 'em off. Then each Schooler in the field gets hooked up with a Chatter at Haven who monitors their situation daily. Those dudes report to the Chatter Boss, who reports to me. You understand what I'm telling you?"

"That—we're organized?" I asked uncertainly.

Tom nodded. "Straight up. Three years back it was just your dad, Sharyn, and me. But slowly we been getting bigger. This month, six more kids'll roll in, including yourself—and that's pretty typical. We're up past 120 Undertakers, with about a quarter of them in the field at any given time. We're good at this, Will. Seriously good."

I considered this. "Tom, it sounds great. It really does."

"Do I hear a *but?*" he remarked, smiling.

"I get what you're saying," I said with a sigh. "I'm sorry. I didn't mean to—"

I started to stand up.

Tom's strong hand fell on my shoulder. "Don't wimp out on me. Nothing you said has pissed me off. Like I told you, I'm impressed you even came up with this concern. Now level with me. Tell me what's on your mind."

"Well, the Undertakers have been around for about three years—almost since the Corpses first appeared, right?"

"Right."

"And in all that time, other than getting bigger and better organized—what have you really *done?*"

Even in the darkness, I saw his expression falter. Instantly I backpedaled. "I'm sorry."

"It's cool," he said quietly, thoughtfully. "You sound like Sharyn is all."

"I do?"

"She's always nagging me that we need to stop playing defense and start taking the fight to the Corpses."

"Are you sure she's wrong?"

"No," the Chief admitted. "Will, do you know who Harriet Tubman was?"

"Who?"

"Harriet Tubman. She was this slave who lived down south about 150 years ago. Ever heard of her?"

I thought that maybe I had, that she sounded familiar due to some half-remembered history class. But I shook my head anyway.

Tom said, "She escaped slavery and came north. Then she turned right around and went back to help free others. Became this major conductor on the Underground Railroad. Know what *that* was?"

This time I nodded. "It was this bunch of safe houses where runaway slaves could hide after they escaped."

"Right. The thing that most people don't get is that the fight against slavery started up long before the Civil War. And it wasn't fought by armies on battlefields but by ordinary folks doing what they could to help themselves and each other."

I nodded, frowned, and looked uncomfortably down at my shoes.

Tom laughed a little. "Good speech, huh?"

I shrugged. "Not bad."

"But the thing is: I believe it," he insisted. "Look, bro. Nobody'd like to really nail the Corpses more than I would. But staying alive in this situation ain't about heroism. It's about practicality. If we attack now, we lose. Straight up. As things stand, the Corpses know we exist, and they're looking for us. But since we don't do nothing to really threaten them, they don't look too hard. Yeah, they've raided a couple of our First Stops, but they still ain't found Haven. And I intend to keep it that way."

"I get it," I said.

"Do you?" Tom asked, and there was something like need in the Chief's expression.

He wants me to get what he's saying.

"We can't be Harriet Tubman forever, Tom," I said.

"That's what Sharyn tells me."

"Maybe she's right."

He nodded. "No maybes about it. But before the time comes to really start fighting, we first got to find a weapon—a genuine lethal weapon—that we can use against the Corpses. And we've got to pick up numbers. We need to finally become the army that you and my sister think we ought to be—the army that your dad dreamed about."

"My dad dreamed that?" I asked.

"Will, your dad dreamed all of this. Ain't I made that plain?"

"I guess so." It just kept surprising me. My dad was everything to me. But as it turned out, he was even more than I'd thought he was.

"Will," Tom said, his manner suddenly grave. "I need you to understand something."

"Yeah?"

"I don't know when the Undertakers'll be ready to start really fighting back. But this much I *do* know: when it happens, it'll be *my* call. I'm Chief, Will—have been ever since your dad died—and that chain of command is what helps to keep us alive. I need your word that you'll respect that no matter what you feel inside. Can you give me that?"

I met Tom's eyes in the dark.

"Yeah," I said. "I mean...yes, sir. I can."

It was a promise that I meant to keep.

At least I thought I did.

CHAPTER 20

THE COOLER PARTNER

Moving confidently in the darkness, Tom led me out of the kitchen and through the nearby door into the training room. Here at least there was light—provided by a single, battery-powered lamp that sat at the edge of the practice area. Kyle was checking the boarded-up windows for cracks and sealing them up with duct tape when he found them.

A sucky job. I made a mental note never to volunteer for Kyle's gig.

Sharyn stood on the mat, her hands on her hips. She grinned her trademark grin. "Well, about time you two showed up. I was about to send out a search party!"

Feeling embarrassed, I didn't reply.

Tom shrugged. "Sorry, sis. We had some stuff to talk about."

"That right? Well, it's late, and we've got to get this dance started. Come on up here, Red." Then more seriously, "You look nervous."

"I am," I admitted, stepping onto the mat. "A little."

"Don't be. We just want to see how you do against a trained opponent. You nailed Ethan easy enough—and even Hot Dog, big as he is. But—"

"Yeah, I get it," I said. "They weren't trained."

"Straight up. Kick off your shoes, and show me your stance." She studied my form. "Good. Now, the thing to remember is that when you're fighting, every move your opponent makes is predictable if you watch 'em close enough. Hand-to-hand's all about reading your enemy, figuring out what they plan to do next, and then getting around it. Got it?"

"Got it," I replied a little skeptically.

She grinned again. "Well, knowing it and doing it are two different things. Anyhow, you just consider this a talent test. Don't plan on winning this fight. Believe me, you won't. We're setting you up with one of our best. Just focus on doing *your* best. I ain't looking for technique here—just instinct. So don't play the game the way you figure I want you to play it. Make the moves that feel right, okay?"

"Okay."

"Any questions?"

"I don't think so."

"Cool! Then let's dance! Will—say hey to your partner."

Helene Boettcher emerged from the nearby shadows.

She was dressed in shorts and a tank top. Her arms and legs were tanned and muscular. Her long hair had been tightly braided. She crossed the floor and stepped lithely onto the mat, her eyes on mine and her expression unreadable.

"Hi," I said, the memory of our last encounter—the terrible things we'd said to each other—suddenly fresh in my mind.

"Hi," she replied flatly.

"Get some helmets on, and wrap your hands, you two," Sharyn directed.

As we did so, I muttered, "I'm—sorry about what happened the other day."

She wouldn't even look at me. "That's nice."

I swallowed. Then I pulled the boxer's helmet over my head. It felt hot and tight.

Sharyn inspected us both. "Cool. Helene, don't get too fancy, but don't hold back too much either. I know you dudes are tight, but I want both of you to kind of put that down for a while."

Helene's face was stone. "No problem."

"Um...yeah," I added.

Sharyn left the mat to stand at her brother's side.

"Begin," said Tom.

Wordlessly and without warning, Helene attacked.

I barely had time to get into my stance before she lashed out with a front kick to my stomach that doubled me over.

Then, spinning on her heel, she delivered a lightning-quick wheel kick that caught my temple and sent me crashing to the mat.

I lay there dazed and wheezing.

From the sidelines Sharyn said, "Rule One, Red: don't assume your opponent'll wait for you to get ready. Got it?"

"Got it," I grunted.

Helene stood over me, and there was no mistaking the hard anger in her eyes.

"Nice hit," I muttered.

"Yeah," she replied.

I staggered to my feet.

Helene stepped suddenly forward, hooked one foot behind my knees, and shoved with both her wrapped hands.

I crashed down onto my back again.

Sharyn sighed. "Ease up, Helene. For now let's give him time to find his stance."

The girl nodded and retreated. With an effort I pushed myself to my feet a second time. My side ached, and I could feel my face reddening. It wasn't getting beaten by a girl that was bothering me. It really wasn't. I'd seen enough of what Sharyn could do to Dave to be past all that.

But to lose this completely was a real blow to my pride.

"Take your time," Helene suggested, a little mockery in her tone. "Catch your breath."

Steadying myself, I set my feet as I'd been taught and raised both my fists.

"Ready?" she asked me sweetly.

I studied her. We were about the same height, although I was probably a little heavier than she was. She, however, had tons of training behind her. I remembered how agile she'd been during our escape from Manayunk. Sharyn hadn't been kidding about this girl being "one of our best."

But she had been wrong about one thing. This was no *talent test*. It wasn't even a sparring match.

It was payback.

There was no way I was going to win this fight.

But that didn't mean I had to lose it badly.

"Ready," I said.

And she came at me—fast.

I fought my instinct to cover up. Instead I remained motionless, my muscles loose but ready, watching her come. Left foot. Right foot. Her braids bounced in her wake. Helene's right arm was cocked, the way Dave's had been earlier in the day. But her left—yes! That was where the blow was coming from. The right arm was a trick!

At the last instant, I pivoted, barely sidestepping her left-fisted gut punch. At the same moment, I hooked my right arm into hers, locked our elbows, and yanked backward. Gasping, Helene overbalanced.

I jabbed my foot into the crook of her knee.

And down she went.

"Sweet!" Sharyn remarked from the sidelines.

As Helene got to her feet, I stepped back and resumed my stance. I supposed that I should feel some sense of victory. I didn't. I'd just knocked a friend to the floor—a girl who'd saved my life.

A girl I liked.

"Sorry," I said.

Helene's hazel eyes narrowed. Wordlessly she advanced again, this time more slowly.

"Fighting ain't just about defense, Will!" Sharyn called.

I nodded, suddenly a little sick to my stomach.

I hated this.

Helene drew closer.

I feigned a right hook and then crouched low, intending to sweep her legs out from under her. But Helene saw right through the trick. Ignoring the fake punch, she jumped over my low-swinging leg and treated me to a single sharp kick to my shoulder. The blow sent me rolling across the mat. I kept rolling, waiting until I was nearly at the edge before regaining my footing.

Helene was already charging forward, her expression hard and determined. From the angle of her body, I guessed that she meant to jump-kick me into next Tuesday.

I didn't think. I just reacted. Instead of trying to block or sidestep, I leapt into a kick of my own. I did it pretty badly, but I timed it right because I caught Helene in the stomach a split-second before she launched herself off the mat.

She went down very hard, tumbling head over heels.

I landed clumsily, spun around, and prepared for a fresh assault.

But Helene lay facedown, unmoving.

"Oh, crap!" I looked up for Tom or Sharyn but couldn't spot them in the deep shadows. "She's hurt!" I yelled. They didn't answer.

I dropped to my knees beside Helene and called her name. No response. Could I have broken one of her ribs or something? Did she need an ambulance? Where the hell were Tom and Sharyn?

"Kyle!" I called, trying to remember if the First Stop Boss had stayed in the training room for my sparring match. Again there was no answer.

Finally, hesitantly, I shoved both my hands under the girl's limp body and rolled her over onto her back.

Her eyes opened.

And she punched me dead in the nose.

CHAPTER 21

THE WAY COOLER PARTNER

I recoiled, clutching at my face. Blood started oozing out from both my nostrils. Tears flooded my eyes. Through them I saw Helene climb to her feet wearing a triumphant expression.

"Never trust a wounded enemy," she said smugly.

I sat back on the mat, tasting blood and staring up at her through a haze of shock and pain. "I didn't!" I cried. "I thought I was helping a friend!"

Helene's victorious smile disappeared.

"She ain't your friend right now, bro," Tom remarked from the shadows. "She's your opponent."

"No!" I exclaimed, close to screaming. "She stopped being my opponent the minute I thought I'd hurt her!"

"You don't want to be thinking like that," Sharyn warned. "Not in combat."

I struggled to my feet, leaving bloody handprints on the mat. I was shaking, but more with anger than pain.

A pair of gentle hands touched my arm. I flinched. From beside me, Helene said quietly, "I'm sorry."

I tried to jerk my arm free, but her grip tightened.

"Turn around," she begged. "Let me see how bad it is."

Reluctantly I obeyed. Helene wiped the blood from my face with a towel, her fingers tentatively exploring the injury. She pressed up on my nose. It hurt but not too much.

She sighed with obvious relief. "It's not broke. But you're gonna have a shiner tomorrow. I'm really sorry, Will."

I pulled away from her, my cheeks burning. A knot of outrage, hot and sour, had formed in the pit of my stomach. I glared at Helene, who offered up a small, apologetic smile. Payback had evidently been made. All was forgiven.

My outrage deepened.

"Let's do it again," said Sharyn from the shadows.

Helene shook her head. "No. I got carried away. We should call it a night."

Tom stepped onto the mat. "Think you're up for another match, Will?"

"Uh-uh," I replied in a thick voice. "I...don't want...to do this...anymore."

"So don't," Tom replied, without expression.

Nodding, I left the mat. Helene trailed after me, but I

wordlessly shrugged off her advances. At the moment I didn't want or need her help.

Then I saw something that gave me pause.

A figure sat hunched over at the back of the room, near the closed hallway door. For a second I thought it might just be Kyle sitting in the dark and enjoying our little drama. But this person was too big to be the First Stop Boss. Besides, Kyle—I now saw—was off to the left, sitting at the edge of the light and reading a comic book.

So who—?

Then I recognized him. Maybe it was the slope of those huge shoulders. Maybe it was the silhouette of his oddly square-shaped head.

But the kid sitting quietly in the dark was Dave.

He wasn't supposed to be there. Tom had made that clear. But here he was, showing uncharacteristic stealth and equally uncharacteristic silence. I knew he'd wanted to watch my private match; he'd said so about a hundred times. But this—

I almost spoke up. I almost announced his presence to Helene and the rest, flashes of suspicion and words like *mole* running through my head. Almost.

But then the Chief of the Undertakers remarked from behind me, "Of course, a Corpse won't give a crap if you ain't in the mood to fight."

I froze.

"You lost," Tom said gravely. "It's humiliating. Believe me, I understand that."

I didn't turn around. My anger suddenly reasserted itself. So what if the Burgermeister wanted to watch? The knot in my gut tightened almost painfully.

He continued, "But if you plan on surviving, you've got to be able to go the distance in a fight—no matter what. Walk away now, and how do you figure you'll ever have the stones to try again?"

"Tom," Helene said, "don't you think he's had enough for one day?"

The Chief ignored her. "Well, bro?"

So, Burgermeister, I thought bitterly, *you want to see a fight? Okay then! I'll give you a real show.*

Slowly I turned. Tom's expression was stony as he met my eyes.

I suddenly understood that all my outrage wasn't really directed at Helene. At the moment it wasn't even directed at the Corpses for taking away my life.

It was directed at this kid right here—Tom Jefferson, Chief of the Undertakers—for pitting me against someone I cared about, a friend.

For wanting to make me into the sort of person who could hurt her.

"I won't fight Helene anymore," I said.

Tom looked disappointed. "That's your call, Will. But—"

I cut him off. "But I'll fight *you*."

A leaden silence fell over the training room. Into it, Sharyn uttered an oath that sounded totally out of character. "Oh—fudge!"

Her brother's dark eyebrows rose in surprise.

"Will?" Helene asked hesitantly. Off in another corner of the training room, I noticed Kyle's attention snap up from his comic. He looked stunned.

I ignored them both. "What about it—Chief?"

Tom studied me. Finally, resignedly, he said, "You're on."

"Whoa, bro!" Sharyn exclaimed. "I don't think—"

"It's what the man wants," her brother interjected calmly. He walked to the edge of the mat, picked up the tape, and started wrapping his fists. They were big fists. "Helene, I'll need your helmet."

Helene looked from me to Tom and back again. Then with obvious dismay, she removed her headgear and tossed it onto the mat.

Tom pulled off his shirt and retrieved the fallen helmet. As he slipped it over his head, adjusting it for size, I was struck by the incredible shape that this kid was in. His chest was broad and heavily muscled. His arms looked as thick as tree branches, especially compared to the twigs sticking out from my own narrow shoulders.

Apprehension gnawed at my anger. I pushed it away and stepped defiantly back onto the mat.

Tom positioned himself in the standard Undertaker fighting stance.

"Bring it, bro," he said.

Seeing his expression—so passive, so controlled—fueled my already fiery anger. Uttering an outraged roar, I charged him, my feet pumping across the mat, my fists at the ready. The moment he was in range, I hurled a right-fisted punch at his infuriatingly calm face.

I was nose-down on the mat before I even realized it had happened.

"Don't fight pissed," Tom instructed. "It just makes you careless. Relax. Be calm. Be in control."

"I don't want a lesson from you!" I snapped as I climbed to my feet.

Whirling around I launched myself into a wheel kick. Tom smoothly sidestepped it and caught my foot in one vice-like hand. In a fluid motion, he gave my ankle a single hard twist.

My body spun in midair—once, twice—before again crashing to the mat.

This time Tom offered no advice.

Frustrated and furious with myself, I staggered back up and resumed my stance. The Chief stood just a few feet away, watching me with eyes like still, dark pools.

I feigned another kick and then instead stepped close and delivered a series of lightning jabs, each of which Tom easily, patiently blocked. I threw just enough punches to lower his guard. Then without warning, I leapt up and kicked him hard in the stomach.

It was like kicking a stone wall. I literally bounced away, lost my balance, and crashed to the mat. Tom staggered back a few steps, grunting in surprise. He coughed and smiled. "Didn't see that coming. Not bad."

I jumped to my feet again, my face burning. Tom was beating me, and so far, he hadn't so much as thrown a punch!

"Fight back!" I exclaimed in frustration.

"If he fights back, he'll waste you, Red," Sharyn muttered.

"Please, Will..." Helene begged.

I ignored it all.

"Who are you mad at, bro?" Tom asked.

"You!" I screamed.

"Why?"

"Because you wanna make me into something I'm not!"

"And what's that?"

"A fighter!"

Tom slowly shook his head. "I ain't looking for fighters. What I need are soldiers."

I yelled until I thought the walls would shake. "I'm *not* a soldier! I go to middle school! Middle school! This is your world, and I don't want to be in it!"

Then I launched myself a third time, driving the heel of my hand up toward his nose, determined to knock the Chief of the Undertakers' head right off his broad, muscled shoulders.

Tom struck like a snake, cuffing me under the chin hard enough to snap my head back. My ears rang. I felt my knees buckle, felt a piece of the mat seem to rise up and smack my cheek.

Everything blurred. There was no pain—only a creeping numbness.

A voice spoke in my ear, calm as always. "You wanna go home, Will? Well, get in line. We all want to go home. But you know what the difference is between you and me? You got a home to go to. That's something I ain't never had. Think about *that*, bro."

Then everything went black.

CHAPTER 22

THE POCKETKNIFE

Here he comes," Tom said.

I opened my eyes. I was lying on my cot in the First Stop boys' dorm. Dave stood close by, wringing his big hands. Helene and Sharyn were over by the door, apparently arguing about something. Tom sat in a chair beside the cot. His shirt was back on. There was no sign of either Kyle or Ethan.

I tried to turn my head. It throbbed something awful. I moaned.

"Sorry about the headache," Tom said, smiling with relief.

I closed my eyes against the pain. "What did you do to me?"

"Gave you a chin tap. Your head snapped back hard enough to knock you cold."

"A chin tap," I echoed. "Did you mean to do that?"

Tom shrugged. "You made it plain that you wouldn't let up, so I figured I'd better keep things from getting out of hand. If done right, a chin tap clicks off consciousness like a switch."

"Is that a street karate move?"

He nodded.

"Where'd you guys learn to fight like that?" I asked.

Tom thought for a moment. "That's a long story for another day."

"Okay," I said. "Guess this means you won, huh?"

"Depends. You still blame me for everything that's gone down?"

I frowned, searching my feelings. "I guess not."

"Then yeah, I won."

"It's funny," I said, opening my eyes again, more carefully this time. "I remember being really pissed. But now it's—I dunno." I looked at him. "You said something to me right before I went out, didn't you?"

"Wasn't sure you'd remember that," Tom replied a little sheepishly. "That was...selfish. I shouldn't have said it. Sorry."

I gave him a thin smile. "Maybe you were pissed too."

"Maybe."

Seeing I was awake, the rest of them closed around me. Helene's eyes were red as if she'd been crying. Sharyn, of course, was grinning. And Dave was making a sour face, like he was looking at something really gross.

"What are you staring at?" I demanded.

"You got a black eye—and this bruise on your chin that looks like a cantaloupe."

I gingerly explored my jaw, which earned me a fresh wave of pain. I winced.

Tom said gently, "Just let it be. You'll be cool in a day or so." He turned to his sister. "That fresh ice?"

"Yeah," Sharyn replied, handing a couple of small ice packs to her brother. "Helene thinks he might need a doctor. I say, she's nuts."

"No, she's ain't nuts," Tom replied. "But she ain't right either. Will's going to be fine. Trust me on this, Helene. I know how hard I hit him."

"What about his eye?" she asked. This was, of course, the injury *she'd* given me.

"What about it?"

"Looks swollen."

Sharyn grinned. "I like it. Gives him character."

Tom said, "That ain't bad either, Helene. No facial bones broken. It may not be pretty, but it won't do him no harm. I promise."

Helene nodded, but she didn't look pleased about it.

Tom positioned one of the ice packs over the lower half of my face and the other carefully over my left eye. It felt funny. I reached up to adjust it. "Uh-uh," Tom told me. "The swelling'll go down quicker if you let it alone."

"Okay."

He smiled. Then he turned to the others. "Could y'all give us this room?"

Helene looked about to protest. But then Sharyn wrapped an arm around the smaller girl's shoulders and led her out. The Burgermeister gave me one more unhappy scowl before following after them, shutting the door as he went.

Tom said, "There's loyalty in that dude. Turns out that while we were in the kitchen before the match, he snuck by us and got into the training room. Very sneaky. But the minute he thought you were really hurt, he came charging out of the shadows. He looked more pissed than you and me put together. For a minute there, I was afraid I'd have to tap *him* too."

"Where's Ethan?" I asked.

"Ethan? In the kitchen. Sharyn chased him out when I carried you in here." Wearing an odd smile, he asked, "Why?"

"Why what?"

"Why ask about Ethan?"

I shrugged. It hurt. "This is the boys' dorm. If he's not here, I just wanted to know where he was."

"Is that right?"

I looked at him. "What's the smile for?"

"Forget it," Tom said. "Listen up. What I want to say—"

I cut him off again. "Why Helene?"

"What?"

"Why, of all people—did you have to pick Helene to fight me? She's the closest thing I've got to a friend around here."

He frowned. "*I'm* your friend, Will. So's my sister."

"I didn't mean it like that."

"Yeah. I know." Tom sighed. "Fact is, we picked Helene tonight because you two *are* friends. We knew you'd be nervous and figured a familiar face might make things easier. Sharyn and me didn't know there was so much trouble between you two. Helene clued us in on that later, after I'd..." His voice trailed off for second. "Anyhow, that ain't the reason I wanted to be alone with you."

I managed another weak smile. "You planning on beating me up some more?"

But the Chief apparently wasn't in any mood for jokes. "I owe you another apology."

"For what? Knocking me out?"

Tom shook his head. "Nope. Ain't even a little sorry I did that. No, this one's because when you first hit our crib last week, I shoved some stuff at you that you weren't ready for."

"I don't get it."

"In more than two years, Will, nobody's ever come to the Undertakers the way you did. Nobody's ever skipped First Stop and rolled straight into Haven. And nobody's ever been shown the shrine on their first day. Know why you were?"

"Because of my dad?"

"Right. And that wasn't fair to you."

I considered this. "I still don't get it. Why wasn't it fair?"

"You'd just had one nasty shock—worse than pretty much every other Undertaker. On top of the usual—getting yanked out of your home, your school, and your life without no warning and dumped into this new hard reality—you also wised up to the fact that your old man had this whole other...well, family. And that he had to keep us secret from you, your mom, and your sister."

I swallowed. A half-dozen emotions spun through my head.

"Yeah," I whispered.

"Well, all that was my fault," Tom continued. "It was me who told Helene to bring you straight in. It was me who tipped you off to Karl's gig with the Undertakers. And it was me who showed you the shrine up front instead of waiting until you were better prepped. All of it my fault." His dark eyes lowered. "I did it because—well, I've been expecting you, bro. Karl's only son. I always figured you'd get the Sight, join up with us, and someday become a great Undertaker. I see now how unfair that was. You were dead right in wanting to kick the crap out of me tonight. I had it coming. And I'm sorry."

He met my eyes again, and it was clear that he meant what he'd said. "It's okay," I told him and was a little surprised to find that I meant it too.

"Yeah?"

I nodded. This time it didn't hurt so much; most of my face had gone numb from the ice packs.

Tom blew out a sigh. "Thanks. In that case, I got a present for you." He pulled something out of his back pocket and held it out to me. After a moment I took it.

It was a pocketknife.

Except that, close up, it didn't resemble any pocketknife that I'd ever seen. About six inches long, it was made of silvery steel polished to an almost mirror shine. There weren't any markings on it—neither from the Boy Scouts nor the Swiss Army. Instead there was a series of six small buttons set along its length, each one labeled with a number.

"Wow," I muttered.

Tom said gravely, "Your dad made it two years back, about a month before he died. For my birthday. Sharyn got her *wakizashi* sword that day."

"My dad made this?"

He nodded. "And it ain't left my body since…until now."

"It's big," I marveled. "How many blades does it have?"

The older boy shook his head. "This ain't no normal pocketknife. See these buttons?"

"Yeah?"

"Watch." Tom reached for the closed knife, his thumb tapping the button marked *1*.

What popped out the end of the tool looked less like a blade than it did a thin, twin-pronged tuning fork.

"What is it?" I asked, frowning.

"A lock pick. It'll pick most any lock in under thirty seconds. Takes some practice though. I'll make sure you get time to work with it over the next week."

"Wow," I said again.

Another press of the *1* button and the lock pick withdrew. Tom's thumb tapped button number *2*. Two more prongs, much larger than the first, emerged from the knife's other end.

"Another lock pick?" I asked.

"Nope. Watch." Tom held the button down. An arc of blue electricity sprang to life between the tips of the two prongs. I gasped in surprise.

"It's a Taser," Tom explained. "One hundred and fifty thousand volts—enough to drop a grown man—or a Corpse—and keep them down for a while. But handle with care. Don't mess with it until you learn how."

"Jeez!"

Tom released the *2* button, and the Taser retracted with a *snap*. His thumb pressed number *3*. This time a genuine blade emerged. "Five and a half inches of high-carbon steel," he told me. "Ain't much it won't cut. It's also balanced."

"Balanced?"

Tom spun around and whipped his arm out. The knife

flew across the room, whirling end over end until it hit the opposite wall and stuck there.

I felt my eyes widen. "Whoa!"

Grinning, Tom retrieved the knife.

Buttons *4* and *5* released power screwdrivers—one bladed and the other Phillips-style. Number *6* activated a flashlight, small but very bright. "The battery's rechargeable," Tom explained, handing the knife back to me. "It lasts about a week. I'll give you the charger too."

"My dad made this?" I asked again.

"Sure did."

"And Sharyn's sword? Did he make *that* too?"

He nodded.

I frowned and said, "I don't think so."

"What?"

"Tom, I loved my dad—but he couldn't change a light switch without shocking himself. I mean, one day when the bread got stuck in the toaster, he tried to pry it out with a butter knife and got half-electrocuted. Mom almost called an ambulance."

He looked confused. "Straight up?"

"Straight up."

"Well, that makes no sense. Your father told me he made them—the pocketknife and the wakizashi both. He even made a joke about it. *Dream children*, he called them."

"Maybe he had them *made* someplace," I suggested.

Tom considered this. "The sword maybe. But the

knife? Uh-uh. Sharyn and me know this city, and I'm telling you there ain't no such shop in Philly. Sure, there's a couple of custom knife makers, but there's nobody who could put a thing like this together. I always figured your old man had some kind of workshop at his house, maybe in the basement, with some high-tech tools. I swear I half-expected you to already have something like this."

I shook my head. "No way."

Tom laughed a little nervously. "Well, guess we just have to just chalk it up to one of life's little mysteries."

"I guess," I replied, although I wasn't happy about it. My dad making Japanese swords and super pocketknives? Not likely!

I cleared my throat. "Anyway, I can't accept this."

"Yeah, you can."

"But my dad gave it to you for your birthday!"

"That makes it mine to give to his son," Tom replied matter-of-factly.

"But why?"

The Chief leaned close. "Partly because I *am* sorry for all the stuff I dumped on you when you first blew in—and partly because I *do* expect major things from you, Will. You got guts. More than I seen in any recruit in a long time—if ever."

"Guts? Yeah, right, Tom. I'm scared to death!"

"We're all scared to death," the older boy said with a shrug.

"So far the only brave thing I've done was challenge you to a fight."

"And how many first-week Undertakers do you figure do that?"

"Dave challenged Sharyn on his second day!" I replied.

Tom chuckled. "That was more stupid than brave. Besides, all Dave did was act tough and try to scare a girl. Well, he wised up quick to how far that crap flies with my sister."

"She's a good fighter," I said. Then correcting myself, I added, "A good soldier."

"You got no idea."

"You're a good soldier too," I added.

"Thanks, bro."

"You might even be better than she is."

Tom laughed again. "Just do me a favor and don't tell Sharyn you think that. I don't need the bruises."

I smiled. "Okay." Then I hefted the knife again. "Are you sure about this, Tom?"

"Way sure."

"If you ever want it back—"

"I won't. But thanks for the offer."

"Thanks for the gift."

"So...we're cool?"

"We're cool," I said.

"Good." Tom stood. "Rest up. You got the morning off, but after lunch, it's back to business. You've still got six nights on that cot before you and the rest of the recruits grad to Haven. And Will?"

"Yeah?"

"Promise me you won't *play* with that pocketknife. It ain't a toy. It's a tool and a weapon. Make sure you learn the buttons. The last thing you wanna do is pop the wrong thing and end up cutting or zapping yourself. Sharyn won't dig it when I tell her I gave it to you. She figures you're too young."

I replied, "Tell her that there are children in the Undertakers but not a lot of childhood."

Tom grinned. "Couldn't have said it better myself."

CHAPTER 23

THE LONG LAST NIGHT

After the field trip, things at First Stop changed.

Tom and Sharyn met with each of us in turn, asking us which crews—if any—had appealed to us. Dave liked the Monkeys, Ethan the Chatters. Maria and Harleen favored Hacking, while Amy, always the quietest of the bunch, just tended to cry when asked to commit herself. Nobody had even mentioned the Brains so far.

For myself, I was thinking Schooler, although when pressed, I couldn't quite say why. I couldn't tell one end of a hammer or test tube from another and was a loss at computers, and the idea of talking on the radio or flipping through newspapers all day made me almost physically ill.

In fact, the only thing I *had* shown any talent for since coming to First Stop was combat.

Besides, Helene was a Schooler, and for reasons I couldn't explain, that mattered.

Fortunately it wasn't a decision that I had make right away. All new Undertakers started their lives at Haven as Moms working under Nick Rooney—a gig that could run anywhere up to three months depending on recruitment.

Three months! I could barely believe I'd been away from home for almost two weeks!

But lately I'd kind of gotten used to ignoring such thoughts.

It was now my last night at First Stop. Lights out was hours behind us, and both of my roommates were asleep. But not me. I lay wide awake on my cot, turning Tom's pocketknife over and over in the faint city light that filtered through the edges of the boarded-up window.

Tomorrow we'd all be going to Haven. At least we'd be out of this dingy dry cleaners and back someplace where the air didn't smell like rat droppings.

It struck me with a shudder that I could barely remember what my bed at home felt like. The thought tightened that now-familiar knot in my stomach.

The pocketknife. Think about that instead.

Tom had always believed that my dad made it. I knew that couldn't be right. Still, I was pretty sure that he hadn't picked it up at Kmart either. Alone in the dark over these past nights, I'd explored every one of its gadgets. There wasn't a single serial number or manufacturer's mark on it anywhere. Wherever this thing had been made, it hadn't been done on some assembly line.

Besides, it was too—well—*perfect* for that.

Every one of its springs sprung soundlessly. Every one of its buttons clicked smoothly. I'd asked for and gotten enough stupid crap for my birthday and Christmas to recognize quality when I saw it.

So where had it come from?

Footsteps.

I glanced over at the shut bedroom door.

More footsteps—tentative, sneaky.

Faint light peeked under the closed door. It floated past, barely there at all.

It might be Kyle, of course, doing his First Stop Boss thing. Except it hadn't sounded like Kyle, who had a pretty heavy footstep. These steps had been light, soft—maybe barefoot. Nobody went barefoot at First Stop. The floor had too many splinters.

Weird.

It was curiosity more than anything that got me out of bed. I pulled on my sneakers. As I tiptoed past Dave's bunk, the Burgermeister rolled over in his sleep, mumbling something about Baby Ruth candy bars and a girl named Sarah. Against the opposite wall, Ethan never stirred.

I gingerly opened the door, remembering its squeaky hinges, and peeked down the corridor. Despite the lousy light, I could just make out someone standing at the end of the hall. She—for the person was too small to be anyone but one of the girls—was peering out into the training room.

As I watched, the mysterious girl opened the training room door just enough to allow her to slip quietly through.

What the heck…?

I followed, tiptoeing along the grimy hallway and finally pausing almost exactly where the girl had just been standing. The training room door stood partway open. Through the gap I could see two Undertakers playing cards by the light of a battery-powered lamp.

The boy was Kyle.

The girl was Tara Monroe, the Monkey Boss. Apparently it was her turn to play senior Undertaker on site at First Stop.

I was almost certain that Tara hadn't been the girl in the hallway just now. So where was *she?*

Neither of the escorts noticed me slip into the shadowy training room. I looked around, searching for some sign of where the unidentified girl had gone—and spotted a quick flicker of light off to my right. It came from the front of the empty shop—there and gone in an instant, but it was enough.

Cautiously I followed that light to the open threshold that connected the training room to the unused storefront. Here the front wall was entirely glass and all boarded up. The door leading to the street, through which customers had once come in with their shirts and trousers, stood firmly padlocked. The floor was layered in dust.

Nobody was supposed to be in here. There were too many gaps in the boards where they might be spotted from the street, even at night.

But someone was here. I could just make out a female voice coming from the opposite side of the long narrow room. I squinted but couldn't see anyone. Whoever she was, she must be crouched behind the dusty old Formica counter that ran along the far wall.

I inched closer, my heart drumming.

Gradually the words became more distinct and their tone more urgent.

"...I can't. They'll hear me. They're playing cards in the next room. No, I asked. They never had a key to the front door—only to the big steel one that leads into the alley. But the front is just wood. Can't you just, you know, kick it in?"

I paused. I didn't know what I was listening to, but it sounded wrong. Worse, I still couldn't tell who was talking. Slowly, not even daring to breathe, I slipped Tom's knife from my pants pocket.

The voice whispered, "Who? Oh, yeah. He's here. But why's he such a big deal? I mean, it's Sharyn and Tom you really want, right? They're the chiefs. They run the whole show. Look, we're all headed to Haven tomorrow. Why don't you just wait one more day?"

I wondered if I should run back and fetch Kyle and Tara. I vaguely remembered Tom telling me to do that very thing if something just like this happened. But maybe this was innocent. I didn't want to get anyone in trouble, didn't want to be a snitch.

The girl whispered, "No, I don't know for sure if Will's going with us. Is he why you won't wait? I still don't see—"

At the sound of my name, my already hammering heart shifted into overdrive. I suddenly leapt around the corner, my thumb pressing the pocketknife's *6* button.

Its flashlight illuminated the face of Amy Filewicz.

She was hunkered down behind the counter, barefoot and dressed in gray sweats—no Barbie pajamas at First Stop. She stared up at the light, wide-eyed with horror, the color draining from her cheeks. With one hand she pressed a tiny cell phone to her ear.

Her other hand gripped a kitchen knife.

A big one.

CHAPTER 24

THE MOLE

What are you doing?" I demanded, although I already knew the answer. Amy was a mole. And surprisingly my first reaction was relief.

I knew it wasn't Dave!

She stared up at me, her face ashen, her lower lip quivering. She was utterly silent.

And then she wasn't.

Jumping to her feet, Amy shrieked into the cell phone, "Will's found me! He's right here!"

Then she dropped the phone and lunged at me with the knife.

The attack was so sudden and savage that the kid I'd been two weeks ago would have been dead before I had time to blink. But this Will Ritter had spent many hours in combat exercises, and my body reacted automatically before my mind could really process what was happening.

Instinctively I sidestepped, grabbed Amy's wrist, and twisted hard.

The girl cried out in pain. The knife fell from her fist, clattering to the dusty floor.

"Tara!" I screamed. "Kyle!"

Cries of alarm rose from the training room, followed by approaching footfalls.

Amy's pain turned to panic, but instead of pulling away, she stepped forward and drove her knee up toward my stomach. I saw it coming and twisted so she caught more rib than belly. It still hurt, but at least I didn't lose my wind.

Wide-eyed and snarling, the girl's head lashed downward, her teeth biting into the back of the hand that clutched her wrist. I yelped, the beam of my flashlight splashing crazy shadows across the wall. Desperately I flipped the knife over, pressed the *2* button, and tapped Amy's shoulder with the Taser.

Big mistake.

Electricity raced down the girl's arm and—since I was still holding her—right up my own.

I was knocked backward—all of my limbs going numb and the pocketknife flew from my hand. I landed hard, raising plumes of dust. Blearily I watched Amy stiffen and then sink to the floor, her fearful eyes turning glassy.

The footsteps reached the threshold.

"Will?" Tara asked urgently. "What's going on?"

Beside her, Kyle held up the battery-powered lamp. He shone it around the room.

"Amy?" he asked, bewildered.

Tara knelt beside me on the floor. I tried to say something, but my lips felt like they'd fallen completely off.

"What happened here?" the Monkey Boss asked me.

"M-m—" I stammered. "Mmmooo."

"What? I don't understand."

Kyle rushed to Amy's side, still holding the lantern. She'd been stunned too and lay twitching against the wall, her hand inches from the fallen knife.

"Nnnnnn," I struggled, trying to warn him.

"Come on," Tara suggested. "Let me get you outta here."

She came around and lifted me by my shoulders. She was surprisingly strong.

I managed to raise one arm and point feebly in Amy's direction. Concentrating, I yelled, "Mmmmoooollllle!"

Tara blinked. Then as I watched helplessly, her confusion became understanding and her understanding became alarm. Suddenly and not very gently, she dropped me back to the floor and started forward.

The boy knelt beside Amy, trying to soothe her. He touched her shoulder.

"Kyle!" Tara exclaimed.

Still twitching but regaining more control with each passing second, Amy managed to reach out and close her small hand around the nearby knife.

What happened next is forever burned in my memory.

The blade came up hard and fast. Kyle gasped, his eyes going horribly wide.

At the same instant, the padlocked front door burst open.

Corpses poured into the room.

There were four of them, all Type Twos or early Type Threes and all dressed in police uniforms. I hadn't seen one since the Laundromat, other than in pictures, and I'd almost forgotten the horror of them. Their bodies reeked of death, the stench flooding my nostrils and bringing tears to my eyes. The uniforms they wore were moist with the fluids expelled from their putrid bodies, and their hair hung in dead strands from atop their slick, grotesquely decayed faces.

"Kyle!" Tara wailed.

But the First Stop Boss didn't reply. He was slumped with his back against the wall, clutching at his stomach. The lamp had fallen from his hand and now lay on the floor at his feet. By its light, I could see Amy's pale face, her own eyes almost as wide as Kyle's. She was trying to stand up. The knife was still in her hand. There was blood on it.

Meanwhile, the Corpses began to spread out, trying to block off both of the room's exits.

Still standing over me, Tara tore her eyes away from Kyle and drew a water pistol, firing a stream into the face of the nearest Corpse. He let out a sound a bit like a whimper. Then he sort of staggered off to one side, crashing blindly into one of his pals and knocking him over. The two of them tumbled to the floor, raising dust.

Apparently unconcerned, the remaining two spread apart, trying to outflank us.

"*We. Want. Boy!*" one of them said in Deadspeak.

Tara's only reply was to level her pistol at them, holding them at bay. Her expression was frightened but determined.

Sensation had returned to my arms and legs. I was still dizzy and a little nauseated, but that might have been as much from the smell of the dead bodies in the room as from the Tasing I'd given myself.

Turning my head, I peered over at the room's far corner where Tom's pocketknife lay.

"Get up, Will!" Tara told me. "Quick!"

But I was suddenly thinking that wasn't such a good idea.

Instead I rolled over, scrambled to my knees, and shot forward.

In the shadowy room, the nearest Corpse didn't spot me immediately. I managed to crawl right between his spread legs, my hand reaching for the pocketknife.

"Will!" Tara cried.

"Look out!" Amy suddenly exclaimed at the same moment.

With an outraged moan, the Corpses both turned.

Tara fired, catching one of them in the back of the knee.

The Corpse stumbled immediately, struggling to keep its balance as its whole leg went numb. For the moment, at least, he was as helpless as his fallen buddies.

That left only one—the one nearest to me.

Throwing myself forward another two feet, I groped for the pocketknife just as a slimy fist clamped around my ankle.

Suddenly I was dangling half a yard above the dusty floor, caught in the iron grip of a lifeless hand.

I struggled, my arms flailing, the blood rushing to my head.

A voice, horribly close, growled, "Looking for something, boy?"

I twisted around and caught sight of the dead man's hideous lipless grin.

Burying my fear, I offered up a smile of my own.

"Found it, thanks," I said, holding up Tom's pocketknife.

Then swinging my leg around with all my strength, I drove the blade of my foot into the Corpse's raised armpit. I could only hope it worked as well on a cadaver as it had on the Burgermeister.

It did.

The Corpse's expression twisted in shock. Its greasy fist opened, dropping me to the floor with a bone-jarring *thud*. Gritting my teeth, I somehow managed to push away the pain, burying it in the same grave as my fear. Then I sat up and shoved the pocketknife's Taser against the Corpse's pants leg.

The sound reminded me of a whip crack.

The Corpse's body shuddered and collapsed beside me.

I climbed unsteadily to my feet.

All four Corpses were now down, although the first two—the one Tara had shot in the face and the one he'd then collided with—looked like they were about to recover. Worse, I could hear footsteps outside the storefront.

More were coming.

I glanced over to where Kyle sat. His back was against the wall, and the front of his shirt had turned red with blood. Amy still stood over him, motionless as though in shock. Then as if sensing my gaze, she turned and looked at me. There was fear in her eyes, but it was mixed with a terrible, burning hatred. She looked like she was about to say something—about to curse me out maybe. Instead she ran for the open door, shouting for help.

Tara and I both went to Kyle. He looked up at us, his face deathly pale, his hands clutching his stomach. When he tried to say something, a trickle of blood rolled out the corner of his mouth.

Each of us took an arm, and working together, we half-walked and half-dragged him back out into the training room.

Behind us, footfalls—a lot of them—were rapidly approaching the storefront.

Tara said, "Listen up, Will. You need to take Kyle out of here. Go into the back and wake the other recruits. Get them all out through the alley door."

"What if they're watching that door?" I asked.

She considered this. "Go out the kitchen window instead. It's got a loose board. Take Kyle's water pistol and wrist radio. Keep him alive, Will. You hear me?"

"I hear you," I said.

She nodded. "Go! I'll hold them off as long as I can."

"But you can't—"

"Go!" she repeated. "Be brave!"

She let go of Kyle then, and suddenly the kid's full weight was pressing down on me, drowning any further protests. With an effort, I started walking him toward the door to the kitchen and the dormitory hallway. He was conscious, but only barely. And although he did his best to help support his weight, it got harder with every step.

Behind me, a fresh wave of Corpses stampeded in through the dry cleaner's shattered front door.

CHAPTER 25

FIGHT AND FLIGHT

Kyle was heavy, and he was badly hurt.

Still, he kept trying to help. Every time I stumbled while the two of us struggled down the short corridor toward the dorm rooms, he would reach out a hand to the wall to steady us. And each time he did so, he left behind a bloody handprint that added to the dark red trail following us all the way from the training room.

If the Corpses got past Tara, I thought, they'd have no trouble tracking us.

There wasn't much time.

The latch on the door to the boys' room was loose. I knew that. So when we neared it, I didn't bother with the knob. I just kicked the door in and shined the flashlight from Tom's pocketknife on the faces of the two sleeping boys.

Dave and Ethan snapped awake, blinking against the glare.

"Hey, dude!" the Burgermeister complained. "Shut that thing off!"

"Get up quick!" I exclaimed. "Corpses are attacking! Right now!"

Five horribly long seconds passed.

Finally Ethan gasped, groping for his glasses with trembling fingers. Dave, on the other hand, grinned and jumped to his feet. "Cool! Point me at them!"

"We're getting out here!" I told him.

"No way! I owe those dead dudes some payback!"

I groaned. "Look, I'm waking the girls! Help me with Kyle. He's hurt!"

"Hurt?" Dave blinked. "How?"

"Come on! We don't have any time!"

Something in my tone got the Burgermeister moving. Nodding grimly, he scooped up Kyle as if the older kid weighed nothing. As soon the weight was off me, I ran to the girls' room.

Maria and Harleen responded faster than the guys had. "Where's Amy?" Maria asked as she pulled on her shoes.

"She was a mole," I replied flatly. "She set us up."

Both girls cried in unison, "What?"

I heard a cry from the training room. It didn't sound like a noise that a Corpse would make. I felt myself go cold.

"Hurry!" I told them. "Don't take anything! Just come on!"

Long seconds later, all the recruits had gathered in the darkened hallway. "We're going out the kitchen window," I said. "Dave, you take care of Kyle."

"He's bleeding," Dave said.

"I know. Amy knifed him."

"I don't *believe* this...!" Harleen whispered.

"Worry about it later," I told them. "For now we need to find a place to hide and then call for help. Stick together, and keep it quiet. Okay?"

Anxious nods all around.

Suppressing my own rising terror, I used the flashlight to lead us hurriedly into the kitchen. "Ethan," I said. "That board's loose. See if you can move it."

"Okay," he said. Crossing the room, he climbed up onto the old countertop and pulled aside the half-inch plywood covering the room's only window. The glass was long gone, and the alley beyond the missing pane was dimly lit.

"Dave, you first," I commanded. "Be careful with Kyle. Then the girls. Ethan and I'll bring up the rear. Hurry!"

Dave obeyed. They all did—to the letter.

And I suddenly wondered: *When did I get elected leader?*

But I buried that thought along with my pain and fear. There wasn't time for it.

A scream—very human—split the air. Everybody froze. I spun around, my breath catching in my throat. My every instinct was to run out there. Tara was in trouble—big trouble.

But I remembered her final words to me.

Sick with guilt, I hissed to the others, "Keep moving!" Then I pulled Kyle's pistol from my waistband.

Out in the hallway, the training room door burst open. Footsteps approached.

"Your turn, Will!" Ethan called urgently. "Come on!"

"You go!" I replied. "I'll watch your back!"

"Don't be stupid! You need me to hold the window open!"

Of course it was true.

The first Corpse appeared at the kitchen threshold. Another cop.

Swallowing back a scream, I gave him a faceful of saltwater. As he recoiled, I crossed the kitchen at a run, launched myself over the counter, and blindly leapt headfirst through the open window.

Remembering my Undertaker training, I tucked myself into a ball at the last second, using my upper back and shoulders to break the fall. It worked—sort of. I stayed conscious and didn't break any bones, but my whole body stung from at least a dozen nasty scrapes. Harleen helped me to my feet.

We were all there, huddled in a filthy alley behind the dry cleaners.

All but one.

"Ethan!" I spun around just in time to see the skinny kid hop through the window after me. Corpses closed in behind him, moving horribly fast.

"Hurry!" I screamed.

A second after Ethan jumped clear, the window board swung shut. It would slow them down but not for long.

"Get to the street," I told them all.

Once again they obeyed without question. And once again I didn't permit myself time to wonder why.

Though it was past midnight, this *was* Philadelphia, and traffic sounds were everywhere. However, this particular nameless street looked pretty deserted.

"Now what?" Dave asked, finally struggling a little with Kyle's weight. The injured kid looked like he might have passed out in the big recruit's arms.

Good question.

No sign of Corpses in the alley—yet. But it wouldn't take them long to figure out where we'd gone.

I had Kyle's wrist radio but couldn't risk the time to use it. Better to find a hiding place and then call for backup.

Struggling to keep myself calm, I scanned the street. Just storefronts, all dark, although there were lights on in some of the upper floors. Apartments maybe? Could we knock on a random door and ask for sanctuary? Sure. Six grubby kids begging some old lady to hide them from the cops. Oh, and let's not forget that one of them is bleeding all over the place. Fat chance.

Then I spotted a Dumpster across the street, shoved against the front of a building that looked like it was being demolished. It was one of those large industrial waste containers, seven feet tall and maybe twice that long, with the top of it open all along its length—a big steel box.

Not a great hiding place but large enough for all of us and better than nothing.

"There!" I said.

As we started over, a figure suddenly emerged from a shadowed doorway on our left. "Hey, kids—wanna go to a party?"

Gasping, I turned my flashlight into the stubbly face of a man—a living man—filthy and dressed in little more than rags. He was smiling, but there was this look in his eyes that I didn't like at all.

Maria asked fearfully, "Can you help us, mister?"

"Why sure, darlin'," the man cooed. "Why don't you just come with me?"

He reached for her. His fingernails were long and grimy with dirt.

Without even realizing I was going to do it, I reached over and tapped the guy with the Taser.

He went down like a sack of wet sand.

"What'd you do that for?" Maria demanded, tears shining on her face. "He might've helped us!"

"Don't think so," Dave muttered. "Good move, Will."

"Yeah," Harleen added. "Good move."

Nearby a police siren blared.

"Keep going!" I said. "We'll hide in that Dumpster."

We crossed the street at a run.

Gathering alongside the waste container, I told Dave to lay Kyle down gently atop a pile of cardboard that had been lashed together at the curb—probably for the recycling trucks. He did so, and while Harleen stayed with Kyle, the Burgermeister positioned himself beside the Dumpster and laced his fingers.

Ethan took the first boost, scaling the seven-foot steel wall and tumbling clumsily inside. He was followed by Maria and then Harleen. After that Dave hoisted me up to the lip of the box, and between the two of us, we managed to get Kyle inside. It wasn't easy, and it didn't do the injured kid much good, but we managed it. Finally, with as much grace and silence as a drunken gorilla, the Burgermeister pulled himself up and into the huge Dumpster after us.

The container was almost completely empty, with only a few broken two-by-fours lying around. It was a lucky break—the first we'd had all night.

"What did you do to that man back there?" Maria demanded crossly.

"Hush!" Harleen hissed, although I could tell that she was curious. Ethan and Dave were too, for that matter.

I held up Tom's pocketknife, pressing the *2* button. "It's a Taser. I zapped him."

"But what for?" Maria complained.

"Keep it down!" Dave hissed.

I didn't have time for this. Turning away from them, I checked on Kyle. He was unconscious, his face pale in the flashlight beam, and he'd lost a lot of blood.

Swallowing, I strapped on Kyle's wrist radio.

Someone caught my arm. It was Maria. "I want to know why you did that!" she said, accusation in her eyes.

Before I could answer, Ethan did it for me. He sounded frightened and utterly spent. "He did it because that guy wasn't gonna help us, all right? Couldn't you see that? My dad always says there are monsters in the city—all kinds of monsters. I guess he's right."

Maria glared at us both, but she said nothing more.

CHAPTER 26

TRAPPED

The radio didn't work.

"It's basically just a cheap Walmart watch with some generic cell phone parts built into it," Steve had cheerfully explained during one of tech lectures. "But don't get your hopes up. This phone dials only one person: our on-duty Chatter. All you have to do is press this little silver button on the side."

Well, I'd pressed it like crazy and—nothing. Not even static. Had it broken sometime during the fight in First Stop or maybe when I climbed into the Dumpster?

Either way it was bad news.

I struggled to stay calm. By now there could be twenty Corpses out there looking for us, and we had no way to call for help!

The others were all watching me. Maria was quietly

crying. Harleen had an arm around her. Ethan's mouth moved wordlessly, as though in prayer. Beside me, the Burgermeister stood almost at attention, regarding me as if I was his undisputed commander.

I'm no leader! I don't want this!

"Busted?" Dave whispered, pointing to the watch.

I nodded glumly.

"It's broke?" Maria exclaimed too loudly. Beyond the Dumpster's high gray walls, the police sirens had gone silent. I wasn't sure if that was a good sign or not.

"Nobody panic," I said softly, holding up the watch. "These things have trackers in them, remember?"

"GPS locators," Ethan corrected absently.

"Whatever. It means that they can find us. There'll be a squad of Angels here before you know it. We just got to stay put and keep quiet."

"Yeah," Dave immediately agreed.

Maria started trembling. "I can't stay here!" she suddenly wailed. "They'll find me again! I can't! I can't!"

"Hush, Maria," Harleen cooed, doing her best not to sound scared. "Nobody's gonna find us."

"Shut her up!" Dave hissed.

I raised my hand, demanding silence. Amazingly I got it.

There were footsteps out on the street, neither loud nor hurried. Methodical—like maybe someone was searching.

I met and held everyone's eyes, putting all my newly discovered and totally unwanted authority into that look.

"Be quiet!"

It worked.

The footsteps drew closer.

It was funny how I could tell the difference between dead and living footfalls. It was a subtle thing. When they weren't running like crazed gazelles, Corpses tended to shuffle—not quite like zombies in the movies, but close enough that I could catch it.

And *this* shuffling was very close. Maybe just a few yards away from the Dumpster.

I glanced at Maria. Harleen was gripping the girl now, holding a hand tightly over her mouth.

If she screams, we're dead.

The footsteps stopped. A voice spoke. "*No. Find. You. Still. Smell. Blood?*"

Another voice replied, this time in English. "You know the rule. Speak English."

"*Why. Speak. English? Nobody. Hear. Us.*"

"It's the rule." Then, after a groan: "So?"

"*What. So?*"

"I don't smell them. Do you?"

"*No. Smell. Them. Sweet. Blood. Buried. Under. Odor. Garbage. Vermin.*"

"They're not here. Let's go back."

A long silence followed. I closed my eyes, gripping

the half-empty water pistol so hard that my knuckles went white.

"*Agreed. First. Check. Dumpster.*"

Maria jumped a little. Harleen clutched her even tighter, almost pinning the smaller girl against the Dumpster wall. Nearby, Ethan clamped both his hands over his mouth to stifle a scream.

The first Corpse complained, "*No. Want. Smell. Bad.*"

Dave picked up a broken two-by-four, hefting it like a club. He looked pointedly at me. I shook my head, pressing a finger to my lips. Even if we could somehow take out these two Corpses, more would certainly come—possibly a lot more.

Disappointed, the Burgermeister nodded.

The second Corpse snapped impatiently, "*Obey! Check. Dumpster. Master. Blame. Us. If. Boy. Escape.*"

His companion groaned, "*Agreed! Agreed!*"

The footsteps approached.

A new voice called in English, "You two! Anything?"

The first Corpse replied crisply, also in English. "Nothing!"

The new voice came closer. "Nothing what?"

"Master!" the first Corpse barked. "I mean, nothing, Mr. Booth!"

"Nothing, is it?" This voice sounded different than the others—more authoritative and smarter. "When did you two come through?"

"A week ago, Mast—I mean, Mr. Booth!"

"A week! And you were assigned to *this* task?"

The second Corpse replied nervously, "The others were sent out along the prey's known travel routes. We were left here to check this short stretch of street."

"So Captain DeAngelo assumes the brats are making their way to their mysterious HQ, does he?"

"Yes, Mr. Booth!"

A groan. "DeAngelo's a fool! These are recruits! They don't even know where to go! More likely they've found some awful hiding place to await rescue. Did either of you consider this?"

"Of course, Mr. Booth!" both Corpses barked.

"And yet you've found nothing?"

"N-no, Mr. Booth!" they stammered together.

"Idiots!" the master spat. Then before I even knew what was happening, something—probably a dead fist—slammed into the Dumpster's steel side.

Maria pulled free from Harleen and shrieked in terror. Harleen gasped and clamped her hand back down over the girl's mouth.

Too late.

The silence that followed seemed as deep as the grave.

Ethan began to quietly sob.

"Well—what have we here?" the master hissed. Then mockingly, "Did I get to the truth?"

All of a sudden, I knew who was out there.

Get to the truth with Kenny Booth.

Apparently the news guy wielded some level of authority among his Corpse buddies.

Booth said pleasantly, "Mr. Ritter?"

My head nearly spun with terror. I fought it with everything I had.

We're dead!

No! The Undertakers are coming! They have to be!

"Mr. Ritter," Booth said again. "I know you're in there."

I figured I had two choices: talk or keep quiet. If I kept quiet, Booth would just send his rotting cronies into the Dumpster to find us. If I talked, however, I might be able to buy us a little time.

"I'm here!" I called.

"Ah!" Booth replied. I could almost hear the smirk. "And I'm guessing you're not alone in there, are you?"

"Keep guessing," I replied.

"Well, as it happens, Mr. Ritter," Booth said calmly. "I don't want them. All I wanted out of this little raid was *you*."

I felt my stomach roll over.

"What for?" I asked, my voice cracking.

"Plenty of time for all that later. Come out now—unarmed—and maybe I'll leave your little friends right there, safe in the trash. Now doesn't that sound fair?"

I looked around, my mind reeling. Dave was shaking his head. The rest were looking at me with a kind of hopeful horror. Suddenly they saw a possible way out.

All they had to do was give *me* up.

"I...don't think he wants to hurt you," Ethan said quietly. "Maybe—"

"No way!" Dave exclaimed, leaving me almost weak-kneed with gratitude. The Burgermeister might not have been the sharpest knife in the drawer, but he had courage—and loyalty. Right then I needed plenty of both. "Say that again, and I'll pound you!"

The smaller boy trembled but shut up.

"Are you listening, Mr. Ritter?" Booth asked.

"I'm listening," I replied, steadying myself. There had to be a way out! Frantically I scanned the Dumpster. Nothing but smooth steel. Except—wait a minute. What was that *thing* jutting out from the far wall, right next to where Harleen was still cradling Maria?

Frowning, I stumbled past Ethan and Dave, carefully stepping over Kyle's limp form. As they all watched, I knelt beside Harleen and examined the thing I'd spotted.

It was a lever.

And it opened a small hatch at the base of the Dumpster.

I waved Dave and Ethan over. The bigger kid glowered at the smaller one, but they both obeyed. Within seconds we were all huddled together at the rear of our steel cage—all except Kyle, of course.

I wonder if he's dead...

No time for such thoughts!

Booth suddenly called, "I need a decision, Mr. Ritter! Shall we make a deal?"

I ignored him. Speaking in fast whispers, I explained to the other kids what I hoped was a halfway workable plan. I was still counting on the Undertakers riding to the rescue like Han Solo at the end of *Star Wars Episode IV*. The problem, of course, was that I couldn't be sure that Haven even knew we were in trouble. True, they could use the GPS to track us here, but that required someone actually knowing that they needed to be looking!

So for now at least, we had to fend for ourselves.

Or die trying.

CHAPTER 27

GAMBIT

Okay…here's…the…deal," I said through the Dumpster's wall. I was doing my best to sound terrified. It wasn't hard. "I'll come out. But you have to let my friends go!"

Booth replied, his tone utterly sincere, "Well, that just sounds right as rain to me, Mr. Ritter."

"You promise you won't hurt them—or even chase them?"

"If I have your promise that you'll come out unarmed. None of those clever little water pistols."

"Deal," I said.

"Deal," Booth echoed.

I glanced down at Kyle. The boy had stopped moving.

"Don't forget him," I whispered to Dave. He nodded.

I didn't dare look at the other kids. If I did, I might lose my nerve.

"Be careful," I heard Harleen say.

Nodding and trying to keep my stomach down, I began to scale the Dumpster's inside wall. My sneakers caught and slipped more than once, but I finally managed to swing one foot over the top edge.

If Dave could have helped, it would have been easier.

But that wasn't part of the plan.

"The water pistol, Mr. Ritter?" Booth said.

I wasn't ready to look at him—not just yet. So, keeping my eyes averted, I pulled the gun from my waistband and let it fall to the street as gently as I could, hoping—praying—it wouldn't break.

"Very good," the Corpse purred. "Now watch yourself coming down. I don't want you injured."

I'm gonna die.

I tried to push the thought away like I'd been pushing away my fear and self-doubt all night. This time, however, the idea refused to be pushed. It kept coming back. I felt like crying.

Mom... I'm scared.

Closing my eyes, I eased myself down the far side of the Dumpster and dropped clumsily to the sidewalk.

The Corpses closed immediately around me. I found the strength to face them.

Dead Man Kenny Booth was by far the best dressed. He was also the freshest of the bunch. The other two wore police uniforms and were clearly Type Two. I could smell the decay rising off them, and the flies—a lot of flies—wouldn't leave them alone. However, Booth was a Type One, wrapped in a cadaver so fresh that its original owner had probably died that morning. That and the way the other two had referred to him as *Master* made me think for the first time that maybe all Corpses weren't created equal.

Almost without thinking, I crossed my eyes.

And Booth's Mask was there—the familiar handsome face, perfectly groomed blond hair, and broad white-toothed smile that had made him the most popular TV news anchorman in town. This face—his illusionary self—seemed better suited to his tailored duds than the slimy, lifeless, milky-eyed reality.

I wonder what he *sees. When Kenny Booth gazes into a mirror, which face looks back?*

"Nice suit," I muttered.

"Why, thank you, Mr. Ritter," Booth said. "Clothes are rare where we are from. Most of my people find them a nuisance, but I've come to recognize their value. It's not what we do that brings us power but rather how we are perceived by others. And good clothes are all about perception, wouldn't you say?"

"I guess so."

The dead man raised one fist, in which he clutched a box of candy—Sweet-Rox, to be precise, made right here in Philadelphia. Absently he fished out a handful of the hard, colorful, fruit-flavored morsels, opened his mouth absurdly wide, and tossed them inside, where his swollen tongue wrapped greedily around them.

He sighed.

I felt my stomach flip-flop.

The crazy thing was that I'd had seen Kenny Booth do this a thousand times. The whole city had. Booth gulped down Sweet-Rox by the fistful, even when he was on TV. It had kind of become his trademark—so much so that the candy company had hired him as their spokesman. This had caused a bit of a stink a while back, as I recalled—a television journalist pitching a commercial product. But I'd never been much for watching the news, so I didn't remember how it all had ended.

Except that Kenny Booth was still on TV every night and still gulping his Sweet-Rox.

How dizzyingly weird it was to see the *real* Kenny Booth doing it—this animated carcass. It was like something out of a screwball nightmare.

"It's the sugar," Dead Man Booth admitted, as if reading my expression. "I crave it! It gives me energy and keeps me sharp. Do you know what I mean, Mr. Ritter?"

Of course that didn't make a bit of sense. He was walking around in a dead body that was no longer capable of digesting any sort of food. So there was really no way for Booth to get a sugar rush.

Nevertheless I replied, "Sure."

"I'll bet you're a sugar man yourself, aren't you?"

I shrugged but didn't answer.

Still smiling, Booth faced his two cronies. "Climb up into that Dumpster," he commanded pleasantly, "and kill the rest."

"What?" I screamed.

"It stinks in there," one of the Corpses complained.

Booth glowered.

"Then can we at least, you know—have some fun while we're at it?" the other one asked.

"Indulge yourselves," Booth replied dismissively. "Just make sure you get rid of the leftovers. I don't want them found—ever."

Cursing, I demanded, "Why didn't you just do that right away?"

He grinned at me. His teeth were yellow. "And risk injuring *you?* My prize? Certainly not! Mr. Ritter, you don't recognize your importance!" Then to his cronies, "What are you waiting for? Get in there and take care of those brats!"

"Yes, Mr. Booth!" they replied in unison.

I watched as the two dead cops flanked the Dumpster and scrambled up its sides. They moved fast—far faster than I had—clearing the top in seconds. They landed inside with dull *thumps* like hammer blows.

Booth's smile turned cruel, expectant.

He's waiting for the screams to start.

"You promised you wouldn't hurt them!" I snapped.

The Corpse thoughtfully tapped his chin with one finger. Then his grin was back, wider than ever. "I lied."

I pulled Tom's knife from my pocket.

"So did I," I told him.

Then I shoved the Taser's twin prongs into Kenny Booth's tailored midsection and pressed the *2* button home.

The stolen body stiffened. To my horror, partially congealed blood spilled from his mouth and nose. He toppled over. I knelt beside him, still pressing the Taser prongs tight against his stomach, careful to avoid direct contact. Tom had told me that enough Tasing could force a Corpse to Transfer. Well, that was what I was going for. Maybe I couldn't kill this *thing*. But I could do what I could do.

From inside the Dumpster, I heard one of the Corpses yell, "They're gone! There's nobody in here!"

Booth's body jumped like a landed fish, his eyes wide and sightless and his tongue protruding from between his teeth. The bag of Sweet-Rox flew from his grasp, scattering its colored contents along the street just as two rotting heads popped up over the rim of the Dumpster, confusion playing over their slimy features.

"Now!" I cried.

The kids ran from behind the far side of the Dumpster, having gotten out through the hatch while I'd been making my noisy climb out of the steel box.

"Run!" I shouted.

"What about you?" Dave called back. Kyle hung limply in his arms.

"I'm right behind you!"

Booth's cronies spotted the running recruits and uttered matching cries of outrage.

Finally, reluctantly, I pulled the pocketknife away from Booth's now-motionless form. Running back to the Dumpster, I snatched up my dropped water pistol. Then I fired a shot up at the first Corpse, who was trying to clear the rim. The saltwater nailed him squarely in face. He flailed and toppled forward, landing badly on the concrete right beside me.

I ran after the others.

After a dozen yards, I risked a hasty glance back. So far the Corpses weren't following us. Booth lay exactly where I'd left him. Maybe he was trapped, with the body he'd stolen rendered useless by the Tasing. Maybe he'd stay there until another cadaver became available. Steve had told us that the Transfer range was short—possibly even line of sight.

All of a sudden, a chill danced down my back.

I looked for Dave and spotted him ahead of me. Kyle's motionless form still hung in his arms.

"Burgermeister!" I called. "Watch it! I think he's—"

That was as far as I got.

Kyle's dead hands flew up and locked around my friend's throat. Except it wasn't Kyle anymore.

The First Stop Boss was gone forever.

This was Booth.

Dave gasped and dropped the boy, but the Corpse inside stayed with him, shoving the bigger kid back with astonishing strength. The Burgermeister fought furiously, but nothing he did seemed able to pry the hands off his neck. I ran toward them, screaming at the others to do something, but none of them moved. They simply stared, frozen with either shock or horror, watching the two boys crash to the street and start rolling in a frenzy of combat.

I reached them seconds later, with the pocketknife in one hand and the water pistol in the other. The pistol was close to empty, and I wanted to conserve it. On the other hand, if I Tasered Booth, I'd get Dave too—and that wouldn't help our chances of escape.

So I chose the pistol, firing it right into what had been Kyle's ear.

Booth let out a funny moan. His hands slipped from Dave's throat. With a roar, the Burgermeister hurled the Corpse off him, sending the body flying through the air before it crashed to the asphalt.

"Thanks," he gasped as he struggled to his feet, coughing. "I owe you one."

"Forget it," I said. "Let's go!"

He turned to do just that—and stopped.

Two police cars, their lights flashing, cut across the intersection, blocking our way.

Maria started to scream.

Four Corpses emerged from the cars, all dressed in police uniforms. There were two Type Twos and two Type Threes—a messy bunch, all drippy and moist.

"Come on!" I called to the rest. "The other way!"

We all turned.

The second of Booth's rotting thugs had escaped the Dumpster and was now standing fifty feet away, watching us. A couple of moments later, Booth, still wearing poor Kyle's body, joined him. Both their faces split into identical toothy grins.

They had us, and they knew it.

"Everybody stay together!" I cried. I shouldn't have bothered. The other recruits were already gathered close around me, all of them shaking with terror.

I still had the water pistol, although I didn't think there was more than a single squirt left in it.

Booth and the Dumpster Corpse took a few wary steps toward us. I raised my gun and they stopped, although they kept smiling. Seeing Booth in Kyle's body was creepy in the extreme. It was all I could do to remember that what I was looking at was a monster, not an Undertaker. Just to drive home the point, I briefly crossed my eyes. The look on the TV guy's Mask did nothing to calm my fear.

Desperately I looked around. The surrounding buildings were all dark, with their doors undoubtedly locked.

We were trapped.

I swallowed down a rising panic.

"Nowhere to run, Mr. Ritter," Booth declared.

The Corpses began to close around us, boxing us in.

"What do we do?" Dave whispered.

I don't know! Who died and made me *boss?*

Kyle, that's who.

"When I give the signal," I said, willing my voice to remain steady, "we're gonna run for that window right there." I nodded toward a nearby storefront that—unlike its neighbors—had no bars on it. "When we get there, grab a rock or something and break the glass. Okay?"

Dave nodded. "No problem."

Except it *was* a problem. The Corpses were fast, and I wasn't even sure there'd be a handy rock for the Burgermeister to grab. Besides, I honestly didn't think we'd get halfway to the curb before they jumped us. But maybe with luck, one of us would make it and be left with the barest chance for survival.

One out of six. Some leader I turned out to be.

My heart was pounding so loud!

"On three," I said. "One."

I felt the others tense up, ready to run. Apparently even Ethan and Maria trusted me.

"Two."

I've gotten them all killed.

A voice announced, "What this? Y'all having a party?"

We spun around. So did the Corpses.

A half-dozen kids stood atop the police cars, Sharyn among them. She was clutching Vader in both hands. The rest of them all had Super Soakers—big ones.

The nearest of the Corpses pounced at her, moving with horrific speed. He leapt up onto the hood of the cop car, his teeth bared and his hands outstretched. I opened my mouth to shout a warning, but Sharyn only smiled.

"Let's dance," I heard her say.

Then in one fluid motion, she swung her sword and cleaved the cadaver's head from its shoulders.

After that things happened very fast.

The remaining Corpses—all but Booth—launched themselves at the kids on the cars. Although their lips never moved, the air was suddenly awash with Deadspeak. No words this time—just roars of terrible, inhuman fury that almost sent me screaming.

But the Angels *didn't* scream. Instead they raised their Soakers and fired.

These were no water pistols.

The streams of water that struck the Corpses were as hard and straight as laser beams. Each dead cop's forward momentum suddenly stopped as if he'd hit an invisible wall. Almost simultaneously they crashed to the street, twitching helplessly.

The Angels kept on firing.

The Burgermeister literally shrieked with delight,

clapping his hands together. The others only watched in mute amazement.

Moments later a half-dozen more Angels—these riding Stingrays—poured through the narrow gap between the police cars. They skidded to a halt in front of us.

"Need another ride, dude?" Chuck Binelli asked me with a grin.

I felt like sobbing with relief. I tried to say something clever, but it all came out as, "Ack!"

"Well said! Hop on!"

I wasn't sure why I waited until the other recruits had all mounted their own rides. It just seemed like the right thing to do. Then finally I threw my leg over the back of Chuck's banana seat.

"Thanks," I told him.

"It's what I live for," he replied cheerfully.

"Mr. Ritter!"

The voice was laced with such rage that I felt a fresh chill dance down my spine. Despite my every instinct, I turned and looked.

Kenny Booth stood beside the Dumpster, out of range of the Soakers. He was still wearing Kyle's body and was pointing one of Kyle's index fingers directly at me.

"This isn't over, boy! Do you hear me? This isn't over!"

"I know," I whispered.

Then the Undertakers fled the scene, leaving its terror and chaos behind us.

CHAPTER 28

CASUALTIES OF WAR

No one spoke during the long ride to Haven—except when Sharyn ordered us all to stop so she could check that we weren't being followed. When the Stingrays slipped down the spiraling tunnel and made the jump through the brick wall, no one uttered so much as a *yahoo*.

I was off the back of Chuck's ride the moment we stopped. Ignoring the stares and questions everyone was throwing at me, I went looking for Tom.

I found him at the Chatters station, hastily debriefing Sharyn.

Sharyn was saying, "...straight up. It's a miracle any of them are alive! Hot Dog rode with me and wouldn't stop talking about how Will kept them together and risked his own butt to save them."

Tom considered this. "Any sign of Amy?"

"Nothing. Deaders probably snatched her." She sighed wearily. "We've got to get these kids some grub and then beds for the night."

"Nick'll handle that," Tom told her. "You promised to let *her* know how it went."

Sharyn nodded. "I know." Then she walked off, her dreadlocked head lowered.

"What happened to Tara?" I demanded.

Tom actually gasped in surprise. "Didn't know you were there!" He laughed nervously.

"The Corpses," I pressed. I could feel bile rising in my throat. "Did they kill her?"

He gave me a long look. "No..." he replied hesitantly. "She's the one who called us and told us what went down."

"And then the Angels tracked us with the GPS in the wrist radio."

"Yeah," Tom said.

"Where is she?"

"The Infirmary."

I hadn't known there was such a place, although I guess it didn't really surprise me. The Will Ritter from a week ago might've said something stupid, like: "Is she hurt?" Instead I asked quietly, "How bad?"

Tom grimaced. "Bad."

"I want to see her."

"Will—that probably ain't such a good idea."

"I want to see her," I repeated.

Tom studied me. "Come on."

He led me across the Big Room toward a large sectioned-off area with a heavy curtain stretched across its only entrance.

"What do you think happened to Amy?" I asked.

Tom shrugged. "She's probably dead by now."

I frowned, confused. "Why would the Corpses kill her? She was working for them!"

"We've run into this before," he explained, sounding miserable. "Once a mole fails, the Corpses take them out. Amy's job was to find Haven, and she blew it."

I shook my head. "Maybe that was her original mission, but I overheard some of what she was saying to them right before the attack. Booth didn't want Haven anymore. He wanted—me."

I glanced at Tom, who replied, "Yeah, I figured that."

"You did?"

He nodded. We'd reached the curtain.

"What's so special about me?" I asked.

Before Tom could answer, Sharyn appeared. She looked from one to the other of us, tears in her eyes. Slowly, meaningfully, she shook her head.

"Will wants to see her," Tom said.

"She…uh—ain't in good shape, Red. The Deaders, they…well, she's messed up pretty bad."

I recalled Steve's lectures.

Suddenly I *didn't* want to go in there.

But then I remembered the girl's sacrifice. Had that really been less than an hour ago?

"I kind of have to do this," I said quietly.

Sharyn regarded me. Then she stood aside and drew back the curtain. Swallowing, I stepped through it.

When I was eight, I fell off my bike and broke my arm. My parents rushed me to the local emergency room—the only time I'd ever set foot in a hospital. I remembered the place as being bright and noisy and incredibly clean.

Haven's Infirmary was nothing like that.

There were a dozen cots, a table, a sink, and a bunch of medical books. A short thin boy moved about with an almost desperate urgency. He wore surgical garb: green linen pants and a matching short-sleeve shirt. The front of the shirt was bloodied. So were his latex gloves.

Then I saw why.

Tara lay on the farthest cot, looking pale and terribly small. She'd been horribly beaten, and it was all I could do not to retch at the sight of her. Instead, mustering every ounce of my nerve, I approached the bed and looked down at this girl who had risked everything to give First Stop's recruits a fighting chance.

The Corpses had done their work savagely well.

"Who are you?" the short boy snapped.

"He's Will Ritter," Tom replied from the doorway.

The stranger blinked. "Oh," he said, his anger vanishing. "Hi. I'm Ian McDonald."

Tom explained, "Ian's our medic. His old man's a doctor."

"A surgeon," Ian added. "A great one. He works at the University of Pennsylvania."

So why isn't your dad here?

I just kept looking at Tara. "We have to get her to a hospital."

Ian looked helplessly over at Tom, who approached me and said, "Will—if we drop her at an ER, the Corpses'll find her inside of an hour. Then they'll either quietly ice her or..."

"Or what?" I demanded.

A small voice whispered hoarsely, "Or make...me talk."

I gaped down at the cot. It hadn't occurred to me that she might be conscious!

Tara met my gaze with her one remaining eye. When she spoke she winced in obvious pain. "I...hear you got... everyone out. I knew...you could."

"Don't talk," Ian scolded gently—like a doctor.

I had no idea what to say. My mind locked on a dreadful fact that no one seemed willing to openly admit. Tara was dying, and there wasn't anything that anyone could do about it.

Perhaps for the first time, I think I truly understood the evil that had come into my life. Until then the Corpses—while terrifying—had been almost like childhood monsters, like the imagined "things" that once lived under my bed. Only children could see them. Run or they might grab you!

Well, Tara had been grabbed.

And my childhood was over.

Trembling, I knelt beside the cot. It was all I could do to look her in the eye.

"Thank you," I said. It sounded completely lame.

"No problem," she replied, actually managing to smile. The Burgermeister had said the same thing back on the street, when things had been their most desperate. It had been a lie then, and it was a lie now—courage in the face of tragic certainty.

Valor.

Before now that word had meant almost nothing to me. Suddenly I understood it with awful clarity.

"Do me...a favor...." Tara whispered.

"Anything," I replied. Tears poured down my face. The familiar knot in my belly now felt as cold as the moon.

"When all this is over...tell my pop...I was brave."

Sobs exploded from my throat. Burying my face in my hands, I cried for most of a minute. Around me, no one spoke.

Some of my tears were for Tara and her awful sacrifice. But the rest of them—I'm ashamed to say, maybe most of them—were for myself, for everything I'd lost, for everything that had been *taken* away from me. I cried because I couldn't keep it inside any longer, and I went on crying until I felt empty—wrung dry like an old sponge.

Finally I looked back at the girl on the cot and whispered, “I will.”

But Tara’s eyes were closed, and she’d gone very quiet.

And that gentle, valorous smile was still on her lips.

CHAPTER 29

AFTERMATH

Kenny Booth's an even bigger deal in the Corpse world than in ours," Tom explained. "Seems the others call him *Master*. He's got a hold of Kyle's body. And worse—it looks like he's hunting Will."

Held in a secluded corner of the Big Room, the meeting consisted of nothing more than a loose circle of folding chairs occupied by the crew bosses—plus me. I was easily the youngest one there, and I could feel the weight of all their eyes on me.

"Now, we ain't sure why they're so interested in him," Tom continued. "But a good guess'd be that they're trying to figure out why his dad was the only adult who ever got the Sight."

"That makes sense," Steve remarked. "The Corpses' biggest weakness is our ability to See them. If that ability spread to everyone—well, they'd be exposed."

"They'd be history!" Sharyn amended.

Her brother nodded. "So they might be looking to snatch Will alive—for study."

I supposed that the idea of becoming a lab rat for some Corpse mad scientist ought to frighten me. Oddly, it didn't.

I felt too numb.

Last night's events had pretty much trashed Haven's morale. There was less enthusiasm, and absolutely nobody smiled. I felt it too. In fact, sadness seemed to have moved into my heart to stay.

After catching a few hours of sleep in the boys' dorm, I'd been awakened around midmorning by an uncharacteristically subdued Sharyn. Following a hasty breakfast, she'd escorted me directly to this meeting.

Dragged along by events as always.

"So how'd they even get in to First Stop?" demanded Alex Bobson, the irritating kid I'd met back on my first day. He'd been named the new Monkey Boss, replacing Tara. "I mean, they tried twice before, and both times we saw them coming a mile away." He glared at Steve. "What happened to all those cameras of yours? The motion sensors?"

Steve blanched. "The cameras were all working fine. But the motion sensors had been disabled. I'm not sure how."

"Rats," said Elisha Beardsley, the Hacker Boss. She was a pretty, slightly overweight girl who now reminded me painfully of Tara. "Rats kept setting the alarm off, especially at night." She swallowed. "So Kyle started turning the sensors off. Tara told me. It's been more than a year since the hit on our last First Stop. I guess he figured by now it was safe."

Steve groaned.

Alex glowered. "Jeez, Elisha! Why didn't you tell somebody Kyle was doing this?"

The girl looked nervously around. "Tara asked me not to. They—liked each other. She was my friend."

"Your friend!" Alex exclaimed. "Some friend! You should've—"

"Enough," Tom said. To my surprise, Alex obeyed immediately, looking like a mean dog suddenly put on a short leash. "Throwing blame around gets us nowhere," the Chief continued. "If nothing else, this tragedy should teach us about following the rules and regs. Elisha, you should've reported what Tara and Kyle were doing. Alex, it ain't your place to kick her butt over this. It's mine."

"Sorry," muttered the new Monkey Boss.

"Look," Tom said, "yesterday we got hit harder than we've ever been. It's one thing to know that war's dangerous but another when two of our own get killed on the same night. Losing Tara and Kyle makes me sick. But they were both Undertakers, and they wouldn't want grief blinding us to what's important."

"He's right," said Sammy Li, the Chatter Boss.

Sharyn managed a smile. "Of course he is. He's my brother, ain't he?" Everyone laughed halfheartedly.

Then I said, "It was my fault."

"What?" Tom looked over at me, surprised.

"I should've signaled Kyle or Tara when I first followed Amy out into the training room."

"Why *didn't* you?" Alex demanded.

I shrugged. "I didn't want to snitch on her—not until I knew what she was up to. It never occurred to me that she might be…"

"Yeah," Tom replied gently.

"You should've made some noise!" Alex insisted, his eyes blazing. "You're right! It *is* your fault! They're dead because you were too stupid to—"

"Alex!" Tom snapped so sharply that the other boy actually flinched.

The Chief spoke calmly, addressing everyone. "Despite being only twelve years old and despite having been an Undertaker for less than two weeks, Will got himself and four recruits out of an active combat zone. He also managed to bring a wounded Undertaker along with him. It ain't his fault that Kyle died. Fact is, he kept his cool under pressure—even after almost sacrificing himself for his crew."

I made bad calls that nearly got them all killed.

Tom continued, "I won't have nobody in Haven saying a single thing against him. Think back on your own first weeks. Could any of you have done what he did?"

"Not a chance," Steve admitted.

"No way," said Sammy Li.

"Pretty cool," remarked Nick Rooney, the Mom Boss.

"You hear me, Alex?" Tom asked.

Alex Bobson's face reddened. "I hear you."

"Good," the Chief said. "Now that we got that settled, looks like we need us a new First Stop. Elisha, get your crew to work hunting down foreclosures. You know the drill. Find me a condemned building with some space, running water, and a nearby fuse box that we can tap into."

"No sweat," the girl replied.

"Sammy," Tom said, "keep covering the police bands. See if anything's getting said about what all went down last night."

"Sure, Chief."

"And Nick, get the new recruits hooked up. Give them spots with the Moms."

Nick Rooney nodded. Then he winked playfully at me. "Hope you can handle a mop, kid!"

But Tom shook his head. "Uh-uh. Not Will. The others."

"Will's not going into the Moms?" Alex asked, frowning.

"I want to start him on Angels training."

A shocked murmur rumbled around the meeting. Only Sharyn looked unsurprised. I gaped at Tom, my grief, guilt, and general misery momentarily forgotten. The Chief met my eyes and smiled.

"Um—no offense and all," Steve said carefully, "but isn't he a little young?"

"A *little* young? He's twelve!" Alex exclaimed. "There's never been an Angel younger than fourteen!"

"That's true, Tom," Sammy added.

"It ain't really about age," Tom explained patiently. "It's about—and I know how this sounds—the warrior instinct. Will's got more natural talent than anyone I've ever met. Look at what he did last night!"

"He still had to be rescued, didn't he?" Alex pointed out.

"That was from a lack of training and weapons—not a lack of talent," Tom replied.

An unhappy silence followed. A few people glanced my way—some supportively; others resentfully.

Finally Sharyn suggested, "Why don't we ask him?"

"What?" Alex demanded crossly.

"Well, it's real easy to just dump him onto my crew. Me? I'd love to have him. But this is risky duty. Maybe we ought to see how Will feels about it."

Tom nodded. "Girl's got a point. So, Will, what do you think? Does going Angel do it for you?"

For half a minute, I didn't reply. Then, looking up, I said flatly, "I want to fight the Corpses."

Alex snorted. "Jeez! Who doesn't? That's no answer!"

I turned to him. Although not particularly big, Alex had the kind of tough, arrogant demeanor that, once upon a time, I might have found intimidating.

Those days, however, were gone.

"You don't get it," I told him. "I don't want to make little raids, the way the Angels do now—showing up in the nick of time and rescuing kids from the Corpses. I want to *fight* them. I want to make them pay for what they did to Kyle and Tara, what they did to Amy—what they did to *all* of us." After a pause I added, "I want to *kill* them—every last one of them."

Another heavy silence fell over the circle.

"We all want that," Sharyn replied quietly.

"Yeah? So far I'm not seeing too much proof of it."

"Will—" Tom began.

"No!" I snapped. "I know what you're going to say. We're Harriet Tubman. We're on defense. We're outnumbered and outgunned and outclassed. If we start an open war, we'll all be killed. Right, Chief?"

Tom frowned, but he said nothing.

It was Nick Rooney who replied, "Right."

I stood up. "Wrong! You've all played it that way for years now, and this morning, two Undertakers and an innocent girl are dead. You know why that is?" I didn't wait for an answer. "It's because the Corpses *are* fighting an open war. They've got no problems at all attacking us. After all, what's there to be afraid of? If they kill a few of us, all we'll do is say how sad it is and start looking for a new hiding place!

"Well, not me! Look, I know I'm new around here.

I know I'm young. Most of you probably think I don't know what I'm talking about. But I'm done hiding! I'm going to make those worm sacks pay for what they did! And if you won't let me do it as an Undertaker—then I'll do it on my own!"

I fell silent then, my face burning. I didn't sit down but instead stared straight at Tom, whose expression had turned thoughtful. Sharyn seemed like she might be fighting a smile. The rest of the bosses looked completely shocked. I wondered if anyone had ever spoken out like that at one of these meetings.

At last, wearily, Tom rose to his feet. Everyone watched him. No one spoke.

The Chief of the Undertakers met my eyes, and despite all of my bravado and righteous anger, I lowered my gaze.

"Will," Tom said evenly. "I want you to leave this meeting. Now."

I swallowed. I suddenly felt like crying. I didn't.

Instead I turned and marched out of the circle.

CHAPTER 30

BOMBSHELL

Haven was about kids, and kids are about games and television.

The Rec Hall was the largest sectioned-off area of the Big Room—and with good reason. Inside it were smaller plywood rooms that included everything from air hockey tables to video games—all for free. This made the Rec Hall easily the most popular place in the Undertakers' HQ.

And the TV room was easily the most popular place in the Rec Hall.

Six older but working twenty-five-inch televisions had been lined up along the walls. Each TV was currently being watched by a handful of off-duty Undertakers, and these groups were frequently bickering over their competing volume levels and selection of programming. Cartoons here. Sports there. Game shows over there.

There was one TV showing CNN, which I honestly didn't think I'd watched for more than five seconds in my life.

It was a noisy place.

I'd come here from the meeting because I couldn't think of anywhere else to wander. Curious eyes watched me as I slipped through the rain of wooden beads that covered the Rec Hall's only entrance. They followed me as I moved dejectedly down the short corridor toward the video arcade.

At least fifteen kids were there, sharing the dozen available machines, with the Burgermeister easily towering over the rest. He was playing Mortal Kombat, and as I watched, Dave's cartoonish, muscle-bound fighter victoriously turned its hapless opponent into sushi.

The Burgermeister threw his big fists skyward. "I rule!"

"Nice job," I commented.

He beamed. "There's my man! How'd the meeting go?"

"Um," I began, noticing the way the other kids were eying me. "Let's go next door, okay?"

"Sure!" Dave replied loudly. "One of you dudes take my game. Me and my man here need to talk!"

Inwardly I sighed.

We went into the air hockey room next door, which was currently unoccupied. "So? The meeting!" Dave demanded.

"Keep your voice down," I told him. "These aren't real walls, ya know."

"Right. Sorry. What happened? Did they talk about us? Where they're putting us, I mean?"

"The Moms," I said. Then as the Burgermeister moaned, I added, "Tom wanted to put me into the Angels."

"What? You kidding?"

I shook my head glumly.

"Man! That rocks! Think you can get me in too? I mean, maybe not right away...but in a couple of months? Seriously I don't think I can stand doing the dishes and collecting trash. What am I, a maid?"

"I don't think it's gonna happen," I said.

"You don't think what's gonna happen?"

"I don't think I'm going to be an Angel."

Dave's expression slackened. "Huh? Why not?"

"Because I don't think I'll be around here much longer."

I told him what happened at the meeting, finishing up with my own long, stupid speech about finally striking back at the Corpses.

"Anyway," I concluded, "I just mouthed off to the head honcho—right in front of all his under-honchos. Do you really think he can keep me around after that, no matter who my dad was?"

Dave thought about it all for a full minute before latching onto exactly the wrong point. "So it's true what everyone's been saying? Your dad was the cop who started the Undertakers?"

I laughed weakly. "Yeah, I guess so."

"And he was the only adult to ever See the Corpses?"

"Well, at least until Tom and Sharyn turn eighteen."

"Whoa! Like, no wonder you're so good!"

I frowned. "What?"

"I'm just saying that you must have, you know, inherited all your game from your old man."

"My game?"

The Burgermeister rolled his eyes. "Your fighting skills, dude! And the way you always know what to do!"

I groaned. "Dave, I almost got us killed last night."

"Yeah? Well, if I'd been in charge, we'd never have gotten outta the kitchen! You think any of those other geeks could've done better?"

I felt utterly flabbergasted.

"I'll tell you something else," Dave continued. "That thing about taking the fight right to the Corpses sounds dead-on to me! If you do get kicked out, I'm going with you!"

Before I could form a reply, a new voice added, "Me too."

Helene stood in the doorway, smiling.

I hadn't seen her since the night we'd sparred. That had been more than a week ago.

"Hi," I said.

Her smile widened. "Hi yourself."

Dave said, "Helene, right?"

"Right. And you must be Dave Burger."

"That's me!" The boy grinned proudly. "Except everybody calls me the Burgermeister."

I hadn't actually noticed anybody beside me calling him that but decided not to say so.

"Well, um...Burgermeister," Helene said, her smile faltering, "I kind of got something private to talk to Will about. Could you...?" Her voice trailed off. She flushed.

I suddenly felt like crawling under the cement floor.

Dave looked back and forth between us. "Oh! I get it! Hmmm...think I'll go catch me some SpongeBob." He gave me a hard slap on the back. "Don't do nothing I wouldn't do."

And off he went, whistling.

Helene said nervously, "I guess maybe I should've waited until later, huh?"

"Maybe."

"Is he going to—talk about us or something?"

"Probably," I said.

"And that doesn't bother you?"

"I've got an army of Corpses who want to do experiments on me," I said. "*That* bothers me."

Helene lowered her eyes. "Yeah. Listen, I meant what I said just now. The crew boss meeting just ended, and Sharyn told me what went down. If Tom kicks you out, I'm going with you. I think a bunch of others might too."

"I didn't say what I said to rip the Undertakers apart," I told her.

"I know that." She came closer and whispered, "Truth is, a lot of us have felt like fighting back for a long time. But Tom's always shot down the idea. He says we're not ready yet—that we've got to increase our numbers."

"I've heard his argument."

Helene nodded. "But while we're picking up kids, the Corpses are multiplying too! Our best guess is that they control a third of the cops, including the chief of police. There's even a Corpse on the city council! We don't know where they're coming from, but more are coming all the time. So no matter how fast we grow, we're always going to be outnumbered."

I considered this. "I can't believe Tom doesn't realize that."

"He says he does but that it doesn't change things. He says that right now, staying alive has to be our first priority."

"And yet Tara and Kyle are dead," I remarked bitterly.

Helene's expression twisted into a moment's grief. "Yeah."

"Tom's a good leader," I told her.

"He's a *great* leader," Helene agreed at once.

"And a good guy," I added.

"That too. But he's wrong, and you're right. We've got to start fighting back—before the Corpses take over the whole city."

I studied this pretty girl and wondered vaguely if I still had a crush on her. I wasn't sure. Right now I just didn't seem to have any room for those kinds of feelings.

"Will?"

"Yeah?"

"Um…I'm really sorry about what happened at First Stop."

Thinking she meant last night's Corpse attack, I replied, "What for? You weren't even there."

She scowled. "Not *that!* Last week! When I beat you up!"

"Oh."

"Anyway, I'm sorry."

I shrugged. "I had it coming. I was a jerk talking to you the way I did."

She grinned. "Well, maybe a little. So—we're cool?"

"We're cool."

Abruptly Dave's voice boomed from the direction of the TV room. "Yo, dudes! Get in here! Quick!"

Alarmed by something in his tone, Helene and I shared a wary look and ran out together.

This time there were a lot more kids in the TV room, and the sets were all tuned to the same channel: NBC local news. There, behind a news desk on some City Line Avenue sound stage, sat Kenny Booth. Of course, he was still wearing Kyle's body, only now it was wrapped in a fancy tailored suit.

"Look at this!" Dave exclaimed, pointing wildly at the screen. The other kids shushed him.

Words ran below Kyle's gray, dead face.

NBC News anchor Kenny Booth announces his bid for mayor.

Kenny Booth was speaking, his voice authoritative and trustworthy. It was Kyle's voice, but naturally nobody could recognize that but us. "So in light of Mayor Runston's resignation and with the emergency election just two weeks away, I feel a sense of community obligation to offer my services to the city of Philadelphia."

"Holy crap!" Burt Moscova muttered. I looked over and saw him standing beside his brother Steve.

"I realize that this will be a shock to many of my more loyal viewers. It certainly came as one to my own director, Pete Reubens, when I informed him of my intentions this morning. But please know that I haven't made this decision lightly. Philadelphia has suffered a terrible blow with the loss of Mayor Stuart Runston, especially under such circumstances. I feel compelled—no, check that—obligated to present myself as a candidate for his post. If elected, I will bring to City Hall not only my long experience with the day to day affairs of this city that I've come to love in the three years that I've lived here but also an honest man's determination to avoid my predecessor's political and moral stumbles.

"I thank you."

Silence fell over the Rec Hall. All eyes were staring glumly at the televisions, which were now all playing the same car commercial.

Suddenly the Burgermeister laughed and barked, "A Corpse mayor!" Then, looking around, he added, "What's everybody so down about?"

"What's everybody so down about?" Steve echoed incredulously. "We just heard Kenny Booth say he's running for mayor!"

"Yeah?" Dave asked. "So what? Who cares who's mayor? I couldn't have told you who the last one was!"

Steve threw up his hands in disgust. "Don't you get it? If he wins, that Corpse will effectively control the entire city! Never mind that he could promote other Corpses to important positions! Never mind that the office of mayor of Philadelphia is often a good stepping stone to the Pennsylvania governor's office in Harrisburg! As mayor, Booth could send the whole police department after us! He could use every resource this city's got to hunt us down!"

The color drained from the Burgermeister's face. "Oh," he muttered weakly.

"Yeah!" Steve snapped. "Oh!"

I glanced over at the curtained doorway. Filling it, with his sister beside him, stood Tom.

Our eyes met.

I said, "We can't let this happen."

CHAPTER 31

DISSENT

At eight p.m. on Tuesday, the Undertakers gathered.

It was a pretty big deal—one that took some time to set up, especially considering the forty Schoolers who had to be called back from the field. But finally, all 122 Undertakers were onsite—something that, according to Helene, was very rare.

And usually meant trouble.

The kids had all come together in an open area of the Big Room—some standing; others sitting Indian-style on the concrete floor. An unhappy murmur rumbled through the crowd. It reminded me of the impatience in the air right before a school assembly, except that instead of boredom, it was nervousness that had stuck ants in our collective pants.

Tom moved through the crowd, greeting almost everyone

by name. Finally he climbed onto a folding chair that Nick had set up for him. There, standing tall and in easy sight of everyone, the Chief of the Undertakers spread his arms.

The murmurs stopped.

He cut right to the chase—no empty speeches for Tom Jefferson. "Undertakers, Kenny Booth just announced on the news that he's making a run for mayor." The murmuring started up again as those who hadn't yet heard this news reacted to it. Tom waited for the chatter to die down. Then he said, "Now, as y'all must know, Philly's old mayor, Stu Runston, resigned two weeks ago after getting nailed in an appropriations scandal—the same scandal that's cost the jobs of half the city council. It's the biggest political shake-up this town has ever seen. At least a dozen city officials are looking at resignation or even jail time."

I hadn't heard any of this, although Helene, standing beside me, nodded sagely.

Dave asked, "What's an *appropriation?*"

No one replied.

Tom continued, "It's a situation that we've been monitoring real close, especially since we suspect the Corpses are somehow behind it. Thing is, they ain't never before tried anything quite this big—and we ain't been sure if this is really them or just normal human stupidity.

"But Booth's announcement today settled all that.

"This here scandal has totally fouled up the city structure, leaving what's called a *vacuum at the seat of power*. Bottom line: the way things stand, there ain't nobody really in line for mayor, and Philly needs a mayor.

"The city charter's got this special election amendment that allows for an acting mayor to be elected to finish out Runston's term. That election's been called for the first Tuesday in November—two weeks from today.

"So—two weeks ain't a lot of time for a mayor's campaign. But then Kenny Booth ain't your normal candidate. Even though he's only been in town for a few years, he's gotten himself a big fan base. Fact is, he's the most trusted news dude on this end of the state. Y'all have heard of him. Maybe before you started Seein', some of you even liked him. If so, don't let it bum you out. Everybody likes him."

"Now, there are other candidates—a whole bunch, in fact. But ain't none of them as respected as Booth. That's why we think Booth really has a shot at becoming the mayor of Philadelphia."

He paused, letting his analysis sink in. This time, when the murmuring started again, Tom talked right over it.

"We always figured the Corpses were after some major political power in our world. But so far none of them's ever gotten this close. Seems they're finally making their first big move. I know I don't got to tell y'all that a Corpse mayor would make our troubles a whole lot worse.

"Now, a good friend told me a little while ago that we can't let this happen. Well, he's right. But stopping it ain't gonna be easy. To start with, the Hackers are digging up whatever dirt they can on Kenny Booth. Of course, we already got a file on him and on any other Corpses with high-profile public gigs. But for this, we've got to look harder and find something that we can use to cost him this election."

I listened, frowning.

Beside me, Dave whispered. "Who cares about the election? I say, let's waste the jerk!"

Helene replied, "How? Even cutting their heads off doesn't do anything permanent!"

"Shhh!" I snapped.

Tom's tone grew somber. "There's another thing. We lost Tara Monroe and Kyle Standish to the Corpses last night at First Stop—betrayed by a mole. They both gave their lives so the recruits they were assigned to protect could get away safely. Their deaths are a tragedy—both to the Undertakers and to me personally—made all the worse because it seems Booth has decided to take Kyle's body as his own for now.

"I'm grievin', and so should y'all. But remember that Tara and Kyle would want us to keep up the fight."

He lowered his head. "At ten o'clock there's gonna be a memorial for them both. Obviously we don't have Kyle's body. But Tara's will be laid out on a cot, covered with a sheet, and I know I don't got to tell y'all that that sheet ain't to be messed with. This is about grief, Undertakers... and it's about respect.

"Now, each of you who wants to will get the chance to say something about either Tara or Kyle or both. Talk as long as you want. But when it's done, let it be done. Later tonight her body'll be dropped off outside a local hospital. I really wish we could do more than that. But this is war."

When he raised his head again, the Chief's eyes were shining with renewed conviction. "Starting tomorrow, we go after Booth. But in the next two weeks, it'll be situation normal for most of y'all. Schoolers get back to their gigs. Chatters and Hackers keep doing their things.

"On top of all that, we'll be staying on Kenny Booth like gum on his shoe! We're going to go everywhere he goes, see everything he does. We *will* find something that we can leak to the media or to another candidate to bring him down! And we're gonna do this in Kyle and Tara's memories! Undertakers, are you with me?"

The crowd cheered explosively. Applause, whistles, and wild shouts filled the air.

"Are you with me?" Tom asked again, louder this time.

The crowd cheered again, even more powerfully than before.

When things settled down, he said, "Go on and ask me stuff. Whatever you're feeling, put it out there."

Tom spent the next half hour fielding questions. Some were pretty smart: Can we get electronic bugs inside Booth's office or house? Can we try to somehow squirt him with saltwater in front of cameras? Should we volunteer to help out some of the other candidates? Tom promised to consider all these ideas.

Other questions were less smart—or maybe just less mature: If Booth becomes mayor, will he order the cops to shoot us on sight? What if the Corpses kill off all the other candidates to make sure that Booth wins? Can we hunt down the First Stop mole and kill her? These Tom handled with patience. No, even if he wins, Booth can't order Seers to be shot in the streets. No, the Corpses are too smart to start assassinating candidates. And no, we're not going to kill a girl who's just as much a victim as anyone else.

The Undertakers, he stressed, don't kill people.

We're just kids, and Booth knows it. In fact, he's counting on it.

At last the meeting ended. Tom reminded everyone to stay for the ten o'clock memorial. Almost immediately the gathering broke up into little groups—all discussing the goings-on.

I watched from a distance as Tom jumped off his chair, went straight to Elisha Beardsley, and started talking to the Hacker Boss.

"That was pretty short, huh?" Dave remarked. "I don't

think he talked for more than five minutes, and the rest of it was stupid questions."

"Not all stupid," I said.

Actually the stupid questions seemed like the only ones he really had answers for.

"It's always like that," Helene told them. "Tom keeps these things short. Anything more than, like, ten minutes, and everybody starts falling asleep. We're Undertakers, and we're not used to sitting and listening to speeches. We need to be doing something."

"Can't argue with that," I said. Without another word, I headed off toward Tom and Elisha. As I got close, I overheard a little of their conversation.

Elisha said, "He doesn't go every Sunday night—just once a month or so."

"And you dug this up how?" Tom asked, clearly impressed.

"His private calendar on the NBC-10 network."

"Way cool, Elisha!"

Grinning proudly she said, "The truth is, Heather's the one who finally broke through their firewall. She worked on it all afternoon."

"I got to remember to thank her for the effort," Tom promised.

"You should. Heck, she already thinks you're dreamy." Elisha laughed, and Tom made a playful show of pretending to punch her.

"Where's he go on Sundays?" I asked, marching right to them.

Startled, the two kids looked at me.

I added, "We're talking about Booth, right?"

"Um—hi, Will," said Elisha.

"Keep digging," Tom instructed her. "Find out how he gets there and how long he stays."

Nodding, Elisha disappeared into the dwindling crowd.

I turned to Tom. "Where's Booth go on Sunday nights?" I asked again.

"Bro, we need to talk."

"We *are* talking."

"You know what I mean."

Of course I did. "Sorry about this morning," I told him.

"Don't be," Tom replied. "You said what you felt."

"I thought maybe I embarrassed you in front of the crew bosses."

The older boy grinned. "Well, you did *that* too."

"Sorry," I said again.

"Thanks. But that ain't what we need to talk about."

"Tom, are you gonna kick me out?"

"What?"

I steeled myself. "I mean—I understand if you are. I just want to know so I can—well, get ready, I guess."

To my surprise, Tom burst out laughing. "Will! If

I tossed out every Undertaker who got in my face at a bosses' meeting, my own sister would've been out on the streets years ago! Forget it! It ain't important."

"Oh. Sorry. Then what *did* you want to talk to me about?" I asked, although inside I was sighing with relief.

"Well, if you'd quit your apologizing, I'd tell you." He was still laughing.

"Sorry," I repeated before I could catch myself.

With an effort the Chief got his amusement under control. Then in a more serious tone, he said, "Listen. I think we'd better hold off on the Angel thing."

I frowned. A moment ago I'd been deeply relieved not to be exiled. But now I was just as deeply disappointed. "How come?"

"Well, partly because some of the bosses ain't digging it. Now, if it was just that, I'd say let's ride it out. But the other part is that right now, you ain't in the right frame of mind for that kind of work."

"The right frame of mind?" I asked, suddenly irritated. "What's that supposed to mean?"

"You're pissed off—and you got every right to be. But an Angel in the field's got to stay cool. Anger can make you reckless, and I won't risk nobody running off and going outside the scope of a mission. It can get their fellow crewers into trouble."

"I wouldn't do that!" I exclaimed.

"Didn't say you would. But you *are* pissed."

"Of course I'm pissed! Look at everything that's happened! Look at Tara and Kyle!"

Tom shrugged. "Just give it a month. Until then I'll put you on any other crew you want. Then when you're more settled, we'll try the Angels thing again. I still do think it's the place for you—once you're really ready for it."

"I'm ready now!" I insisted.

"No, bro. You ain't."

"But in a month, the mayor's election'll be over!"

"I know."

All of a sudden, I got it. "You're afraid I'm gonna go after Booth!" I snapped.

"Crossed my mind."

"Would it be such a bad thing?"

"It could get you killed," Tom said. "I figure that counts as a bad thing."

"So what? It's my life, isn't it?"

Tom's eyebrows rose. "Maybe you should tell that to your mother and Emily, huh?"

I looked away.

Tom waited.

Finally, feeling defeated, I said, "Do I have to be a Mom?"

"Not if you don't want to be."

"The other recruits'll get jealous."

Tom shrugged. "They'll get over it."

"Why do I get special treatment?"

"Because you're a special case," he replied. "You know that."

And I did, although I still didn't entirely understand why. Could it really be because of who my father was? Tom seemed—well, smarter than that.

"I'd like to try out the Brains," I said.

Tom looked surprised. "You wanna work for Steve?"

"Is that okay?"

"Sure. I just didn't expect it. Well, go ahead and report to the Brain Factory whenever you're ready. Make sure you tell Steve it's only for a month."

"Okay." I walked glumly back to where Dave and Helene still waited. The girl was twirling her hair nervously. Dave cracked his knuckles.

The Burgermeister spoke first. "You getting kicked out?"

"No," I replied. "But he's holding off on my Angel training."

"Why?" asked Helene.

"He thinks I'm too—emotional, I guess."

She considered this. "So where *is* he putting you?"

"He gave me my choice. I asked for the Brains."

Dave grimaced. "What for?"

I ignored the question for now. "Booth's got something going down on Sundays. That's what Tom and Elisha were talking about. Apparently it's something that he does every month."

"*What* does he do every month?" Helene asked.

"Tom wouldn't tell me."

"Guy's a jerk," the Burgermeister spat.

"No, he's not!" Helene replied impatiently. Then to me: "He's just trying to protect you."

"I know," I said. I met Helene's pretty hazel eyes. "Know anybody on the Hackers crew?"

My question surprised her. "A couple of kids."

"Anybody named Heather?"

"Sure. Heather DiSalvino. We went through First Stop together. Why?"

I hesitated. Helene was my friend, but she was also an Undertaker and loyal to Tom, despite her promise that if I left, she'd go with me. Still, I couldn't pull off what I was planning alone, could I? "Think you can find out from her where Booth's going one Sunday night a month?"

Now it was her turn to hesitate. She looked worried. "Will..." she began.

"I'm not saying I'm going to *do* anything. I'm just curious," I insisted. It was a lie, and we both knew it.

Dave frowned, clearly confused.

"Will..." she repeated.

"Come on, Helene. Please?"

She blew out a long sigh and reluctantly said, "I'll try."

I smiled. "Thanks."

She smiled back. "Sure."

CHAPTER 32

CONSPIRACY

Assembling a radio watch is all about patience and the right tools."

I was in the Brain Factory, and Steve had just removed the back from a cheap digital watch. As I looked on—the dutiful student—he used a pair of tweezers to expertly fit a tiny transmitter/receiver and an even smaller GPS chip into a space only slightly roomier than a pea. "It's actually easier than it looks. You just solder the TR and the GPS right onto that silver prong beside the battery."

"What about a speaker and microphone?" I asked.

"That's why I picked this brand. It has a memo function so the wearer can record voice messages. The TR chip simply taps into that."

"Cool," I said.

"You try the next one," Steve suggested.

So I did, taking the tweezers and miniature soldering pen. I flubbed the first one but nailed the second. Steve had been right. It wasn't hard.

"Good! Just add it to the stockpile. The Angels are always breaking them. Sometimes it's all I can do to keep up. Come on, the new batch of saltwater should be ready."

As we crossed the Factory, the four other Brains treated me to curious, sidelong glances. Everyone at Haven had been doing that all week, ever since news had spread about that last night at First Stop.

Being a reluctant celebrity was something else I'd gotten used to.

As we passed one of the Brain Factory tables, a crewer named Zack showed up with a box in his arms. This he unceremoniously dumped onto the tabletop, spilling an assortment of gadgets.

"These are broken," Zack reported.

The pile included two Super Soakers, a dozen or more water pistols, a bunch of radio watches—and something that looked a bit like a small crossbow. Maybe a foot long, it was made mostly of wood with a steel cable stretched between its tips.

"What's that?" I asked.

"Grappling gun," Steve replied. "What happened to it this time?" he asked Zack.

The boy shrugged. "Jammed when firing. We still don't have the launching coil right."

Steve groaned, picking up the crossbow and eyeing it from different angles. "Got banged around too much," he pronounced. "You can see it. Here—the seam in the wood is cracked."

"A grappling gun?" I asked. "Seriously?"

"When it works," the crewer replied. "Which isn't often."

"And who broke it?"

"Angels," Zack replied. "Who else?"

"It's for scaling walls," Steve added. "Fires a three-pronged grappling hook up to fifty feet straight up. The Angels use it for recon. So far it's a prototype—the only one we've got." He sighed. "Okay, log them and scrap them. Except the bow. Let's look that one over again. I still think it's got potential."

Zack nodded. "If you say so." He didn't sound convinced.

Moving on, Steve and I next stopped in front of a big pot sitting atop a lab table's hot plate. "Check the timer and temperature," the Brain Boss told me.

I obediently examined the contents of the pot—five gallons of tap water with seven ounces of sea salt mixed carefully into it. The concoction smelled—well, salty. A thermometer that floated inside read just over one hundred degrees.

"Temp's right," I reported. "And it's been brewing for half an hour."

"Then it's ready," replied Steve.

We spent the next ten minutes funneling the water into a dozen old soda bottles for storage.

"Where'd you learn to do this?" I asked.

"Make saltwater?" Steve said. "It's not exactly difficult."

"No. I mean, how did you find out that saltwater worked on the Corpses?"

"Oh…" He grinned. "You really want to know?"

"Sure."

The other Brains groaned. Apparently they'd heard the story before.

"Know what *serendipity* means?" Steve asked me.

I shook my head.

"It means 'lucky accident.' It happens sometimes in science. In the nineteenth century, an English doctor named Edward Jenner discovered—by accident—that people who came down with a mild bug called cowpox never got the much nastier smallpox. This resulted in the development of the first vaccination. In fact, the word *vaccination*, comes from the Latin word *vacca*…which means 'cow.'"

"Okay," I said, suddenly feeling like I was back in science class. "But what's that got to do with Corpses and saltwater?"

"It was discovered the same way."

"By accident?" I asked. "Serendipity?"

"Right. Back in school I got this idea for a science fair. I did a salinity test."

"A what?"

He looked at me as if astonished that I didn't know. "Salinity: the dissolved salt content in a body of water. I did a study. I used sea salt to manufacture four types of water: brine, seawater, brackish water, and fresh."

"But—fresh water doesn't have salt."

"Sure it does," Steve said. "Just very little. Less than five hundred parts per million."

I shrugged. "Okay. So where do the Corpses come in?"

Steve replied, "While I was working on my science project, I started Seeing them."

"Huh?"

"He was in the school lab after hours," one of the Brains, a girl named Lisa, said with a sigh.

"It was two days before the science fair," a boy called Andrew added.

"A janitor came in, and he was a Corpse!" Zack chimed in.

"Steve freaked out, giving himself away immediately, so the dead janitor attacked him!" said another girl whose name I didn't know.

"Quit it!" Steve snapped. "I'm telling the story!" Then to me, he said, "I kept my cool."

"He freaked," the girl said again.

"Quit it, Kelly! Anyway, I grabbed the only weapon I could find—a beaker filled with the seawater I'd made—and threw it in the Corpse's face. All of a sudden he started twitching and just kind of fell over. Then I ran the hell out of there!"

"I'll bet you did," I remarked.

"Later on, after Burt hooked me up with the Undertakers, I suggested to Karl—your dad—that we try the same thing again. And it worked! Something about saltwater disrupts a Corpse's control over its host body." He laughed. "Serendipity!"

I didn't quite get the joke, but I laughed along anyhow. "Cool! So your brother brought you into the Undertakers?"

Steve's smile faded. "Yeah."

"But isn't he younger than you?"

For a long moment, Steve didn't answer. Then Zack did. "He is—by almost a year. But Burt had already started Seeing and had run away from home before Steve got into the science fair."

Frowning, Steve muttered, "Not everybody gets the Sight at the same age."

"Because some go into puberty later than others, huh, boss?" Andrew chimed in. They all laughed a little. Steve blushed a deep scarlet. This was obviously an old joke in the Brain Factory—a little bit of fun at the head guy's expense.

A couple weeks ago, I might have joined in.

Not anymore.

"I don't know," I said casually. "Seems to me that a lot of kids would be *dead* if Steve had started Seeing when he was supposed to."

The laughter faded. Steve looked at me, surprised.

I continued, "I mean, if Steve hadn't gotten into that science fair, we wouldn't know about the salt thing. And without that, the Corpses would've killed a lot more Seers than they have—including me." I offered my hand to the boy. "Sharyn's right. You *are* a genius."

Steve stared at the hand. Then he shook it. "Thanks," he said, and something told me that he meant it in more ways than one.

Everyone else went back to their work, looking a bit embarrassed. Steve cleared his throat. "Um...you want to get another batch started?"

"You got it, boss."

As I washed out and refilled the pot, Steve fetched the big bottle of sea salt, which the Undertakers bought in bulk.

"Think you can manage this on your own?" Steve asked me. "I've got a little work to do."

"I'm good."

I watched Steve leave, walking tall, and smiled to myself. Then I set about grinding up some of the big chunks of salt by using a special ceramic bowl and a knobby hand-held gadget combo that Steve called a mortar and pestle. The idea was to pound the salt crystals as small as possible. That helped them dissolve faster in the hot water.

Once I finished pounding, I weighed the salt carefully, making sure I was using the right amount. Too much and the mixture would gunk up the guns. Too little and there wouldn't be enough salt in the water to affect the Corpses.

"Psst!" said a voice.

I looked up, startled.

Dave stood just beyond the limits of the Brain Factory, waving frantically. I glanced over my shoulder. Steve was busy at one of the lab tables, messing around with what looked like little chunks of Styrofoam. Thankfully none of the other Brains were looking my way just now.

"What?" I asked the Burgermeister, keeping my voice low.

"Helene wants to see you. She's got something."

I felt a twinge of excitement. At last! We were running out of time. Tomorrow was Sunday. "Where?"

"In the TV room."

"I'll be there soon," I said. "Now beat it."

"Right." And off he went, big hands in his pockets and whistling, drawing odd stares from everyone he passed.

I sighed and went back to work.

Shortly afterward I asked Steve for a bathroom break.

"No problem," he told me.

It was two o'clock, and the Rec Hall was largely empty, most of the crews being busy elsewhere. In fact, the only kids on hand were Moms, who mostly pulled morning and evening duty. A group of them, including Maria, Ethan, and Harleen, was watching a soap opera.

"Will!" Harleen called.

I waved. "Seen Dave?"

"He and that Helene girl went back into the arcade," Ethan reported.

Beside him, Maria giggled. "I think they like each other."

I smiled halfheartedly and headed down the short hall to the video game room. It was empty—except for Dave and Helene.

The two of them stood close together, the boy towering over the girl. Both were studying a sheet of paper that Helene held in her hands.

"What's going on?" I asked.

They looked up.

"Fort Mifflin," Helene said.

"I still don't get it," Dave complained. "What the hell is Fort Mifflin?"

Helene shook the paper impatiently. "*This* is Fort Mifflin!"

"Well, duh! But what *is* Fort Mifflin?"

"Slow down, will you?" I demanded. "What about Fort Mifflin?"

"That's where Kenny Booth's going tomorrow night," she replied. "That's where he goes about once a month."

"How'd you find out?"

"It wasn't easy. Heather wouldn't tell me a thing, and just try to pry something out of Elisha once Tom's told her to keep quiet. The thing is, there's this other Hacker named Justin. I think he…" Helene's voice trailed off, her face reddening.

Dave chimed right in. "He kind of likes her!"

Helene shot him a look that would have melted stone.

"Yeah?" I said. All of a sudden, I felt strange—almost sick to my stomach. I didn't know what the feeling was, but I absolutely knew what it wasn't.

It wasn't jealousy.

No way.

"He wants to be her boyfriend!" Dave continued cheerfully.

"Um…so this Justin kid told you that Booth goes to Fort Mifflin?" I asked, starving for a change of subject.

"Yeah," Helene said sourly.

"The old Fort Mifflin?"

"Uh-huh."

Dave interrupted, "Will somebody please tell me what the heck Fort Mifflin is?"

"It's an old Revolutionary War fort," I told him. "It's down near the airport."

"And that's where Booth is going tomorrow night?" asked the Burgermeister.

Helene nodded. "Around midnight."

As it happened, I knew something about Fort Mifflin. It stood south of the city, right on the banks of the Delaware River—a walled fort that once defended Philly against the British. A century later, during the Civil War, it became a military prison. Now it was a museum—one that I'd visited on a class trip. Actually I remembered it as being pretty cool.

"What does Booth do at Fort Mifflin in the middle of the night?" I wondered aloud.

Helene replied, "That's what Tom and Sharyn want to know. The Angels are heading there to keep an eye on the comings and goings."

"From inside the walls or outside?" I asked.

"Outside. A safe distance away—at least according to Justin."

"Uh-huh," I said. I'd expected as much. "So what's the paper?"

"A map of the fort," Dave replied. "Helene's boyfriend printed it out."

She groaned and handed me the sheet.

It was a color map, pretty rough, labeled with the words *Walking Tour of Fort Mifflin*. It showed the sharply angled walls of the roughly star-shaped fort encircling a handful of rectangular buildings identified with labels like *Artillery Shed*, *Parade Grounds*, and *Commandant's House*. The entire compound was surrounded by a genuine moat with just three bridges.

Booth'll be there.

I thought about Kyle and Tara, and that now-familiar anger flared up again inside me.

And so will I.

"Thanks, Helene."

"Sure," she replied with an embarrassed shrug.

I turned to leave.

"Whoa, dude!" Dave said quickly. "What's the plan?"

"I'm going there tomorrow night."

"Not without me you're not!" the Burgermeister insisted.

"Guys—" Helene stammered. "Wait a minute—"

"I think I'd better go alone," I told Dave.

"Not a chance! You think I want to stay here and scrub toilets? I've got to be out there where the action is!"

"Guys!" Helene exclaimed loud enough to startle us both into attention. "Neither one of you is going anywhere. Tom won't let you."

"I won't be asking him," I said.

At that, Helene's mouth dropped open.

Her reaction pissed me off a little—or maybe it was the Justin thing. I snapped, "Well, what did you think I wanted to know this stuff for?"

"You told me you were just curious!" she replied harshly. "You didn't say anything about running out there without Tom's okay!"

I wasn't sure how to respond to that. It was true that I'd lied to Helene about why I wanted the Booth info. But I was also pretty sure that she'd *known* I was lying.

But if so, then why had she gone along with it?

"Look," Helene pleaded, "forget about all the trouble you'd get into—"

"What kind of trouble?" Dave interjected.

A good point. What sort of discipline did the Undertakers have? What could Tom do to me? Give me a detention? A time out? Send me to bed without supper? I'd never heard of anything like that happening in Haven. Was such a high level of cooperation and obedience a result of everyone's common effort against the Corpses? Or could Tom's personality really be so strong that more than a hundred kids followed the rules all the time?

What did that say about a leader?

And why was I finding it so easy to defy that leader?

Because I'm a special case.

I smiled humorlessly.

"I don't know what kind of trouble," Helene admitted, sounding exasperated. "But trouble. Besides that, you can't get out—not without somebody knowing it. There are motion sensors all along the tunnel."

My smile overturned. I hadn't thought of that.

"No sweat!" Dave said cheerfully. "Will's going to think of a way around that. Ain't that right?"

"Guess I'll have to," I said.

Helene threw up her hands in disgust. "You're both crazy! What do you think you're going to do even if you *do* manage to get to Fort Mifflin?"

"What Tom won't do," I replied. "I'll sneak in and find out what's going on."

"You mean *we* will, dude," Dave corrected.

I sighed and then relented. "Okay. *We*."

"Booth's a Corpse," Helene pointed out. "There's no way for you to kill him."

"I know that, Helene. I'm not an idiot. I'm not gonna charge in there and start yelling at him. I'm just gonna find out what he's *doing* there!"

Half a minute passed during which Helene studied me with a look on her face that I couldn't quite identify. Admiration? Respect? Worry? Surprise?

Finally she said, "Well, in that case—*I'm* coming too."

CHAPTER 33

MASTER PLAN

To pull off our unauthorized mission, we required three things: equipment; wheels to Fort Mifflin, meaning three bikes; and some way of getting past Haven's motion sensors.

Late Saturday afternoon I went around the Big Room and quietly collected the gear we'd need, including squirt pistols, bottled water for the trip, and a few energy bars. All this I stuffed into three backpacks, which I hid in a dark corner of the Brain Factory where nobody would notice them, least of all Steve.

The second and third obstacles took a bit more thinking. Because the Stingrays were kept out in the open—in the roped-off corral—just swiping them wasn't an option. Fortunately, by dinnertime, Helene had an idea. "We didn't always use Stingrays," she explained during a quiet powwow that the three of us shared in the cafeteria. "In one of the front storage rooms, there are a bunch of older bikes. The room's close to the ramp, so if we go in quiet—one at a time—we can probably get three bikes out without anybody seeing us."

"What about the jump?" I asked.

She looked thoughtful. "I've got a way around that one too—I think."

"You *think?*" Dave remarked nervously.

That just left the motion sensors.

Once again it was Helene who came through—this time at Sunday's breakfast. She dropped onto the cafeteria bench between Dave and me, deposited her tray on the table, and bent her head close to ours. "Good news," she whispered. "The tunnel sensors are programmed for one-way throughput."

"Was that English?" the Burgermeister asked, his voice low.

"It means that they only detect motion coming *into* Haven from *outside*, not the other way around. As long as we're heading out, they won't pick us up."

"Until we come back," I whispered.

If *we come back*.

"Well—yes. But by then everybody'll know we're gone anyway."

She was right, of course.

"Yeah," Dave muttered sourly. "Real good news."

But it *was* good news. It meant that we were ready.

The *coming back to Haven* part would have to take care of itself.

That evening the three of us hung out in the TV room, watching whatever was on. My eyes kept straying to the clock, and the minutes dragged like hours. It was all I could do to sit still and stare at the tube. More than once Helene elbowed me for fidgeting.

Finally the time passed, and with wordless nods all around, we each left the Rec Hall one at a time a few minutes apart. Nobody noticed. I went last.

The few kids in the Big Room were busy and either so tired or so deeply involved in their tasks that they never even looked up.

I had no problem at all getting into the storage room unnoticed. By the time I slipped inside, Helene and Dave had already picked out their bikes. Most of the best rides had been dismantled for spare parts, and the leftovers looked pretty lousy. Dave had selected a big old Schwinn, while Helene had settled for a green Huffy. I grabbed a rusty red Roadmaster.

"The Angels already left," Helene told us. "I checked. Once they were gone and I was sure nobody else would be going out through the tunnel, I dropped this hunk of plywood over the jump, from ramp to ramp. Tom keeps it handy just in case we have to get everyone out in a hurry."

That sounds like Tom, I thought, and I felt a sharp pang

of guilt. The Chief would undoubtedly see what we were doing as a betrayal, even if the three of us did manage to do some good out there.

I patted my jacket pocket, feeling the comforting weight of the pocketknife.

After tonight I'll probably need to give it back.

But I have *to do this.*

"You guys ready?" I asked.

They both nodded.

"Then let's go."

We departed one bike at a time—walking, not riding. Nobody stopped us. Nobody shouted an alarm. Nobody so much as looked our way.

Within a minute we were pedaling up the spiral tunnel, and a minute after that, we were on the darkened Philly streets.

We rode in silence to the Tenth Street subway station. Fortunately bicycles were welcome on city trains, so it was pretty simple to catch the R1 to Philadelphia International Airport. After that it was just a matter of getting through the airport and then mounting up for the one-and-a-half-mile ride to historic Fort Mifflin.

It was more biking than I'd ever done in my life. The same seemed true for Dave, who huffed and puffed atop the Schwinn, which was clearly too small for him. Only Helene pedaled along without breaking a sweat, keeping to the side roads and following the route we'd mapped out ahead of time. The October night was cold, and cars often jetted past us, creating currents of air in their wakes that threatened to tip our bikes. Worse, because we were riding right by the airport, huge planes kept flying low over our heads, so loud and so massive that I almost lost my balance more than once.

Finally, with relief, we turned onto the less-traveled Fort Mifflin Road.

Here, amid wooded marshes, we switched our headlights off, fearful of alerting the Angels, who were undoubtedly already in position. I felt almost dizzy with nervousness as the low, sharply angled walls of the two-hundred-year-old fort came into view. There were lights on inside it, and cars were already filling the North Gate parking lot.

A *lot* of cars.

It was time to get off the streets.

As planned—and with the fort still a quarter-mile away—Helene led us down a dirt side road. Minutes later we parked our bikes near some railroad tracks around a bend that was flanked by trees and tall grass.

From there the three of us set off on foot, hurriedly crossing a dimly lit access road that serviced the fort's administrative offices. We kept low and moved quickly, mindful of the vehicles that were arriving with increasing regularity. Booth, it seemed, wasn't the only midnight visitor, and the last thing I wanted was to be caught in the headlights of an advancing car.

We finally reached the northern edge of the moat. From this point, I could see two obvious entrances. One, the North Gate, bridged the moat fifty yards to our left. The other, the Main Gate, was nearer to the parking lot.

Both entrances were brightly lit and clearly guarded.

Fortunately we'd already mapped out another way in.

"The wildlife refuge is on the south side of the fort," I explained. "That's where the footbridge is. We'll follow the moat until we get there. And keep it quiet."

The hike proved to be longer and harder than I'd expected, leaving us scratched, muddy, and very cold. By now, voices had begun to emanate from inside the fort. Sharing nervous glances, the three of us crossed a narrow footbridge that spanned the moat. We then approached the high brick façade that formed the fort's angled southern wall.

Wordlessly Dave bent over, laced his fingers, and offered me a boost. I took it and was startled to find myself all but thrown over the top of the wall. I landed on a flat, grassy battlement. Helene followed a moment later, and together the two of us managed to haul the Burgermeister up to join us.

Breathlessly we turned and faced the ancient fort's bright and noisy interior.

CHAPTER 34

SPEECH

Buried in shadows, the three of us made our way cautiously down from the earthworks and onto the fort's green. Moving as quickly as we dared, Dave, Helene, and I soon reached the centuries-old artillery shed, which was constructed more like a big mound of earth with tunnels beneath it than like an actual building. Once there I motioned for the others to stay low. So far we hadn't been spotted, and I wanted to keep it that way.

"This is a creepy place," Dave muttered.

"That's because of all the ghosts," Helene replied.

The Burgermeister scowled. "That ain't funny."

"That's because I'm not kidding," she told him.

"It's true," I said. "Fort Mifflin's like the second-most haunted place in the country. There's got to be a dozen ghost stories connected with this place. I thought everybody knew that!"

"*I* didn't," Dave complained. "Thanks loads."

Carefully we peered around the edge of the mound.

"Wow," Helene muttered.

Fort Mifflin's parade ground was filled with the walking dead. There had to be hundreds of them, dressed in everything from military uniforms to surgical garb. Their milky eyes darted this way and that, and their feet shuffled anxiously, as if they were waiting for something.

"Jeez," Dave mumbled. "There's a lot of them."

"Let's get closer," I whispered.

"Closer?" Helene quietly exclaimed.

I led them around the artillery shed and past the blacksmith's shop. Finally we settled into the shadows surrounding the two-story commandant's house. From there we had a pretty good view of the goings-on.

And just in time too.

As we watched, Kenny Booth appeared. He moved through the crowd, still wearing Kyle's body, and stepped confidently up onto a platform that had been erected in the center of the parade grounds. Kyle's cadaver was a week old now and not as fresh as it had once been. The skin had turned gray, and the hair had begun to fall out. The result was a grotesque, twisted shadow of the Undertaker who had given his life at First Stop.

It made my stomach turn to see Kyle's body so abused. *Desecration* was the word that came to mind. I hadn't really known the boy whose skin this Corpse now wore, but he'd surely deserved better treatment than *this*.

Besides, Mr. Would-Be-Mayor was wearing a fancy suit and tie that I was pretty certain poor Kyle wouldn't have been caught dead in—no pun intended.

"I hate seeing him in Kyle's body," Helene said.

"I know," I replied. "Try focusing on his Mask instead."

Taking my own advice, I crossed my eyes, watching not Kyle's face but the older-looking, perfectly grooved visage of Philly's favorite news guy. It helped a little.

Behind me the Burgermeister grumbled, "I really wish I knew how you guys did that."

I almost assured him that he'd learn but stopped myself. To be brutally honest, I wasn't sure he ever *would*.

On the platform, Kenny Booth raised his fists skyward in a triumphant salute. The crowd roared. "Brothers and sisters!" The Corpse spoke loudly in Kyle's voice. It was unsettling, but at least he was speaking English. Suffering through a speech given in Deadspeak would have been *too* much! "For years we have returned to this place, drawn to its long and bloody history, to meet in secret. But tonight is no ordinary gathering! Tonight, safe from human eyes, we revel in the knowledge that we are about to enjoy our first great victory on this place called Earth!"

"They must have Corpse police posted on the roads around the fort," Helene whispered, "making sure nobody gets close enough to hear any of this."

I nodded. "It'll make it harder to get back."

Booth continued, "Earlier this week, as planned, I announced my candidacy for the office of mayor of Philadelphia. My years spent smiling for the human cameras, cultivating the trust and respect of this city's foolish natives, have finally borne fruit. In two weeks I will become the first of our kind to seize genuine control over a major Earth city! Then, in time, I shall bore deeper into the world of human politics. In a month, City Hall; in five years, the governor's mansion in Harrisburg; and in ten... the White House!"

"This dead guy thinks big, doesn't he?" Dave remarked.

"Ugh," Helene moaned softly, shaking her head. "I can't keep that Mask thing going. It gives me a headache."

"Me too," I admitted reluctantly. I uncrossed my eyes, resigned to having to witness Booth is his stolen Undertaker body.

Booth declared, "In the three years since we established our foothold on this world, I have worked tirelessly toward increasing the scope of our invasion. Our brethren have now begun to infiltrate every metropolitan area on the East Coast. Still it is only fitting that it is here, where our campaign began, that I have taken this glorious step toward final triumph! Brothers and sisters, I—and I alone—have given us our greatest success to date! This is my success. My glory!"

The cheers of the Corpse crowd were almost deafening.

Dave scowled. "He's talking like he's already won the election."

I watched the *thing* on the platform, feeling anger churn inside me like molten lava.

"So before we begin tonight's festivities," Booth said, "each of you must once again declare your loyalty to me! For I alone can bring us total victory! I alone can make us masters of Earth!"

What followed seemed less like an oath of loyalty than a cry of worship. There could be no doubt that Booth, no matter whose body he wore, was the boss of the Deaders.

This guy's evil even by Corpse standards.

Booth spoke again, this time in a more serious tone. "We are not, however, without our enemies, brothers and sisters. As all of you are aware, almost from the moment we arrived in this place and began taking their bodies for our own, there have appeared among these pathetic humans those who can See." A hiss of general loathing rumbled through the crowd. "At first we believed these cases unique, and we removed each threat as it appeared. After all, these Seers were nothing but human children, to whom adults barely listen, much less believe.

"But then there appeared one adult with this power—a policeman named Ritter. Of all the humans, he came closest to discovering our secrets—and revealing us!"

Another group hiss.

I felt a surge of pride.

That's my dad this stinking cadaver is complaining about!

Then Booth grinned savagely, his thin lips pulled back against surprisingly white teeth. "But eventually I dealt with him myself, brothers and sisters. And sweet it was to take that puny man's life!"

This was followed by a roar of appreciation. For a moment I thought I might explode with rage.

"Easy, Will," Helene whispered, touching my arm.

Easy, Will.

I forced myself to keep still and listen.

Booth went on. "With his death, however, we face his legacy—these brats who somehow share his Sight. They plague us! Organized and well led, they infiltrate the city's schools, spiriting away other Seers before we can find and deal with them. And their goal, brother and sisters? Their goal is to build an army to stand against us. Us!"

As one, the audience of walking dead laughed. It was a harsh, raspy sound that hurt my ears.

Booth sneered, "They call themselves *the Undertakers*. They strike at us in the night and then flee, unseen, to their hidden lair. But they are merely whelps romanced by a child's delusion of battle and glory. We have tolerated them, for what can they really do? Their weapons cause us no lasting harm. At worst they rob us of a handful of Seers each year. So after a few token attempts at discovering their lair, we had all but forgotten them...

"Until now."

Booth's expression twisted in anger. "Today we have a new enemy: the son of Karl Ritter. Long have we watched this human child, waiting for him to shows signs of his father's inexplicable ability. But when he did, the Undertakers—the cursed Undertakers—spirited him away like all the rest! Now they have him, and the spy that we slipped in among their newest trainees failed to secure him for us."

The audience hissed their collective displeasure. It suddenly struck me that the crowd's reactions to Booth's speech seemed almost childish, cheering the good points and booing the bad ones.

This isn't a secret meeting. It's a pep rally!

And the "big game" they intend to win is me!

"We must have William Ritter, brothers and sisters! We must take him apart, cell by cell, and learn from him just how these humans are able to penetrate our illusion. Then there will be nothing to stop us!"

A new cheer followed, more raucous and terrible than any of the others.

I felt sick to my stomach.

"As mayor I shall bring the whole of this city's resources to bear against the Undertakers. We will find their hidden lair and scratch that persistent itch once and for all! At the same time, we will take possession of Ritter's only son!

"I state this as my blood oath to you!"

Booth's audience went into an almost animalistic frenzy,

hopping up and down, flailing their arms, and cheering with their rotting, swollen tongues. All of them were dead. All of them wrapped in the stolen bodies of men and women who had once been real people with real lives.

These were invaders, yes. And killers. But they were thieves too.

They stole dignity.

"What's that?" Dave whispered, pointing.

All three of us craned our necks to see.

A small contingent of well-dressed Corpses was marching through the crowd, approaching the podium. At the sight of them, I felt my anger fade, replaced by a growing dread.

The Corpses went suddenly, ominously quiet.

"Oh, no..." Helene whispered.

Nestled in among the contingent, looking small and terrified, walked Amy Filewicz.

Her clothes were soiled and torn, her hair matted, and her face grubby and tear-streaked. Suddenly, despite what she'd done, I felt sick at heart to see her. Whatever was happening, Amy was right in the middle of it, and she clearly didn't want to be.

"Here," declared Booth, "is a whelp whose mind was turned to us by the *pelligog*. She was placed into the Undertakers' training center, originally to discover the location of their lair. Later, however, when we learned that William Ritter was among her fellow trainees, she was ordered to help us capture him. But in the midst of the attempted capture, the quarry escaped—after this little brat tried to kill him without permission!"

Her Corpse escorts scooped Amy up under each arm and deposited her on the platform. There she stood, staring wide-eyed up at Booth, who smiled wickedly down at her.

"I don't blame you for failing us, child," he said soothingly. "After all, failure is the way of your kind. Instead, tonight you will have the honor of validating the promise I've made to my brethren. Tonight your blood will seal my oath!"

He touched her face with his slimy, decaying fingers. She flinched and trembled but didn't try to run. The Corpse grinned and licked his lips with a black tongue that glistened hideously in the harsh parade ground lights.

His fingers settled around the girl's throat.

With an almost electric shock, I grasped what was about to happen.

He's gonna kill her—right now!

I didn't think. I just reacted. No way was I going to watch this innocent girl get murdered to satisfy some sick ritual!

"No!" I exclaimed, yanking the water pistol from my belt and charging out of the shadows.

"Will!" Helene screamed loudly—too loudly.

On the parade grounds, hundreds of dead eyes turned toward us as if pulled by a common string.

CHAPTER 35

DISASTER

My heart seemed to seize up inside my chest as the realization of what I'd just done came crashing down on me. Cold, bitter terror flooded my mind. Desperately I clutched at Tara's father's words.

Be brave.

But then something my own dad had sometimes said bubbled up to the surface.

There's a difference between courage and suicide.

Well, it was too late to worry about that now.

Feeling suddenly terribly foolish, I brandished my pistol at the motionless wall of Corpses. There were so many of them! They looked hungrily back at me—all dead eyes and rotting fists that opened and closed in eerie unison.

On the platform, Kenny Booth grinned, still clutching the terrified, trembling girl.

"Well, Mr. Ritter," he purred, "this *is* a pleasant surprise." Then to the mob, he barked, "Take him alive and undamaged!" His grin widened. "At least, mostly undamaged!"

A rumbling chuckle rolled through the mass of Corpses as they slowly advanced.

I knew I had eight good shots in my gun—maybe nine. Then they'd be on me.

How stupid am I?

I'd jumped to Amy's rescue without a thought, much less a plan. But I couldn't imagine having done anything differently. Booth had been about to murder the girl, and the idea of just standing there and watching it happen—

No.

No matter how things turned out, I was proud of what I'd done.

I'm sorry, Mom. Kiss Emmie for me.

Abruptly the lights flooding the parade grounds went out.

I blinked into the sudden darkness that was rendered even deeper by the cloudy night. Then my Undertaker training kicked in, and I didn't bother wondering what had happened. It was an opportunity, and I took it.

I had no idea if the Corpses were as blinded as I was, but I had no intention of waiting for my eyes—and theirs—to adjust.

Turning sharply left, I ran across the width of the parade grounds. Some fifty feet to my right, I could hear the wall of Corpses collapsing into chaos as the walking dead all jostled each other in the confusing blackness. Moving as quickly and quietly as possible, I skirted the main force of their numbers before cutting in and hurrying toward where I hoped the platform waited.

I reached it seconds later, almost running into it in the dark. Hastily I climbed up onto it and squinted into the surrounding black, desperately trying to spot Booth and Amy. For several agonizing moments, I couldn't see them.

Then the Corpse himself came to my aid, calling out into the crowd, "Spread out! Cover the exits! Don't let him escape again!"

There! Ten feet away—a tall silhouette clutching a smaller one. I could just hear the terrified girl's sobs.

Silently I drew closer. Booth's head was turning this way and that, scanning the darkness.

I'm right here, Deader! Just give me a few more seconds.

I considered using Tom's Taser to drop the monster but worried that its light would alert the others. No, the gun would be better—although first I needed a diversion.

Turning, I fired three quick bursts of saltwater out into the crowd of Corpses below the platform. Within moments the air was flooded with groans of helpless outrage. I heard bodies collide and crash down to grassy floor of the parade grounds.

Nearby, Booth stiffened.

He knows I'm here. But he's too late.

Smiling in the darkness, I changed my aim and fired again.

Now it was Kenny Booth's turn to groan.

The Corpse staggered away, his arms out in front of him like a sleepwalker, looking for all the world like the zombie I knew I wasn't supposed to call him. He wandered toward the edge of the platform, and as I watched, did a clumsy sideways tumble off it. It occurred to me, with satisfaction, that the mud down there would ruin his fancy suit.

I ran to Amy's side.

Injured and terrified, she jumped when I took her hand.

"It's me—Will," I whispered. "Come on."

"Wh-what?" she stammered.

My eyes had mostly adjusted to the darkness, and I could easily see her grimy, tear-soaked face now that I was closer. She evidently recognized me too because she started to say something. I clamped my hand over her mouth. "Shut up, and stay close!"

Amy nodded fearfully.

I led her to the rear end of the platform, and once there, I helped her down onto the grass. Then, using the big, blocky silhouettes of the fort's half-dozen buildings as landmarks, I navigated the darkness, making my way back toward the commandant's house.

I was halfway there when the lights came back on.

I felt my heart leap into my throat. One moment, Amy

and I were moving like ghosts through nice, shielding darkness, and the next, we were pinned by dazzling light.

Amy screamed, squeezing my hand so hard that my knuckles went white.

Dozens of walking cadavers surrounded us, littering the path of our escape route. Once again, all their heads turned in my direction.

This time, however, they didn't come at me slowly.

This time they charged.

I pulled Amy toward the only gap I could see in the Corpses' ranks. One of the cadavers, a female, lunged at me, and I fired into her face, driving her back. Another approached from my left, and I whirled and sprayed salt-water at that one too. The Corpse fell away just as the last of my ammunition dribbled from the pistol's plastic barrel.

Fighting panic, I dropped the gun and fished out Tom's pocketknife, releasing its Taser.

But in my heart, I knew it was hopeless. There were too many of them, and they were everywhere. In seconds a dozen Corpses would descend on us, and it would all be over.

Then something small, round, and blue whizzed over my head.

It struck the nearest Corpse full in the face and exploded, stopping him in his tracks and dropping him to the grass, where he spasmed like an upended turtle. Before I could really grasp what was happening, another of the *somethings* caught a second Corpse in the chest, sending it staggering spastically off in a new direction. Then another. And another. Within moments the sky will filled with colored orbs, each about the size of my fist.

Water balloons.

I nearly laughed out loud.

There had to be dozens of the things raining chaos down on the hoard of walking dead, transforming them into a panicked mob.

Still clutching Amy's hand, I spun around.

Angels lined the west wall battlements. Each was armed with a funny-looking slingshot, and each had a huge sack a small water balloons hanging from his or her belt. As I watched, they methodically hooked balloons into their slingshots' leather pouches, took aim, and fired. In this manner, working as one, the ten of them were each able to launch perhaps a dozen projectiles per minute into the night air!

Sharyn's eyes found mine, and for once she didn't smile. Instead she paused in her firing routine just long enough to quickly gesture Amy and me toward them.

I nodded. Then I looked back toward the commandant's house for Dave and Helene. At first I spotted neither one, but then Helene came rushing around the corner, her pistol at the ready. She shot first one Corpse and then another before giving me a heroic wave.

Grinning with relief, I waved back—

—only to watch in horror as a Corpse caught her from behind.

Helene screamed and thrashed, but the dead man knocked her gun away. Then, his milky eyes triumphant, he clamped one slick, decaying hand over her mouth and yanked her savagely back into the shadows.

Screaming, I shook free of Amy and started forward.

Another Corpse appeared in front of me. This one was flailing wildly, blinded by one of the water balloons, and completely unaware of my presence. Nevertheless, as I tried to get around him, he changed direction suddenly—and with the thoughtless power of a hurricane, he body-slammed me. The blow was both accidental and incredibly powerful. I felt my feet leave the grass, saw the darkened sky tumble past me, and then heard a terrible *thump!* as my head hit a rock.

I tried to get up, but my arms and legs wouldn't cooperate.

Helene! I called silently.

And then everything went black.

CHAPTER 36

ANGEL

William?"

I opened my eyes. I was lying on a cot under a thin blanket. My head ached. My shoulders and arms ached. My legs and chest ached. In fact, it felt like my hair ached.

But the worst was the light. It was dazzling—utterly blinding, as if the Corpses had decided to torture me by strapping me right up against one of those huge parade ground lamps.

"William?"

Definitely not a Corpse. Their voices didn't sound so sweet—almost musical. Mom's did. I could definitely remember my mother sometimes sounding like that.

But of course it couldn't be my mom. She was part of another time. Another life.

"William?"

Slowly my bleary gaze settled on the woman who was

leaning over me. She was pretty and fair-skinned, with a thick mane of blond hair. It seemed to fill the air around her with its luminescence.

Kind of like a halo.

The woman smiled the single-most beautiful smile I'd ever seen. "There we are." Her voice had an odd, echoing quality, as if she were far down a tunnel. But she was so close!

"Who—?" I began, but she put a finger to my lips.

"Shhh. Don't speak, William. Not yet. You've been rather badly hurt."

No kidding.

I tried to remember. There'd been this blinded Corpse. It had plowed into me. Jeez, it had been like getting hit by a truck.

"I don't have much time, William. So just listen. I knew your father. I once gave him something of great value that he then presented to Tom Jefferson. I think you can guess what it was."

The pocketknife. Had to be. So this woman had given my dad that strange gadget? Who was she? I tried to voice these questions, but her finger stayed on my lips—gently but firmly silencing me.

"Don't speak. Before I go, you'll have the chance to ask one question—just one. So I want you to think about it before you ask. But don't ask yet. For now, just listen to me. Will you do that?"

I nodded, suddenly understanding that all this light was coming from *her*—from this strange woman. I supposed I should be afraid, but I wasn't. Instead I felt perfectly calm. And I experienced another feeling too—one that I hadn't felt in a long time. Not since I'd been a little kid. Not since—well…

Not since I'd believed in Santa Claus.

"William, you have a destiny. You think you know what it is, but you don't. You think it's all about fighting the *Malum*—the Corpses—but it's more than that. Much more. This battle is just the beginning. But that doesn't mean it isn't important. It's very important because everything that will come later—all the rest of your destiny—depends on it. You need to remember that, William. You and your fellow Undertakers—you *must* win."

I realized that I was probably dreaming—that I was likely still lying on the Fort Mifflin parade ground, waiting for some Corpse to stomp me dead. Or maybe I *was* dead, and this angel had come to take me to Heaven. But then why would she be telling me about my destiny? What destiny could I have if I was dead?

Hey, that could be my one question: *Am I dead?* No. That was stupid.

"I have to go now. But before I do, I will leave you something. It'll be here." Her hand slipped briefly under my pillow. "When you wake up, you will find it. Use it, William. Use it well."

She smiled again. "And now you may ask your question. One question, William, and I will answer it. It's not *my* rule. It's merely *the* rule. So think carefully before you ask it."

Even after her finger left my lips, I stayed quiet, considering. A thousand questions churned like a whirlwind inside my throbbing skull. They all seemed important. How was I supposed to choose? One question? That wasn't fair!

But then, quite abruptly, a single question pushed the rest away. I felt almost guilty for having hesitated.

Swallowing, I whispered, "Is...Helene dead?"

The golden woman—for that was how I'd started thinking of her—seemed pleased, as if I'd passed some test. For a long moment, she didn't answer but merely gazed at me with an expression that once again reminded me vaguely of my mom.

"No, she isn't. But she's in terrible danger, William. She's being held prisoner at Kenny Booth's home in Roxborough."

The words seemed to charge through me, driving away my aches and pains and filling my limbs with fresh energy. Helene was alive! But what about Dave? Amy? The Angels? I tried to say something more, but the woman shushed me.

"I'm leaving now, William. Don't worry though—we'll see each other again."

"When?" I asked, fairly spitting out the word.

But she was already gone.

CHAPTER 37

RECRIMINATIONS

Will?"

I opened my eyes.

Another woman hovered over me, younger than the one before. This one wasn't blond or fair-skinned—but at least she was familiar.

"Good," someone else said. "He's awake."

Sharyn managed a weak smile. "Yeah. How you feeling?"

I uttered a painful croak. "Helene?"

Sharyn's slight smile faded completely. She glanced up at Ian MacDonald, Haven's makeshift doctor.

"Will," Sharyn replied gently, "there ain't no easy way to say this. Helene's dead."

I shook my head. "Uh-uh. She's alive, and I know where they're keeping her."

The girl's expression went strangely blank. She and Ian shared a worried look.

They don't believe me. They think I hit my head too hard or something.

"Hey, really!" I insisted. "Booth's got her at his house up in Roxborough!"

"Roxborough," Sharyn repeated. Then hesitantly she said, "Red—I saw that Corpse grab her. Then I saw you go down. We had to move to get you before the Corpses did—ended up shooting our way out of there and boosting a Deader's car so we could bring you back here, with you being knocked out and all. You ain't talked to nobody since then. So how do you know this?"

I frowned. What could I tell her? Sharyn clearly figured I was delusional already. What would she think if I started describing a golden woman with shining hair?

"What about Dave and Amy?" I asked.

"Dave got tagged by a Corpse," Ian said. "Broke his collarbone. But he'll be fine."

"And Amy's safe," Sharyn added. "Pretty freaked out though. I don't like even thinking about what the Corpses done to her."

I nodded miserably, wracked by conflicting emotions. Last night I'd gone out without permission and rescued Amy. I couldn't help but be proud of that accomplishment.

But had it be worth Helene's loss?

"How bad am I hurt?" I asked Ian.

The boy sighed. "You probably have a minor concussion. And of course, your right arm is broken."

I blinked. "It is?" I looked down at the limb, which lay across my chest atop the thin blanket. It was bent at the elbow and held rigid with splints. I wiggled my fingers experimentally. "It doesn't hurt."

Ian scratched his head. "That's good, I guess. We don't have an X-ray, so I can't tell how bad the break is. All I could do is set it and hope for the best. Still, I haven't given you any pain pills, so you should be, well, hurting pretty bad right now."

"I'm not," I insisted. "In fact, I feel fine." I started to sit up, but Sharyn pushed me firmly back down.

"Chill, Red! You ain't going no place."

"Sharyn," I said, trying to control my frustration, "I'm telling you, Helene's alive! Booth's got her at his house. We can get her back!"

Sharyn replied gently, "Maybe we can and maybe we can't. But *you* sure can't. Not with no broken arm."

"I—don't think my arm's broken," I said, twisting it back and forth inside its stiff wrapping. "I don't feel anything wrong with it."

"Um, shock can do that," Ian suggested.

"I'm not in shock!" I exclaimed. Again the two of them shared a worried look. I felt like exploding. "I'm fine! Now, we've got to go get Helene!"

Then a third voice said—quiet but as hard as stone—"No, we don't."

Tom filled the Infirmary's curtained threshold, his expression grim and his eyes fixed on me. "Sharyn, Ian, give us this room."

Sharyn looked like she was about to say something but changed her mind at the last second. Reaching over, she gave my good shoulder a friendly squeeze. Then she wordlessly followed Ian out.

Tom waited until they were gone. Then he approached and said, his tone cold, "How you feeling?"

"Okay," I replied. Actually, I was suddenly nauseous.

"Dave's got a broken collarbone."

"Ian told me."

The Chief nodded. "He'll be out of action for at least a month. Now, there ain't no way to really set a broken collarbone. So he's just got to carry his right arm in a sling to keep from stressing the fracture. We can only hope it'll heal straight."

I bit my lip but said nothing.

He reached the foot of the bed. "And then there's Helene."

"Tom, she's not—" I began, but he gestured for silence.

"Do you know what keeps Haven running, Will?"

"Huh?"

"Haven. The Undertakers. All of this. You know what keeps it running?"

At first I didn't know how to reply. Then I did.

"Loyalty?" I asked, my stomach churning.

"That's one word for it. 'Nother might be *discipline*. 'Nother might be *duty*. In the two years that I've been Chief, ain't no one ever done what you did last night. No one. Truth is, we ain't really got no rules or regs for this. I mean, there's no brig or a jail or nothing like that. And it ain't like we can just kick you out onto the street. Not with the Corpses wanting you so bad."

All of a sudden, I felt like crying. I fought it—hard.

"So," Tom continued, "what're we going to do with you? I suppose I could get the Monkeys to build a cell and then lock you up in it. But then I'd just need to assign somebody to feed you and take you to the bathroom. Besides, half the kids think what you pulled last night was courageous—my sister's one of them. They'd probably freak if I locked you in some cage. So—I'm stuck, ain't I?"

"Tom," I began. "I...I'm sorry."

He studied me. "Are you?"

With an effort I met his eyes. "No," I admitted finally. "I'm not."

"Didn't think so." Tom shook his head. "Thing is, this is the kind of crap your dad might've pulled—the kind of crap that got him killed. The difference is that Karl didn't take orders from me. *I* took orders from *him*, so I couldn't say nothing when he went off on his personal crusades."

I risked sitting up. It proved easier that I thought it would be. The sling on my arm seemed more of a nuisance than anything else. "Tom…" I said hesitantly, "don't punish Dave. All he did was go along with what I wanted to do."

"And what exactly *did* you want to do, Will?" Tom asked evenly.

I flushed. "I wanted to find out what Booth was up to at the fort."

Tom nodded. "But what made you figure I didn't want the same thing?"

"You wouldn't even go into the fort!" I snapped. "You were gonna just stay outside and watch who went in!"

"And so you decided it'd be better to sneak inside for a real close peek?"

"Look, I know it was risky! And I know that Dave got hurt and Helene got caught because of it. But we had to hear what was going on! I mean, how can we fight the Corpses if we don't even know what they're up to?"

Reaching into his pocket, Tom extracted a flat stone about the size of a quarter. He tossed it to me. I caught it left-handed and then looked at it in surprise. It didn't have much weight. It wasn't even a real stone. It seemed to be made of Styrofoam painted granite gray. "What's this?" I asked.

"A wireless short-range transmitter," he explained. "Steve whips them up for us. Last night after the Angels arrived at Mifflin, Sharyn used her slingshot to fire a bunch of them over the wall and onto the parade grounds. They're heavy enough to travel but light enough and soft enough to make no noise when they land. The Corpses never knew a thing—they were a few more rocks among thousands. But using them, we managed to hear every word of Booth's pretty little speech."

I blanched. I suddenly recalled the strange project that Steve had been working on in the Brain Factory yesterday while Dave and I had been making our plans.

Tom continued, "How'd you think we knew when to show up and save your sorry butt? From the second that Sharyn heard you charge into the middle of that nasty blood oath ritual of theirs, she tagged your voice and came running. If she hadn't, then all three of you—four, including Amy—would be dead."

I gulped. "I…didn't know about this."

"No, you didn't. But then it didn't occur to me that I was supposed to tell *you* everything. Of course, I wasn't figuring on your little stunt last night." Tom sat down on the edge of the cot and held out his hand.

Feeling oddly small, I returned the stone. "Was it Sharyn who shut off the parade ground lights?"

"Nope. Helene. According to Dave, after you took off—ready to go toe to toe with a few hundred Corpses while armed with one little water pistol—Helene split in another direction. Seems she figured out that the lights they were using all plugged into the same portable generator. So while you was playing hero, she slipped around to the generator and shut it off."

"Smart move," I remarked.

"Undertaker training. She'd have made a great Angel. Before long, though, the Corpses clued in and turned the power back on."

"Yeah." After a long moment, I added, "I—just couldn't let them kill Amy."

"I know."

"You wouldn't have done anything different."

Tom scowled. "Will, I'd have done *everything* different."

I scowled right back, "So—what? You'd have let Amy die?"

Tom slowly, reluctantly nodded.

"I don't believe you!" I exclaimed.

"Don't judge me too quick, Will. This is war—and wars have casualties. Before you go around patting yourself on the back for saving that poor girl, 'member that Helene's dead because of what you pulled."

"But she's alive! Booth's got her at his house up in Roxborough!"

For the first time, he faltered. "How d'you know that?"

"Because a—" I caught myself. *Because a golden woman told me in a dream?* "Well, it's just a feeling—but a strong one."

Tom's expression made no bones about his opinion of my *feeling*.

"Do you know what's going down in the Big Room right now?" the Chief asked.

I shook my head.

"Packing. Everything's getting boxed up and loaded into vans."

"Vans? Like back at First Stop?"

"Actually we keep a half-dozen big white vans around for emergencies. We're rich, remember? Bought them used and park them in a month-to-month garage down the block. A few of us—Sharon and me included—know how to drive. Even had Elisha hack into the DMV databases and whipped us all up some nice licenses. Fake names and addresses, of course."

I asked, "But why are you packing at all?"

For the first time, I hear real anger behind Tom's words. "Thanks to your stunt, the Corpses got Helene, and she knows Haven's location. By now, chances are they've wormed that info out of her and then likely killed her. The Corpses don't keep prisoners alive for no good reason—believe me."

"That's what you said about Amy," I protested. "And they kept *her* alive!"

"Booth wanted to use her as a sacrifice," Tom replied flatly. "A little bit of showmanship in front of his Deader flunkies. But last night's Corpse lovefest is over. He won't have any use for Helene."

"You *don't* know that!" I pressed.

"Then let's talk about what I *do* know. I know that now, after three years, the Corpses got our location. So we need to be gone before sundown. I don't figure they'll risk a major attack during daylight hours. We have to abandon Haven, Will."

It was like being hit in the chest with a sledgehammer. "It's my fault."

"Yeah, it is."

"But—where will you go?" I couldn't bring myself to say *we*—not anymore.

"I've had a place lined up for more than a year now. Nobody knows about it but me and Sharyn. The trick'll be keeping the Corpses from tracking the vans. They must be watching the building by now. But we got ways around that."

I stammered, "Tom...I..."

The Chief gave me a hard look. "Sorry now, Will? Now that you see the real damage you've done?"

I squeezed my eyes shut. "Leave me here."

"What?"

"When you go tonight, leave me behind."

"Don't turn martyr on me. It's stupid."

"I mean it! It's my fault! I've messed up everything! You should just leave me here!"

For a long moment, Tom didn't reply. I waited, my shut eyes flooding with tears.

Finally, and to my horror, the Chief of the Undertakers said quietly, thoughtfully, "I should."

In the heartbeat that followed, I found myself wondering where I would go and how I would survive alone.

Then Tom added, "But how would I feel the next time I visited Karl's shrine, knowing that I handed his only son over to the Corpses?"

I waited.

"When we go," Tom said, "you're coming with us."

It took all my courage to open my eyes—and when I did, I still couldn't see past the wash of tears. When at last my vision cleared, the expression on Tom's face had softened. The coldness was gone, replaced by a deep sorrow.

I hurt him.

And that knowledge dug more deeply into my conscience than I'd ever have imagined.

"Thanks," I muttered, the words coming out in a pathetic squeak.

Tom nodded. "I'd better let you rest."

"I don't want rest," I insisted. "I'm fine. I wanna see Dave and Amy."

He considered it. "Your call. Dave's laid up in the boys' dorm. Amy's next door in the girls'."

"Okay," I said.

Tom rose and walked to the door. He looked somehow smaller than he had the other day when he'd addressed the full gathering of the Undertakers. His shoulders were slumped, and his head had lowered.

I did that to him, I thought, and in that moment, I hated myself.

"Catch you later," Tom said.

"Yeah," I replied.

And then I was alone in the Infirmary.

CHAPTER 38

THE GIFT

I lay back on the bed, feeling utterly miserable.

My solo war against Booth had gotten one friend hurt and possibly killed another. It had also alienated Tom and forced the Undertakers to abandon their headquarters.

On the other hand, I *had* rescued Amy.

But no, I hadn't even done that, had I? I'd *tried* to rescue her but had only ended up getting myself knocked unconscious. In truth it was Sharyn and the Angels who'd saved Amy.

Guilt warred with sadness, grief with regret, until I wasn't sure what I was feeling.

Worst of all, Helene was in trouble, but nobody even believed she was alive. And I was stuck in this Infirmary with a broken arm.

I wiggled my fingers again.

Except it didn't *feel* broken.

I strained against the splints, turning my wrist experimentally. Nothing. No pain at all.

Frowning, I examined the wrapping. It was just an elastic bandage. I'd worn one like it back when I'd hurt my knee playing soccer. That one had been secured with a little silver clip. This one was simply knotted.

Once again, acting more from gut instinct than reason, I worked at the knot until it came free. The stretched bandage loosened immediately, whipping around my arm so fast that it actually slapped me in the face. Then two wooden sticks—paint stirrers, I saw—tumbled to the blanket.

I extended my elbow, ready for a shock of pain.

Nope.

If my arm really was broken, then it was a funny kind of broken!

I sat up on the cot, waiting for my head to throb. It didn't. I waited to feel dizzy or nauseated. Again, nothing. I felt fine—better than fine. Energetic.

I remembered the golden woman.

Did she…heal me?

It was a crazy idea, but what other explanation was there? Of course, in order to heal me, she'd *have* to be real. But how could I know for sure one way or the other?

Quite suddenly I recalled the gift she'd given me, and I looked excitedly down at my pillow. Could there really be something under there? Only one way to find out. I reached one hand under the thin foam cushion and felt around.

Nothing.

Then—something.

I pulled it out.

A pocketknife.

I gasped.

It wasn't Tom's. For one thing, this one was gold instead of silver and had eight buttons instead of six. For another thing, Tom's pocketknife lay in a cardboard box under my cot, along with my shoes and backpack. Apparently the Chief hadn't been angry enough to demand it back.

Not that I needed it anymore. It seemed that I now had one of my own.

But what kind of angel goes around handing out pocketknives?

I tapped the *1* button. There was the familiar lock pick. The *2* button was my old friend, the Taser. I tapped the *3* button. Out sprang a balanced throwing blade, just like on Tom's knife. Then the *4* button. Again, just like the other knife: a screwdriver. The *5* button too. Pressing *6* produced the flashlight.

That left the two new buttons.

Hope neither of these turns the knife into a hand grenade!

Feeling both excited and a little foolish, I tapped the *7* button. A little cylinder about the size of a quarter popped out one end. I studied it, frowning, then pulled it close to one eye, closing the other.

It was a telescope.

How it worked was beyond me. But there was no denying that it worked extremely well. There was a dial on the side of the cylinder, and when I rolled it, the magnification increased. At its highest, I could clearly spot the cobwebs that laced the ceiling of the Big Room, high overhead.

Cool!

I tapped *7* again, and the cylinder retracted.

Then I looked at the *8* button.

What's the worst that could happen?

I pushed it.

The lights went out.

Uh-oh.

I sat in breathless silence as, beyond the Infirmary's walls, kids exploded into cries of alarm. Somebody called out fearfully, "Is it them? Is it them?" Then after half a chaotic minute, Tom's strong voice boomed out—calm but urgent—"Listen up! I want Angels on the roof and in the tunnel! Gear up for combat! Everyone else, stand clear! Invasion regs are in immediate effect!"

Further commotion followed. Something crashed loudly to the concrete floor. This was followed by additional shouts and then footfalls—a stampede of them.

I wondered if I should say something to someone.

Um—I think I did this.

Yeah, right. Like I wasn't in enough trouble already.

Instead I simply sat there, listening to Haven mobilize for what they all thought was an impending attack.

Long minutes passed. I half-expected someone to check on me. No one did. Tom probably figured that I was safer where I was—safer and out of the way. He was right, of course.

I betrayed him.

The knowledge was like a weight around my neck.

I'd meant it when I'd told Tom I was sorry. I hadn't realized how important his trust had been to me until I'd lost it. The look on the Chief's face when he'd left the Infirmary had felt like a punch in the stomach.

But if I had to do it over again, would I do things differently?

No way.

I ran my fingers over the pocketknife's smooth surface and stared blindly into the surrounding darkness.

Helene was alive. This pocketknife proved it. How else could it have gotten under my pillow if the weird lady hadn't put it there? And if her visit was real, then her answer to my one question had to be real too.

Helene was being held captive in Kenny Booth's house in Roxborough.

And Tom's not going to do anything to help her because he thinks I'm nuts.

I could show him the pocketknife, tell him about the

golden woman and what she'd said. But given my bad rep right now, what were the chances that I'd be believed? As things now stood, Tom would never accept anything that I told him, regardless of the evidence. Even if I did present the Chief with the angel's pocketknife, Tom would probably confiscate it for study and send me back to Ian for some aspirin or something.

Suddenly I knew two things. The first was that if anyone was going to save Helene, it would have to be me. The second was that whatever I did, I'd have to do it alone.

I'm not going to betray him again—not ever. This time the only person I'll risk is myself!

Then, almost desperately, I thought, *If I can find Helene and bring her back, maybe he'll forgive me.*

Finally after what felt like an hour but was probably more like ten or fifteen minutes, Tom's voice spoke out loudly again. "Stand down, Undertakers! Looks like it's just a power failure! The fuses somehow blew! Sharyn, keep the defenses up, just in case. But the rest of you, chill. We're cool! The light'll be back on any—"

And just like that, they were.

"There you go," Tom said, laughing with what sounded like genuine relief.

I scared the crap out of everybody.

I looked down at button *8*, marveling at it. I remembered a time when I'd been a little kid and my father had taken me down to the Manayunk Canal. A fish had jumped out of the brown murky water, momentarily glistening in the midmorning sun. It had been there for only a split-second, but I remembered gasping at the strange, almost otherworldly beauty of it.

I felt kind of like that now—awed by something new and beyond myself.

I wonder what they'd do if I turned off the lights again.

Despite everything, I nearly laughed.

And deep in my mind, a plan began to form.

CHAPTER 39

DAVE IN A SLING

I tried to make as little eye contact with anyone as possible on my way to the boys' dorm. Around me, the Big Room was a hive of activity, with kids packing up computers, telephones, printers, and other equipment. The illusionary curtain at Haven's entrance had been replaced with a wooden ramp, along which heavily laden hand trucks were being paraded.

The Undertakers were evacuating in a hurry.

Despite my best efforts, I couldn't help catching a few kids' expressions. Some were sympathetic. Others, like Alex Bobson, looked pretty nasty. No one spoke to me, which was just fine.

The Burgermeister sat on his bunk in the dorm, his injury preventing him from assisting with the move. He was alone, staring moodily into space when I walked in.

"Dude!" he exclaimed, instantly brightening. He climbed to his feet, a clumsy process given that one of his beefy arms hung in a sling.

"Hey," I said, whipping up a smile. "How's the collarbone?"

"No biggie. Hell, my grandma hits harder than those Corpses!" Dave couldn't quite match my grin. "But what's with you? Tom said you broke your arm."

I shrugged and waved with the "bad" hand. "Nope."

"That's cool."

"Yeah."

His face fell. "Helene's dead."

I said, "No, she's not."

"What?"

"She's alive. Booth's got her in his house up in Roxborough."

To my surprise Dave let out a great whoop of joy. "Yeah! All right! So when do we go get her?"

I said flatly. "We don't."

"What?" Dave asked again.

"Tom doesn't believe me."

"He doesn't? Why not?" Then, warily, "Dude—how do you *know* she's alive?"

"You wouldn't believe me either if I told you."

Dave's face clouded. "Will, um—you sure you're okay?"

I shrugged and changed the subject. "Listen, Burgermeister. I'm sorry."

Dave blinked. "What for?"

"For talking you into coming with me last night. For getting you hurt."

The Burgermeister laughed. "Dude, I was the one who talked *you* into letting *me* tag along, remember? Jeez! Last night was the first solid action I've seen since joining this screwy outfit! You got nothing to be sorry about!"

"Yeah, I do. Turns out the Angels had the whole fort wired for sound. They heard everything we heard. We might as well have stayed here."

"Yeah? Tell that to Amy."

I didn't bother pointing out that it had been the Angels who'd really saved Amy. Nor did I remind him that, yes, Amy was free but at the cost of Helene's safety.

Instead I simply said, "I'm gonna get her."

"Who? Amy?"

Despite myself, I laughed. "Helene!"

"Yeah? Are you?"

I nodded.

"Is Tom gonna let you?"

"I'm not gonna tell him. I'm not gonna tell anybody… except you."

The Burgermeister's eyes widened. "Dude, you're going to do it again?"

"I have to. She's alive, Dave. I can't leave her behind! I mean, she didn't leave me behind, did she—back at my school?"

"Hey, Will, you don't got to convince me! I'm behind you all the way. When do we leave?"

"Not *we*. This time, I go alone!"

Dave's face darkened. "No way! I'm going too!"

"It's really great that you want to," I replied, "but we both know you can't—not with that sling."

"Oh. Right." The Burgermeister dropped dejectedly down onto his cot. When he looked up, I was astonished to see tears in his eyes. "Dude, if you do this—they'll never let you back in."

"I know."

"You won't even know where to go—not once we make the move. Tom ain't told nobody where the new place is."

"I know that too."

"You'll be on your own."

"Not if I rescue Helene."

Dave considered that. "Yeah. I suppose that's true." Then, frowning, "So what is this—like, good-bye?"

"Guess so."

We silently studied each other, sharing the kind of moment that, two weeks ago, would have seemed awkward and embarrassing. Now, however, with all that had happened and all that would happen, it felt completely natural—

—and horribly sad.

Dave stuck out his free hand. "Good luck, Will. And take care of yourself."

I took the hand, feeling Dave's meaty paw completely envelop my own. It didn't matter. We were equals. We were peers. We were friends. "You too, Burgermeister." I smiled wanly. "See you around."

Dave's reply sounded strangely adult. "I hope so."

I checked the girls' dorm, but Amy wasn't there. Instead two girls I didn't know eyed me disdainfully before telling me that Nick Rooney had lured the former mole off to the kitchen for something to eat. I muttered a thank you and left.

I passed the skateboard track, where two boys were running the course, performing complex ollies and 180 backsides that, to my eye at least, looked pretty skillful. When they saw me, they both took a final half-pipe side by side and landed smoothly in my path, smiling and snatching up their boards. One of the boys was Chuck Binelli. The other was Burton Moscova, Steve's younger brother. Both were Angels.

"Hey, man!" Chuck said.

"Hey," I replied flatly. The last thing I wanted to do was trade small talk with anybody. "Um—shouldn't you guys be off filling up boxes or something?"

Chuck grinned. "We did our share. Then me and Burt told Sharyn we needed a break. She said okay, so long as we stick around in case of an alert."

"That was half an hour ago," Burt added, also smiling. "I think she forgot about us."

"Oh," I said. I hadn't thought Haven *had* any goof-offs. Finding out that it did was both a relief and a disappointment. After all, kids were kids.

Chuck's manner turned serious. "Look, we know it sucks about Helene—but we wanted you to know that what you did last night was pretty cool."

I shook my head. "I shouldn't have gone out without Tom's okay. It was stupid."

"Stupid?" echoed Burt. "I seem to remember you facing down a couple hundred Corpses with a single water pistol."

"I remember that too," Chuck added.

I shrugged.

"Pretty cool," Chuck repeated, smiling.

I supposed that all these compliments should cheer me up a little. They didn't. Instead I kept thinking about Helene—Helene in trouble.

"Thanks," I replied glumly.

Chuck leaned closer, lowering his voice. "Listen, Will. A few of the other Angels are thinking about staying behind after tonight's evac—standing up and fighting when the Corpses come."

I frowned. "You'd be killed!"

"Maybe," Burt replied firmly. "But it has to be better than running."

No wonder Tom's upset.

Have I destroyed the Undertakers?

I felt a sudden, desperate urge to run off and apologize to Tom and Sharyn.

And especially to my dad.

"Anyway," Chuck said, "we, uh—just wanted you to know that."

"Thanks," I said, halfheartedly.

Both boys nodded. Then Burt burst out, "Look, Will, we're not saying that we're actually going to hang back. We're not that dumb. But we're thinking about it! All this time, we've been about keeping low. Staying hidden. All defense. No offense. Know what I mean?"

Of course I did.

"Well, since you've been around, that's changed. More of us are getting less interested in playing it Tom's way—in *playing it safe*. We want to start really hitting back! And that's because of your example."

I frankly hated this idea but didn't know how to say so.

Feeling uncomfortable, I decided to try a change of subject. "So what happened with the lights a little while ago?"

Burt uttered a nervous little laugh. "That was messed up. At first Tom figured the Corpses had killed our power, especially after the roof spotters said that the outage hit every building for at least two blocks around. But then my brother checked the fuses. Turns out they were blown."

"Which ones?" I asked.

"All of them."

An odd chill danced up my spine. "What—um, what could do that?"

"Who knows? Steve replaced the fuses, and everything went back to normal—except all the other buildings were still out. My brother says that the only way that can happen is with some kind of freak power surge—or maybe an EMP."

"EMP?"

"*Electromagnetic pulse*," Chuck explained. "According to Steve, they can burn out pretty much any electrical device in their range."

"Oh," I said. "Um—do they happen a lot?"

Chuck laughed. "About as often as you get struck by lightning!"

Burt added, "Steve says the only things that can cause an EMP are really big electromagnets—the kind that only the U.S. Army's got—and nuclear explosions. And since we're all still here, looks like the explosion thing didn't happen."

"Oh," I said again. "So he thinks this was the army?"

"I don't know what my brother thinks," Burton replied with a shrug. "I rarely do."

An electromagnetic pulse? Was that what button *8* did on my new golden pocketknife? I couldn't imagine what possible good something like that could be.

But then abruptly I could.

I cleared my throat. "Well, I'm sure Steve'll figure it out."

"Of course!" said Burt at once. Beside him, Chuck looked less sure.

"In the meantime, though," I continued, "I, um, got to go."

"Yeah, everybody's busy," Chuck replied. "But, hey—about that thing we told you? Maybe if you, like, went with us to talk to Tom, we might get him to change his tactics or something."

"Maybe," I replied, faking a smile. "I'll think about it."

I hurried away, trying to ignore the enthusiastic thumbs-up that both guys gave me. I felt foolish, embarrassed, and horribly guilty.

CHAPTER 40

OUTCAST AMY

The cafeteria was empty except for Nick and Amy. The Mom Boss stood at one of the counters, dipping a pair of long tweezers into one of three small bowls. Amy stood beside him, smiling wanly, although there was bright, eager interest in her eyes.

As I approached, Nick lifted the tweezers out of the bowl, cupped his long-fingered hand under the girl's chin, and dropped the tweezers' sticky contents onto her ready tongue. Amy chewed, swallowed, and sighed.

"Told you," Nick said, grinning. "Nothing like candy to make you feel better!"

Amy smiled.

"Now how about some of the grape?" he suggested.

"Sure," she replied, nodding.

"Hey!" I said, announcing myself.

Neither kid looked particularly happy to see me.

Nick said flatly, "Oh—hey, Will."

Alongside him, Amy's face had suddenly paled. I offered her a smile. She looked away.

"Figured you guys'd be packing," I remarked, trying to sound friendly.

"Almost done," Nick replied, motioning toward a stack of boxes piled atop one of the cafeteria tables. "Amy was helping me. Then we kind of got sidetracked."

"Oh," I said.

"You want some candy-coated something?" he asked me.

"Candy-coated what?"

"Well..." The Mom Boss conducted a quick inventory. "We got peanuts, cashews, milk chocolate, and pretzels. Take your pick."

I looked down into the three bowls. Each contained a different-colored syrup heated over a separate hot plate. "How's this work?" I asked.

"Nothing to it," Nick replied. He gingerly picked up a chunk of chocolate with the tweezers and dipped it into the red bowl for a few seconds. "There!" he declared, removing the morsel and blowing gently on it. "Hold out your hand. Don't worry, this stuff cools fast."

"It's cherry," Amy offered shyly.

Shrugging, I let Nick drop the misshapen confection into my palm. I sniffed it and then popped it into my mouth. I vaguely recalled these homemade candies from my first day in Haven, but I hadn't tried them since. They were better than I remembered.

"Good," I said, still chewing.

"Yeah!" Nick remarked, grinning. "Try something else. The peanuts are my favorite."

"Not right now," I told him. "Actually I was kind of hoping I could talk to Amy for a minute." At the sound of her name, the girl went even paler.

Nick's usually pleasant face darkened. "Well, the thing is, Amy's kind of helping me right now."

"It won't take long," I pressed. "I promise."

"Don't you think she's been through enough, Will?"

"I'm not going to upset her."

"Why not? You've upset just about everybody else around here."

I was about to reply, but Amy beat him to it. "It's okay, Nick. I'll talk to him."

Nick looked at her, his expression softening. "You don't have to."

"Yeah, I do."

Scowling at me, the Mom Boss reluctantly nodded. "Then why don't you both grab that table over there? In the meantime, I'll finish coating these candies. We'll need them when we get to the new place—for morale."

He wants to keep an eye on us.

Sharyn had once described Nick as a *born nurturer*. I wasn't sure exactly what that meant, but there was no mistaking the pleasure the boy took in looking after the Undertakers' most struggling underdogs. Everybody in Haven knew that if you were unhappy or frightened, you could always count on big Nick to cheer you up.

Or try to.

If anybody fit that bill, it was Amy Filewicz.

After all, two Undertakers had died because of Amy's betrayal at First Stop. Brainwashed or not, I imagined that most of Haven's residents wanted nothing to do with her.

But Nick had taken her under his wing.

It was hard not to like a kid like that.

"Sure," I said. "Thanks, Nick."

I sat down beside Amy at the farthest table, feeling the Mom Boss's watchful eye on me. For a long uncomfortable moment, neither of us spoke.

Then Amy whispered, "You hate me."

I blinked. "What?"

She didn't repeat it.

"Amy, why would you say that?"

A single tear traced a lazy path down her cheek. "I tried—" She swallowed and then regrouped. "I tried to kill you."

I saw no point in pretending otherwise. "Yeah, I know."

Amy buried her face in her hands and cried. I awkwardly patted the girl's shoulder. Nick gave me a look of plain, undisguised loathing.

"It's okay," I muttered.

"No, it's not!" she told me miserably. "Everybody tries to pretend it's okay. But then I see the way they look at me when they don't know I'm watching. I hear some of them whispering when I walk by. They think I betrayed the Undertakers—and I did. They think I might still be working for the Corpses—but I'm not!"

"Everybody's freaked out over what happened last night," I told her gently. "I left Haven without permission to find out what Booth was up to. I've got to be honest: I didn't even know you'd be there. But that's how it all worked out. And in the middle of it, Helene got snatched by the Corpses. Some of the kids are blaming me. I think maybe the rest are blaming you."

"I killed Kyle," she said, her face ashen.

"But you couldn't help it. The Corpses were controlling you."

She shook her head vehemently. "It doesn't work like that! When they first caught me about a month ago, they took me to Kenny Booth's house. He's got this room in the basement where he keeps these—spider-like things, only they've got ten legs instead of eight. He told me not to be afraid and that his people had come to *help* Earth. He promised to put an end to war and disease and starvation. He promised to help all humanity. I guess that, scared as I was, I kind of wanted to believe him, even if he did look…"

"Dead?" I finished for her.

She nodded, still crying.

I could imagine Booth's oily charm taking advantage of this innocent girl's fears—his dead guy appearance notwithstanding.

But Corpses helping humanity? Not likely.

"Then he had his two servants grab me and make me lay face down on a table in that basement room. Mr. Booth took one of those spider-things and just dropped it on the small of my back. It started to...dig its way into me, burrowing right into my skin! It hurt! Oh, Will, you've got no idea how much it hurt!"

No, I don't. I shuddered. *But I can imagine.*

"After a while this funny kind of—I don't know, *calm* settled over me. Suddenly, everything that Mr. Booth had told me wasn't just believable. It made, like, perfect sense. I wanted to prove myself to him, wanted to do anything he asked me to do. And I told him so.

"He said they would teach me how to use special equipment that they had. Then I'd be asked to infiltrate a camp of rebels who were fighting against his people—against humanity. He said that he wanted to shut their camp down. So he arranged for his people to pretend to chase me into a part of the city where he knew the Undertakers would rescue me. They did, just as he'd planned, and they brought me to First Stop. The rest I guess you already know."

"Yeah," I replied. "Amy—what happened that last night?"

"They gave me this little cell phone. Mr. Booth warned me to only use it once—on the night before we were supposed to go to Haven. He was afraid that if I used it more than that, it might be detected. So I hid it in my sock and waited until Monday night. Then I snuck out of bed and went and called Mr. Booth.

"I told him that the next day we'd be going to Haven. But Mr. Booth wasn't interested in waiting until tomorrow. Instead he wanted to raid First Stop that night and capture—you."

"Me," I echoed, feeling sick to my stomach.

Amy nodded. "He didn't tell me why. He said you were dangerous—very dangerous—and that getting you was all of a sudden more important than finding Haven. That's when you showed up." The girl looked away, blinking against fresh tears. "I tried to...kill you...because I was afraid of you. I thought you were evil. I thought all the Undertakers were. Then when Kyle came in, I was so scared. I didn't even realize I'd grabbed the knife...."

"What happened after you ran out?" I asked, changing the subject.

"I went right to Mr. Booth, who was nearby in a police car. At first he pretended to be happy to see me. But when I told him that I'd tried to kill you, he got really mad and had me thrown in the trunk.

"After that I don't remember much. When we got back to Booth's house, the Corpses gave me a needle right here—

in the back of my neck. All of a sudden, my mind changed. I think whatever they gave me killed the spider-thing. I don't know for sure. All I *do* know is that I remembered what I did to you and the rest of the Undertakers, and I felt—well, just awful."

More sobbing. I wondered if I should hug her or something. I didn't have a lot of experience hugging girls, and doing so now seemed embarrassing and uncomfortable.

What would Tom do?

With a sigh I put my arm around the girl and let her head fall to my shoulder. There she cried, softly but deeply, for several minutes, soaking my shirt and clutching at me with her tiny hands.

"It's okay," I said. But we both knew it wasn't. Amy would face what she'd done over and over again in her dreams for the rest of her life.

And in that moment, I hated the Corpses more than ever before.

Booth especially.

Wiping her face, Amy pulled away, offering a small, grateful smile. "Anyway," she said, sniffling, "yesterday afternoon they drove me down to that fort and locked me in one of the buildings. Mr. Booth said even though I'd failed him, he had one more way in which I could help his people help humanity. I told him that I didn't want to help him do anything! That I hated him! But he only laughed and told me it didn't matter what I wanted. It never had. Then he left, and after a while, it got dark. I heard voices and then some Corpses came for me."

She looked up at me with doe eyes. "I knew they were going to kill me. But *you* saved me."

"No, I didn't," I replied. "I tried—but they'd have gotten us both if the Angels hadn't shown up."

"The Angels wouldn't have shown up if it wasn't for you. They would've let me die. If you hadn't stuck your neck out for me, that's what would've happened." Then in a shy voice, she added, "Thanks."

Feeling tongue-tied, I simply shrugged.

"I—I don't know what I can do to pay you back," Amy stammered.

"Maybe there *is* something you can do for me," I said.

"Sure," the girl replied, still sniffling.

"Tell me exactly where Kenny Booth lives."

CHAPTER 41

A FORCE OF ONE

I spent the afternoon quietly getting ready.

It wasn't easy. Everywhere I went, I drew stares—some friendly; some not. Many whispered nasty comments or made even nastier gestures. A few smiled or offered me thumbs-up signs and little winks, as if we shared some dark conspiracy.

Either way, the attention made sneaking around next to impossible.

Collecting the necessary supplies was the most difficult part. Most of the Brain Factory equipment was already packed. That meant waiting until the crew had gone to lunch and Steve finally took a bathroom break—that kid seemed to have a bladder the size of City Hall! When at last the Brain Boss left to take a whiz, I moved in and quickly rummaged through the boxes until I found what

I needed. Then I hurried off, leaving Steve and his crew none the wiser—hopefully.

Next came a trip to the kitchen, where—ironically enough—I had to wait for the Brains to *finish* their lunch. Finally alone in the roped-off area, I gathered up some supplies, which included a fistful of snacks and lemonade packets from the fridge. I stuffed it all into my backpack, along with the rest of my stolen gear.

The ramp was unguarded and crowded. Spotting an opportunity, I stepped up behind a girl I didn't know who was struggling with a crate of telephones and wiring. Wordlessly I grabbed one end of the crate and heaved right along with her. She repaid me with a tired smile. Together we hauled the load up the long, spiraling tunnel and out onto Green Street, where an unmarked white van stood waiting, already half-filled with Undertakers stuff.

Seeing it, I wondered vaguely if the Corpses were already watching the building, and if so, what would keep them from just following the truck to the new hideout.

But that was Tom's problem, not mine.

The nameless girl and I delivered our burden. Then with hasty thanks, she hurried back into Haven for more.

The only other kids outside were two Monkeys named Jonathan and Adam. They both eyed me distrustfully but said nothing as I smiled and strolled away.

With a relieved sigh, I turned the nearest corner, vanishing from sight. My plan was to walk up to Market Street and catch the 61 bus up Ridge Avenue and into the Roxborough section of the city. This would take me straight through Manayunk—a prospect I didn't relish. Being so close to home was a lure that I could've done without.

Still, if I wanted to reach Helene, there was simply no other way.

"Hey, Red!"

I spun around, almost leaping out of my shoes. A figure emerged from the shadowy alley that ran directly behind Haven. Instinctively I drew my water pistol.

"Yo!" Sharyn cried in mock alarm. "Watch where you're pointing that thing! You might muss up my hair!"

My shock ebbed. I lowered the gun and said nothing.

"Out for another stroll?" she asked.

I still didn't respond. I felt heartsick and defeated.

"That backpack sure looks heavy," the dreadlocked girl observed. "Got a lot in it, huh?"

I shrugged.

Sharyn leaned casually back against Haven's brick rear wall. "Word is that your arm ain't busted after all. It's got Ian all in a tizzy. He can't figure it."

For the first time, I spoke. "Well, it's not like he's a real doctor."

"Straight up. But he's the closest thing we've got to one, and he ain't usually wrong about stuff like this. Anyways, I saw you myself last night, right after that Corpse knocked you flying. Your arm was broke. I'd bet a year's pay on it—that is, if I got paid anything." She laughed her musical laugh.

I shrugged again.

"Not feeling too talkie now, huh?" Sharyn remarked. "Your first day all over again, ain't it? After everything that went down last night, I guess you're pretty freaked."

"Yeah," I replied.

Sharyn nodded sympathetically. Her smile faded. "Will—do you really figure Helene's alive?"

I nodded.

"So now you're off to rescue her. That right?"

I swallowed. Then I nodded again.

"So you're gonna—what? March into Booth's crib, trash the bad guys, grab the damsel in distress, and just split?"

I faltered. "I—guess so."

Sharyn chuckled. "If Helene ever found out you was thinking of her as a damsel in distress, she'd kick your butt!" Then more soberly, she added, "And you're planning on doing this all by yourself?"

"I'm not risking anybody else," I told her defiantly. "Not this time."

She studied me. "So let's just say, for saying's sake, that Helene *is* still breathin', which ain't likely, and that you're gonna boost her all on your own—which ain't likely even more. She'll be guarded. You figure on taking on the world with a water pistol for the second time in two days?"

"I've got another one in my backpack," I said defensively.

"Oh—so it's *two* water pistols against the world?"

I didn't reply.

Sharyn laughed. "You're your old man's son. No doubt about that!"

She stepped toward me.

"Wait a minute!" I protested.

She paused in mid-step.

I struggled to find the right words. "Look, Sharyn, we both know that if you want to stop me, you can. It's just that—"

"Who said I wanted to stop you, Red?" she asked.

I stared at her, uncomprehending.

She sighed. "Will, I love my bro. Tom's more'n just a cool dude—he's a great man. After your dad died, he kept this place running with nothing but guts and brains. In fact, until you came along, I would've said there wasn't anything that could challenge his leadership around here."

"I'm sorry about that," I said at once. "I didn't mean to—"

She cut me off. "But that don't mean I always agree with him. See, Tom's all about organization, security, and defense. I ain't never been too good at just sitting back and waiting for my problems to come at me, dig? So we knock heads a lot. I've been saying for years that we ought to start laying some serious fight on the Deaders. But he's always figured we ain't ready yet. And in the end, I always go along because—well, he's Chief, and I wouldn't trade him for nothing or nobody. None of us would. Tom Jefferson *is* the Undertakers."

She looked at me, her expression complex.

"Truth is, you and me think the same. Neither of us is like Tom. We can't turn our backs on what we feel just because it's *best for everybody*. Tom won't order nobody to go after Helene, won't risk another life for a girl who's probably already iced. He'd go himself, of course. I know he wants to—pretty bad. But he ain't going to do that neither. You know why that is?"

I shook my head.

"Because my brother puts Haven ahead of everything else. Sometimes it half-kills him, but he does it anyhow—just because it's the right thing for him to do. He won't go running off to boost Helene because he's needed here."

I said quietly, "I'm not."

Her eyebrows rose. "Will, if you was anybody else, I'd give you a quick chin tap and drag your sorry butt right back inside. But you ain't anybody else. Fact is, even though you're one of the youngest kids we got, I'd trust you with my life—and that ain't something I say easy. So I'll let you go, but that don't mean I can't up your odds a bit." Reaching back into the shadows of the alley, Sharyn produced a Super Soaker. "I want you to take this."

I took it. It wasn't a particularly big gun—it had maybe a pint of saltwater in its reservoir—and it seemed easy enough to carry and conceal under my coat.

When I looked back at Sharon, she wore an odd expression—and she was holding her sword in both her hands.

"And this," she said.

I looked from her to Vader and back again. "Sharyn...I can't—"

"Your dad gave this to me before he died," she said. "It's only right I should loan it to *you* now." She smiled a little nervously. "And get this, Will. That's what it is: a loan."

"I wouldn't know how to fight with it," I said, gazing at the sheathed short sword.

"Ain't so hard," she told me. "You swing that there sharp edge at Corpses."

I reached out and took the sword. It was heavier than the Soaker—but somehow it didn't *feel* heavy. There was a funny balance to the weapon, and when Sharyn showed me how to wear it across my back and under my jacket so that it didn't show, it fit so well that I could almost forget it was there.

Almost.

When this was done, Sharyn put her hands on my shoulders and said grimly. "You know everything that went down at First Stop was about snatching you."

"Yeah. I know."

"If you get yourself caught, you'll be giving Booth just what he wants most. You'll be making his day!"

"I know that too," I said.

"But you're going anyway, ain't you?"

I nodded. "I have to."

"For Helene?"

Another nod.

Sharyn sighed. "I wish I could go with you. Fact is, I *should* go with you. Helene's my friend too. But I can't. That kind of betrayal—coming from me—would kill him." We both knew who *him* was. "And that's a line I ain't never going to cross."

"I understand," I said. Then on impulse, I reached into my pocket, pulled out Tom's silver knife, and handed it to Sharyn. "Give that to Tom. Tell him that this time, I really *am* sorry."

"Ain't you gonna need this, Will?" Sharyn asked, accepting the pocketknife.

I thought of the other one that I was carrying and shook my head. "No, I don't think so."

Slowly the dreadlocked girl nodded. "Then you go get her, Red," Sharyn told me gravely. "And you bring both your sorry selves back safe."

"Where to?" I asked. "You'll all have abandoned Haven by then. How will we find you?"

Her grin returned. "Don't worry over it. *We'll* find *you*. But there's just one last thing before you go."

"What's that?"

She was on me so quickly that my mind barely registered it. One minute, we were standing on the sidewalk four feet apart, and the next, her arms were around me, pulling me into a fierce hug. Her body was warm and muscular, very athletic, and she smelled of soap. She kissed my cheek and whispered, "Mind your training—Undertaker."

Then she disappeared into the shadowy alley.

I stared after her, my cheek tingling and my face burning.

"I will," I said to nobody.

Then, armed with a backpack, a sword, and a Super Soaker, I continued up the street, feeling ready for whatever the rest of the day might throw at me.

After all, I was an Undertaker.

CHAPTER 42

BREAK-IN

Just after six o'clock, as night was about to fall over the Roxborough section of northwestern Philadelphia, I crouched in the bushes across the street from what had to be the biggest house in this part of town.

Kenny Booth lived here—news anchorman, celebrity, mayoral candidate, Corpse. And somewhere inside, he was holding Helene captive.

Big surprise: the place was guarded. In fact, I was watching the guards right now, peering through my new pocketknife's cool miniature telescope. Dressed like bankers, the dead guys grimly patrolled the manicured grounds surrounding Booth's three-story mansion. They carried no guns that I could see, and being Corpses, they probably wouldn't use them anyway.

Nevertheless, I needed to do this quietly.

The ride up here had tempted me. Really tempted me. I mean, it was *sneak-downstairs-on-the-night-before-Christmas* tempting, except not in a good way. The bus route had taken me up Ridge Avenue, right past my middle school. I was shocked to find my heart aching a little at the sight of it.

A month ago, I'd hated the place.

Now I longed for it.

Worse, my house had been just a few blocks away. I could have yanked the stop cord and run down there in less than ten minutes—all downhill. Close. So close that I could almost feel my mother's presence.

But I'd stayed on the bus.

Once again I pushed such thoughts away, needing to focus on the here and now. On Helene. On Booth. On how best to get in there.

There was probably a burglar alarm. Maybe motion sensors. Maybe even cameras. Without a plan, I wouldn't get ten feet inside the gates.

Fortunately, I *had* a plan.

Still hiding in the bushes, I lifted my gilded pocketknife, watching the way the glow from the streetlights danced along its facing side.

Use it well, the golden woman had told me.

I intended to.

Swallowing, I pressed the *8* button. I half-expected to feel something: a shock, a jolt, *something*. I didn't.

But every light within view winked out: the streetlamps and the lights in the windows in every nearby house. Even the cars traveling along this narrow side street rolled silently to a stop, their headlights dark, their drivers confused and alarmed.

EMP, I thought, marveling.

I popped out the telescope again and surveyed the grounds around Booth's house. To my surprise, I could see clearly—very clearly—although everything had a strange greenish cast.

This thing's got night vision!

Awesome!

Better still, there was now no sign of the guards. Perhaps they'd been called inside when the blackout hit. Whatever the reason for their disappearance, my chance had come.

Pocketing the knife, I quit the bushes and crossed the street, wearing Vader across my back and clutching Sharyn's Soaker in both hands. I stayed low and kept to the shadows. I'd be lying if I said I wasn't scared, but it was a fear that I could control—maybe even use. I was going into battle, and the fear would keep me sharp.

Cautiously I tapped the front gates with my fingertips. No alarm sounded. I gave them a firm tug, but they wouldn't budge. Then I saw that a thick black chain was laced through the bars and fastened with a big padlock.

Shouldering the Soaker, I pulled out my pocketknife.

I could use the lock pick—had, in fact, practiced with it a lot back at First Stop. But I had another idea. Tapping the *3* button, I watched the knife's five-inch blade pop into view.

Ain't much it won't cut, Tom had said.

Feeling a little foolish, I ran the blade against the lock's steel shank. I honestly didn't expect anything to come of this experiment, other than maybe a dull edge.

But the knife bit into the steel—deeply.

"Whoa," I whispered.

I started sawing.

Five strokes was all it took for the lock to pop open in my hands.

"Cool," I muttered as I freed the gates. Then I opened them, slipped through, and tossed the chain and padlock into a nearby hedge.

The grounds sloped upward for about a hundred feet before reaching the house. Thanks to the EMP, all the windows were dark. Hopefully Booth would need time to find and reset the popped fuses. Right now, light was my enemy.

I scanned the grounds one more time with my telescope. Nothing. Satisfied, I started silently up the hill, keeping to the shadows and avoiding the driveway.

Undertaker training.

The main entrance would be well-guarded. Fortunately I spotted another door along the north wall and headed for it, using the trees for cover. Once there, I paused, listening furiously for the slightest noise. There was nothing but the distant sound of traffic floating in from beyond the EMP's effective range.

I tentatively tried the knob.

Locked.

Crouching down, I slipped the pocketknife's pick into the keyhole and held down the *1* button. There was a faint whirring noise.

Ten seconds later, the door's bolt clicked free.

I gingerly pushed the door open and slipped into a dark, roomy kitchen that was thankfully deserted. Islands with high countertops offered good cover, and I used them, half-crouching and half-crawling over to an archway that led into a big formal dining room.

Here the floor was thickly carpeted, and I was able to cross the room in silence, watching out for chairs and other furniture. At the far end, I found another archway, bigger this time, that led into a foyer beside the front door.

It was very dark.

I stopped at the threshold, listening again. Faint voices. Deadspeak.

"*Fuses. Blown.*"

"*How? Why?*"

"*Unknown. Investigating.*"

"*Intruder?*"

"*Unknown. Security. Broken.*"

"*Girl?*"

"*Basement.*"

"*Keep. Guard. No. Two. Guards. No. Mistakes.*"

"*Obey.*"

So Helene was in the basement, apparently alive.

I swallowed back my relief. I hadn't found her yet.

Footfalls. I ducked behind the archway wall just as the door across the foyer opened. A Corpse emerged—a Type Three by the look of him. He seemed pissed as he shuffled wordlessly down the hall to his right.

Then moments later, out came Kenny Booth.

Still in Kyle's body.

I silently fumed.

He appeared to be waiting for something or thinking about something. In either case, he wasn't moving, and that was a problem.

I stayed put, crouching in the shadows, my legs turning to hot rubber.

A minute passed. Then two. Booth didn't budge, watchful but not alarmed. I concentrated on keeping still and breathing slowly—in and out, in and out—praying that my pounding heart wouldn't give me away.

From elsewhere in the house, I heard Deadspeak, the tone urgent. "*Come. Kitchen. Now.*"

Booth uttered a groan. Then he stalked off, the feet inside his expensive shoes making sickeningly squooshy sounds as he walked. I watched him disappear through a door at the end of the hall. Then I straightened up and silently stretched my stiff muscles.

I wondered where the basement door might be. In my own house, it was under the stairs. Booth's place was, of course, much larger, but the layout didn't seem all that different. Here was the foyer and front door, with a wide staircase that led to the second floor. With any luck, the correct door would be somewhere below those steps.

But first—

I crossed the foyer, careful about the noise I made, and checked out the door through which Booth had emerged. Unlocked. I slipped inside.

It was an office and pretty fancily decorated. The only other door looked like a small closet. The windows all had their drapes drawn so only a sliver of moonlight filtered through, splashing over the surface of a huge oak desk. Behind the desk sat a leather chair big enough to accommodate a shopping mall Santa Claus.

I rummaged through what I assumed was the private desk of the smartest and most powerful Corpse in Philly. But this wasn't just a random search. No, I was looking for something in particular, and it had to be here. It just had to be!

In the second right-hand drawer, it was.

I grinned.

Bingo.

CHAPTER 43

RESCUE

I'd no sooner finished doing what needed doing in Booth's drawer when the lights came back on.

A lamp on the desk suddenly flashed to life, blinding me. I reached out with my hand to shut it off, only to end up tipping it over. It rattled loudly to the desktop.

Cursing, I quickly righted it—but too late. Outside the office door came footsteps, followed by Deadspeak.

"*Noise. Here. Crash.*"

"*Open.*"

The second voice had been Booth's.

I raced across the room and into the closet, diving in amid an assortment of oversized trench coats and other outerwear. No sooner had I shut the closet when the hallway door burst open. Heavy footfalls filled the small room. I readied Sharyn's Super Soaker. Shooting my way out wasn't my first choice, but I'd do it if I had to.

Booth's voice: "*What? Noise! What?*"

"*Nothing. Empty.*"

"*Noise? Cause?*"

"*Unknown.*"

"*Search.*"

I steeled myself. This was bad. If I fired on these two, the noise they'd make might alert the whole house. I frowned, thinking furiously. If only the lights were still out!

Why can't they be?

Frantically I pulled out my gilded knife and held it up. Then I said a little prayer and pressed the *8* button.

The lights went out again.

I had to swallow back a triumphant cry.

"*Lights. Off. Fuses. Fixed.*"

"*Not. Fixed. Check.*"

"*Search?*"

"*Too. Dark. Later.*"

"*Obey.*"

More footfalls, these heading out of the room.

I waited until the only sound was my own drumming heart. Then I slipped out of the closet.

The hall door had been left standing open. Peeking carefully out into the foyer, I listened for the slightest noise. Nothing.

My Soaker at the ready, I made my way toward the rear of the house. I skirted the staircase, avoided a couple of small accent tables, and once almost tripped over a fancy

Oriental runner. I could only hope that I wasn't wrong about where the basement door should be.

I wasn't.

I found it roughly below where the staircase ended overhead. Cautiously I tried the knob. Unlocked. As quickly as I dared, I opened the door and stepped onto a small landing with a flight of wooden stairs descending into near-perfect blackness.

I headed down, mindful of every step. There were creaks, but they were pretty muffled, and by the time I reached the basement's bare concrete floor, I was fairly sure my presence had gone undetected.

There was light here, faint and some distance away. By its glow, I was able to get my bearings. The basement was roomy and looked a bit like a laboratory, filled with weird and frightening equipment. I recalled Amy's tale of being dragged down here and having had a spider of some kind dropped on her back.

I shuddered involuntarily.

Don't give into it. Use the fear, but don't let it control you.

Taking a slow, steadying breath, I inched toward the source of the light. It was a kerosene lamp sitting on the floor in front of a closed metal door that was flanked by two Corpses. Both Type Threes, they had the look of guards but inattentive ones. As I neared, I heard them talking to each other in nervous tones.

"*No. Like.*"

"*Agree.*"

"*No. Need. Us.*"

"*Agree.*"

"*Foolish. Job.*"

"*We. Obey.*"

"*Agree.*" This last word was uttered reluctantly. Neither of these guys wanted to be here, and standing in the dark as they were, guarding a metal door, who could blame them? Then I remembered what Booth had said about posting guards outside the *girl's* room.

It was time to relieve these two clowns of their posts.

Stepping into the light, I raised the Soaker. I tried to think of something clever to say—like they do in the movies—but I couldn't come up with anything.

So I just fired.

Sharyn's Super Soaker launched a stream of saltwater with the force and velocity of a major league fastball. It caught the first Corpse full in the mouth, driving him back into the concrete wall beside the door, where he stood twitching uncontrollably. The second started forward, his rotting fingers reaching for me. I nailed him in both eyes. The dead guy screamed and retreated, clawing at his face.

Then I dropped the Soaker and pulled Vader from its scabbard.

I'd never wielded a sword in my life before now—but this one felt oddly *right*. I gripped it with both hands, samurai-style, and taking a deep breath, leapt forward and swung it at the blind Corpse.

The blade seemed almost to sing through the air.

The Corpse's head came right off.

"Jeez!" I heard myself say.

But I didn't stop.

Instead I spun on my heel and slashed the other guy—the one twitching against the wall—right across his midsection. As always, there was no blood. This guy's blood was long gone. But the twitching pretty much stopped.

Then his body split in two at the waist. His top went one way and his bottom the other. The two halves flopped on the basement floor with gray, shapeless *stuff* awash in sticky, lumpy fluid spilling out of them.

Okay. That's gross.

Their cries had stopped, but I figured the ones they'd already made would be heard. I had to move fast.

The door was held closed by a heavy metal bar. I sheathed the sword and pulled on the bar with both hands. After several fevered tugs, I managed to first slide it off one of the brackets and then topple it clear of the other.

I yanked the door open, shining my pocketknife's flashlight into the small room beyond.

A frail-looking figure blinked up at me from one corner. Her clothes were torn, and there were cuts and bruises all over her bare arms.

"Helene?"

She cringed. I stepped inside.

She reached toward me, looking scared. "Will? Is... that you?"

I placed the light under my own chin, letting her see my face. "Sure, it's me," I said, annoyed at the way my voice cracked. "You didn't think I'd just leave you with these Deaders, did you?"

Unsteadily, Helene stood, her hand still reaching out toward me as if she were afraid that I might not be real, that her fingers might reach me and find nothing there but smoke and light. "Will?" she asked again, nervously, hopefully.

"It's me," I insisted. "I swear it is!"

"Are you...alone?"

"Just me," I replied, doing my best to smile.

Something in my tone seemed to convince her because she suddenly came forward and threw her arms around my neck, sobbing. Feeling awkward, I let the hug go on for a few precious seconds. Then I pulled away gently but firmly. "Come on. We don't have a lot of time."

I led her out of the room and past the four pieces of the two guards. Holding Helene's hand, I headed straight for the stairs—this time using my flashlight to guide the way.

Halfway there, the lights came on a second time.

"Oh, crap," I muttered.

Helene's hand tightened on mine.

"It's okay," I told her without looking back. "My gun's still got plenty of juice. I'm pretty sure we can—"

A slender arm coiled around my neck from behind. Before I could say another word, it dug into my windpipe, cutting off all air and sound.

Then a voice—sweetly familiar—whispered in my ear. "Yeah, I'm sure we could have."

I struggled, but Helene's grip was strong. I thought about using my Taser but gave up the idea immediately, remembering my hard lesson at First Stop: never zap somebody that you're in physical contact with. Instead I jammed my elbow backward, catching the girl in the ribs. She grunted in pain, and her grip around my neck slackened. Then I grabbed her elbow, twisted my head, and pushed upward—a move we'd learned in training.

I slipped free of Helene's grasp and spun around, facing her. "What are you doing?"

She didn't answer. She simply attacked, throwing a lightning punch at my face. I blocked it—but only just—and had to block another and then another, retreating all the while. The pocketknife fell from my grasp as Helene drove me backward, keeping me on the defensive. Then as we neared the stairs, she suddenly dropped into a crouch and swept out with her leg, catching me in the knees and sending me crashing to the floor.

I landed hard but immediately rolled, employing another First Stop technique to regain my feet. I spun around just in time to dodge another punch.

I let her fist sail past me, sidestepped her, and hooked

one leg behind her knees. With a hard shove, I pushed her to the floor. Then I lunged for my pocketknife.

I'd nearly reached it when Helene caught my ankle, tripping me and sending me crashing down. She scrambled on top of me, small but strong, cursing and pulling my hair. I ignored the assaults, concentrating instead on getting to the pocketknife.

Only another foot. Six inches.

A small hand reached past me and snatched it up.

"Looking for this?" Helene asked. Suddenly she was up off my back.

Sensing what was coming, I tried to scramble clear.

Too late.

An electric jolt raced through my body. I shuddered and flopped onto my belly on the cold concrete just as heavy footsteps came charging down the stairs.

"It's okay," Helene said. "I've got him."

"Good girl," Kenny Booth replied.

CHAPTER 44

CONFRONTATION

I told you this wasn't over, didn't I, Mr. Ritter?"

I lay paralyzed, the first victim of my new pocketknife's Taser. Helpless, I could only watch as Kenny Booth knelt over me and yanked the sword and backpack off my shoulders, twisting my arms as he did so. It hurt, but I couldn't even cry out.

Straightening, he unceremoniously dumped the backpack's contents onto the cellar floor, taking a quick inventory. "Two water pistols, one silly water rifle and—of course—Sharyn Jefferson's famous sword. Armed for bear, I see."

He gazed disdainfully at the two Corpses I'd cut down. With a disgusted sigh, he crossed the room and opened a closet door set against one wall. It was buried so deep in the shadows that I hadn't even noticed it before.

From inside, he removed two long black zippered bags. I'd seen enough movies to recognize what they were and to realize that both bags were currently occupied. Hoisting one onto each shoulder, he hauled these back across the basement, somehow supporting both of them on Kyle's thin shoulders, and dumped them in front of me. Then he unzipped each bag.

The cadavers inside looked like Type Twos at best. My stomach gave a sickening lurch. I wondered how many more he had stuffed in that hidey-hole.

"Well?" Booth said. "What are you two oafs waiting for?"

The chopped up body parts stopped twitching, and the cadavers in the bags opened their eyes.

"A child," Booth told them both as they sat up. "You let a human child best you."

"*Sorry. Master*," one of them said in Deadspeak. Both looked sheepish.

"*Boy. Table*." Booth commanded in the same language. "*Now*."

The Corpses shook themselves free from their bags. Both were naked—a fact that didn't seem to bother them but which did nothing for the state of my stomach. Wordlessly they picked me up by my arms and feet and carried me a short distance to a strange metal table. There, I was placed facedown atop cold steel, my arms outstretched onto special shelves that were mounted to the table's sides. At Booth's direction, straps were fastened around my wrists and ankles.

Through it all, Helene watched him adoringly.

Stupid! I should have seen this coming!

Fear rose in my mind like bile. I swallowed it down. Sharyn's teaching came back to me.

Keep your head, no matter how bad it gets. Crying never helps. Neither does begging. Look for an out.

"Actually, Mr. Ritter," Booth purred, "your timing couldn't be better. Right now, twenty of my people are preparing to raid your little Green Street warehouse. You see, lovely Helene here was kind enough to give us all the particulars, weren't you, dear girl?"

"Sure, Mr. Booth," Helene replied immediately.

Booth continued, "I had intended to instruct my people to be careful who they killed. After all, I couldn't risk one of them unintentionally taking your life, now could I? Not after having you slip through my fingers—not once but twice."

I heard him take a step closer, his voice lowering to a hoarse whisper. "But now that you've paid me a visit, I'll have my underlings tear apart every Undertaker in Haven right before they burn the place to the ground!"

Reflexively I thrashed, trying to punch or kick him. My arms and legs only twitched a little. My cry of outrage sounded like a strangled gurgle.

"Don't worry," Booth remarked. "You should be

recovering any time now. When you do, I have some questions for you."

The three Corpses and one human girl waited patiently as the crippling effects of the Taser shock slowly wore off. After a couple of long minutes, movement returned to my limbs, and my tongue no longer felt like a big ball of cotton inside my mouth.

"He's pretty much recovered," Helene observed.

"Glad to hear it." Booth stepped around the table, forcing me to turn my head to follow him. "There we are," he said, sounding pleased. "I must say, you impress me, young man. To get this far—and all on your own..."

"Who said I was on my own?" I bluffed. "There are a dozen Undertakers outside right now. They'll be storming this place any second!"

"Is that so?" Booth looked amused. "I rather doubt it. Whatever you did to burn out all the fuses in my house has again been corrected, as you see. That means that my security measures are in place once again. If anyone else sets foot on my property, I'll know. So I think it's quite safe for us to have our little chat."

"I won't tell you anything!" I exclaimed, wishing my voice didn't sound so obviously terrified.

"That's exactly what your girlfriend said, but we were able to convince her of a few—truths."

"Yes," Helene added. "They were."

I stared at her. She met my eyes defiantly. She didn't

look brainwashed—but then, neither had Amy. "What did they do to you?"

"Just what Mr. Booth said," the girl replied evenly. "They made me see the truth."

"The truth?" I cried. "They're monsters!"

"No. They're saviors."

"She's quite correct, Mr. Ritter," Booth said. He wrapped one of Kyle's slowly rotting arms around Helene's slender shoulders. "We're not the beasts that your Chief, Tom Jefferson, would make you believe."

"Tell that to Tara and Kyle," I spat back.

"They got what was coming to them," Helene said. "They shouldn't have gotten in the way."

"A clever girl," Booth remarked with a nasty grin. Then his smile vanished, and he stepped forward, waving the gilded pocketknife in front of my nose. "So let's get started, shall we? My first question: where did you get this?"

"Tom gave it to me," I lied.

"No," Helene said. "Tom gave you *his* knife. That one was silver and was given to him by your father two years ago. This one's gold, and I've never seen it before."

Booth leaned close. He smelled utterly putrid, although he'd tried to disguise the smell with some kind of fancy cologne. I wondered why he bothered. Non-Seers couldn't smell the stink of his decaying flesh. But of course I knew the answer.

Arrogance. This guy might like to look down on us humans, but he liked pretending to be one of us even more.

Booth continued, "So my question stands. Where did you get this, Mr. Ritter?"

"I'm not telling you a thing!" I exclaimed, the words half-wrapped in a sob.

The Corpse brought its black, peeling lips to right beside my ear. "Yes, you will, Mr. Ritter. Soon you'll tell me everything I want to know—and gladly. Willingly. Even eagerly. Because soon we'll be good friends."

Then he straightened, turned to Helene, and said. "My dear, first let me thank you for participating in our little trap. You did very well indeed!"

"Trap!" I said. "You knew I was coming?"

Booth glanced at me. "The moment the lights went out, I suspected some clumsy rescue attempt. So I asked Helene to throw on her old, torn clothes and rub some dust in her hair. Then I positioned her in the basement's prisoner room and stationed two guards outside her door. Her orders were to pretend relief when she was liberated and then turn on her liberators at the proper time. I never imagined the liberator would be you, of course. That was just a happy surprise." He turned back to the girl. "Why don't you go upstairs and get cleaned up?"

"Okay," she said.

"But please be quick, my dear. I need you back down here as soon as possible."

"No sweat," Helene replied. Throwing a final glare at me, she disappeared up the stairs. Booth watched her go, smiling thinly.

"What did you do to her?" I demanded.

Booth faced me. "In my language, it's called *pellikoa*: 'mind bending.'"

"You brainwashed her!"

"A ridiculous term. No, Mr. Ritter. Your friend has had her attitude adjusted. You'd be amazed how many behavioral differences can be achieved simply by altering someone's brain chemistry. But please—why don't I show you exactly how it works?"

The Corpse walked over to a closed cabinet. Unlocking it with a key from his pocket, he extracted what looked like a large cylindrical tube, perhaps eighteen inches in diameter. Smiling, he brought this over to my table, placing the container atop a small wheeled cart and lifting its lid.

The rustling sound from inside was so eerie that it sent shivers down my spine. Then Booth tilted the cylinder so that the overhead light washed over its contents.

I gasped.

It was a *ball* of spiders—a huge, undulating mass of creatures, hundreds of them, all climbing in, around, and under each other. Except that Amy had been right—they weren't spiders. They each had ten legs, five yellow eyes, and a needle-like stinger almost an inch long sticking out where its nose should have been—a bit like a mosquito's, only a whole lot bigger.

"These are *pelligog*, Mr. Ritter—one of the few creatures capable of surviving the journey between our worlds. They're difficult to handle, very aggressive, but also very useful. You see, *pelligog* enjoy a collective consciousness. The members of any single nest share a single mind. This grants them an unusual capability.

"Simply put, a *pelligog* burrows into the flesh of its victim's spine, introducing certain chemicals into the host's central nervous system. After that, hosts become very—cooperative. They retain their will and their intelligence, but their loyalties shift entirely to whoever controls the nest as a whole. That is to say: *me*."

I stared at the spiders, or *pelligog*, or whatever they were and felt what little courage and determination I had left abruptly crumble. The idea of one of those *things* digging its way into me—for Booth could surely have nothing else in mind—terrified me beyond anything that I'd experienced so far.

An icy cold fear clamped around my guts. Uttering a single, desperate whimper, I began to struggle uselessly against my wrist and ankle bonds. All the while I stared, slack-jawed in horror, at the soccer-ball-sized mass of scuttling parasites inside that cylinder.

Suddenly everything that had gone down from the moment I'd stepped out of my house and seen Dead

Man Pratt—everything that had happened to bring me to this single terrible moment—all came crashing down around me.

I'm only twelve! I shouldn't be doing this! I should be home watching TV and going to school and playing with my friends! The only things I should have to be afraid of are homework and math tests and which girl might or might not like me! I'm not a soldier! I'm a boy! I'm just a little boy!

I tried to lend words to some of this, but all that came out was a half-strangled, "Please..."

Booth leaned close. "What was that, Mr. Ritter? I didn't catch it."

Every inch of my body seemed to be shivering. "Please..."

The Corpse came even closer. "Do you want your mommy, William? Do you want to run back to her arms and pretend you've nothing to fear? Do you want to go home?"

Yes, I do! I want to go home! Daddy! You lied to me! You told me there were no monsters! But there are! There are!

Again, I whispered hoarsely. "Please...don't..."

But of course he would.

I knew he would.

CHAPTER 45

SECOND GAMBIT

Booth chuckled. Then, straightening, he replaced the lid on the cylinder. I nearly fainted from relief. "Although invaluable," he said, "the *pelligog* have one limitation. Because an entire nest is but a single mind, it requires an entire nest to modify the behavior of a single victim. Therefore only one person at a time can be controlled in this manner. It's an annoying obstacle.

"So you see, Mr. Ritter, I can't infect you while your little friend remains under my control. Fortunately she has outlived her usefulness. So when she comes back downstairs, I will destroy the *pelligog* inside her body, thus freeing her mind. Then I will place a new creature on your bare back, thus claiming yours. Finally, once your loyalty is completely ours, you can watch as I personally snap Helene's neck. Does that sound like a workable plan to you?"

Horror-struck, I had to fight to keep myself from doing even more useless begging. Somewhere inside me, I felt something *shift*—as though Booth's boasting had somehow turned some of my terror into anger.

I had one more trick to play—something Helene hadn't warned the Corpses about, mainly because she didn't know about it.

It was a chance—a slim chance—but better than nothing.

If I could keep my nerve.

Booth said, "But before all that, there's something I'd like to share with you. Because you were at my gathering last night, I don't need to tell you who killed your father."

"No," I said. "You don't."

"Would you like to know exactly how I did it?"

I swallowed but didn't reply.

The Corpse chuckled. "I led Detective Ritter into a trap that night. He came to a rundown building expecting to meet with an informant who would give him information about us—specifically our real purpose in your world. Instead he met me, and I stabbed him with a filthy kitchen knife and left him to bleed to death. Normally we don't like to use weapons. In our culture such external means of combat are considered crass, even cowardly. I'd have preferred to end your father's life with my bare hands. Sadly, we needed his death to look like the work of common street thug, and a beating or strangulation would have been a bit less...tidy."

I listened to this walking worm bag casually describe my dad's murder, and I felt my resolve strengthen.

Keep talking, you lump of rotting flesh, because every word that comes out of your mouth makes me a little madder—and a little less afraid.

"So what *is* your real purpose?" I demanded. "And don't give me that crap about being here to help us because I'm not buying it."

Booth laughed again. "But we *are* here to help! We're here to put an end to wars and disease and poverty in the most certain way possible!" Then the Corpse leaned close again until I nearly choked on the stink of him. There were maggots in his mouth.

"We are the *Malum*, Mr. Ritter," he whispered with his festering tongue. "We are the Unmakers of Worlds. For countless ages my people have searched the ether between universes for places in which life thrives. And when we find one, we invade, infiltrate, and consume it, leaving nothing behind."

"Why?" I gasped.

The corners of his lipless mouth turned upward. "Because life is precious, Mr. Ritter—and we *Malum* reserve it for ourselves alone. All other forms of sentient existence are an abomination to us. So now we have come to *this* world in *this* dimension and have discovered life more plentiful here than anywhere else we have seen. So many humans—so confused, so in conflict. The end of your culture, the extinction of your race, will be our greatest triumph!"

I stared up at him, caught between disgust and horror. The Corpse, the *Malum*, stared right back at me, and for the first time, I thought I detected a strange agelessness to him, as if the thing inside Kyle's body had existed for a long time on many different worlds, using many different names.

Yes, he *was* ancient. But he was also overconfident—absolutely convinced of his own superiority and his own destiny to win.

Light footsteps tapped eagerly down the basement stairs. Moments later Helene reappeared, wearing fresh jeans and a clean blue T-shirt. The dust had been hastily brushed out of her hair.

"Ah! There you are, my dear!" Booth said cheerfully. "Looking as lovely as ever. Feel better? Didn't I promise you I'd let you clean up as soon as your task was done?"

"Yeah, Mr. Booth," she replied. "Thanks."

"Not at all. It gave William here and myself a chance to chat. Now, Helene, I'm afraid that I need to give you a small injection. Honestly, there might be a little pain, but something tells me you're tough enough to handle it."

She lifted her chin. "I'm tough enough."

"Of course you are." Booth nodded to one of his thugs. "Please bring me the *pelligog* dispatcher."

"*Obey*," the naked Corpse replied in Deadspeak. From

a nearby cabinet, he fetched an enormous syringe, which Booth accepted.

"This concoction is made from the crushed bodies of *pelligog*," he explained to me. "When injected into a host, it kills the parasite, thereby severing the nest's influence. The victim's normal brain chemistry is immediately restored, and more to the point, the nest is free to seize control over another mind. Attend." The Corpse then addressed Helene again. "My dear, will you turn around please?"

She didn't look happy about it, but she did it. I watched helplessly as Booth placed one slimy, maggot-riddled hand on her shoulder. Clutching the syringe in his other fist, he jabbed its needle into the base of Helene's neck with cruel force.

She screamed.

"Leave her alone!" I cried, pulling uselessly at my bonds. The Corpse ignored me, drawing the now-empty syringe out of the girl. Then he turned her toward me.

Helene's face contorted with pain. Her entire body shuddered. I felt awful watching her, but there was nothing I could do. Besides, what Booth had done would supposedly free her from the spiders' control, and that might give us both a tiny shot at escape—before it was my turn.

Gradually Helene's expression softened. Bewilderment flashed across her face, followed by a terrible awareness.

She screamed again, this time in heartbreaking anguish. She fell to her knees, burying her face in her hands.

"Oh, Will!" she wailed. "I'm sorry! I'm so sorry!"

"It's okay," I said, but she didn't hear me. Wrenching, guilt-wracked sobs bubbled up from her throat, drowning anything I might say. I tried anyhow, shouting over her cries. "It wasn't your fault! They made you do it!"

She lowered her hands. "No! It's not like that. I knew I was betraying you! I wanted to! I was sitting in that room, looking forward to it!"

"Because the spiders made you!" I persisted. "That's what they do!"

"Enough!" Booth declared. One of his thugs wordlessly yanked Helene to her feet by the hair. He then pinned both her arms, holding her in an iron grip.

Booth smiled wickedly. "Your turn, Mr. Ritter. What friends we'll be!" He turned and reopened the *pelligog* cylinder.

Just the sound of that writhing, undulating bug ball was enough to nearly cripple my resolve. But then Booth reached inside and drew out one of the ten-legged needle-nosed monstrosities—and my sanity almost slipped altogether.

Use the fear!

"Lift his jacket and shirt," Booth ordered his other thug.

With terrible effort, I focused on the tear-streaked face of my friend.

Nobody our age should have to endure this. Nobody!

"Helene," I said, trying to keep my voice steady. Blinking, she met my eyes. "Remember: don't test anything unless you've seen at least three other people test it first."

She stared uncomprehendingly at me. I felt my jacket and shirttail pulled roughly up past my shoulder blades, revealing the pale, freckled skin of my lower back.

"Three times!" I repeated.

Understanding dawned in her large hazel eyes. The barest hint of a smile touched her lips. "Yeah, I remember."

"Stop babbling, Mr. Ritter," Booth cooed. "And don't struggle. It'll only hurt more if you do."

Then his thug said in Deadspeak, "*Box. On. Back.*"

"Box? What box?" Booth replied absently. A pause. "What *is* that strapped to his—?"

Gritting my teeth, I squeezed both my fists as hard as I could.

The rectangular saltwater reservoir strapped to my lower back—the heart of Steve's prototype weapon system—instantly exploded in the Corpses' downturned faces. Booth groaned and stumbled backward, his limbs flying in every direction at once. The spider-thing was hurled over his shoulder, where it smashed against the concrete wall of the basement. Booth's henchman clutched his face and then collapsed, falling into a twitching, helpless heap on the floor.

At the same moment, Helene dipped her head forward and then slammed it up and back, right into the last dead guy's face. More from surprise than pain, I suspected, he loosened his hold on her just for a second. Instantly she spun on her heel and drove a devastating kick into the creature's kneecap. Then as the Corpse doubled over, she slammed both her fists down against the base of his neck—a human nerve center.

The naked thug crashed to the basement floor, twitching.

"Get me loose!" I cried. "Quick!"

Helene unstrapped my wrists and ankles, fairly yanking me off the table and hugging me with a fierceness that, despite our predicament, made me squirm and blush. "You're a genius!" she exclaimed. "Do you know that? An absolute genius!"

"Thanks. Um—we should get out of here."

"Not without weapons," she said.

We ran over to my emptied backpack. Helene grabbed the Super Soaker. I took Sharyn's sword. Everything else we left behind.

"Wait a second," I said. I went to Booth, who was still writhing on the floor. Reaching into the Corpse's trouser pocket, I recovered my pocketknife. Then, standing over him, I said, "That body you're in belonged to an Undertaker. You can't have it anymore."

I lifted Vader and let it come down.

Off went the Corpse's head.

Helene and I retreated up the stairs at a run.

CHAPTER 46

THE SUN ROOM

At the top of the landing, I peeked out the cellar door. The hallway appeared deserted. "How many Corpses does Booth keep around?"

"Four altogether. There'll be two more guarding the front door."

I nodded. "Then we'll go out the back. I came in through the kitchen. You know a better way?"

She thought for a minute. "Yeah, I think so!" She led me down the hall, through a nearby door, and then out into a long narrow room that looked like it made up most of the rear of Booth's big house. One wall was lined with fancy family room furniture. The entire opposite wall was all glass from ceiling to floor.

"He calls this his sun room," Helene explained. "He spends a lot of time here reading newspapers and watching TV."

"Corpses watch TV?" I asked, surprised. I tried to imagine a bunch of milky-eyed dead bodies gathering around the tube to catch *Scrubs* reruns.

"Booth likes to pretend he's human."

"Yeah, I noticed that. Is there an outside door?"

She pointed. "Down at the end. A sliding glass door. Outside, there's a path down the hill. Booth showed it to me this morning, back when we were—pals." She shuddered at the memory.

"It wasn't your fault," I told her.

She met my eyes. "It feels like it was."

"Let's go."

We ran the length of the sun room. To our left, the night beyond the windows was so dark that only our reflections showed. I really hoped there weren't any Corpses out there. If there were, the two of us would be pretty hard to miss.

The room ended at two doors. One was Helene's sliding glass escape route. The other looked more ordinary and probably opened into an unexplored part of the big house.

Just as we reached the first door, the second one *erupted*.

It didn't just burst open. It was literally ripped off its hinges and hurled aside, where it shattered a nearby widescreen television.

No more Scrubs *reruns.*

The Corpse leapt into the sun room. He was a Type Two, his skin still slick but turning a dark, mottled gray.

He was also totally, hideously naked.

"Hello, Mr. Ritter," he hissed.

At the sound of my name, I let my eyes cross. Suddenly the Deader's Mask became visible, showing a handsome, telegenic face that was twisted by rage.

Booth!

I didn't bother wondering how he'd accomplished the Transfer. It didn't matter.

Helene raised her Soaker, but she wasn't nearly fast enough. With one hand, Booth slapped the rifle from her grip. With the other, he shoved her hard in the chest, knocking her down and sending her body sliding back across the tile floor.

"Helene!" I cried.

Her head struck a bookcase with a loud *clunk*. With a groan, she went limp.

Desperately I lashed out with Vader.

He dodged me, moving much faster than I would have thought possible in that rotting body. I came at him a second time, but he caught my wrist, holding the sword at bay. With his other hand, he clutched my throat, easily lifting me up onto my toes.

Both hands squeezed.

I felt the sword fall from my grasp and clatter to the tile floor. At the same time, my breath was cut off. Frantically I reached for the pocketknife in my pocket.

The Corpse's face split into a hideous smile. "Not this

time, Mr. Ritter," he hissed. Still clutching me by my neck, he shook me savagely. I felt like a rag doll in a dog's mouth. I tried to hang on to the pocketknife, tried to hit the *2* button and release my faithful Taser—but the shaking was just too much. I dropped it.

Booth tightened his grip and lifted me higher until my feet actually left the floor. The pain was terrible. I clawed at his hand, tearing off bits of rotted flesh, but he felt none of it.

"Like my new body?" he asked. "I don't. I took it because it was there in the closet, available. *Any port in a storm*, I believe is the human expression. Getting out of the body bag was problematic, but I managed it."

Back at First Stop, Steve had theorized that a Corpse needed to actually see its target body before possessing it. Apparently he was wrong about that. Too bad I'd never get the chance to tell him."Tell me something, Mr. Ritter," Booth said. He was carrying me deeper into the sun room now, walking casually, as if clutching ninety pounds of kicking and struggling twelve-year-old didn't bother him in the least. "Have you ever heard of a *caste system*?" He didn't wait for an answer. Just as well—I couldn't give him one. He said, "It describes a society in which the members are separated into specific classes based on cultural status, education, wealth, or even intelligence. On my world, such a caste system exists. Most of the *Malum* that you've encountered, for example, have been from our warrior caste. They're bred for loyalty and prowess but not necessarily intellect. I, on the other hand, represent the leader caste. We are born to rule—to be cleverer and more resourceful than our lesser brothers and sisters.

"Let me give you an example. My underlings are still trying to recover from the damage you and your little friend did to them below. I, however, was able to manage a Transfer and escape the basement in time to—how's the saying go? *Cut you off at the pass?*"

My vision blurred. His voice was starting to sound very far away. Seeing this, Booth slowly turned me around, and with a casual flick of his wrist, he tossed me against the wall. I hit it hard and collapsed into a heap on the floor, clutching at my bruised neck.

"A good effort, Mr. Ritter," he said, "but it's over now. The *pelligog* await. There's no escape. There never really was."

"No!" I croaked. I tried to stand, but my head spun, and I fell back down on my butt.

Suddenly an image of my mother, heartbreakingly vivid, flashed through my mind. Blearily I looked up at the looming cadaver. "You won't...get our planet," I coughed.

"No?" he asked. "And why not?"

I did my best to sound tough, to sound confident. It didn't go very well.

"I'll...stop you..." I gasped.

"Is that so?" He knelt down in front of me. He smelled

of the grave, of death. "Another human cliché comes to mind: *You—and what army?*"

The entire rear wall of the sun room—fully sixty feet of glass—shattered all at once.

Booth leapt to his feet and spun around.

Figures emerged from the darkness, stepping over the broken shards and spilling into the ruined room. There were two dozen of them at least, and each one brandished a Super Soaker. In the center of the line, a tall, dark-skinned boy came forward with a slightly shorter dreadlocked girl right beside him.

"That'd be us," Tom said.

CHAPTER 47

RAISING THE STAKES

At first I couldn't believe what I was seeing. I blinked, trying to focus through a haze of pain and dizziness.

They'd come. Heck, it almost looked like *all* of them had come!

For just a moment, Tom's eyes found mine. The Chief smiled.

He doesn't look *mad.*

I moved my gaze over to Sharyn.

She winked at me.

Booth glowered, his milky sunken eyes accessing this new threat that seemed to have appeared out of nowhere. Then to my surprise, the Corpse smiled and said, almost politely, "Mr. Jefferson, is it?"

It was Sharyn who answered. "Ain't nobody but!"

Booth's smile widened. It wasn't a pretty sight. "This is a rare treat. I've heard so much about you."

"Same here," Tom replied.

"I'm surprised you made it past my security now that the power's back on."

The Chief shrugged. "It ain't as good as you think it is."

"Really? I'll have to have my people look into that. And my two guards?"

Tom brandished his Super Soaker. "A bit under the weather just now. As for those twenty Corpses you sent into Haven—they just found the place deserted. Go figure."

Booth seemed unperturbed. "Ah! But we watched you load your van. By now my associates have followed it to your new hideout!"

Tom smiled thinly. "And which van would that be? By the time the one we loaded hit the streets, four more that look just like it were already tooling empty around the neighborhood—all headed to different spots all over town. Your thugs found nothing, believe me."

At that, Booth actually laughed. "I see! How wonderfully clever of you. But then I would expect nothing less from the leader of a group that has managed to so effectively evade me over these past few years."

"Thanks."

Booth's smile vanished, replaced by a menacing sneer. "Of course, I wasn't trying all that hard. After all, what threat did your so-called Undertakers really pose? A few stolen Seers. Some boldly dramatic rescues. Nothing more troublesome than that."

Tom's expression was stone. "All that's about to change."

"Really? Ready to raise the stakes? Are you sure, boy? Because tonight, you *have* become troublesome. After this I will hunt your little Peter Pan underground movement to every corner of this city. And I won't rest until every one of you meddling brats is dead!"

"Big talk," Sharyn remarked, "seeing that we're the one with the guns."

"Fire away with your toys!" Booth declared, spreading his huge arms wide, naked as a jaybird. "I'll return as strong as ever! I *will* be mayor of Philadelphia, and when I am, there will be nothing to keep me from turning the whole of this city to the single purpose of your utter destruction!" The Corpse laughed mockingly. "You're nothing, Mr. Jefferson! A boy playing general—commander of a children's army. Even with your toys and tricks, you're no match for us! No match for me!"

"That right?" Tom asked, unperturbed. A slow smile crept over his face. He handed his Soaker to Sharyn. She accepted it without question, although I could read the sudden apprehension in her eyes.

Tom took a step forward. He glanced first at me and then at Helene, who still lay motionless on the tile floor. "You're good at beating up children, ain't you, Booth?" the Chief of the Undertakers said. "How's about trying your luck with a cooler partner?"

Booth's grin widened.

This is what he wanted!

The Corpse hissed, "My pleasure—Undertaker."

Booth launched himself forward with such blinding speed that I reflexively cried out a warning. I couldn't believe that even Tom, as good as he was, could possibly defend himself against something that fast.

He could.

The boy sidestepped the dead man, sticking out his foot at the last moment. With a frustrated howl, Booth tripped, crashing down onto the tiles. The Corpse recovered instantly, springing to his feet with tiger-like grace, his milky eyes wide with anger.

Tom turned to face him, smiling thinly. Along the shattered glass wall, the Angels were swapping nervous looks. Sharyn's trademark grin was gone. For the first time, I could see real fear on the girl's face—fear for her brother.

Raising one hand, Tom waggled his finger Booth's way.

And the Corpse came, but more slowly this time, never taking his eyes off his prey. Tom waited, calm but expectant, not retreating a step.

"Get him," I muttered.

The instant he came within striking range, Booth lashed out with one lightning-quick fist. Tom ducked it. Then came the other fist. Tom ducked that one too, his head bobbing and his body weaving with each new assault. I noticed that he didn't attempt to block a single swing. Doing so—given Booth's far greater strength—would have been disastrous. Instead the Chief, with his usual calm confidence, was simply arranging not to be there when each blow connected.

This went on for perhaps half a minute, although it seemed longer, and with each dodge, Booth grew more and more angry. Finally, with a frustrated roar, the Corpse suddenly hurtled himself forward, meaning to body-slam his irritating opponent halfway across the long room.

This time Tom didn't duck. He didn't even crouch. He picked his moment and then launched himself into a single hard kick. The blade of his foot caught Booth in the midsection. Reflexively the Corpse doubled over.

Tom then grabbed the cadaver's decaying right arm, twisted it up behind his back, and with a single brutal yank—*snapped* it off.

Sharyn let out a little whoop of victory, although she still looked frightened.

Booth staggered a few steps and turned around, accessing the damage. He felt no pain, of course, but there was no way to miss the humiliation in his eyes.

"You'll pay for that," he hissed at Tom.

Tom merely smiled, still clutching the disembodied limb.

The Corpse advanced again, the fingers of his remaining hand open and reaching for his opponent's throat.

Tom swung the arm like a baseball bat, with terrific force, catching Booth squarely in the side of his head.

There was a sickening *crunch* that made me wince.

When I looked again, Booth was standing completely still. His head was *sideways*, half-hanging off his neck, his eyes unfocused. Tom looked him over for a few seconds. Then he dropped the severed arm and stepped close to the helpless dead guy.

In his native tongue, Booth slurred, "*No. Can. Kill. Me.*"

The Chief calmly placed his open palm on the Corpse's quivering chest. "Don't want to," he said. Then he pushed.

Booth toppled like a tree, landing on his back, his head lolling horribly on what was left of his broken neck. Still, he didn't—couldn't—move. He was trapped inside a human body, and a human body had its limits.

Tom knelt down beside the fallen Corpse. When he spoke again, it was through clenched teeth. "What I want is for you to get this message, you decaying sack of meat. We been fighting now for three years—but it's been what you might call a defensive kind of fight. Well, that's done.

"As of this moment, the Undertakers declare war on your kind. As of now, we're going to start hitting back—hard. Maybe I can't kill you, but I can kill your plans. You think we were trouble before? Well, now we're going to be a hornet's nest. Everything you build, we'll tear down. Every victory you think you've won will turn out to be a defeat in disguise. Everywhere you turn, whatever you do, there we'll be. You want to know why?"

Tom leaned close. "Because you're tearing up folks' lives. Because you're killing innocent kids. Because you're messing with our city and our world. And the part that bugs me most? You're a tourist!"

Then he straightened, turned his back, and said to Sharyn, almost casually, "Got your sword back, sis?"

She grinned and held up Vader, recovered from where it had fallen from my grasp. "Got it!"

"Use it."

As the Angels gathered around and Sharyn went to work, Tom went to Helene. He pressed his fingers to her throat and then his hand to her forehead. Then he turned to me. "She's got a good bump, but she'll be okay."

Relief washed over me. Elsewhere in the room, hidden behind a circle of Angels, Sharyn's sword was going up and down, over and over. I realized with a shudder that she was doing more than just decapitating Kenny Booth. She was cutting him to pieces.

But it won't kill him. He'll be good as new by morning.

Unless—

Tom came and stood over me, smiling and offering his hand. I took it, and he pulled me to my feet. "You cool? We saw what was going down through the windows while we were coming up the hill out back but couldn't get here in time to stop it. You breathing okay?"

My throat was sore, but I was getting air. I nodded.

"Nothing broke?"

"I...don't think so."

The Chief shook his head, marveling. "Ian'll be beside himself. He was sure you came out here with a busted arm."

"I'm fine." Then, lowering my head, I added, "Tom, I'm sorry."

He shook his head. "Don't be. It's me who's sorry. I've been so busy trying to play it safe that I forgot the first rule of any army. You never leave a soldier behind—whatever the odds. It took my sis to bring me around. After you left, she cornered me. She told me what you'd done and what exactly she thought of my *defensive war*."

I was shocked. "She shouldn't have done that!"

"Yeah, she should've. I needed it. She told me that Will Ritter was twice the leader I was because you were willing to go into the heart of the enemy camp—alone—to rescue a comrade in trouble. She was dead right, and I'm ashamed that it took me so long to see it."

I felt a glow of pride, but it didn't last. Suddenly alarmed, I cried, "Tom! There's two more Corpses in the basement! I hit one with saltwater, and Helene dropped the other. But with the way these things heal—"

The Chief held up a hand. "No sweat. It's cool."

"But—"

Tom reached out and slid a hand into the breast pocket

of my jacket—a pocket I almost never used. It came out holding a rock.

Except, of course, it wasn't a real rock.

I gasped. "You planted a bug on me?"

"Sharyn did," he replied, "when she hugged you outside Haven right before you split. She figured it might come in handy. But it's short range—so we couldn't pick nothing up until we got right up to Booth's front gate. By then you and Helene had escaped into this room and were already in trouble. But we *did* hear Booth talking all about his dudes in the basement. The same Undertakers that I sent to handle the front door guards took care of them too. They won't be going no place for a while."

I looked from him to the rock and then back again. I laughed shakily. "Well, in that case, what the heck took you people so long?"

A perplexed look flashed across Tom's face. "Funny thing. We drove up here in one of the vans and got most of the way up Ridge Avenue when the engine suddenly died—along with every other car on the road, the streetlamps, and even the lights in the neighboring buildings. No matter what we did, that sucker wouldn't start again, so we had to all come the last quarter-mile on foot!"

I stifled a laugh. I'd have to explain that—later.

"Well, your timing was perfect!" I exclaimed. "That was one awesome entrance!"

"That was Sharyn. She's got this thing for being dramatic. Speaking of which—yo, sis! You done over there?"

The dreadlocked girl raised her sword. The blade wasn't bloody—Kenny Booth *had* no blood—but the girl wielding it looked like she'd broken a sweat. "I think he got the message!"

"Cool! Let's move out!"

Sharyn issued the retreat order. The Angels immediately turned and exited out through the shattered sun room windows. As Tom went to Helene, scooping her up effortlessly in his arms, I ran over and recovered my fallen pocketknife.

On the way back, I looked down at what was left of Kenny Booth. There wasn't much. Sharyn's efforts had reduced him to a pile of parts—a collection of twitching gray bits of human being. I felt bad for the guy—the living human—who'd once owned that body. But at least the *thing* inside it now wouldn't be going anywhere. Something told me there wasn't another handy cadaver for him to Transfer into here in this sun room.

"Nothing a couple of Sweet-Rox won't fix, right, Mr. Booth?" I asked.

One of the milky eyes inside what little remained of the Corpse's head fixed on me.

I grinned.

"Coming?" Tom called.

"Yeah!"

Together the two of us—with Tom carrying Helene—

exited through the shattered windows and headed down the hill after the rest of the Undertakers.

Halfway across the lawn, however, alone and out of earshot from the others, Tom suddenly stopped. "Hey, bro—hold up."

I paused, curious. He studied me for a moment and then said, smiling, "Know what I think?"

"What?"

"I think Karl Ritter would've been proud of his son tonight."

I looked back at him. Tom stood bathed in the glow of the moon, with Helene's limp form cradled in his arms. That image of the Chief of the Undertakers seemed somehow to define him, and it was one that I knew I would remember for the rest of my life.

You came for us tonight. You may say that Sharyn talked you into it, but I don't quite believe that. Nobody could talk you into anything if you didn't already secretly want to do it. You wanted to come. You just needed somebody to show you how.

You're the Chief of the Undertakers—my Chief—and I promise you this: I'll fight for you. I'll never betray you again. And if necessary, I'll die for you.

I met Tom's eyes, feeling more grown-up than I ever had before.

Quietly I replied, "I think he would've been proud of *both* his sons."

For the first time since I'd known him, Tom's face crumpled. A tear—just one—traced a path down his cheek.

"Will…" he whispered. "You honor me."

"Come on," I told him. "Let's go home."

CHAPTER 48

POP GOES THE WEASEL

I stand here before you all today, the victim of what can only be called *domestic terrorism*."

I stood beside Helene, watching the television along with pretty much every other onsite member of the Undertakers. We filled the new TV room, which was a bit roomier than the old one had been—although, overall, the new Haven wasn't as large as its predecessor.

Just more interesting.

Late last night, the Undertakers had forever abandoned their Green Street warehouse, having moved—lock, stock, and barrel—into a forgotten subbasement of Philadelphia's enormous City Hall. Located on Broad and Market streets, the mammoth century-old building concealed entire levels beneath its official cellar that hadn't been used or even visited in fifty years or more. This Haven wasn't a single big room but rather a warren of passages and chambers of varying sizes.

At least now there'd be some more privacy for everyone.

Not that our new lair was perfect. Far from it.

For one thing, the Undertakers weren't leasing this space, as we had on Green Street. Instead we'd become what Tom called *squatte*rs, tapping into the city's utilities without anyone knowing about it. It was, he'd explained, a somewhat more *wobbly* existence—but at least the Corpses couldn't dig through city records to find us.

For another thing, the living conditions weren't quite as comfortable. The brick walls were cold, the air dank, and the lighting lousy. Worse, for now at least, the only way in or out of New Haven was through an abandoned service tunnel that ended at a neglected metal door half a block down a subway tunnel that serviced the Broad Street Line.

Getting all the equipment in here had been a ton of work, although Tom's decoys had done their job well. We were pretty confident that the Corpses had lost us in the maze of darkened city streets. Even so it had taken the rest of the night to smuggle everything out of the truck, down an unused service stairway, and safely into underground Philly. Lookouts had been posted all up and down the surrounding streets, and their frequent warnings had really slowed down the effort.

And finally, there was the issue of the cats.

Apparently City Hall's basements were infested with them—big, wild cats that had originally been introduced down here to deal with the rat problem. They'd since had kittens, and those kittens had produced kittens, and so on, until there were whole generations of them in these tunnels that had never seen sunlight. For the most part, the creatures stayed out of view, although a few of the kids claimed to have caught glimpses of their small, darting forms in some of the more remote corridors. Others had reported hearing strange meows in the dark—very creepy sounds!

The Monkeys were already working on these problems. Soon there'd be new, concealed entrances at carefully selected spots in and around City Hall. Cameras and motion sensors would watch for intruders. Portable heaters and gadgets called *dehumidifiers* were already helping with the cold moist air. Special traps would capture any wild cats that got too close. These would be released elsewhere.

Inside of a week, Tom promised, we'd be secure and comfortable, and nobody would ever know we were here.

"Last night my home was the site of a ruthless attempt on my life by a gang of underage criminals calling themselves the Undertakers."

It was six o'clock on Tuesday evening, almost exactly twenty-four hours since the battle in Roxborough. That was how long it had taken Kenny Booth to Transfer to a new body. The cadaver behind the NBC-TV podium, dressed impeccably and wearing an expression of righteous indignation, was obviously Type One and would no doubt last its Corpse master a good long time.

"As yet the police don't know who they are. But their motivations were made clear to me. They want me to withdraw from the mayoral race. They want me to abandon my promise to the people of this city to bring order to these streets again. They invaded my home, injuring my staff and causing many thousands of dollars worth of property damage—all in a cowardly effort to intimidate me into submitting to their demands."

"Nice tie," Chuck Binelli remarked.

"Yeah," Burt Moscova agreed.

"But I say to them and to you, the people of Philadelphia, that I will not surrender my values to these terrorists. I will not abandon what I know I must do. I have dedicated my future to this glorious city, and nothing and no one will turn me from that path!"

On the television, Kenny Booth the Corpse grinned hideously. At the same moment, I was grimly aware that a city full of Sightless people was watching a good-looking television journalist flash his brilliant, toothy white smile. Of course I could have crossed my eyes and witnessed that smile for myself.

I didn't bother.

"I hereby reaffirm, with all my heart and at no small personal risk, my candidacy for mayor of Philadelphia!"

Cameras flashed. Booth fielded questions. He looked

entirely comfortable, entirely in control, a man—a dead man—in his element.

The mood in the new TV room was somber, to say the least. Nobody said anything. Everyone simply stared at the screen, scowling or sighing or shuffling their feet.

Then from the doorway, a strong voice spoke. Every head turned.

"Don't sweat it, Undertakers," Tom said. With his sister alongside him, the Chief moved among us, looking every bit as confident as Booth had just now. He came at last to stand right beside the TV, which still showed Booth singing out answers to questions with all the flair of a movie star. Sharyn, in the meantime, took the remote control away from Alex and muted the sound.

"Booth can babble on all he wants!" the Chief of the Undertakers declared. "We got our new crib and our new plan. We're going after them. We're going to start hitting back at the Corpses with everything we've got. Somehow we'll find a way to make the whole world See the way we do. In the meantime, though, we'll be kicking old Booth in the butt every chance we get.

"By now y'all have heard the other promise that Booth made to us last night, away from cameras and reporters. Starting today they'll be coming after us. They'll hunt us down if they can. The gloves are off. This is now open war. Well, I say, bring it on, Deaders! We'll be ready!"

He didn't quite get cheers, but there were at least smiles

and a few supportive words as he crossed the room again and came to stand beside me, Sharyn, and Helene.

"We're with you, Chief," Helene whispered.

"I know it," he said. "Thanks."

"Can you turn the sound back up?" someone asked.

"What for?" Sharyn demanded.

"Come on!" That one came from Alex, who was frowning impatiently.

With a groan, Sharyn switched off the mute. Booth's voice once more filled the room.

"No, I don't believe in personal vendettas. The damage done to my home is repairable, the cost covered by insurance. The injuries to my brave staff members were, overall, not serious, and all will make full recoveries. As for my own hurts"—he grinned again, looking right into the camera—"let's just say I heal quickly.

"I'm not interested in vengeance—only justice. And once I'm mayor, I will vigorously pursue justice against the so-called Undertakers and against anyone else who breaks the laws of this fine city."

"*Hypocrite* don't seem to say it," Sharyn observed.

But I barely heard her. I was watching Booth, who had fallen back on his famous trademark. The bag of Sweet-Rox was once again in his hands, and between questions, he'd begun tossing back big handfuls of the colorful candies.

"I swear to y'all," Tom remarked to no one in particular, "sooner or later we're gonna get that dude."

I felt a slow smile spread across my face. "With a little luck," I said, "it might just be *sooner*."

On the TV, Kenny Booth suddenly started coughing. He excused himself and tried to recover. The coughing worsened. Within seconds he was gasping and clutching at his throat. Someone screamed for the paramedics. Someone else demanded that the cameras be shut off, but they just kept running. The gasps turned into gurgles, and the gurgles into strangled croaks. Booth's expression had gone from confident to confused to terrified in the space of a few seconds.

Then, with maybe a million people watching, Kenny Booth exploded.

It happened so fast and so completely that nobody—not us and not the people on the TV with the candidate—realized it right away. One minute, Booth was standing there, gripping the podium, looking pained and desperate. The next, he just sort of burst like an overripe melon.

This was a Type One cadaver—and a fresh one at that—apparently not even embalmed. There was blood. A lot of blood. It splashed the walls, splattered the camera lenses, and covered the podium like a coat of red paint.

On the NBC-TV sound stage, pandemonium broke out. People ran in a dozen directions at once—some screaming; others shouting orders. The cameras bobbed and then steadied. After several tense moments, another newsman—nicely human this time—stepped into the frame, a stunned expression on his face. Booth's blood was on his face and clothes.

Blood that he could obviously see and feel! Booth's illusion was gone.

When he spoke, his voice was flat with shock. "Ladies and gentlemen, something terrible has happened. It seems that Kenneth Booth has..." As if just now realizing it was there, he began to wipe at the blood on his face with one trembling hand. "My God! Get this off of me! Somebody—"

What he said after that, I don't think anyone in Haven heard. We were all staring at the podium—at the spot where Booth had been only moments before, at the gore he'd left behind.

Something stood there.

The shape was roughly man-size but without mass or substance. We only saw it for a few moments, but in those moments, we could all tell two important things. First, whatever it was, it wasn't human—wasn't anything like a human. And second, it was dying.

No one in the studio saw it; that much was clear. You had to be a Seer. The thing writhed and thrashed as if in pain, looking as if it were searching for some escape—another body maybe?

Then, as we watched, it just sort of ceased to exist—collapsing in on itself and crumpling up like a wad of paper before vanishing with a strange little *pop*.

Sharyn switched off the TV.

This time no one complained.

Haven's TV room was wrapped in a kind of shocked silence. For half a minute, no one spoke. I wasn't even sure anybody was breathing.

Then Burt whispered, "What'd we just see?"

Nick replied, "I think...he's dead. A Corpse is dead!"

"But that's impossible!" Chuck exclaimed. "I mean—isn't it?"

"It couldn't survive without its shell," Steve suggested. "Whatever happened to Booth, it utterly destroyed his stolen body, leaving the thing inside exposed."

"But how?" Alex demanded. "How in the world...?"

I stayed quiet, although I couldn't keep the smile completely off my face. Glancing around, I found Helene looking pointedly at me. "William Karl Ritter," she demanded, sounding for a moment like my mother, "what did you *do?*"

Every head in the room turned my way. I suddenly felt like I'd been pinned by a spotlight. Even Tom and Sharyn were gaping at me, open-mouthed.

My cheeks flushed.

"I—um..." Having so many eyes on me made me uncomfortable. Finally I just focused on my shoes and said, "Before I headed up to Booth's place last night, I took some lumps of sea salt to the kitchen and dipped them in the melted candy dishes. I let them cool and put them in a little brown bag. Then later—when I was hiding in

Booth's office—I found his sack of Sweet-Rox in one of the drawers and—well, I added the salt candies. I just thought that, you know, if we couldn't kill him from the outside..." My voice trailed off.

"...maybe we could kill them from the inside!" Helene finished. "Will! You're a genius!"

For one horrible moment, I was afraid she might hug me again.

Dave, still in his sling, suddenly exclaimed, "Awesome!"

Then *he* hugged me.

"I...don't...believe...it!" Tom stammered. It was the first time I'd ever seen the Chief struggle for words. "I... just...don't...believe...it!"

"But what did it do?" Alex Bobson demanded. "I mean, he just kind of..."

"Burst!" Elisha Beardsley offered.

"Yeah!" the new Monkey Boss exclaimed. "Yeah! Like a balloon!"

"Every cell in the host body suddenly lost cohesion... violently," Steve pronounced sagely. "What sort of physiology would allow for...?" His voice trailed away.

"Pop goes the weasel!" chirped Harleen Patel.

"But is he dead?" Amy asked hopefully. "Is Booth really dead?"

For several moments no one else spoke. Finally, with a shaky, slightly unbelieving laugh, Sharyn replied, "He just exploded! I figure that's a good sign!"

Helene clamped her hands over her mouth like a girl at Christmas. Then she spun in a circle, threw both her arms in the air, and jumped fully three feet off the floor. "Will did it! He did it!"

The entire room erupted into wild cheers. Suddenly dozens of kids descended on me, scooping me up and carrying me out through the door and down the dark, moldy subbasement passage. I laughed until my sides hurt, riding atop a wave of hands that bore me the length of Haven and out into the large chamber that was now serving as a general workroom.

All that fuss—it was embarrassing.

But I'd be lying if I said I hated it.

CHAPTER 49

THE PRODIGAL SON

An exhausted Susan Ritter opens the door of her Manayunk home and fishes into her rusty mailbox with trembling, nail-bitten fingers. The street is quiet. Even her neighbor, Mr. Pratt, who's been so attentive lately—always asking after Will—seems to have finally taken the hint and left her alone.

It's been more than two weeks now. The school has offered little in the way of explanation—other than that Will and a girl she never heard of ran out of class one morning. Apparently a teacher was injured. The circumstances are sketchy, and Susan can't shake the feeling that everyone—even some of the police—is keeping things from her.

Emily is in the living room watching Dora the Explorer. *The little girl knows full well that her brother is missing, and her mother senses that she is suffering the loss, despite her tender years. Susan sometimes has to force herself to tend to the child. Other times, she clings to her like a lifeline. After all, Emmie is the only one left of her once whole and happy family. First Karl. Now Will. Dear God.*

In the days since the disappearance, there'd been a lot happening, with police, school board representatives, relatives, and neighbors constantly stopping by. But as a week passed and then two, these visits grew less and less frequent. Susan still calls the police twice a day, hoping for news. They still talk to her. They're still kind.

But now, except for daily visits from her sister, everyone leaves her alone.

Susan isn't sure which is worse: the constant attention or this terrible feeling of abandonment. Will is out there somewhere, and every fiber of her being wants to search for him. But there's Emmie to consider—beyond the simple terrible reality that she has no idea where to look.

So she does the only thing that she really can do. She goes on with her day, her life, without him. Just as she did after Karl died.

It is agony.

What little sleep she manages to get is always fraught with dreams: Will in trouble. Will in pain. Will calling out to her, his pale, freckled face awash with tears. She often wakes either screaming or crying, which sometimes frightens Emmie. Then the two of them, mother and daughter, clutch each other on the bed until this meager comfort finally lulls them both back to sleep.

Susan reflects on all this as she flips through the mail. Junk and bills. Always more bills. She's taken a leave of absence from work, but she can't keep that up for much longer. There's still food to be bought and a mortgage to pay.

Her hand stops at an unstamped white envelope. It bears no return address—no address at all, in fact, except for one word—scrawled in blocky letters that she recognizes instantly.

Susan feels her heart skip a beat.

Mom.

Feeling a sudden chilling mixture of excitement and terror, she drops everything else and tears the letter open. Inside is a single sheet of lined paper.

Dear Mom,

I'm okay. I'm sorry I can't come home yet. I'm also sorry I can't tell you where I am. There's this stuff I have to do—important stuff. I know you're sad. I'm sad too. I know you're probably real worried about me. But I really, really want you to trust me. Scary things are happening, and I have to fight them. It's a fight that Dad started before he died, and now it's my job to finish it. I know you don't understand, but it's really safer if you don't.

I'm not alone. I've made some good friends, and we're all working real hard so I can come home.

Until then, you've got to be real careful, so burn this letter. Take care of my sister, and try not to worry *too* much. I know I used to tell you to stop babying me. That I wasn't a kid anymore. Well, it wasn't true then. It's true now.

I miss you.

Love,

Will

Susan reads and rereads the letter, feeling her heart pound in her chest. What is this? Obviously, someone dropped it into her mailbox, probably during the night. A terrible joke? But it's Will's handwriting! She's certain of it!

He's alive! Somewhere out there, alone in the world, her son is alive!

Slowly Susan re-enters her home and closes the front door. Vaguely, running on autopilot, she locks it. Then she walks past the living room, where Emily in sitting too close to the television.

"Sit back, Emmie," she says flatly, as though in a daze.

The girl nods, shifting herself maybe six inches.

"I'm going to lie down for a while, baby. Come upstairs if you need me, okay?"

"Okay, Mommy."

Susan climbs the stairs and enters her son's empty bedroom, clutching his letter so tightly that her fingers ache.

Will's room is just as he left it: the bed poorly made; his pajamas in a heap on the floor. Her sister frequently offers to tidy things up, but Susan always refuses. "He'll do it when he gets home," she insists, repeating the statement over and over again, almost like a prayer.

Now she sits down on Will's rumpled bed and reads the letter a third time.

He's alive. Her stunned mind can barely grasp it. As for the other, more confusing parts of the note—well, there'll be time enough to try to figure out what they mean later.

Susan lays back on her missing son's bed, tucks her missing son's pillow under her head, curls up into a ball atop her missing son's blanket...

And begins to cry.

CHAPTER 50

THE ROAD AHEAD

Something very rare was happening at Haven: a genuine party.

Not surprisingly it had been Sharyn's idea to celebrate the Undertakers' first real victory. Tom had agreed but only after insisting on twenty-four hours to make absolutely certain our new HQ was completely secure. His sister had called him a wet blanket, but she'd gone along with him.

A few kids were sent out for chips, dips, and sodas. Others went looking for streamers and noisemakers. By nightfall on the day after Kenny Booth had exploded on live television, Haven was awash in music, food, laughter, and dancing.

For a short time, the Undertakers got to be kids again.

Sharyn whirled around the room, talking to everyone

and pulling people out onto an uncluttered section of the workroom floor that she'd designated as a dance area. She hijacked control of the sound system that the Monkeys had just finished setting up and used it for karaoke, singing a half-dozen rap songs before passing the mike onto Chuck who, as it turned out, could manage a decent Elvis impersonation.

I quietly hung back, watching the goings-on from a corner of the room. Helene was twirling around the dance floor with the Burgermeister, who was blushing beat red and clearly enjoying himself.

I spotted Tom standing near one of the doorways and walked over to him. We swapped smiles.

"Cool party," Tom said halfheartedly.

"Lot of noise," I said.

"Yeah," Tom replied.

"Afraid somebody'll hear?"

Tom shrugged. "It ain't likely."

"Guess it's your job to worry about stuff like that, huh?"

"Guess so."

I suddenly didn't envy this guy.

Hesitantly I asked, "Do you think the Corpses'll replace Booth?"

Tom considered this. "Given what he told you about their caste system, they'll have to. In a month or so, some new member of the leader caste will show up—maybe not as a news anchorman but as *someone*. That's the bad news. The good news is that it'll be a long time—years, maybe—before they get back to the point where they can take another shot at the mayor's office."

"But what about the Corpses in other cities?" I asked. "Other leaders?"

"One thing at a time. We've declared war in Philly. Let's start here, okay?"

"Okay."

The Chief glanced sideways at me. "Had enough of the party for a while?"

"Yeah," I admitted.

"Then come on. I wanna show you something."

He led me out of the workroom and down a passageway, past more than a dozen smaller chambers that had already been turned into living quarters. We passed the new kitchen, Steve's new Brain Factory, and Karl Ritter's newly recreated shrine.

Be proud of me, Dad.

We came to an unmarked, rusted metal door, which Tom opened, having to pull hard against its ancient hinges. Then with a finger to his lips, he motioned for me to follow. Beyond was a flight of cement stairs leading up.

We climbed to another door. This one opened into what appeared to be a city government records room. Dusty boxes of papers filled tightly packed shelves. It didn't look like anyone had been in here in years.

"Where are we?" I asked.

"Still in City Hall's basement," Tom told me, "but a higher level—one that's still in use. It's pretty late, so the building's mostly empty. A few janitors. A couple of guards maybe. As long as we don't make no noise, nobody'll bother us. Just stop when I tell you to, dig? There are a few security cameras."

"Okay."

Tom clearly knew the route well, making me wonder just how many times he'd come this way—and why.

The two of us moved higher into the enormous municipal building, avoiding the elevators and instead climbing long winding staircases past floor after floor of offices, meeting rooms, and public halls. We saw nobody. Once or twice, Tom stopped me with a gesture—his dark eyes watching the sweeping movements of a ceiling-mounted video camera. He waited until the lens turned away before hurrying us along.

Finally we reached the seventh floor, where a small museum offered displays about the building's long history.

"This…what you…wanted…to show me?" I asked, leaning over to catch my breath as I tried to recall the last time I'd climbed so many steps. The Chief, I noticed with dismay, didn't look tired in the least.

"No way." He waggled a finger. "Saved the best for last."

Groaning, I followed him to a single elevator. Beside it was a sign that read TO TOWER.

Suddenly I knew where I was.

I'd been here years ago with my family, although in the after-hours gloom, I hadn't recognized it. This was City Hall's Tower Museum, with its elevator that would carry us to the observation platform at the top of the building, right below the enormous statue of Billy Penn.

Tom produced a key, flashed another smile, and used it to activate the elevator. We rode it up through the shell of the century-old, five-hundred-foot tower, behind the enormous clocks that decorated each of its four sides, and finally to the entrance to the outdoor platform.

My exhaustion forgotten, I fairly leapt out of the elevator as soon as it opened, pushed through the door to the observation deck, and bounded out into the brisk October air. Tom trailed after me, laughing.

The city of Philadelphia lay spread out before us—a vista of lights and motion, glistening skyscrapers filling the blocks between the cold, black ribbons of the Delaware and Schuylkill rivers. I circled the observation deck, seeing the city from every angle, gawking at the thousand different colors and hearing the distant rumble of traffic on the streets forty stories below. Then I craned my neck, gazing up at the statue of the city's founder. William Penn had been a Quaker. He'd come from England looking for religious freedom and had ended up creating a place that he'd called "the City of Brotherly Love."

Well, maybe it wasn't quite that, I supposed. But it was

my home—the only home I'd ever known; a home that I was—that we all were—fighting for.

"Your namesake," Tom remarked.

"Huh?"

Tom motioned up at the statue. "Another William."

I grinned. "Yeah."

Then we both turned and stood for a while in silence, side by side, looking out over the carpet of lights. It was cold, but I didn't mind.

After a while Tom reached into his jacket and pulled out the pocketknife that my dad had given him. For a moment he just gazed at it, turning it over in his strong hands. Mimicking him, I pulled out my own newer version—the one that the mysterious golden woman had provided. I studied it wonderingly.

Tom asked, "Any more visits from ladies bearing gifts?"

I shook my head.

"Mind a question?"

"Shoot," I said

"Why didn't you tell me about the new knife back in the Infirmary?"

I shrugged. "You were already so pissed at me. What was I supposed to do, start talking about an angel coming to my bedside, leaving me a present, and whispering about my destiny? You'd have thought I was nuts!"

"Think so?" the Chief asked, his tone serious. "Bro,

I'm leading a gang of teens in a fight against cadavers that have been reanimated by alien *things* from who-knows-where. Trust me, I'm a bit more open to weird ideas than you might imagine."

"Okay," I said. "If she shows up again, I promise you'll be the first to know."

Tom smiled gratefully. "Cool. Thanks." Then looking back down at the knife in his hands, he remarked, "So she was the one who gave this to your dad."

"Yeah."

"And she knew that he gave it to me?"

"Uh-huh."

Tom looked thoughtful. "Then I figure that means she's okay with me having it."

I looked up at him. "I can't think of anybody better." Then I grinned and held up my own knife. "At least, not now that I got one of my own!"

The two of us shared a laugh, but it didn't last. As beautiful as it was up here, there was simply too much uncertainty ahead. Downstairs, everyone else was celebrating. But I just couldn't bring myself to do that. Not now. Not yet. Not with all we still had to do. And something told me that Tom felt the same way.

That's why he brought me up here.

True, the Undertakers had won a battle today—our first—and an important one.

But the war was just beginning.

Tom said quietly, "*The Unmakers of Worlds*."

I nodded. "Think we'll find out exactly what that means?"

"I imagine so—eventually."

We fell silent again.

I breathed in the city air and looked up at the stars. It was late. Emily would be in bed by now. Mom would be watching TV. Tomorrow they'd go to church.

Life. My normal life.

"Miss your mom?" Tom asked, as if reading my mind.

I nodded.

"And your sister?"

"Yeah."

"Still want to go home?"

"More than ever," I replied wistfully.

"Good," he said. "It gives you something to fight for."

"I know," I replied. Then, glancing up at him, I asked, "Do you really think we can do it, Tom?"

"Do what?"

"Beat the Corpses?"

"Yeah," Tom replied without hesitation. "We can."

"How can you be so sure?"

"You want my honest answer?" he asked.

"Of course."

"You might not like it."

I shrugged. "Try me."

The Chief of the Undertakers put one arm around

my shoulders and squeezed. It was the same gesture he'd done before—back in the shrine on my first day at Haven. At the time I'd resented it. At the time I'd been frightened and confused. Well, I was still frightened—no doubt about that—but I was no longer confused. I knew what I had to do now, and as uncertain as my life was and would surely continue to be, that was better than nothing.

"Because of you, Will," Tom said quietly. "I think we can win...because we got *you*."

ACKNOWLEDGMENTS

These days, writing the book is only the beginning. I'd like to express my heartfelt appreciation both to my amazing agent, Ann Behar, and to my equally incredible editor, Rebecca Frazer, for believing in Will, Helene, Tom, Sharyn, and the rest of the Undertakers as they begin their adventure.

I'd also like to thank Josh Hahn, master of theatrical makeup, for his work on the homemade YouTube book trailer; Christine Breller, the mutual friend and fellow writer who brought us together; and Dr. Lyle Back and Kim Back for their support during the filming—as well as for the loan of their son, Griffin.

And finally, my gratitude goes out to Griffin Back, the talented young actor who—in the book trailer—became the first person ever to play Will Ritter. May he not be the last!

ABOUT THE AUTHOR

Ty Drago is an author, editor, publisher, business analyst, family man, and Sicilian Quaker (not necessarily in that order)—clearly a modern Renaissance Man. Or something. For the past twelve years, he's served as editor/publisher of *Allegory*, an online magazine of science fiction, fantasy, and horror.

The Undertakers marks his debut in youth fiction.

Ty makes his home in southern New Jersey with his wife Helene, daughter Kim, son Andy, two cats, and a dog.